Bring us back an oul' bucket of ice

An Eirestown Féile

By Michael Collins

Acknowledgments

Thanks to my father Michael Collins for his advice and creative insight, for being a sounding board during the editorial process, and for introducing me to the song, When I Mowed Pat Murphy's Meadow.

For my mother Elizabeth, a special thank you for cherished, childhood memories of Templemore, Ireland - where I spent all my summers, as well all the other motherly things.

A heartfelt thanks to my dear friend Johnny Williams, whose constant support, love and inspiration have been a blessing.

And last but not least, a special thank you to Pete St. John, for graciously allowing me to use the lyrics of his classic Irish song, The Fields Of Athenry.

Introduction

Everyone has heard about Ireland – or Éire as it is also known. That fabled land full of magic, madness and the odd flash of Celtic genius.

Ireland!

A land spoken of in every corner of every Irish pub and house in the world. Where they drink Black Stuff and sing and dance up and down the streets like the cast of Riverdance.

A proud and noble land: a land full of brave warriors and cunning leprechauns. A land brimming over with fiddle players, and even greater fiddlers. A land of singers, musicians, storytellers, poets and weavers and spinners of blarney and cod-ology, a land of great intellectual tomfoolery, wisdom, wit and even greater Craic.

But we are not here to talk about Ireland.

For beneath an eerie green mist, the very heart of Ireland herself is to be found in a humble hamlet known as Eirestown. A magical mist, which comes and goes, opening the doors to an alternate, mysterious Universe. An impenetrable green mist, beneath which Ireland's greatest secret is literally kept under wispy emerald wraps.

An even greater mystery is the actual location of Eirestown, for each morning when the green mist lifts, the residents never know which county of Ireland they'll wake up in.

Eirestown!

A town which is not spoken of in every corner of every pub and house in the world, not yet anyway, and a town which has brought Shillelaghs into the twenty first century, along with a few other iconic Irish bits and bobs.

And even though you have never heard of Eirestown, as you read you will discover how the residents of this humble abode, along with the help of a few of those Shillelaghs, saved the whole world from the expansion plans of a megalomaniac. A good for nothing scoundrel, hiding behind a mask of corporate respectability, who was intent on creating, and subsequently profiting from, the greatest climactic crisis since the dinosaurs were wiped out by a meteor 60 million years ago.

Welcome to the first Eirestown Féile (pronounced fay-la) which is Gaelic for a festival of words.

Chapter 1

Fight Him For His Boots

Sure wasn't it a beautiful Saturday morning in Eirestown. Over the town a green mysterious mist was slowly rising to reveal a clear blue sky and, in the distance, south of the town, the Wicklow Mountains glistened under the brilliant morning sun. A few minutes later, the green mist had lifted completely, leaving Eirestown somewhere just outside Dublin.

Along the Laffy river bank a couple of birds were making grand music chirping: When Eirestown Eyes Are Smiling. While in the river itself, several green dolphins were flying in and out of the water, chasing each other silly, leaving trails of inimitable, cackling laughter in their wake.

Meanwhile the main square of Eirestown hummed with the hustle and bustle of commercial life, what with the shops eager to take the week's wages off anyone who cared to spend them. Danny Boy's Toys, ShamRock&Roll Music Shop, Limericks From Counties Other Than Limerick, An Cabáiste agus Bagún Deli (The Cabbage And Bacon Deli), and a travel agent established to promote local tourism called, You'd Be Mad To Go Anywhere Else, were already open, some even serving customers. However, one shop was still closed, and the queue of children waiting outside were growing more and more impatient as the seconds dragged on.

"Good morning to ye!" chirped QuickMIC, screeching to a halt outside a shop called Technological Shenanigans, where an angry queue was waiting for him. "'Tis a grand morning, isn't it?"

QuickMIC, a microprocessor powered Shillelagh, with micro-robotic arms and legs, was usually very quick indeed, what with his MIC (Microprocessor Integrated Circuits) getting him around the place. But he was running a little late today and an apology was in order. These human children could be a fiery lot, much worse than the adults in some cases.

"Morning is it?" moaned Fin, the first child in the queue, who was in an awful mood altogether. Hadn't he been up half the night with excitement, waiting for QuickMIC's shop to open, and sarcasm was getting the better of him. "Sure I make it nearly lunch time, meself."

"Nonsense, Fin," said QuickMIC, running a comb back through his single curly quiff, and checking his nano-watch, "why the day's not even started."

"I think the watch is as slow as himself," said Fin to the other children, generating a wave of giggles, which rippled the full length of the queue and back.

"Cop yourself on now young man," snapped QuickMIC, slipping the comb back inside his jacket pocket, "and less of that cheek." He searched around in his shoulder bag, a brown leather satchel with a shamrock on the side of it, and pulled out a hair brush. "Anyway, never mind me young fella, have you no shame?"

Fin raised his eyebrows as QuickMIC offered him the brush, "Here now, sure you look like you've been dragged through a hedge by a tractor." With the embarrassment mounting, and a few more giggles rippling behind him at his expense this time, Fin stared in the shop window, trying to ignore QuickMIC. "I've no rake with me, so this'll have to do," QuickMIC went on, but Fin started whistling as if he couldn't hear a word. "Hurry up now," QuickMIC insisted, "or you'll be putting the scarecrows out of business."

Fin's hair was a mess alright and he hadn't even bothered to brush his teeth. He was usually much tidier than this, but wasn't he in so much of a hurry to be first in the queue this morning that he'd forgotten all about his personal hygiene and appearance. Bad hygiene had it benefits though, while the others were squashed into the queue like sardines, Fin had plenty of room, what with the smell coming off him. He didn't really mind this weekly lapse in hygiene and appearance. It was a small price to pay for a prime position in the queue. Saturday mornings at Technological Shenanigans were always magical because QuickMIC would reveal his new stock, freshly ordered from America or China, or he might even reveal one of his own inventions. For as well as owning Technological Shenanigans, QuickMIC was an inventor extraordinaire.

So the hygiene wasn't too much of a problem, but with QuickMIC pestering him and still trying to force the brush on him, Fin shrugged again, and started whistling even louder. However, when a few of the young girls behind him sniggered, and agreed with QuickMIC, whispering that Fin looked like a scarecrow alright, never mind smelt like one, he snatched the brush out of QuickMIC's hands, and raked and patted his matted hair, checking his reflection in the shop window. After a few good oul' rakes, convinced that he looked like a member of a boy-band, he gratefully returned the brush, whispering to QuickMIC, "Do you happen to have any deodorant in the bag?" A few squirts later, Fin smelled like a freshly cleaned computer screen. Unfortunately, QuickMIC had passed him screen cleaning fluid, and Fin had it under his arms before QuickMIC realised his mistake.

"The day's not even started, you say?" several of the other irate customers scowled, harassing QuickMIC as a freshly groomed, fresh smelling Fin returned the cleaning fluid.

Then one young fella shouted, "Never mind the hairdressing tips QuickMIC, why are you so late, have you got a short circuit or something?"

"Maybe he's a screw loose," shouted one of the young girls from the back of the queue. She was as cute as an angle, but didn't she have the tongue of an oul', haggard banshee.

"He'll have a screw loose in a minute alright, if he doesn't live up to his name and get me in that shop quicker than quick," shouted an older child from the middle of the queue, shaking a couple of raised fists in QuickMIC's direction.

QuickMIC's eyes zoomed in and out and up and down the queue, determined to find the source of the latest heckling. Instead of eyes, QuickMIC had bright

LEDs which, depending on his mood, emitted different coloured light. His eyes were also telescopic, therefore he could zoom them in and out to get almighty magnification when he needed to. Sure didn't he also claim that he could see between your very atoms, and even deep into your brain, when he thought you were lying to him.

His eyes a flustered crimson, QuickMIC continued to scan the queue, intent on giving the last abuser a clip behind the ear, a piece of his mind at the very least. But when his kaleidoscopic eyes focussed in on the antagonist's hefty fists, which were still shaking in his direction, all bets were off.

Didn't QuickMIC's eyes turn bright red, a mighty bright red actually, a red so bright that it was usually reserved for the highest levels of danger. He not only changed his mind, he almost powered off with the fright when he saw those threatening, gnarled fists. Fin was a regular, but this complainant was a new customer, and he was literally popping out of his shirt with the muscles. Sure even Mike Tyson himself would think twice about giving young Mr Muscles a clip behind his ears. He may only have been the tender age of fifteen QuickMIC guessed, but he was surely a farmer's son, and looked like he'd been stacking bales of hay since the age of two.

QuickMIC was only 50 centimetres high, about the length of one of the hay-stackers arms. Oh he had hydraulic arms alright, and they were powerful enough, but just look-it - he zoomed in again to make sure he wasn't seeing things - sure Mr Muscles' muscles even had muscles. He was certain that given half the chance, Mr Muscles would loosen more than a few screws alright. It'd be the scrap yard for him this morning, if he wasn't careful.

"Well if you're just going to stand there staring at me, QuickMIC," snarled Mr Muscles down at him, startling what little life he had left out of him, "sure we could be out here for the rest of the day."

QuickMIC un-zoomed his telescopic eyes so fast with the shock that the recoil knocked him over backwards, and he finished up on the floor, having performed a perfect, involuntary back flip. A few moments later, having rolled forward, back up onto his feet, he smiled up at your man nervously, his eyes just shy of anxious scarlet, and said apologetically, "Not a bother Mr Muscles, we'll have the shop open in a nano-sec."

Even though Saturday was his busiest day, QuickMIC was running later than ever before, because his legs had been literally running away with him all morning. An intermittent malfunction in his MIC was causing his stepping motor to go haywire altogether. Which meant that every now and then, instead of taking one step forward, he was taking three, sometimes as many as ten steps back. Hadn't he spent most of the night moon-walking around his bedroom like your man, Michael Jackson.

The moon-walking was bad enough, but he was sorry he ever tried to go down for that cup of hot chocolate at that hour of the morning. Sure didn't he wake the whole neighbourhood up, what with him rattling up and down the stairs all night like a newlywed shillelagh, with a set of pots and pans tied to each ankle. Not one of them got a wink of sleep, and first thing in the morning, a queue had formed outside his house, with a rake of weary eyed neighbours taking turns to look in through his letterbox, gossiping and asking questions.

"Is it himself?"

"It's himself alright!"

"And what the hell is he doing?"

"I'm not sure."

"Is he playing a drum kit by any chance?"

"No, there's no drum kit."

"Sure he might need oiling."

"And himself, can you see him?"

"Ah yes ... oh no, now wait a minute, sure he's gone again."

"Gone where?"

"Oh wait ... look now, he's back. You won't believe this, but he's running up and down the stairs like an eejit."

"Here now, let me have a look," said another woman, her head covered with a black shawl, who'd been up half the night banging on the wall at him. "Ah look ... Sure he looks like one of yer ones from the Hollywood musicals, what's his name ... Gene Kelly. Would ye just look at the cut of him, dancing up and down the stairs like that."

"He's deadly isn't he," said a younger neighbour, peeping in. She glanced back at the eager queue, giving them a running commentary, "Sure he's hopping up and down the stairs like a kangaroo." Lifting the letterbox even higher she gave him an almighty boost of confidence, "Good man yerself QuickMIC, may you hop 'till you drop." Finally she got up and concluded, "He must be in training for the Olympics or something. I'm not codding ye, he's taking the stairs three, sometimes four at a time."

"It's the Olympics alright," shouted someone from the back of the queue, "and with jumps as high as that, wouldn't he make a grand hurdler."

"A high jumper even," piped up another.

"'Deed he would," agreed the young one still holding the letterbox open and about to invite the next voyeur up. "Sure we could stick him in the pole vaulting event as well, and he wouldn't even need a pole. Now who's up next?"

"Here let me have a look, so," said another older neighbour, herself with a grey shawl on. She nudged, pushed and dragged her way to the front of the queue, and peered in through the letterbox. "I'd say yer one was right," she said, agreeing with the first oul' one. "Although, to tell ye the truth, I'd say he's a look of Fred Astaire about him meself." She looked over her shoulder, and nodded wisely before validating her comparison, "Without the top hat and tails, of course." Then she tutted, scowled disapprovingly, turned back and screamed in through the letterbox, "Have you no shame at all QuickMIC? Put some clothes on before me granny looks in."

In the very next moment the granny was pushed to the front of the queue in a wheelchair, nearly knocking half of it over. This oul' one was so old that she had tea and poitín running through her veins. Not only that, but her glasses were so thick that she couldn't see the door, never mind the letter box. So the granddaughter held open the letterbox, while she poked in her walking stick and tried to stab and jab QuickMIC, her ear pressed hard up against the door, and herself using her acute sense of hearing to home in on him. Luckily for him, the stick was way too short, but he got an awful shock altogether when she said she was going home to get an extension.

"The oul' ones are right," said the next young snoop, as the granny was wheeled away cursing QuickMIC, "I'd say he's in training for the dancing alright." She paused to study him a bit longer, and continued, "Although, to tell ye the truth, his moves look a bit more modern to me. Sure I dare say we'll even see him on that show Strictly Come Stepping, soon enough."

With no sign of QuickMIC stopping and with his screams for help getting louder by the step, didn't the neighbours have to give up their snooping and eventually call in the fire brigade to break down his door, and reset his microprocessor circuits, hoping to correct his stepping malfunction.

"That's the fifth carpet this week," QuickMIC said, moaning about his stair carpet, which was threadbare now.

The fire brigade suggested that he get a stair lift, and that, from now on, he also wear some pyjamas around the house. But then the Guards, which is what they call the police in Ireland, turned up and insisted that he wear them, since they'd just received a public indecency complaint.

Didn't the sergeant give him an awful scolding altogether in the hallway, with the tired, excitable onlookers cheering him on through the letterbox. "We've enough odd-balls running around Ireland," he shouted over the cheers and boos, "without having to worry about a microprocessor controlled shillelagh, tap dancing around the town half naked all night."

"Sure I was in my own house," QuickMIC argued, blushing and covering his private parts with crossed palms.

"Keep your curtains pulled from now on, so," said the guard, his sound advice being met by rapturous applause from the crowd.

"And what about my letterbox?" demanded QuickMIC pointing at his door, where twenty sets of eyes and lips vied with each other for prominent viewing and shouting positions. "Sure my privacy's been invaded, and it's been open so much this morning that I might as well take it off altogether. Are you not going to prosecute this nosy, noisy lot?"

At that comment the crowd let a roar of profanities through the letterbox which even had the hardened guard, who'd just spent ten years doing nightshifts in Dublin handling rude, obnoxious, violent drunks, covering his ears.

"Keep your pyjamas on, so," said the guard, "and they'll have nothing to stare in at. Otherwise it's the courthouse for you."

"Look," insisted QuickMIC, shivering from head to toe with the draft, "would you please ask them to close the letterbox before I catch a chill?"

"You'll catch a rap of this across the back of your head first," said the guard pulling out his truncheon and slapping it a few times into his open palm aggressively, before pointing it in the direction of QuickMIC's exit route. "If you don't hop back up those stairs as fast as your name can carry you and get dressed."

As quick as he was, wasn't QuickMIC about to remonstrate with the sergeant again when the letterbox flew wide open once more, and the half blind oul' granny, back with a vengeance and wearing a better pair of glasses to improve her aim, took the wind out of him with a fierce jab of her walking stick, which was now fitted with the extension she'd gone home for.

"That was a grand shot granny," exclaimed her daughter, who was holding the letterbox at one end. "Sure I nearly felt that meself," she added, holding her stomach in sympathy as QuickMIC doubled in two and writhed in agony on the floor.

"She's like one of the musketeers," said the young girl who was holding open up the other end of the letterbox, when the granny executed a flèche, an offensive fencing jab usually reserved for the finesse of a fencer's foil or épée. "That's it now," she suggested, hoping to improve an already near perfect aim, "a little more to the right granny, you have him now!" Not that she needed much help in that department, herself having already fitted a telescopic sight to the walking stick. With the latest co-ordinates relayed, the granny dispatched another almighty poke and the young girl cringed, "Jesus granny, but that was a deadly shot altogether, sure the sergeant won't be able to sit down for a week."

Fending the elongated walking stick off with a few defensive parries of their truncheons, the guards had to carry poor oul' QuickMIC up the stairs on a stretcher, before the fearsome granny could finish him off. Didn't they look like a right shower, stumbling up the carpet-less stairs, with the extension prodding a few of them in their tender nether regions, and himself still doubled in two on the stretcher, heaving, wheezing and coughing, desperate altogether to catch a breath of life.

So the morning hadn't got off to the best start for QuickMIC: what with himself at the mercy of peeping Toms, the breath poked out of his little stomach, and having almost been arrested. But with Mr Muscles currently whipping up another crowd outside Technological Shenanigans, things were going from bad to worse for. He'd only just managed to avoid the courthouse and the hospital, but the scrap yard was still looming.

"Good man yerself," a petite, red haired, freckled faced, eight year old girl yelled from further along the queue, urging Mr Muscle's on, her own fists shaking in the air, "Fight him for his boots, I'm right behind you. We'll loosen a few screws alright, or a few of his boot laces at the very least. How dare he keep us waiting so long!"

QuickMIC didn't wear boots. He wore brightly polished brown brogues, which matched his dark green cord trousers and tweed jacket, with its yellow leather elbow patches. But he was more than sure that this lot would fight him for anything at all dangling on the end of his feet at this moment in time.

"Ahh come on now, lads," pleaded QuickMIC, pulling up the shutters, and hanging on for dear life as his legs involuntarily started to take a few steps back, "I'll have ye all in a minute."

"Another minute," groaned Fin, sniffing under his arms, "sure it'll nearly be time to go to bed."

"I'm more than sure," promised QuickMIC, "that the big surprise I have waiting for ye, will make up for any delays."

"Surprise?" said Fin excitedly.

"You should see the new shipment of technological shillelaghs lads," said QuickMIC, turning a key in the door, his legs starting to run away with him again. "Ye won't believe your eyes,"

"I don't believe my eyes now," said Mr Muscles, as QuickMIC's legs hopped, twisted, turned and distorted like they had a mind of their own, doing everything and anything, except what he actually wanted them to do. "Is that a jig he's doing?"

"I'm not sure," said Fin, "it looks like a hornpipe to me, or a reel even."

"Whatever it is," said Mr Muscles, "I dare say he'd give Michael Flatley a run for his money."

"You're right," said Fin, as QuickMIC's legs became faster and faster, and disappeared in a blur.

No longer able to hold onto the key in the door, QuickMIC succumbed to the intermittent stepping motor malfunction which was back again with a vengence, and didn't his legs carry him away altogether this time. He flew fifty steps backwards instantly, zipping past a freshly groomed Fin.

"Hey where you going?" asked Fin, grabbing hold of one of QuickMIC's flaying arms.

"Nowhere young fella," said QuickMIC, flying back inside the shop as soon as his stepping motor had corrected itself, dragging Fin off his feet, and in through the shop door with him.

Where there was a surprise waiting alright, but it wasn't a surprise anyone was anticipating, especially QuickMIC.

Chapter 2

Forget The Irish Potato Famine

William McCoy The Third was sitting in his plush Manhattan office, waiting for Ryan O'Reilly to answer his phone. While he waited he tapped anxiously on the boardroom table, studying his pristine reflection. Suddenly he flinched and lowered his head to the table to take a closer look. A few strands were out of place. Livid at his hair stylist, he raised the tapping finger to sweep the straggly, blond locks back over a very small balding patch, a patch so small that only he could see it.

Satisfied that he looked like a modern day Adonis once more, he opened his mouth and admired his brilliant white teeth in the sheen of the boardroom table, picking at the front ones with his tapping finger, and smoothing down some wrinkles in the lapels of his white Armani suit. Not bad at all for a forty five year old. High cheek bones, tight skin, good tone. He smiled at himself again, and whispered, "Hey good looking, what you got cooking?"

William McCoy The Third was the CEO of 'Global Realtor And Business intelligence Technology', GRABiT for short, and he had a lot cooking at the moment. As the name suggested, William's father had also been the CEO of GRABiT, and also his grandfather and also his ... well you get the message. It was an age old tradition which he was determined to hand over to his son, William McCoy The Fourth, but not before he'd made a name for himself, and propelled the company to the very top of the Fortune 500, where it would stay forever.

The conference phone was on loudspeaker, ringing away. It didn't do to keep such an important CEO waiting so long, Ryan should have answered by now. He would pay for this disrespect, but not before he'd taken part in the most audacious expansion plans in history. Not since the expansion of the Roman Empire had the earth undergone such a remapping.

"Hello, sir. Can you hear me?" Ryan asked when he finally answered.

"Hey, Ryan my boy," said William pleasantly, "it's great to hear your voice again. How go things over there in the Emerald Isle?"

"Sorry for the delay, sir," muttered Ryan. "Dublin's a bit manic today. It took me a while to get back to the hotel."

"Any luck with the project," asked William eagerly, "have you met many Irish?"

"Not as many as you've probably met yourself there in New York and Boston," Ryan joked. "Half of Ireland seems to have migrated over to the States at some time or other."

William licked his lips and wiped back his flopping, wayward lock again. Sure this was just what he wanted to hear. Why there must be thousands of properties and hundreds of thousands of acres of land unclaimed in Ireland, he thought. He was so excited by the news that he could barely get the next question out. "So there'll be plenty of empty properties over there then?"

"Not at all," said Ryan emphatically.

"Why?"

"Because half of Eastern Europe has migrated to Ireland!" Ryan had been infected by the Irish craic, and didn't he fancy himself as an Irish stand-up, unfortunately the captive audience had other ideas.

"This is no time for jokes, Ryan," said William scornfully, somewhat deflated. "Time is moving on and I've an empire to build. The biggest empire the world has even seen as a matter of fact."

"Sorry, sir," grovelled Ryan, adopting a more serious attitude.

"Never mind," said William ominously, "there's been a change of plans."

"A change of plans?" Ryan asked nervously.

"A change of plans," William confirmed. "Ryan, are you still there?"

Ryan O'Reilly was still there alright, and by the sounds of it, he might be staying there for much longer yet. As part of a punishment, he'd been sent by GRABiT to Ireland almost a year ago now, to do a documentary on the migration of Irish people to America, following the Potato Famine. Ryan had mixed feelings about being sent to Ireland. Like William, he was Irish American himself, and he had often wondered what Ireland was really like. Did they really all walk around saying 'top of the morning to ye', drinking black stuff, chasing leprechauns for pots of gold, singing and fighting? Or were such descriptions just exaggerated stereotypes? Apart from getting to know the real Irish, he had often wondered if it would be possible to find some trace of his ancestors. However, he'd rather have made his own way to Ireland, not be despatched there as penance to do a documentary.

That had been the cover story anyway. However, unbeknownst to Ryan, what William McCoy The Third really wanted to know was how many of the Irish migrants had left unclaimed property and land behind, and could GRABiT get its hands on it by legal, or any other means possible, including the most nefarious ones you could imagine.

Given the scale of his crime, Ryan knew that his punishment could have been much worse. So a year in Ireland hadn't really been that much of a price to pay. Actually, William had paid a much higher price for Ryan's crime, nine million dollars to be precise.

Almost two years earlier, Ryan had walked into a seminar about property development in one of GRABiT's offices on Grand Avenue Los Angeles. The seminar promised anyone attending that they would be millionaires within a year, if they applied a simple formula which had been tried and tested by GRABiT for decades. Twenty, trendy and broke, Ryan fancied himself as a property developer, and signed up straight after the seminar.

Less than a week later, Ryan had been promoted to a GRABiT International Acquisitions Executive high-flyer, and found himself in Cairo buying up slum dwellings faster than they were falling down. This was one of William McCoy The Third's pet projects. He often paid peanuts for slum dwellings anywhere in the world in the hope that one day fortune might turn, and those dwellings would become highly sought after. He'd seen what had happened in Harlem in the 1990's following gentrification and they weren't even slums, so he knew the potential such turnarounds could provide.

"Unfortunately, sir."

"What was that Ryan?" asked William McCoy The Third.

"I said yes," grumbled Ryan, squeezing the life out of his phone, "I'm still here in Ireland. You say there's been a change of plans?"

Another change of plans, this was all Ryan needed. He was hoping to go back to sunny Los Angeles soon, but he knew that a change of plans could take him anywhere.

"Yes," William confirmed once again.

"Nothing to do with Egypt, sir?" Ryan felt his face flush, even though William couldn't see him.

Ryan was doing really well in Cairo during his first month. Like a Wall Street speculator with bottomless pockets, didn't he buy anything that came his way. And word soon got out that some American madman, with more money than sense, was buying anything with or without a roof on, with or without walls in some cases, and he was so trusting he didn't even view the properties.

Even when Ryan found out he'd paid several thousand dollars for a few cardboard boxes, he didn't slow down, especially when William told him that the cardboard boxes would make great tax-write-offs.

Ryan's objective was to spend his funds as quickly as possible and get back home. After only a few months, everything was going really well. The funds were nearly dried up and he now owned more cardboard boxes than Wal-Mart. However, as he was about to purchase a moth infested Bedouin tent, with more holes than a fishing net, William contacted him that fateful day with a *change of plans*.

"The pyramids of Giza, sir?" asked Ryan for the fourth time. "But they're Egyptian national treasures."

"They'll soon be American national treasures," William beamed. "We've already got one on the dollar bill, so it's about time we had the real ones back home."

"If you say so, sir," said Ryan.

"I do," said William smugly, "I do say so. The nine million dollars to secure their purchase will be wired over to you immediately."

William McCoy The Third may have considered Ryan to be a naive, gullible simpleton, but, by his own accounts, he was not completely stupid. Therefore, on first meeting William's contact, a carpet weaver and souk trader who went by the rather dubious moniker of *Al' Stit'ch U'up*, in a major bazaar district known as Khan el-Khalili, Ryan was suspicious to say the least. To be fair, courtesy of a few guttural Arabic inflexions, the name didn't sound quite as bad as it looked emblazoned across the sign above the stall, but the fact that Al' Stit'ch U'up's stall was squeezed in between one stall selling three humped camels, and another stall selling the extra humps, did nothing whatsoever to relieve Ryan of his anxieties.

Having tried to sell him everything under the sun, including the wife's mother for a pittance, with the mother-in-laws of the other two stall holders thrown in for free, three Arabian jewels he called them, Al' Stit'ch U'up offered Ryan an exclusive in the form of a quad humped camel. It was a buy-one-hump-get-one-free kind of special. But such dubious sale tactics only increased Ryan's anxiety and suspicions. Resisting the questionable offers, Ryan was about to walk away when Al' Stit'ch U'up said, "Hol' on a minute there me lad-o and cop yourself on. Sure only a t'ick eejit would walk away from the deal of the century."

"What did you just say?" Ryan couldn't believe his ears. A souk trader in the middle of Cairo, dressed in traditional Bedouin attire at that, using Irish phraseology was something else altogether, but when your man started speaking in a brogue usually reserved for the bars around Dublin port, sure Ryan nearly hopped up onto the four humped camel and rode off into the sunset, if only to convince himself that he wasn't dreaming.

"Ah go-on, go-on, go-on, go-on," said Al' Stit'ch U'up, now that he had Ryan's full attention. Then he started patting each hump on the camel like a bongo player. "Ahh but you'd look grand on this, like one of the gentry, and here look-it," he added, addressing the functional appeal of each hump, "sure there's one hump for yourself, a grand one at that, a hump for the oul' colleen, and a few extras for the snappers. And if ye happen to have more than two babbys, which I'm more than sure a good looking, young virile man like yerself will have," he flexed one of his biceps at this point, before pointing over to the stall selling extra humps, "sure you can always buy another hump from the oul' lad beyond."

Ryan remained silent, but only because his ears still could not believe the mouth out which his eyes were trying to convince him the words were being spoken. Of course Al' Stit'ch U'up, that's Al' to the friends and family members he had not yet sold, took this silence as a sign of buyer resistance, and continued his sales patter, determined to wear poor, dumbfounded Ryan down.

"Are you sure now, young fella?" Al' Stit'ch U'up grinned. "Now won't you be the talk of the town, riding around up there like Lester Piggot himself. Here so, since I'm feeling so generous," his smile broadened, "sure I'll even throw in a few plates of ham sandwiches. And you can even have an extra hump for free, to carry them around on."

"I thought Muslims don't eat ham?" said Ryan.

"Did I say ham?" grimaced Al' Stit'ch U'up, opening his mouth as wide as he could, and demanding that the devil leave him immediately. "Come out of me Shaitan ye blaggard!" And when the devil refused to leave his mouth, Al' started spitting, coughing and tugging at his tongue, determined to drag oul' Shaitan out by his horns. But the devil was persistent, so Al' had no other choice but to send for reinforcements. He called over the other two stall holders, and all three of them cursed, spat and tugged on the foul tongue, in the hope of exorcising the unwanted interloper. A few moments later, satisfied that Shaitan had been evicted, and himself with a tongue almost the same length as the camel stood beside him, he went on, "Forgive me dear oul' lad, what I actually meant to say was that I will throw in an oul' plate of camel sandwiches, to be sure."

"Camel sandwiches?"

"On brown soda bread of course," said Al', with the camel giving him an awfully cold stare altogether. Things were bad enough for the camel, what with him having to wear extra humps and all, making him the laughing stock of the other camels in the caravan, but the thought of ending up between two slices of soda bread gave him a hump of another kind.

"And apart from a little extra chewing," Al' assured Ryan, nearly licking the face off-a himself with his new flopping, dangly tongue, "sure you won't even notice the difference."

Ryan O'Reilly thanked Al', but once again refused the generous offer. However, now that he'd heard an Irish accent, albeit it a most unexpected one, he felt a bit more comfortable with the proceedings, and told Al' the real reason for his visit.

"I've been sent by William McCoy The Third, to purchase the pyramids."

Purchase the pyramids? Ryan still couldn't believe he'd been so stupid. And now with William laughing down the phone at him a few years later, rubbing salt into the wound, he wished he'd never heard of GRABiT. But he had, and William was on a roll.

"No, Ryan," chuckled William, "the change has got nothing whatsoever to do with Egypt."

"Good to hear that sir," Ryan said, trying to contain his relief. "So what has changed?"

"GRABiT has just entered the final phase of our latest project."

"A new project," said Ryan, "that's news to me sir."

"We've kept this baby real hush-hush, Ryan my boy, on a need to know basis, only."

"And now I need to know?" said Ryan, feeling that he was about to be stitched up again, except this time it wasn't Al' Stit'ch U'up doing the darning.

"Correct," William said. "Forget the Irish potato famine, and any spare land or properties those Paddys may have left behind when they migrated. When GRABiT completes this new project, there'll be human movement on a scale that will make those famine migration numbers look like a picnic outing to Central Park."

Chapter 3

The Big Surprise

Technological Shenanigans was every child's dream. A large store full of technological wonders, with stacked shelves you could lose yourself in for hours. All manner of contraptions hung from the ceilings, and electronic shenanigans ran around the floor, climbed up the walls or flew from shelf-to-shelf, and you never knew when, or where, another contraption would turn up.

Didn't the kids love the Cantankerous Cabbage, and it was one of the first things they looked for whenever they came inside the shop. A Cantankerous Cabbage, another one of QuickMIC's recent inventions, was a technological shenanigan which spent most of its time rolling around the floor. But every now and then it stopped, opened up its leaves to reveal an awful grumpy face altogether, and with the dreariest voice you could ever imagine, spoke a phrase such as: "I've the head of a cabbage, but I'm twice as green." Then it would close its leaves and roll away. It said a whole load of dreary expressions like that, "You think you've got it hard, every day they stick me in a pot of boiling water!"; "I'm not just here for the bacon you know, sure I've a life of my own."; "A cabbage's life hasn't got a patch on a humans."; "You're a miserable looking eejit. Cop yourself on. If you had my head on your shoulders, you really would have something to complain about!" Or sometimes it would tell the most un-funniest jokes you ever heard.

In one corner of Technological Shenanigans QuickMIC had a repair club, and for the really lucky ones, there was always his personal laboratory in the back of the shop, where he invented, and experimented. And at the moment, QuickMIC wished he could shut up shop and retreat to his laboratory for a bit of peace and quiet.

The rest of the irate crowd had waited outside until QuickMIC switched on the lights, hopped up onto the runner behind the counter, fired up the till and beckoned them in. And now that they had the counter surrounded, their impatience was spilling over into boisterous frustration.

"What do you mean you've run out?" grumbled Fin, who felt that being first in the queue entitled him to first choice of QuickMIC's latest offerings.

"That's some surprise, alright," snarled Mr Muscles.

"Sure I'm as surprised meself," said QuickMIC, his eyes curious purple.

"I think you could do with a trip to diagnostics," said Fin, "to get yourself a check up."

"He'll need a trip to diagnostics if I go home empty handed," growled Mr Muscles. "Sure McDonalds never runs out of burgers now does it? How can a shop which specialises in shillelaghs run out of technological shillelaghs?"

Poor oul' QuickMIC looked aghast and shrugged his shoulders for the umpteenth time, his eyes turning redder. "Like I say lads, I've only ran out of the new arrivals, there's plenty of shenanigans back there on the shelves. Why don't you run and grab yourselves a Cantankerous Cabbage?"

"I've nearly the full set, already" groaned Fin. "Anyway," he added, "they have me and the oul' lad driven mad. All the miserable yokes do is roll around the house all day. And if you happen to step on one, they get even grumpier."

"They can be a bit trying," admitted QuickMIC.

"*Trying* is one word for it," said Fin. "Sure I'd pay you double to take my Cantankerous Cabbages back," he added, and a few others made QuickMIC the same offer.

"Sorry lads," said QuickMIC, smiling, "no sale or return. And wouldn't they be awfully cantankerous if I took them back. I'm not sure I could cope."

"Come on now QuickMIC," said a young girl, "you must have something else?"

"Sorry I can't help you, young lady," said QuickMIC. "How about Danny Boy's Toys, have ye tried them?"

"This is the twenty first century, is it not?" said Fin.

"And?" inquired QuickMIC.

"Their toys look like they've been sat there for the last twenty of them," replied Fin.

"There's nothing wrong with windup toys," said QuickMIC. "Don't be so ageist."

"Well at least now I know how they feel," said Mr Muscles.

"Who?" said QuickMIC.

"The wind up toys," snapped Mr Muscles. "Sure you have me awfully wound up meself this morning."

"Have you none of those talking Father Jack shillelaghs, either?" one of the young girls asked QuickMIC. "Me mother wanted one of them to give to the visiting priest tomorrow."

"DRINK!" another nine year old girl shouted.

"GIRLS!" Mr Muscles shouted.

"FEC .....," another young fella started to shout, but QuickMIC quickly interrupted him.

"Stop right there," he yelled, bringing the unholy impressions to a swift end. "We've no Father Jack Hacketts either, and that'll be enough of that language."

"Awww," several of young girls chorused, "no Father Jacks either?"

"Sadly," QuickMIC said feebly, "we've had a few complaints about that particular model, and we won't be stocking him anymore."

"What do you mean?" asked Fin. "Father Jack was grand, wasn't he?" All the other children agreed, some even muttering a few more of Jack's phrases under their breaths.

"And by the way," QuickMIC insisted, "it wasn't even Father Jack."

"Are you sure now," said Fin, "it had the look of him?"

"It may have looked like him, alright," admitted QuickMIC, raising his eyes in dismay at another round of foul whispers, "but it was supposed to be Saint Francis of Assisi. He looked rough alright, because he'd only just received the stigmata."

"He'd do us anyway," said Mr Muscles. "So why won't you be stocking him anymore?"

"Well now, let me see," said QuickMIC, clearing his throat and struggling to get the words out, "when the Archbishop of Dublin recently gave his entire congregation Saint Francis of Assisi technological shillelaghs at a special ceremonial mass, to celebrate the anniversary of Padre Pio's canonization, we received a few complaints."

"Complaints?" said Fin.

"If only the congregation had waited until they got home," murmured QuickMIC, "before they took Saint Francis of Assisi out of the box. Within minutes of opening the boxes, Christ Church Cathedral was full of blasphemy and profanities not heard since Lucifer himself was kicked out of heaven."

"Jesus Christ," said Fin, "I can imagine. So not only did Saint Francis look like Father Jack, he also sounded like him?"

"I was informed personally by the Archbishop," added QuickMIC, hanging his head in shame, "that the Pope himself collapsed the next day when he read the headlines in L'Osservatore Romano, the Vatican Newspaper: 'Satan is alive and well and living in Dublin!' I can only assume," QuickMIC continued in his defence, "that Saint Francis had some kind of software error."

"How about Mrs Brown?" said Mr Muscles, teasing QuickMIC. "Me mammy would love one of them technological shillelaghs."

If the pope had been stood in the queue after that request, the children would surely have finished him off. Didn't they spend five minutes repeating every expletive Brendan O'Carroll, playing the part of Mrs Brown, had ever used.

"Mind that language," screamed QuickMIC, in vain, trying to stem the flow of profanities. "Jesus, but ye're only children. Will ye whist!"

"Come on now," said Mr Muscles when the last of the swearing died down, "where's all the latest stock gone? I thought you get a new delivery every week?"

QuickMIC had been wondering that himself. How had he run out of stock? When he locked up last night the displays had been full to bursting, with the latest arrivals from America. He was trying to come up with more excuses when his telescopic eyes, now a curious purple, zoomed into the locks on the display cabinets, and started flashing intermittent red. The display cabinets had all been opened from the inside.

"Hold on a moment lads," he said, about to get an even bigger surprise, "I'll see if I've anything left in the stock room."

Ignoring the mounting complaints, QuickMIC went into the back of the store to confirm his suspicions. The back door had also been opened from the inside.

"Be the hoh-key," he whispered to himself, his eyes changing to mysterious green, "the stock's gone alright."

But he hadn't run out of the latest stock, the latest stock of technological shillelaghs had run out on him.

"AWOL," muttered QuickMIC to himself, his eyes turning bright red, "now this could be dangerous."

Chapter 4

We're Taking Down The Ross Ice Shelf

"By the way," said William, "thanks for the reminder."

"What reminder?" asked Ryan anxiously, still on the conference call to Manhattan.

"Egypt, of course," hissed William, "and that pyramid fiasco you got me involved in. Not that I needed reminding."

Ryan cringed and felt like screaming down the phone that it was William who had created the fiasco not him. But he knew better.

Having told Al' Stit'ch U'up the real reason for his visit back there in Cairo, Al' started panicking.

"Sweet Jesus, Mary and Joseph ... sure why didn't you say that in the first place?" asked Al', blessing himself three times, and putting a finger to his lips, urging Ryan to whisper.

"I never got a chance," whispered Ryan. "I couldn't get a word in edgeways. Actually, if it was left up to you, I'd be riding home on a four humped camel right about now, eating one of the humps for my lunch."

"Sure I'm sorry, and all," said Al' affectionately, "but it's a curse sometimes."

"What is?"

"Don't you know the Irish could talk as long as the day itself, to be sure," sighed Al', "longer even. Sure I don't get a wink of sleep some nights, and the poor oul' wife has started wearing ear-muffs about the house."

"Never mind all that, now," said Ryan. "Are you actually Irish?"

"Irish? Are you codding me or what, to be sure?" Al' nearly fell over with the shock. How dare Ryan question his Celtic lineage. Didn't Al' even grow cabbages in his own back garden, huge cabbages at that, cabbages which were watered and fed on nutrients from the Nile herself, and had him the envy of all the other farmers in Cairo.

"But your name," said Ryan, "it doesn't sound Irish?"

In the end Al' Stit'ch U'up convinced Ryan that his name was a very poor translation of his father's real Irish name, which had been eroded over time, via numerous mispronunciations, and garbled altogether recently by absorption into the colloquial.

"I don't know why you look so surprised," said Al'.

"What do you mean?"

"Sure the Irish are everywhere," Al' stated in a Galway accent. "And you may rest assured," he continued, "that if there is a place where the Irish haven't been, sure it's not worth going."

"They are," said Ryan, "and it isn't," he agreed, as Al' took the extra three humps back off the relieved dromedary, claiming that his father, Alan Mac Giolla

Phádraig, an eminent Irish archaeologist, came to Egypt in search of fame and fortune and hit the jackpot when he bumped into Al's mother, Cleopatra Philopator, who was down the local souk buying a few gallons of camel's milk at the time for her next bath. Hadn't his dear oul' mother, Cleopatra, been excavating her back garden for the last few months, many years before they planted the cabbages of course, in the hope of striking any old Pharaoh's gold, and when she saw Alan, dressed in green khakis, haggling over a new soil core, she was smitten. She immediately offered him a chance to use his newly acquired – and heavily discounted on account of her sultry ways with the souk trader - soil core in her garden, where he could dig away to his heart's content, and promised him a luxurious, milky bath every night for the rest of his life. Even Alan, with the soil core nearly shaking out of his hand with excitement, realised that such offers came along only once a millennium, and that one should never look a gift horse in the mouth, or a gift camel if one was in Egypt.

"Did they ever find the gold?" asked Ryan.

It wasn't clear if they ever found the gold, Al' Stit'ch U'up answered, but no one could doubt that they were the cleanest couple in the neighbourhood to be sure, what with the nightly bath routine. Sure if it wasn't for the lingering smell of sour camel's milk, which followed them everywhere to be sure, they might even have been the most popular, too.

Ryan, although somewhat intrigued by the romantic escapades of Alan Mac Giolla Phádraig of Ballindooly County Galway and Cleopatra Philopator of Heliopolis, was still slightly sceptical about Al's name. So Al' Stit'ch U'up took him for breakfast the very next morning, if only to prove to him how such linguistic, tongue twisting, moniker anomalies like his may develop over time, and to assure him of his integrity, before Ryan handed over the nine million dollars for the three pyramids.

"How do you like the Uum Ali?" asked Al' as himself and Ryan tucked into the Egyptian delicacy the next day.

"Not bad," said Ryan, sniffing at another spoonful, "but it tastes a bit like bread pudding, to me. And, given the choice, I'd rather a fry-up for breakfast."

"And there's the first clue, to be sure," said Al' Stit'ch U'up in a Mayo accent, shovelling another spoonful of Uum Ali into his mouth.

"What do you mean?" asked Ryan.

"Tell me, so," began Al', in a heavy Wexford accent, "do you not find it strange that Egyptians eat bread pudding for breakfast?"

"I do," said Ryan, who admitted that he found it even stranger that Al' spoke with more Irish accents than you'd hear at a sell out GAA All Ireland final at Croke Park.

Al' laughed heartily, before continuing the linguistic history of the spoonful of scrumptious bread pudding about to enter his mouth, and explained that he had spoken and haggled with so many Irish tourists over the years that his voice now contained traces of nearly every Irish accent in Ireland.

"Fascinating," said Ryan.

"Sure you're right, Ryan," said Al' in a jaunty Donegal accent. "And the name, so," he went on, getting back to the pudding's history and repeating Umm Ali several more times in several more Irish accents, slowly distorting the phrasing until the words became *O' M-aalli*, "does it mean anything at all to you?"

"O-Maalli?" said Ryan, pondering the possibilities for a few moments. "Nope, I can't say it does."

A real thick eejit we have on our hands here, thought Al' Stit'ch U'up in a Kerry accent, before making the name of the pudding's origin even more obvious in a thick Dublin accent, "U-Malli as in ... O'Mall-i as in ... O'Malley!"

After a few more O'Malleys the penny finally dropped, and Al' explained that Mrs O'Malley, the originator of the pudding's recipe, had been an Irish mistress of the 19th century Khedive. "So you can see ..."

"That the Irish are everywhere?" interrupted Ryan.

"Not at all," Al' lectured, "you can see how in the same way the name Mrs O'Malley has evolved over the generations to become the name of the famous Egyptian pudding, Uum Ali to be sure, the name Alan Mac Giolla Phádraig has evolved to become my own name, Al' Stit'ch U'up to be even surer."

Now that it had been explained in such great detail, Ryan really could understand how the name Mrs O'Malley had slowly evolved to become the name of the famous Egyptian pudding, Umm Ali, but he was still at a loss with respect as to how Alan Mac Giolla Phádraig could ever have evolved into Al' Stit'ch U'up, no matter how many phonetic mutations, across the generations, he allowed for.

"Hieroglyphs," announced Al', revealing the missing piece of the linguistic, etymological jigsaw, and gently sucking on a hookah, now that they were both seated outside the establishment they'd just finished eating in.

"Hieroglyphs?" said Ryan.

"Cursive, logographic, hieratic and demotic glyphs if you must know," said Al' authoritatively.

Ryan stared at him blankly.

"Grand, so," said Al', back in the Kerry accent now, the coals glowing red hot in the hookah's bowl as he drew on the pipe, "it might take a while for me to explain, but I suppose we could start with the Rosetta stone."

What with his belly stuffed full of bread pudding, and his face full of sweet smelling smoke, Ryan was beginning to feel nauseous, and decided that he'd give Al Stit'ch U'up the benefit of the doubt, if only to get away from the sickly, bellowing clouds.

Five days later, Ryan returned to New York, minus the nine million dollars, with three pyramids, including the Great Pyramid of Khufu, which had been sold to him just outside Cairo by William McCoy The Third's Irish contact, Al' Stit'ch U'up. But it wasn't the pyramids which created an international stir.

Ryan's gift to Central Park Zoo nearly turned Darwin's theory of evolution on its head altogether, until three humps of the Egyptian dromedary fell off when the overzealous zoo keeper gave the camel a bath a few days later and scrubbed the bejaysus out of it.

Also, as old, haggard and belligerent as they were, the three Arabian Princesses, Egyptian jewels Al' Stit'ch U'up insisted Ryan take with him as a security measure, went down a great storm altogether over at the United

Nations Headquarters, where they became employed as Egyptian translators, moonlighting as camel experts and marriage guidance counsellors.

However, the coat of arms he gave to the lads with an interest in genealogy over there in the New York Irish Centre, had them baffled for a long time. Sure they found it terribly hard to believe that the name Alan Mac Giolla Phádraig, more commonly rendered into English as Alan Fitzpatrick, Fitzpatrick itself meaning Son of the Devotee of Saint Patrick, had its roots in the midst of ancient Egyptian history at all. But having ran out of ideas, and having managed to decipher a few of the hieroglyphs on the crest, well the ones that look like harps and shamrocks at least, they came to the conclusion that the Irish really are everywhere, and, more importantly, have been everywhere and even every when. In fact, following advice from a Professor of Genealogy at Trinity College Dublin, the lads are now convinced that the Irish coat of arms Ryan brought back from Egypt - another sweetener thrown in by Al' Stit'ch U'up to cement the pyramid deal - suggesting that Alan Fitzpatrick, aka Al' Stit'ch U'up, is a descendent of Ramesses II, and that his great, great, great, great – they ran out of greats here - granny was Cleopatra VII herself, is authentic. And although the lads can just about live with the claim that Cleopatra VII was born in Spanish Point, County Clare, Ireland on April 1st, 69 BC., and not Alexandria, Egypt, they have serious reservations regarding Cleopatra's betrothed, Marcus Antonius - Marc Anthony the lads call him. For according to the family tree on the Fitzpatrick coat of arms, Marc Anthony was actually born on January 14th, 83 BC., in Thurles, County Tipperary, not Rome. However, despite the lads reservations, the newly discovered Fitzpatrick coat of arms takes pride of place on the first float of the St Patrick's Day Parade in New York, every year.

Three humped camels and authentic Irish genealogy aside, considering that the Great Pyramid of Khufu alone consisted of 2.3 million large blocks, was almost 140 meters high and weighed 5.9 million tonnes, William was intrigued when Ryan phoned him to say he had just cleared US customs at John F Kennedy airport without any problems whatsoever.

But a few hours later, when Ryan turned up at William's office with the three pyramids in a brief case, didn't William collapse on the spot. Ten minutes later, William came round to the sight of the three miniature pyramids, replica paper weights, and there and then made Ryan an offer he couldn't refuse. Either he would work the nine million dollar debt off, or he would become a foundation stone in a new pyramid complex GRABiT would soon be building in Las Vegas, to replace the ones Ryan had failed to bring home.

Of course, unlike the boy king Tutankhamen, Ryan felt that, at the tender age of twenty one, he was much too young to be immortalised in the bowels of a pyramid. So a year later, he found himself working part of his debt off in Ireland, doing a documentary on Irish migration to the states. And now William had Ryan just where he wanted him, a pawn with no other choice but to play his part in GRABiT's expansion plans.

"I'd be very cautious, sir," urged Ryan, trying to steer clear of any more Egyptian references.

"About what Ryan?" said William, stroking Khufu on his desk.

"You mentioned the potato famine, sir?"

"I did."

"Well there's only one thing the Irish love more than their cabbages."

"What's that?"

"Their spuds."

"Then they'll love these new ones," said William Mc Coy The Third.

"You're not about to introduce genetically modified potatoes into Ireland are you, sir?" Ryan gulped audibly, convinced that this was part of GRABiT's new strategy to take over the world. Control their diets and you control the people.

"Excellent guess," said William McCoy. "The latest genetically modified spuds will go down a storm over there."

"Or create a storm sir," said Ryan. "There'll be riots on O'Connell Street, you know." Ryan groped for ways to convince William of his folly. "I'd err on the side of caution, sir. The Irish might be considered thick placid, eejits in some parts of the world, but they know their potatoes, and they'll not forgive such a transgression, sir."

"Well they'll just love the new genetically modified ones, then," insisted William.

"Why are you so sure, sir?"

"These spuds have a lot more eyes," said William.

"Eyes?"

"Yes," said William, "these potatoes have more eyes than a box of sewing needles. They can even see in the dark." William sat back, sipped on his Manhattan cocktail and added, "Oh, I nearly forgot, they have ears, too."

"Ears?" said Ryan.

"Yes ears ..." confirmed William smugly into the conference phone. "These genetically modified potatoes have more ears than a cob of corn. They're great listeners, you know."

"Jesus sir," said Ryan, struggling to contain his disbelief, "you talk about them like they're almost alive."

"Funny you should say that Ryan," said William. "We're debating whether or not to give them a mouth. I believe the Irish love a bit of the old blarney? A bit of craic, eh Ryan?"

"Yes, sir," Ryan said tentatively. "The craic, the Irish love it."

"Well these spuds will have their jackets stuffed with craic," said William joyfully. "Can you imagine the conversations they'd have while they were getting peeled out of those jackets? Why I'm even sure some would talk themselves back out of the chip frying pan."

Ryan had long ago suspected William was going mad. The pyramid affair had been sign enough, but he nearly fainted with the thought that intelligent Frankenstein-esque spuds were headed for Ireland.

"You'll never get them through customs," said Ryan, hoping to talk some sense into this madman.

"Why not," said William sharply, "we'll dress them in the finest clothes, fashionable jackets and all. Actually," he went on, "we'll even give each of them spending money and a passport."

It was only then that Ryan suspected William was pulling his leg. "A passport?" he asked, cautiously. "You're joking of course ..." He hesitated - nothing would surprise him where William McCoy The Third was concerned - and added, "... aren't you?"

"Joking?" laughed William. "Well if it's good enough for East European migration into Ireland, I'm sure it's good enough for our spuds."

"Whew," said Ryan, "you had me going there, sir."

"Nothing wrong with a bit of craic, eh Ryan?" William chortled.

"Nothing at all sir," said Ryan congratulating him, "you're a natural."

After some more laughing, and with Ryan a little calmer, William said, "Now I want you to leave Dublin as soon as possible and head for Eirestown."

"Eirestown?" said Ryan. "Can't say I've ever heard of the place."

"That doesn't surprise me," said William, "I'll have Mrs Baxter e-mail you over directions straight after the call. Please obey Security Protocol 5."

Security protocol 5! GRABiT's highest security level. Ryan pricked his ears immediately. "Sounds serious sir?"

"Very serious," said William. "Once you've found Eirestown, you are to befriend a few people."

"Anyone in particular?"

"Details will follow in the e-mail."

"Do you have a cover for me, sir?"

"Have you heard of shillelagh sticks?"

"Of course sir, everyone's heard of shillelagh sticks."

"But have you ever heard of technological shillelaghs," William asked, "or even iShillelaghs?"

"Can't say I have, sir."

"Then there's your cover," answered William, explaining that a shop in Eirestown specialised in such shillelaghs. "You're doing a documentary about them."

"What's the objective of the infiltration, sir?"

"Sabotage Ryan my boy," said William, rubbing his hands together, "good old fashioned sabotage."

"I don't get it sir," said Ryan, "any clues for me?"

"Here's one," said William, "listen up."

Ryan pressed his ear hard against the receiver, but all he could hear was the clinking of William's ice cubes in his Manhattan cocktail.

Ryan scratched his head. "You're running low on ice?"

"Not a bad guess Ryan, not bad at all. They'll be ice enough soon, ice enough for the whole world in fact."

"Ice?" said Ryan.

"GRABiT is taking down the Ross Ice Shelf Ryan," said William calmly, slurping on his Manhattan, "and I don't want anything, or anyone to get in my way."

Did Ryan hear that correctly? Did William actually say he was taking down the Ross Ice Shelf? A megalomaniac, William often said crazy things like that. But there are not many people who would try and buy the Egyptian Pyramids. However, Ryan doubted that he'd get the Ross Ice Shelf though customs at JFK, without raising a few eyebrows.

"As in ... The South Pole, sir? You're taking down the Ross Ice Shelf in Antarctica?" pushed Ryan.

"No," said William, "that would be a ridiculous idea. It just so happens that I've a shelf in my freezer called Ross, and I'm due to take it down for a spring clean this weekend."

"Ok," said Ryan, wishing he was back in Cairo, buying moth ridden Bedouin tents, the pyramids even, "for a moment there I thought you meant ..."

"Of course I meant the Ross Ice Shelf in Antarctica," William boomed, nearly popping Ryan's eardrum. "You got a problem with that?"

"Me a problem?" said Ryan, tinnitus still ringing in his ear and quickly looking to redeem himself. "Why I'd expect nothing less of you sir. No project is too big for GRABiT. No doubt the Ross Ice Shelf will make an excellent addition to New York's islands. I can see it now ... Manhattan, Brooklyn, Queens, The Bronx, Staten Island and ..." Ryan thought for a few moments, "and ... The Borough of Ross Ice Shelf, where people go to chill."

"Nice idea Ryan, my boy, I like it. But she'll not be coming here."

Ryan pressed William for more details about what exactly taking down the Ross Ice Shelf entailed and how his sabotage mission would fit in. But William refused to divulge any further information until the next conference meeting, which they'd have just as soon as Ryan had carried out some surveillance in Eirestown. Suffice to say, he repeated, that there was going to be human migration on a global scale, and GRABiT were about to become richer than Bill Gates, Geroge Saros and Warren Buffet combined.

"Google's wasted a lot of money mapping the world these last few years," William finally said. "Carpe diem Ryan, carpe diem ...Will you GRABiT, Ryan?"

"Yes sir! With both hands," Ryan exclaimed anxiously, saluting and repeating the company motto to prove his loyalty. You never know, William might have a hidden camera in his hotel room. "GRABiT while you can!"

Chapter 5

I Give You iShillelagh

"Shush ... Shush ... Come on now lads, quieten down, please."

QuickMIC was back from the stock room and up on the runner behind the counter, his arms flapping, trying to bring some order to the crowd.

"I've just remembered," he lied. "We had a mad rush on last night lads, a tourist bus from Dublin, and we sold everything we had."

"What were they like?" asked Mr Muscles.

"They were typical Dubliners," said QuickMIC. "Arrogant laggards down from the city, trying to teach us country boys a thing or two."

"I meant the new technological shillelaghs," said Mr Muscles.

"Oh," squirmed QuickMIC, "the shillelaghs, why you'd have loved them. There were Ninja Assassins, American Green Berets and fierce fellas like that."

"Wow," said Mr Muscles, "they sound fierce."

"They were fierce alright," said QuickMIC, "trained killers everyone ..."

"What's wrong QuickMIC?" said Fin. "QuickMIC?"

"Look at his eyes," said Mr Muscles, "is he dead?"

QuickMIC was frozen on the spot, his eyes jet black. The realisation that troop loads of highly trained killers had gone AWOL from his shop and were on the loose in Eirestown had caused a system reset, which is like a heart attack in human terms. Slowly QuickMIC booted back up, his MIC and software bringing him back to life in a start-up sequence.

"QuickMIC," shouted Fin, waving his hand in front of QuickMIC's face, "are you alright QuickMIC?"

"Grand," exclaimed QuickMIC, his eyes a more relaxed blue.

"We thought you were dead?" said Fin.

"Not at all," said QuickMIC, rolling his shoulders and bending down to touch his toes several times. "I've been having problems with the oul' stepping motor all morning, and needed that system reset. But I'm grand now that I've had the oul' reboot."

With QuickMIC completely rebooted, the children started complaining again.

"Look, lads," said QuickMIC, pulling a parcel from underneath the counter, "we've these just in from Silicon Valley, California, only yesterday. Normally I like to check them out first before I let ye at them. But these are exceptional circumstances." He opened the parcel on the counter and rummaged around inside for a few seconds. He wouldn't normally offer new technological shillelaghs without checking them for quality and safety first, but this was an emergency.

The crowd became very quiet, eyes wide with anticipation. The box QuickMIC had pulled from inside the larger parcel was vibrating vigorously and he was struggling to hold onto it. Intrigued, and slightly concerned, he placed it on the counter where it continued jumping from side to side.

"A hopping box," said Fin, "is that it?"

"Is it full of frogs?" one of the girls asked.

"Hold on a nano-sec," said QuickMIC, picking the box up again to read a bright red label. "Now what does this say... Ahh look, lads ... it's The Cracker Craics."

"The Cracker what?" said Fin.

'The Cracker Craics,' repeated QuickMIC.

"It's himself whose crackers," snorted Mr Muscles.

At the mention of the name The Cracker Craics the box started to distort even more in several places, as if someone, or something, was trying to punch or kick its way out of it. Somewhat startled, QuickMIC threw it back on the counter, where it jumped, hopped and distorted even more violently. Muffled high pitched voices could also be heard coming from inside it.

"Open it quick," said Fin, "they could be illegal immigrants, stowaways or something."

"Are you expecting a shipment of midgets by any chance?" Mr Muscles asked QuickMIC.

QuickMIC ignored Mr Muscles' question and started to pull open the top of the box. Of course he wasn't expecting midgets, but at the same time he didn't want to be accused of suffocating anyone or anything that might actually be in the box. He tugged away at the flaps but never got a chance to finish opening it. The technological shillelagh occupants, six in all, sprang out like a troupe of Jack in the Boxes, and started running and tumbling chaotically around the counter, introducing themselves in various high pitched voices, in what can only be described as a complete state of cacophonous, pandemonium. They were only ten centimetres high, but what they lacked in size, they more than made up for in volume.

"Howya!! we're The Cracker Craics... how's the craic ... are you well? Good man yourself ... and good lady yourself too ... would you like a song ... a jig perhaps ... ahh go-on go-on go-on go-on I'll give you a song ... The craic was mighty ... Ahh be Gawwrrr ... How's the craic ... Sure we're in grand form altogether ... you look grand yourself ... Howya ... The craic was mighty ... Ahh be Gawwrrr .... would you like a jig ... Ahh go-on go-on go-on go-on ... I'll give you a jig ... Howya ... how's the craic ..."

Round and round they went for almost a minute, each of them repeating the same phrases over and over. The children and QuickMIC were mesmerised by all the commotion.

Five of The Cracker Craics were male, and held musical instruments. One had a button accordion, one a set of uilleann pipes, one a three string guitar, and one a two string fiddle. The last scraggily yoke, with even scragglier blond hair held a bodhrán, and he also had a spoon tucked in each sock. He was the percussion section. A few of the lads had missing teeth, like the missing strings or keys of their instruments. Three of them were dressed in tail coats and knee britches with felt green hats, and all of them wore waist jackets. But you should have seen the size of the holes in the scraggily yokes britches, it was a surprise he wasn't playing his knees, knocking them together like blocks of wood, never mind the spoons and bodrhán.

The female Cracker Craic played no instrument, and just clapped her hands between phrases, bursting into a jig every few seconds. She wore a white dress, white apron, green blouse, black, tapped jig shoes and had a Galway shawl wrapped around her shoulders.

At last The Cracker Craics settled down and formed a circle on the counter in the middle of which the female took position. Within seconds they were singing the all time classic, The Fields of Athenry. The female singer had a dreadfully, sombre voice, and although there were some tuning issues, the plaintive sound of the pipes almost had everyone in tears, as she sang mournfully:

"Michael they have taken you away ... "

"I wish someone would take these yokes away," yelled Mr Muscles, raising a fist above the counter, "before I smash them all to pieces."

"You're right," said Fin, surreptitiously wiping a tear from his eye, "they'll have me crying over me white-pudding when I get home."

The tuning issues were getting worse, and it was clear that The Cracker Craics were struggling to hold the crowd.

"I love the song alright," one of the girls said, sticking a finger in each ear. "But this is like finger nails screeching down a chalk board. Make them stop."

"She sounds like a banshee," said another girl. "Switch them off," several screamed repeatedly.

"You're right, lads," said QuickMIC, apologising for the wails, squeaks and other uncomfortable noises which had all the children demanding The Cracker Craics be switched off. "I can only assume they've a got few tuning issues, having been banged around while in transit. I'm sure they'll settle down soon enough; but, not a bother, I'll put them back for now."

He tried to grab The Cracker Craics one by one, but they went into a state of pandemonium again, running and tumbling all over the place, before finally jumping off the counter.

The kids were in hysterics when QuickMIC jumped down from the counter and chased them around the shop. As fast as he was, they were faster, and eventually they all tumbled out the front door, their instruments screeching and wheezing.

"Never mind them," said QuickMIC, hopping back onto the runner behind counter and trying to subdue the laughter. "Here now," he reached into the larger parcel again, "I give you the very latest in technological shillelagh design." He carefully pulled off the last few bits of wrapping. "With the latest technology and all built in, apps and everything lads ... I give you iShillelagh!"

The children gasped in awe, and a whisper passed through them, "Did he just say iShillelagh?"

Chapter 6

Is That Yoke For Peeling Spuds?

QuickMIC had recently started taking shipments of iShillelaghs from America. They were the latest craze in Shillelagh Technological Innovation. iShillelaghs were microprocessor controlled like himself, but also had self learning Artificial Intelligence modules, and primitive emotional responses. They also benefited from the latest in bio-silicon polymers, which gave their skins an almost human like quality.

The crowd gasped again as QuickMIC extended his hydraulic arms and, with a little fanfare, pulled this particular iShillelagh out of the box. Holding up a piece in each extended hand he announced once again, "I give you iShillelagh!"

"Did I hear you right," said Fin, "iShillelagh, as in *I*?"

"You did indeed," said QuickMIC, emphasising the final I, "iShillelagh as in *I*."

"Is that *i* as in Apple *i*?" asked Fin

"Not at all," said QuickMIC, with a wink. "It's *i* as in *I* for Ireland." He smirked, nodded and added, "Or how about *i* as in intelligent, like meself."

"Or how about *i* as in ignoramus, like yerself?" suggested Mr Muscles.

"Good man yourself," said QuickMIC, not wanting to aggravate Mr Muscles and thinking that he was the real ignoramus here, "that's a good one alright."

"Are you not an iShillelagh yourself?" asked Fin.

"Well," QuickMIC hesitated, "without going into too many details, what with all my software updates, and addition of apps, sure I'm as good as," he rotated the iShillelaghs pieces, "if not better."

"I'd say you're better alright," said Fin, "that one looks broke."

"It's not broke," said QuickMIC, explaining that these were a slightly different design from the previous technological shillelaghs. The iShillelagh head and shaft could actually be removed from inside the body. The shaft with the head on was almost 25cm long, with a centimetre of thread on its base. "Therefore we'll just insert it," he demonstrated, screwing the iShillelagh shaft into the body, "and twist until it clicks, like so."

"What makes them so special?" asked Mr Muscles.

QuickMIC laid the iShillelagh on the counter, retracted his hydraulic arms, turned it over on its side, and lifted its hair. "Here look-it," he explained, "all the magic happens underneath this panel," he extended a jewellers head screwdriver from the end of one of his fingers and opened a panel on the side of the iShillelagh's head. The magic revealed, QuickMIC's curious purple eyes zoomed in, and he simultaneously pressed a button on a remote control to turn on a large plasma screen hanging behind the counter, which displayed what his eyes were looking at.

"Wow," said Fin, and all the other children agreed, when they looked up at the screen, where all the iShillelaghs microscopic circuits were magnified.

"You see," said QuickMIC, "he's a bit like meself, full of all kinds of technological wizardry. But these little fellas benefit from all the latest micro and nano-technology."

"Is he alive, then," asked Fin, "does he have the spark from the Tuatha Dé Dannan?"

"Not at all," answered QuickMIC, "he doesn't have the divine spark like meself, from those mythological gods."

"A spark from Eógan you mean?" asked Fin. "Where is Eógan by the way, you haven't sold him have you?"

"He's where he usually is," said QuickMIC, "back there in the laboratory, best place for him."

"So if they have no spark," said Fin "what's so special about these iShillelaghs?"

"They might have no spark," said QuickMIC, "but with their Artificial Intelligence, that's their AI, sure you might not even notice the difference."

"What's that?" asked Fin, gesturing to a corner of the screen.

QuickMIC turned the iShillelagh over, and pointed to the back of its head, "That's a USB port, and over here," he moved his eyes to another part of the head, "we have a SIM card slot."

"What are they for?" asked Fin.

"I haven't a clue to tell you the truth, lads," said QuickMIC. "Like I say, they've only just arrived, and I've yet to fully commission them.

"Go on so," said Mr Muscles excitedly, "fire the oul' boy up."

"Grand so," said, QuickMIC. He screwed the panel back, stood the iShillelagh up, and reached round its back. "Now where is it .. ahhh here we are, lads ... we throw the switch like so ... and its circuits should fire up any moment , now." He took a step back and cautioned the children to do the same, "Stand back now. Like I say, I've not tested this one."

All the children took one step back, and waited for some action.

"He's a very interesting oriental looking chap," said QuickMIC, zooming his telescopic eyes into the iShillelagh's face, "isn't he?"

"He's as interesting as me ma's rice pudding," said Mr Muscles, "does he actually do anything?"

"Just give him a moment to warm up," continued QuickMIC proudly, ignoring Mr Muscles' jibe. "Look at him, forty centimetres high and dressed to kill, eh?"

"Dressed to sleep more like," said Fin, "Is that a dressing gown he's wearing?"

"No young fella," explained QuickMIC, brushing a few creases out of the dark green gown, which had an embroidered gold shamrock motif running through it, "it's known as a kimono. I'd say he's a samurai. Like I say, he's dressed to kill."

"He'll kill me with boredom any minute now," said one of the young girls. "A ponytail, are you sure he's even a he?"

"He's a he alright," said QuickMIC flicking the iShillelagh's black, tied back mane, "and that's not a ponytail. It's a chonmage haircut, the traditional hairstyle of the Japanese Edo period. Sure all the samurai's had them back then."

The children started firing more questions at him, but QuickMIC told them to shush, and be patient. For a few moments the iShillelagh remained motionless, and then off it went, running up and down the full length of the counter, its head rotating 360 degrees as it shuffled along.

"What's it doing?" asked one of the customers.

"Sure that'll be its AI," guessed QuickMIC, "you know, its Artificial Intelligence. He's running around and getting to know the place. He'll be grand in a moment or two."

"He looks like one of yer men from the Chinese chipper," said Fin.

"He's fierce looking isn't he," said one of the girls. "I wouldn't ask him for sweet and sour chicken."

"Judging by the look on his face, I'd say it'd be more sour than sweet," said Fin, to which all the children started laughing.

"Konnichi-wa," interrupted the iShillelagh, bowing politely. "Watashi no namae *PaddySan* wa desu."

"Is that Gaelic?" asked Fin.

"No that's Japanese," said QuickMIC. "He's just said hello and introduced himself as PaddySan."

"PaddySan is it?" said one of the customers. "He doesn't look like a Paddy to me."

QuickMIC picked up the box again, to see if he could find any other details written on it.

"Fuzakeru Na!" PaddySan yelled, drawing a razor sharp sword, almost as long as himself, out of an ornate scabbard hidden beneath his kimono. The sword flew back over his head, and then he pulled it forward with lightening speed, slicing the box QuickMIC was holding in two.

"Jesus!" yelled Fin. All the other children gasped, and took a few more steps back.

A few millimetres to the left and PaddySan would have chopped off one of QuickMIC's versatile fingers.

"Kakate Kina!" PaddySan snarled, slashing the air a few times for good measure. Then he froze, with an awfully aggressive look on his face, holding the sword out in front of himself, as if he were about to chop and slice anything that got in his way.

QuickMIC was a little old for a technological shillelagh, but he kept himself up to date with all the latest gadgets. He had recently installed a Universal Translation Unit (UTU) app, if only to converse with all his international friends over the Internet. However, he was having second thoughts now because his UTU took no time at all translating the Japanese phrase *Fuzakeru Na*! – Don't mess with me! And it nearly went into meltdown when it translated *Kakate Kina*! – Come and get some!

"Fantastic," exclaimed Mr Muscles, the farmer's son, praising the iShillelagh's blade action. "Is that yoke for peeling spuds?" Before QuickMIC could answer, Mr Muscles went on, "Me ma could really do with one of them yokes. Sure she's up half the night peeling spuds." Then he pulled a potato out of his rucksack and threw it towards PaddySan.

"Atamma kitaze," PaddySan yelled, turning to meet the missile, his blade a whirl of flashing steel around the potato.

"What did he say?" Mr Muscles asked QuickMIC, when the potato landed at PaddySan's feet, its peel still intact.

"He said 'You've done it now'," translated QuickMIC.

"Done what?" asked Mr Muscles. "Sure he's not done much himself ..."

PaddySan cut Mr Muscles short, stamping his foot on the counter. The children were stunned and gasped again when the potato peel slid off the spud in a perfect helix. Then they all cheered and clapped.

"Wow," said Mr Muscles, "he'll save me ma hours. I wonder if he can make fries?" Before QuickMIC could stop him he threw another potato at PaddySan. Once again PaddySan's blade became a blur. Sure if it wasn't for several glints of light, you wouldn't think it was moving at all. Less than a second later a pile of neatly cut fries lay at his feet, with another helix of potato peel beside it.

The children were delighted with the sword display, and clapped and cheered even louder.

"Jesus," said Mr Muscles, "but me mammy's going to love one of these little fellas running around the kitchen. How much are they?"

QuickMIC's eyes changed to the brightest red his LEDs could muster. He gulped and told Mr Muscles to remain perfectly still as he struggled to stop the two freshly sliced pieces of box shaking out of his hands.

He was convinced that Mr Muscles was antagonizing PaddySan and that any further movement at all may be interpreted by his AI as some kind of counter attack. If PaddySan was a Spud peeler he was a highly skilled one for sure, but a little too aggressive and erratic for QuickMIC's liking. Mr Muscles might not realise the danger he was in, but QuickMIC was taking no chances - if PaddySan should slice at the box again, as skilled as he was, QuickMIC might lose a finger next time.

As concerned as QuickMIC was about PaddySan and the imminent loss of a finger or two, he was even more concerned about the previous consignment of iShillelaghs which had escaped out of their displays and out the back door overnight, and now AWOL.

If you could find it, Eirestown had a pretty liberal immigration policy, but QuickMIC wasn't sure it was ready for a combined influx of an elite team of American Commandos, supported by a clan of Ninjas Assassins, especially with PaddySan staring him down, waving a razor sharp blade at him.

QuickMIC was considering his options. How was he going to switch PaddySan off without losing a finger, a hand or worse, a shop full of children, when a Cantankerous Cabbage rolled across the counter towards PaddySan.

QuickMIC closed his eyes and the children watched with morbid fascination, convinced that PaddySan was about to make cabbage fries.

The Cantankerous Cabbage stopped in front of PaddySan. PaddySan drew his sword way back over his head and with the fiercest look you could imagine on his face, was about to slice the cabbage in two. Suddenly the Cantankerous Cabbage's leaves opened up to reveal the cabbage's awfully sad face.

The cabbage spoke with as much pathos as a priest giving a eulogy, "Did you hear the one about the Irish man who lost his cabbage? He never found it again. Guess why?" Why, one of the young girls asked. "He said all cabbages look the same," the cabbage responded. The dreary joke delivered, the Cantankerous Cabbage popped his head back into its leaves, closed them up tight, and rolled off the counter, letting out a muted OWWW when he hit the floor.

Nobody dared move, except for PaddySan who started giggling slightly, desperately trying to hold back his laughter, but it was no use at all, and the giggles grew louder and louder. No longer able to control himself, he broke out into fits of hysterical laughter.

PaddySan was laughing so much he could hardly get his apology out: "Suman ne na." But he did, and bowing politely towards QuickMIC, he contorted around the counter in stitches, unable to hold the laughter in, before slipping the blade back into its scabbard.

"I'm not sure about his sense of humour," said Mr Muscles, "but he makes grand fries. How much did you say he was?"

QuickMIC breathed a sigh of relief, put the two pieces of box down, waited for PaddySan to double in two with laughter again, quickly switched him off and said, "I didn't, he's not for sale."

Chapter 7

The Ross Ice Shelf Is Melting

After all the fuss at Technological Shenanigans, Fin was glad to be back at home, but a little angry that he'd not been able to buy a new technological shillelagh, or even one of the latest iShillelaghs.

Fin was in the kitchen of Paddy McGinty's Goat, Eirestown's only public house, and sat at an oak kitchen table, close to the black range which was roaring away, light flooding in through the windows.

Even though it was almost lunchtime, Banbha was tending to a pan of breakfast, which was gently bubbling and sizzling on top of the range. Banbha was twelve years old, had long blond hair, green eyes and, according to all Fin's friends at school, she was extremely pretty, feisty, intelligent and funny. Mind you, Fin couldn't see what all the fuss was about - to him she was just a cousin.

"A Cantankerous Cabbage," haven't you enough of them already?" asked Paht, running a curious thumb up and down one of his braces.

Paht was the landlord of Paddy McGinty's Goat, and purveyor of Eirestown's finest Black Stuff. He was also Fin and Banbha's grandfather, but they didn't hold that against him. He was sat across the table from Fin trying to read The Eirestown Press newspaper.

"Sure you wouldn't believe it was possible, but QuickMIC actually ran out of shillelaghs," said Fin.

"Arthur Guinness never runs out of pints, now does he?" said Paht.

"That's exactly what one of the lads said, but he used Mc Donald's burgers."

"So why another Cantankerous Cabbage," inquired Paht, "they have me driven mad?"

"It was either take him home or let him get arrested," answered Fin, explaining that QuickMIC eventually had to call the Garda Síochána to get the children out of the shop, and this particular cabbage had upset a young guard.

"How did he upset him?" asked Paht.

"He told him a joke," said Fin, repeating the joke: "What do you say to a guard with bad breath who wants to give you a kiss? Nothing at all. You don't want the smelly eejit anywhere near you!"

Paht and Banbha started laughing.

"The spotty face guard didn't like that at all," continued Fin. "He roughed the cabbage up, and nearly gave him a belt of his truncheon."

"Police brutality," said Banbha, "we should report him."

"You had to feel sorry for the guard, though," Fin continued. "He's only been married for a year and because he has an unholy case of halitosis, his wife won't let him anywhere near her."

"Jesus," said Paht. "The cabbage is lucky he didn't end up in a tub of coleslaw, never mind a beating with a truncheon."

"Anyway, forget QuickMIC and his shillelaghs," said Paht, "we've more serious matters to worry about. Look at this," he showed Fin the headlines of The Eirestown Press, 'The World Is Melting'.

"What does it mean?" asked Fin.

"I haven't a clue," replied Paht, "she'll tell me nothing this morning."

The Eirestown Press wasn't like other newspapers. The first thing you noticed was the fact that it contained no words, no pictures, no anything actually. Sure Paht was lucky this daily edition even had a headline, because the front page was also usually blank, apart from the name at the top.

"Have you asked her?"

"'Deed I have," said Paht, "but she's keeping stum."

"You'd never believe me anyway," said The Eirestown Press, ruffling its pages. "Either that, or you'll be terribly sad after hearing the latest news. And I've enough of me own problems without making the whole town sad."

"Ah come on now," said Paht, trying to console the newspaper, "no one will blame you. Sure you're only the messenger."

"Yes," added Fin, "and no one ever shoots the messenger."

"Never mind The Eirestown Press," said the newspaper, "if I tell ye the latest news, they'll be calling me The Eirestown De-pressed."

"Is it that bad?" asked Banbha.

"I'm still recovering from the shock meself," said the newspaper, ruffling a few pages again on top of the table. "I'll need to see a psychologist for counselling or something one of these days. The whole world is going mad except for meself and ye." The newspaper paused for a moment, as if in deep thought and added, "And I'm not too sure about ye."

"Cop yourself on now," said Paht, "we can handle it."

"Are ye sure?" asked the paper.

"We are," they all replied confidently.

"Sure I'm already the scourge of the town after last week's news," the paper bemoaned. "I'm surprised you bought me at all."

"Don't forget," said Fin, reassuring the newspaper, "you're only the messenger."

"You promise you won't get mad at me?" asked the paper, meekly.

"Not as mad as I'm getting now," hissed Paht.

"I'm not sure ..." The paper was becoming more nervous.

"Enough of this nonsense," Paht roared, and a moment later he had The Eirestown Press hanging over the open range, flames licking away at the bottom of its yellowing pages. "Are you going to tell us, or would you like to join yesterday's mute down there in the ashes?"

"Ok, ok," screamed the paper, ruffling like crazy to stop the flames spreading. "Would you like to be told, or would you rather read it yourself?"

"We'll read it," said Paht, patting out a few flames at the bottom of the paper.

"As you wish," huffed the paper, "upon your heads be it. Don't say I didn't warn ye."

"Oh just get on with it," yelled Paht, slamming The Eirestown Press down on the kitchen table. He was growing tired of the daily histrionics, and hadn't even got a word out of yesterday's paper.

"Touchy," said the paper, and it ruffled again, and again, as if shaking the words out of some ethereal scrabble bag.

"Look," said Fin, running his finger under the words as they appeared beneath the main headline, "South Pole demise ... The Ross Ice Shelf is melting ... Recent unexplained acceleration in melt rate ... Rising sea levels and global warming threaten all major coastal regions and beyond ... human abuse of fossil fuels major factor... mass extinction ... mass migration ... climatic catastrophe threatens the earth and all life ..."

"They're going to drown us all, so," said Paht. "Humanity's a screw loose, and is hell bent on destroying itself."

"This sounds serious," said Banbha, "they'll have to be stopped."

"You're right!" announced a diminutive figure, entering the kitchen.

"Ahhh, look," said Fin, "... if it isn't Malachy Malarkey, adopted son of King Cormac himself."

"'Tis!"

"Hold on a minute, Malachy," Paht said, "how did you get in here?"

"Some fool left the bar door open," said Malachy.

"I'll have to put a lock on that door," scowled Paht, the fool in question. He wasn't keen on some of the technological shenanigans QuickMIC invented, and Malachy Malarkey, a technological shillelagh, was one of them.

"Never mind locks you," snapped Malachy Malarkey. "Anymore cheek and you'll find yourself in the dungeons, where you'll be more worried about keys. I'm on the King's business, so whist."

Malachy Malarkey, who often played the Court Jester in King Cormac's Castle, was almost fifty centimetres high. When on official business, as he was today, he wore a green, white and orange harlequin suit, with matching pantaloons; and bells tinkled away on his three tailed Shellenmütze, which is a fancy word for a Jester's hat. Paht was always wary when Malachy was around, since he had fallen foul of his tricks on numerous occasions in the past.

"That's not fair Malachy," said Fin.

"You can shut up too," said Malachy, "I'm here on business with the organ grinder not the monkey," then he sneered at Paht again, "nor the guerrilla."

"We'll whist alright, just as soon as you answer me one thing," said Paht reluctantly. "Does oul' King Cormac have any advice for me today?"

"Yes," said Malachy, nodding his head to ring his bells. "King Cormac suggests that if you breathe in between mouthfuls of food you might lose some weight. Now whist I say, or you'll be eating fried brains."

Strapped to his right wrist, Malachy had an experimental, prototype Zapper which QuickMIC had recently invented. Zapper energy was carried by transparent wires to Malachy's finger tips and he could use it to fire off blasts of 'funny stuff'. Although, to be fair, it wasn't that funny if you got an oul' belt off one of those blasts. Malachy wasn't the best of shots and he was also struggling to control the firing mechanism.

Only yesterday, QuickMIC was in the Paddy McGinty's telling Paht that the 'funny stuff' was some kind of high energy plasma thingamajig, and a zap of it could fry your brains. In that case, most people in the bar doubted it would have any effect at all on Paht. But he was taking no chances. Paht knew better than to argue with Malachy at the best of times, and now that he was wearing the oul' zapper, he'd be an awful little terror altogether. So Paht just grumbled a few curses under his breath, and tucked back into his breakfast.

"Now, Malachy, what would you be needing from the organ grinder on this fine morning?" asked Banbha, throwing a sarcastic smile at Fin.

"As lovely and as courteous as ever Banbha, and looking ever so thin," said Malachy. "Not like your one over there, with the head of a cabbage" he added raising his elongated nose in Paht's direction. "He's eating enough for the whole of Eirestown."

Paht stopped chewing as if he was about to argue back, but got stuck into a rasher when Malachy waved his crackling finger at him.

"Well Banbha," continued Malachy, "it's about the Ross Ice Shelf. As you note, humanity has a self destruct button, and seems determined to finish itself off, and take all life with it."

"Is it really that bad?" said Banbha.

"Possibly," said Malachy. "Sure there's chunks the size of Ireland already crumbling off it."

"How bad will it get?" asked Fin.

The Eirestown Press was about to respond when Malachy interrupted it with a zap across its front page and said, "King Cormac told us in his weekly Council last night, that if the Ross Ice Shelf melts much more, sea levels will rise so much that we'll need bathing suits to go shopping soon."

"And how can I be of help?" asked Banbha.

"If the great grand daughter of a Seanchaí doesn't know how to solve this conundrum," said Malachy, "then we really are all doomed."

"Oh," said Banbha cautiously, slipping another rasher onto Fin's plate.

"Not to mention," Malachy added, "that you're the seventh daughter of a seventh daughter ... and you have the gift."

"What do you mean, she has the gift?" Fin asked Malachy.

"She can see things others can't," said Malachy.

"Is that right?" scoffed Fin. "Sure she can't even see her own reflection in a mirror."

"No one's asking you." said Malachy, pointing a crackling finger at Fin. "At least she's able to look into a mirror without breaking it."

"Are they one hundred percent sure the Ross Ice Shelf is melting?" asked Banbha.

"No," answered Malachy, "there could be other explanations. For example, it could be a seasonal variation, or part of a longer natural cycle, but King Cormac's concerned enough to require your services."

"Oh," said Banbha, "well I'll have to think about it ..."

Just then the muffled sound of a booming bass line grew louder outside in the back yard, and it had everyone in the kitchen hopping:

'Now old Paddy McGinty's Goat had a wondrous appetite,
and one day for breakfast he ate some dynamite.
A big box of matches he swallowed all serene
and out he went and swallowed up a quart of paraffin.
He sat by the fireside, he didn't give a hang,
swallowed a spark and exploded and exploded with a bang.
So if you go to heaven you can bet the dollar note....
that the Angel with the whiskers on is Paddy McGinty's Goat.'

"'Tis Donn-Dubh," said Paht, "on that bass powered contraption of his, sure he'll have the whole town hopping if he doesn't stop. Why he has to play that song every time he turns up here, is beyond on me." Paht pressed the palms to his ears, and shouted, "And what the hell does he want at this hour of the morning?"

"I don't know," said Banbha, covering her own ears, "but perhaps he'll be able to lend a helping hand."

Chapter 8

Mostly Harmless

QuickMIC was on the phone, talking to DumbHK's 24/7 Customer Support.

Technological Shenanigans had finally emptied after a further hour of continual harassment from the young crowd, almost culminating in a mini riot. On three occasions QuickMIC had to wrestle PaddySan out of Mr Muscles' hands. Eventually, after a sixth trip into the stock room, QuickMIC found an old box of Mallet-Heads which he hoped would be enough to placate the crowd.

The Mallet-Heads were the more traditional knobbly, shaped shillelaghs made from blackthorn, like the ones Irish people sold to tourists. Of course QuickMIC's mallet-heads had some inbuilt functions, but most were pretty dim, because they relied on older technology, with primitive software. This meant they had limited range when it came to speaking, and could only manage the odd phrase like, "Take me back to Ireland," or "I'm a stick of shillelagh," or 'Top of the morning to ye," or "I'm only a stick but I'm not that t'ick."

In the end however, the Mallet-Heads were not enough to pacify the irate children, and QuickMIC had to phone the guards to get them out. Unfortunately, he nearly got arrested himself when some of the Cantankerous Cabbages decided to annoy a few of the guards.

Digital Universal Microelectronic Business Hong Kong, DumbHK for short, was located in the heart San Jose's Chinatown, Silicon Valley, California. QuickMIC had been doing business with them for a few months now, and all had been going well, until this recent turn of events.

It had taken QuickMIC over an hour to get an answer from DumbHK's 24/7 IPC (Instant Priority Customer) Support Service, and he was on the verge of blowing a fuse.

"What do you mean PaddySan's mostly harmless?" said QuickMIC, somewhat rattled by the DumbHK customer service rep's lackadaisical attitude. "Sure he tried to kill me and my customers!"

The DumbHK rep apologised profusely once more. At least QuickMIC thinks she apologised. She hardly spoke a word of English and QuickMIC's UTU was struggling with the snippets of Mandarin she was using in the middle of garbled English sentences.

QuickMIC had phoned DumbHK for four reasons: Firstly, to complain that PaddySan had nearly assassinated him and his customers. Secondly, he wanted a refund for The Cracker Craics, who ran out of the shop without so much as a goodbye. Thirdly, not only did he want another refund, but he also wanted to know how worried he should be about the consignment of commandos, ninjas and special service personnel which had gone AWOL last night. And fourthly, after some reconsideration, he also wondered how worried he should be about

The Cracker Craics. After all, noise pollution was a big enough problem these days without him getting arrested for promoting it.

"So let me get this right," said QuickMIC to the DumbHK rep, addressing his first concern. "You're saying that PaddySan is mostly harmless?"

"Yes." The rep said, confirming her earlier assurances.

"Like a lion in the jungle is mostly harmless you mean?" said QuickMIC scornfully. "Unless you meet that lion on a dark night and he's not eaten all week. Is that it?"

QuickMIC was right about the DumbHK rep, her English comprehension wasn't the best, and she didn't have a clue what an *iron* had to do with anything, let alone what a hungry iron would be doing roaming around the jungle in the middle of the night. But for the umpteenth time, she reassured QuickMIC that PaddySan may have a few teething problems, or unforeseen technical glitches, but DumbHK would update his software drivers immediately and remotely, via wireless technology, just in case there were any bugs or viruses.

"A few teething problems, you say" said QuickMIC haughtily. "I'll buy him a tooth-brush, wha'?"

The sarcasm was lost in translation.

"Tooth-blush?" The service rep became even more intrigued. What would anyone want with a blushing tooth? Perhaps it was QuickMIC who needed his drivers and software updating she suggested.

"I beg your pardon," snapped QuickMIC, "but I'll have you know that I keep my drivers, software and electronic bits and pieces up to date myself."

Blushing teeth aside, QuickMIC was assured that he'd get a full refund for The Cracker Craics. He was also intrigued to learn that they'd actually been sent to the wrong address. The Cracker Craics had been ordered by the Irish diva Louise Walsh, to enter this year's I-Factor, the Irish-Factor singing contest, and they should have been delivered to his Dublin address. They were probably on their way there now, the rep claimed, using their inbuilt GPS.

Louise Walsh, always the greatest supporter of Ireland's talent, had decided to take no chances in this year's contest, the DumbHK rep explained. The Cracker Craics were a dead cert. The only problem Louise had now was getting the I-Factor's Groups category; or the Slightly Deranged category, the English diva Simone Cowell had commented, when Louise outlined her plans.

"And what about the other batch, the assassins and commandos?" said QuickMIC, addressing his third point. "Not only did they break out of the shop, some of them are 70 centimetres high. I've never seen iShillelaghs that tall before."

The DumbHK rep apologised once more and promised to reimburse him for any damage to the shop. She then said that the height issue had been due to a translation problem, the catalogue should have read 70 not 7 centimetres. She also reminded QuickMIC that he bore some responsibility for any concerns, because the batch had been shipped as beta-prototypes with a large warning in the catalogue: Caveat Emptor.

QuickMIC knew this Latin phrase meant Buyer Beware, but he was fascinated by the latest developments in iShillelagh AI and keen to get his hands on them. He also figured that a hand full of little iShillelagh characters, 7 centimetres high, no taller than a tea cup, could do him no harm. He said he hadn't realised that Buyer Beware actually meant you had to watch your back, just in case one of these iShillelaghs attacked you.

Don't worry, said the rep, they wouldn't harm him or anyone else.

"And they have a new autonomic system," concluded the rep in perfect English, "that's what gives them a certain level of independence. So don't worry about them at all, they'll be back after a little reconnaissance."

As for PaddySan's erratic behaviour, the customer support rep finally managed to allay QuickMIC's fears, assuring him that the latest designs would take a day or two to settle into their new environment and acclimatise.

"Forget the demonstration with his sword," she said, "he was only playing."

"Playing?" scoffed QuickMIC, counting his fingers again to make sure that they really were all still intact. "Sure I'd hate to see him when he gets serious."

And anyway, she went on, there really was nothing to worry about since all the iShillelaghs were programmed to obey the three laws of Robotics Asimov had devised. And The First Law stipulates that a robot cannot harm a human being.

"Does that first law include psychological harm?"

"Cop yourself on now," said the rep.

QuickMIC looked again at the fingers which had been holding the box when PaddySan sliced though it, and zoomed his telescopic vision into their very molecules. PaddySan may not have harmed him, and I suppose he wasn't actually human, but he could have swore there was a layer of atoms missing from the side of one finger. As far as he was concerned that was close enough, and he remonstrated with rep again, for at least twenty minutes, only to find that she'd put the phone down nineteen minutes and fifty nine seconds ago.

While QuickMIC drank chamomile tea to steady his nerves, PaddySan spent most of the morning in the kitchen, sharpening his samurai sword on a block of water stone. In between sessions of sharpening he would spurt out statements like 'Shinji mae na!' which QuickMIC's UTU informed him meant, "Just die already!" and 'Ano yarou', which his UTU informed him to just forget about.

After a few hours waiting for PaddySan to settle down, QuickMIC had gone through two boxes of camomile teabags trying to steady his nerves, and had spent so much time in the toilet, he seriously considered just dragging his mattress in there. As QuickMIC dropped his last tea bag into the cup, after one last furious sharpening session, PaddySan did eventually settle down. Putting his katana back its scabbard he closed his eyes and appeared to be sleeping. Delighted and exhausted, QuickMIC flew up the stairs into bed, to the flat above Technological Shenanigans. Sure after all the commotion his nerves were frazzled, and didn't he need an oul' siesta himself, to recharge his batteries, not that he had batteries mind.

But QuickMIC was taking no chances, before he slipped into bed, he double locked his bedroom door, placed a chair under the door handle, and a large kitchen knife under his pillow. Safely secured, he gave a deep yawn and lay down his weary oul' head, in the hope of getting forty winks or so.

Chapter 9

Bursting Out Of Mi Knickers

"Well," said Donn-Dubh, entering the kitchen of Paddy McGinty's Goat, "tis a grand day."

"It was," said Paht, scowling again at Malachy, "and peaceful as well Donn-Dubh, until you turned up on that blasted bass powered contraption."

Donn-Dubh had discovered Eirestown one morning many years ago by mistake. He'd flown in from London for a stag do in Dublin. Unfortunately, he had only just turned 18, and this being his first time away from home, he got a little bit carried away.

Drinking himself silly in the Temple Bar region, he soon lost the stag and the entourage and staggered around numerous pubs all night long, searching for them. As dawn broke, Donn-Dubh found himself peering into an inviting green mist, just outside Dublin City.

Unable to resist the beckoning green mist, he entered and woke up three days later in Paddy McGinty's Goat, his head thumping, and with half the town staring down at him.

"What you all looking at," asked Donn-Dubh kissing his teeth, "yu never see a black man before?"

"Oh, black is it, now?" said Paht.

"Yeah, man, black," said Donn-Dubh defiantly. "You got a problem with that?"

"Oh, no," said Paht, "we've seen many a black fella in here, alright. It's just that ..."

"What?" said Donn-Dubh.

"Are you sure you not one of the little green fellas?" Paht felt it necessary to clarify his question when Donn-Dubh looked at him like he might just have escaped from the local lunatic asylum, "A little green fella in disguise I mean."

"What?"

"A leprechaun man," said Paht, "are you sure you're not a leprechaun? If you are, you're perfectly safe here. Sure I'll even put the oul' pot of gold in the pub's safety deposit box."

"Me," repeated Donn-Dubh, pointing at himself, "a leprechaun in disguise?"

"So you are a leprechaun," Paht said, completely misunderstanding the rhetorical nature of Donn-Dubh's statement. "Sure I knew it."

"Me," repeated Donn-Dubh yet again, genuinely surprised to be at the centre of such a bizarre case of mistaken identity, "a leprechaun in disguise?"

"Yourself," said Paht, pointing back at him. "And I don't blame you for one minute."

"You don't?"

"I don't," said Paht, tipping his head forward sagely. "Since that last economic meltdown, leprechauns have been disguising themselves in all sorts of ways."

"They have?"

"'Deed they have," said Paht, "to safeguard the oul' pot of gold, you understand. Bejaysus," he went on, rubbing his chin between two well informed fingers and a financially astute thumb, "if the treasury could get its hands on a few of those pots me boyo, we could say good bye to the ECB forever. So no wonder you're all disguising yourselves these days."

"We are?"

"'Deed ye are. Sure only last week we had a gang in here that looked like Bob Marley and the Wailers, and the week before, Elvis himself made an appearance."

"But we knew they were leprechauns," shouted one of the onlookers.

"They didn't fool us at all," shouted another.

"We did indeed," laughed Paht. "Poor oul' Bob Marley was only two foot high, maybe less, and his hat took up a foot of that."

"Never mind him being leprechaun," said another, "he was small enough to be a pygmy."

"And," said Paht, pointing at Donn-Dubh's head with a questioning finger, "what do you call them scraggily yokes on your head?"

"Dreadlocks," snapped Donn-Dubh.

"Ahh, sure, now, but you should have seen the height of poor oul' Bob," said Paht, "and himself with the dreadlocks dangling down past his backside," he bent down, and hovered one of his palms just over his knees, "down to here somewhere," he struggled to stretch lower, "as far as his ankles if I remember correctly"

"You're right," said one of the women. "I'd say the yokes were even longer. Didn't he give the floor a good oul' sweep whenever he got up to buy a drink."

"I could have done with him around the house," said another, house proud woman. "I'd save a fortune on sweeping brushes." She caught Donn-Dubh's eye and asked him, "Are you interested at all in a domestic cleaning position yourself?"

But he just raised his eyes and kissed his teeth angrily.

"I'll take that as a no, so."

"Those yokes on his head are too short to reach the floor, anyway," said another woman, "unless you turned him upside down, and yourself and the oul' lad grabbed a leg each. Never mind a sweep, sure you could give the floor a real good buffin' as well."

"Sure I can see that for meself," said your one. "The green yokes are short, I'll give you that alright, but wouldn't he make a grand job, dusting the shelves."

"As for Elvis," said Paht, interrupting the domestic goddesses, "we knew it wasn't himself. Sure he wasn't much taller that the fiddle he was holding and he played it a bit too well for my liking."

"He did indeed," said another oul' lad. "Didn't he know more jigs than meself, and I'm playing with The Chieftains half my life. He was a leprechaun for sure, aren't they all born with a fiddle in their hands."

"So your disguise doesn't fool us one bit," said Paht, smiling down at Donn-Dubh. "Now hand over the pot of gold, and I'll keep it nice and safe for you."

"Look," shouted Donn-Dubh, "do *I* really look like a leprechaun bruv?"

"Quickly lads, the mirror," Paht commanded, and a mirror hastily made its way, hand-by-hand, via a human chain, from the bar to the table Paht was standing at. "Here you are, so," Paht said winking and handing the mirror to Donn-Dubh, "take a good look at yourself, and tell us you're not a leprechaun, Mr Leprechaun."

Donn-Dubh peered into the mirror and got the shock of his life. Then a memory flashed across his mind. He had drunk himself so silly that he'd forgotten that when they first landed in the Temple Bar, all the lads on the stag had asked a face-painter to paint them a patriotic green, and he even got his dreadlocks painted green.

"It's a grand disguise alright, sure the oul' green mop on your head had us all confused for ages, didn't it lads?" continued Paht. It did, agreed the crowd, as Paht handed Donn-Dubh a pint of the smoothest, most velvety Black Stuff he'd ever seen. "By the way," Paht smiled, "drinks are on the house for the little green fellas. So you may drink your fill."

"Look man," huffed Donn-Dubh, his confused, green face looking back out of the mirror at him, and himself twisting a few strands of green, matted hair, "like I say, these are dreadlocks, and they should really be black, the same colour as my face."

"But your face is green, man," argued Paht. "Now drink up, you couldn't draw a better pint from the Laffy itself, and it'll put a little colour back in your cheeks."

"Very funny," said Donn-Dubh sarcastically, gulping down a few sups of the pint, grateful for the hair-of-the-dog.

"No," apologised Paht clumsily, "sure I only meant ..."

"I know what you meant," said Donn-Dubh winking a green eyelid at him.
Then he suddenly had a brainwave. Pouring some of the black stuff into his hand, he proceeded to rub it into one of side of his face.

"It's a novel drinking style," said Paht, "sure some of these leprechauns have strange ways."

Donn-Dubh smiled at his reflection and it smiled back, when he looked in the mirror. It was working. His black skin was starting to show through where the green paint was being rubbed away. "Look," he said, "like I say, my skin is actually black." And then he explained how he'd ended up with a green face and hair.

"So there's no pot of gold, then?" said Paht dejectedly, when Donn-Dubh had finished his stag night story.

"Look man," said Donn-Dubh, glugging on his pint, "do you really think I'd be sat here with a bunch of weirdoes obsessed about leprechauns looking at me, if I had a pot of gold in my pocket?"

"Jesus man, so you've no gold? Pass me a phone quick," yelled Paht.

"Who're calling?" asked another, when the phone was passed from behind the bar

"My travel agent."

"Are you going somewhere?"

"Not now, I've to cancel that holiday to the Maldives before they bank my deposit," answered Paht. "And listen here you, you blaggard," he snapped, as Donn-Dubh relished the last few drops of his refreshing pint.

"What?"

"It'll be five Euros for the pint."

Donn-Dubh had settled in grand these last few years, sure it was as if he'd never lived anywhere else except Eirestown. The green face was long gone, but he kept his dreadlocks green, and considered this a patriotic gesture to his new found home. Everyone had grown to love him, except when he blasted his Jiggy-Reggy music, a fusion of Reggae and Irish music, first thing in the morning.

And this morning was no exception. Although he'd switched off his bass powered bicycle when he parked it outside Paddy McGinty's Goat, the bass hopped off the walls of the back yard, flew in behind him when he opened the door, and started echoing and reverberating around the kitchen. No one could hear a word.

"Well!" Donn-Dubh shouted again.

"Well!" Malachy, Banbha, Fin and Paht screamed in unison.

"How're ye?" screamed Donn-Dubh even louder, only this time he nearly burst everyone's eardrums, including his own, because Banbha had just opened the kitchen window to let the bass out.

"Be the hoh-key," said Paht, with how're ye still ringing in his ears, "we'd be all well and grand if you stopped shouting and left that contraption of yours at home."

"Sorry," whispered Donn-Dubh.

"What was that?" said Paht, cupping his hands behind both ears. "I think the poor oul' eardrums have drummed their last."

"I said I'm sorry."

"And to what do we owe this honour," said Banbha closing the window quickly, just in case the bass changed its mind and flew back in.

"Mi was just passing," said Donn-Dubh, with only a slight hint of his patois roots modulating his voice, which had been softened and modified by his many years in Eirestown, "and thought mi would visit me oul' friends. Oh and good mornin' yu highness."

"Cop yourself on now Donn-Dubh," snapped Malachy, "we're on first name terms many the year now."

Donn-Dubh doffed his hat, which was quite a feat considering the size of the tricoloured, domed shaped beehive, under which he kept his green locks, "Good morning Malachy. You may be a friend but when you're acting in an official capacity, you know yourself, respect is due."

"And less of that hat nonsense," added Malachy. "I've seen the inside of more doffed hats than a leprechaun's seen pots of gold. Although, I must admit, I've never seen such an ingenious use of a green, white and orange duvet."

Donn-Dubh apologised once more to the further annoyance of Malachy, patted his bulbous hat and asked everyone, "Do you like it? I've just bought it from QuickMIC."

"Intriguing," said Banbha.

"He's only just finished inventing it," Donn-Dubh explained. "Sure you wouldn't believe some of the technological contraptions he's got in there these days."

"It's an interesting hat, alrigth," said Malachy. "But are you sure it's not just a duvet wrapped around your head?"

"No," insisted Donn-Dubh, patting the hat again with both hands, "it's a hat alright. But I'll have you know that it's not just any old hat."

"What do you mean?" asked Malachy.

"Name three items," said Donn-Dubh, "quickly now."

"Hammer, keyboard, hat stand."

Three times Donn-Dubh reached into the folds of his hat, which looked more like a turban folded in on itself over-and-over by an origami expert, and pulled out the items one by one. When it came to the hat stand, he had to kneel down and get Paht to help pull it out.

"That's amazing," said Malachy, stepping forward to reach into fresh fold of the hat, "here, let me have a go."

"No!" yelled Donn-Dubh, trying to pull his head back out of Malachy's reach.

Sadly, Donn-Dubh wasn't fast enough. Malachy had managed to embed his hand deep between two folds of the hat, and was rummaging around.

"Aha," Malachy exclaimed, convinced he had something in his grip. What he didn't realise was that something actually had him in its grip. But as soon as he did, didn't Malachy start screaming and hollering, pulling his hand out of the folds rapidly, to find a lobster's pincers firmly clamped on one of his fingers.

"Sorry," said Donn-Dubh, "sure I tried to warn you. It's a security device. Stops anyone else from rooting around in there, yu know."

Malachy knew alright.

"Be the love of King Cormac," Malachy screamed, shaking the lobster from side to side until it released its vice like grip.

The poor oul' lobster fell to the floor and scurried back to Donn-Dubh. "You've scared him, now," Donn-Dubh shouted at Malachy, bending down to pick up the lobster. "It's ok, Snippy-Snippy... there ... there." Donn-Dubh stroked and kissed Snippy's pincer. "I won't let that nasty, little shillelagh hurt you again." After a few more strokes, he tucked Snippy back into a luxurious fold.

"That's a grand contraption," said Paht, "gets rid of pests wha'." He winked at Malachy. "I could think of a few things to keep in there meself."

"QuickMIC couldn't invent one big enough for your head," said Malachy, still blowing and sucking on his bruised finger.

"Now, Donn-Dubh, will ye have a cup of tea?" interrupted Banbha, wrapping a plaster around Malachy's finger.

"Only if you put a dash of this in it," said Donn-Dubh, reaching under another fold of his hat for a small bottle.

"Would that be a bit of that fiery Jamaican Rum?" asked Paht with a conspiratorial wink of his eye. "If it is, sure I wouldn't mind a sup or two of that me-good-self." He proffered Donn-Dubh his bucket sized mug, and rubbed his lower back. "Sure me bones have been creaking and playing up these last few days, and I'm in awful need of lubricating."

"Lubricating is it?" said Banbha, finishing off Malachy's plaster. "With all the fat and oil you're eating, never mind lubricating, sure you'd give Topaz, Texaco and Shell a good run for their money."

"I'm only surprised you haven't stuck a handle on the side of his head," agreed Malachy, "and turned him into a chipper pan."

"'Tis not rum," said Donn-Dubh to Paht, "'tis only semi-skimmed milk. I'm on a diet, sure that full cream, Irish stuff has me nearly bursting out of me jeans."

"For the love of King Cormac!" yelled Malachy, gently blowing on his swollen finger. "We're discussing the end of civilisation as we know it. Not only is the Ross Ice Shelf melting, but we're about to be swept away by tidal waves, or drowned in ice cubes, and these two are comparing knickers sizes."

"I said mi jeans," Donn-Dubh blurted out, his cheeks almost glowing red. "I never said I was bursting out of mi knickers." His tongue tripping over itself with the shock, he tried to regain some level of dignity, "Not that I wear knickers, yu understand."

"And I'll have less of that knicker talk in front of the young lady," said Paht.

ZZZZZZAAAAAAAPPPPPPPP!!!
ZZZZZZAAAAAAAPPPPPPPP!!!

Chapter 10

An Cabáiste Agus Bagún Deli

"Will those simpletons buy the cover story, Ryan?"

"To tell you the truth, sir," said Ryan, reporting the results of his initial surveillance, "Eirestown might not be the backwater place you think it is."

"What's that?" asked William The Third.

"Well," said Ryan, unsure of how to broach the $3000 dinner bill, "if we were to measure a societies progress in terms of the sophistication of their palate, Eirestown would be right up there."

"Sophisticated?"

"And a little expensive, sir," added Ryan, hoping to soften the blow.

"I'll not have any employee of GRABiT eating like a pauper Ryan," bellowed William, convinced that a plate of cabbage and bacon would be no more than a few dollars.

"Thanks sir ... but, like I say, the level of sophistication in this town is unprecedented, and their cuisine is unrivalled."

Ryan's first meal in Eirestown had not only been an eye and mouth opener, it had also been a wallet opener. Sure the wallet had been opened so wide that it had nearly burst at the seams. Luckily he had a GRABiT company credit card, to help stitch it back up again.

"Sophisticated palates?" William was intrigued to say the least. "You call cabbage and bacon sophisticated?"

"I'm afraid you'll find that things have moved on here a little, sir."

In the heart of the Town Hall Square, whilst carrying out his initial reconnaissance operations, Ryan had stumbled upon 'An Cabáiste agus Bagún Deli', which was Gaelic for *The Cabbage And Bacon Deli*. An intriguing establishment which was promoting and celebrating the fact that it had just received its *fourth* Michelin star.

A *fourth* Michelin star? Ryan thought that the highest Michelin ranking a food establishment could be awarded was three stars, so he couldn't resist perusing the menu as to the possible reasons for such stellar recognition. And it soon became clear that there was a level of sophistication belying this humble abode known as Eirestown.

An Cabáiste agus Bagún Deli's menu, which covered every centimetre of the glass front, reflected an unusual range of internationally renowned fusion food - modern interpretations on Irish classics, and Ryan was at once captivated, confused and at times dumbfounded.

Running his finger along the window, up and down the menu, he came to the conclusion that the influx of immigrants into Ireland, since the sprouts in Brussels had started pumping money into the economy all those years ago, had introduced the Irish palate to a universe of tastes beyond the planetary influence of the humble head of cabbage. These were new and uncharted flavours to him, which made demands on even the most refined, sophisticated and discerning of American taste buds.

A cornucopia of delicacies continued to perplex Ryan as his eyes flew up and down An Cabáiste agus Bagún Deli's menu, stopping every now and then to savour the delights on display. There were delicacies from all over the world, including:

Tom Yum Cabbage and Bacon soup, Cabbage and Bacon burgers, Cabbage and Bacon meatloaf, Cabbage and Bacon sandwiches, Cabbage and Bacon Panini, Cabbage and Bacon kebabs, Southern fried Cabbage and Bacon with cabbage crusted fries and a cabbage coleslaw, Special Fried Cabbage and Bacon with bean sprouts and carrots, Fried sliced Bacon in oyster sauce with Cabbage, Crispy Aromatic Cabbage and Bacon served with hoi sin sauce, sliced spring onions, cucumbers and pancakes; House Special Cabbage and Bacon stuffed bamboo shoots with chestnuts, Cabbage and Bacon jalfrezi, Truffle Crusted Bacon with potato gnocchi, ground mushrooms wrapped in Cabbage, and a brown butter chardonnay.

"Such versatile ingredients," Ryan mumbled under his breath, while his finger raced ahead. "No wonder the Irish love their cabbage and bacon."

By the time Ryan got to the dessert list he was salivating, and had his face pressed so hard against the shop window he could almost lick the menu:

Cabbage ice cream garnished with sweet cured Bacon toppings, Bacon au chocolate with criss-cross delicate Cabbage wafers, raspberries covered with a caramelised cabbage cage.

However, his taste buds did summersaults worthy of an acrobat when they saw some of the French offerings, which took pride of place in the centre of the shop window:

CUSINE FRANÇAISE DE L'EIRESTOWN
~~~~~~~~~~~~~~~~~~~~~~~~~~~~~~

Hors d'oeuvre:
Soupe au lard crouton et chou
(Bacon and cabbage soup with croutons)
Assiette de selection de lard et chou
(A platter of bacon and cabbage dips)
Tarte provencale et sa salade de chou au lard
(Provencal tart with cabbage and bacon salad.)

Les Salades:
Salade Eirestown
(Eirestown salad, mixed cabbage leaves salad with poached egg and bacon.)

Les entrees:
Le plateau des Paté maison au lard et ses garnitures de chou
(A selection of homemade bacon pate with pickle, chutney and cabbage)

Les crustaces:
Quatre grands huitres creuse de Laffey
(Four large rock oysters fresh from the river Laffey)
Les cuisses de grenouille et Escargots beurre au lard et chou
(Frogs legs and snail with cabbage and bacon butter)

Les viandes:
Plat du jour - Notre spécialitee la côte d'Lard, pomme frite et chou et chou rue
(Dish of the day - House special Irish bacon ribs with chunky chips, cabbage and cabbage gravy)
Le Tête de Lard, pomme frite et salade au chou
(Head of pig with chunky chips and cabbage salad)
Lard a l'Orange, fenouil, polenta, pommes de terre à la Boulangère et chou
(Bacon shank a l'Orange with fennel, polenta, and oven baked potatoes and cabbage)
Chou Rouge Braisé d'Alsace et d'Lorraine
(Red cabbage, with bacon slices braised in red wine vinegar and spices)

Les Desserts:
Tulipe au Fraises du Eirestown crème chou avec nonperils doux lard
(Eirestown tulip style strawberries filled with cabbage cream and sprinkled with sweet cured bacon bits)

Plateau de fromages de Eirestown
(Cheese board from Eirestown)
~~~~~~

Even though it was barely lunchtime, no longer able to resist temptation, Ryan entered the premises and finally settled on the house special bacon ribs, followed by *Tulipe au Fraises du Eirestown crème chou avec nonperils doux lard* and *Plateau de fromages de Eirestown*, all washed down with a bottle of *Domaine de la Romanee-Conti Vin d'chou*. The Cabbage wine was a delicacy in itself, and worth every cent of the $500 per bottle.

After his third glass of *Vin d'chou*, Ryan asked to meet the *commis de cuisine,* to thank him personally.

Paddy Roux, who claimed to be a distant cousin of the legendary French Chef Michel Albert Roux, also known as Michel Roux, Jr. to his friends and family, and under whose exacting auspices Paddy trained in Paris, was only too happy to oblige. And over another bottle of the modestly priced *Domaine de la Romanee-Conti Vin d'chou*, he took great pride in clarifying the matter of the fourth star. An Cabáiste agus Bagún Deli was so sophisticated he maintained, so adventurous, so cutting edge and revolutionary, "*C'est manifique!*" in fact, that the Michelin Reviewers had no other choice but to create a new category of *fourth* star. So enthralled was one of the Michelin inspectors, himself a three star chef, that he was currently employed as a kitchen porter, washing pots and dishes in the hope that he would one day learn the culinary secrets of An Cabáiste agus Bagún Deli.

But a few hours later, after his visit to culinary heaven, Ryan was in virtual hell, taking part in another conference call with the devil himself, William McCoy The Third, CEO of 'Global Realtor and Business Intelligence', GRABiT for short. And he was worried that he had bitten off more than he could chew in An Cabáiste agus Bagún Deli, three thousand dollars more than he could chew, actually.

"Three thousand dollars?" William nearly choked on the olive on the end of his cocktail stick.

"Three thousand dollars," he repeated. "Did you feed the whole of Eirestown, the whole of Ireland even?"

"I did wonder if Paddy Roux," said Ryan, timidly, "he's the *commis de cuisine* in An Cabáiste agus Bagún Deli, had got the dollar-euro exchange rate wrong, sir."

"Well if he did," declared William, "with exchange rates like that, never mind *commis de cucisine*, he'll make *Ministre des Finances* in no time at all."

"I'm not sure Paddy Roux will ever make *Ministre des Finances* sir," Ryan replied informatively, "but with his culinary skills, I'm sure he'll be head chef at the Palace of Versailles one of these days." Ryan reached into his pocket and pulled out a leaflet, "Sir, you've got to see this menu to believe it. Here I'll fax it over to you now."

William poured another Manhattan as his office fax machine fired up, and stabbed at another olive on a side dish. "Three thousand dollars?" he repeated again in disbelief as Ryan squirmed on the other end of the line. "Didn't you check the prices first?"

"I did ask Paddy Roux for a price list," clarified Ryan, "but he told me that anyone who had to ask 'how much' couldn't afford to eat there. And being an

American and all ... I wanted these country bumpkins to know that we are still the richest economy in the world."

"We might still be the richest economy in the world at the moment," agreed William, "But with prices like this it won't be long before Eirestown holds the title."

"Sorry, sir, but I was hungry."

"And thirsty I see," gulped William. "$500 dollars a bottle," he continued, struggling to pronounce the name, "*Domaine de la Romanee-Conti Vin d'chou.* Never heard of it. What kind of wine was that?"

"Cabbage wine sir," said Ryan, cringing.

"What," stammered William, "surely that's not possible?"

"I know what you mean, sir," said Ryan innocently, "I didn't believe it myself at first. But Paddy Roux said that at $500 a pop, never mind a head of cabbage, he'd get a bottle of wine out of a head of anything."

"What next," barked William, "Vin du Shamrock?"

"Hey, that's a great idea sir," began Ryan convivially, "I'll have to mention that next time I go to An Cabáiste agus Bagún Deli for an oul' tipple."

"There'll be no next time, Ryan," said William sternly. "It would have been cheaper to fly you back to New York, buy you a meal in Le Bernardin on 7th avenue, and fly you back to Eirestown again. Were these ribs off the side of a twenty four carat golden calf by any chance?"

"No sir," Ryan hesitated, adding a little Irish twang, "just plain oul' bacon ribs. But I'm telling you sir, these ribs were to die for, and that cabbage jou. MMMMM – MMMMM - MMMMM."

"To die for, you say?" hissed William down the line. "It might just come to that yet."

Ryan pleaded his case immediately, he didn't think his culinary foray into the delicacies of An Cabáiste agus Bagún Deli justified him losing his life. And never mind that, he had only just arrived in Eirestown, the sabotage mission hadn't even started yet.

"Sir, it really was all part of the reconnaissance," Ryan carried on, pleading his case. "To know how a people think, you have to know their habits, especially what they eat, don't you think?"

"Well do me a favour Ryan," said William, sighing.

"Anything sir!"

"Next time you want to know what they think, or even eat," William placed his mouth as close as possible to the conference phone microphone and screamed: "Google it!"

And with that, William hung up and walked over to the fax machine.

$3000! William McCoy The Third had been under increasing pressure from several shareholders to grow the company these last few years, the last thing he needed now was to have to explain lavish dinners like that on company expenses at the next AGM.

But here was the proof in his hands, hot off the fax, Haute cuisine, and in Eirestown of all places. Ryan was right, perhaps William had underestimated the simpletons over there. Such suspicions were further confirmed when he read the fax starting at: *CUSINE FRANÇAISE DE L'EIRESTOWN* ...

And by the time William got to:

Tulipe au Fraises du Eirestown crème chou avec nonperils doux lard ...

He was salivating so much he seriously considered booking a flight to Eirestown for dinner that evening, but overcame temptation, saved GRABiT $3000 and settled for a $2999 plate of *pommes frites* at Le Bernardin on 7th Avenue, served with the finest fillet mignon money could buy.

Chapter 11

Do I Look Like A Penguin Bruv?

Having just let off two rounds, like a gunslinger in a Spaghetti Western, Malachy calmly blew the smoke from the top of his finger, where blue and green sparks were still hissing and crackling. He'd been waiting to extract a little revenge from Donn-Dubh for the lobster attack. Paht got a ZZZZAAAAAPPPPPP just for the hell of it.

"Mi dreads man," groaned Donn-Dubh, picking up a couple of singed, green locks from Paddy McGinty's kitchen floor. "What was that for?"

"How about for not having a No-Entry sign on that hat of yours," frowned Malachy, wriggling his throbbing finger in Donn-Dubh's direction, "is that a good enough reason?"

Paht didn't say a word, despite the fact that half of one of his side burns lay smouldering on the plate next to his rashers. He didn't want to risk losing the other half.

"What you on about anyway?" Donn-Dubh inquired, trying to stuff his dreadlocks back under his hat. "What do you mean the end of civilisation?"

Banbha, who was struggling with the laughter and might burst out of her own knickers at any moment, quickly brought Donn-Dubh up to speed about the Ross Ice Shelf and the fact that the scientific community thought it was melting due to Global Warming.

"Man, that's easy to sort out," said Donn-Dubh, still fumbling around under his hat.

"Go on, so," said Malachy, finger poised.

"Just get the Chinese to build a huge refrigerator, and refreeze it. Init."
ZZZZZZAAAAAAAPPPPPPPP!!!

"Malachy, will you stop that," groaned Donn-Dubh as a double blast of the funny stuff whizzed past his ears. "Personally, I think it's a very good idea."

"Me too," said Paht. "Sure there's a billion Chinese and they could build a refrigerator the size of a planet in no time."

"Whist you, if you carrying on eating at the rate you are," said Malachy to Paht, "you'll need a refrigerator the size of a planet."

"Here's your tea," said Banbha to Donn-Dubh. "Now please sit down at the table," and she pulled out the chair next to Paht. "And come on now Malachy, give the lads a chance. It wasn't such a bad idea, was it?"

"No, not bad at all," gloated Malachy, "except we'd have to build ten thousand new coal power stations to generate enough electricity to fuel a fridge that size, and we'd also have to mine every last remaining bit of metal from Mother Earth herself to build it.

"Oh," said Donn-Dubh, taking a sip of tea, "I never thought about that."

"Oh indeed," said Malachy. "Sure it's a classic Catch 22 situation. The very solution would only increase the pollution, and hence the speed of melting. We'd be knee high in iced water before they'd dug the coal out, never mind started the manufacturing process. So if you don't mind ..."

"What?" said Donn-Dubh and Paht.

"Keep your thoughts on the matter to your good selves. And we'll just stick with Banbha's solution. After all, she's the one with the gift."

Banbha's eyes widened at this comment and she quickly turned back to the kettle to hide a slightly reddened face: "More tea anyone?"

"Unless of course," Malachy giggled nervously, "Banbha was also planning to get a billion Chinese to build a continental fridge?"

"The thought never crossed my mind," Banbha lied, quickly racking her brains for another solution.

"What's that?"

From the corner of his eye, Malachy saw a Cantankerous Cabbage rolling towards him. The cabbage stopped, opened its leaves and said:

"Did you hear the one about the Irish man who wanted to build an igloo? He found the loo alright, but no matter how hard he tried, he could never find the IG."

Suddenly Paht shouted, "Igloo, that's it, I've had a brainwave."

"I'm sorry to tell you," said Fin, "your brain waved good bye a long time ago."

"Ow!" Banbha gave Fin a clip across the back of his head with the rolled up Eirestown Press, and along with the paper, Fin also let out an ow or two.

"We'll build a modern day Hadrian's Wall," Paht said, "to hold back the Ross Ice Shelf."

"Go on," urged Malachy, surprised that Paht had a brain at all, never mind one that waved.

"We'll get yer ones ... you know the ones..." said Paht. "They're always talking blubber."

"The Eskimos ..." Donn-Dubh nodded, on the ball now.

"Right, the Eskimos ..." Paht concurred excitedly. "We'll get yer ones, the Eskimos, to build us a wall out of ice blocks. A wall across the full length of the Ross Ice Shelf. That ought to do it."

"Grand," said Donn-Dubh, "because if Paddys are known for one thing, it's definitely construction."

"And," asked Malachy scornfully, "where will we get the trillions and trillions of ice blocks, such an elegant solution would require?"

"From the Ross Ice Shelf, of course," said Paht, oblivious of the sarcasm.

"So let me get this straight," summarised Malachy, "you want us to dig trillions and trillions of ice blocks out of the Ross Ice Shelf to build an ice wall to stop the Ross Ice Shelf melting, is that it?"

Paht and Donn-Dubh nodded their approval.

"Let me explain a few things," Malachy said. "Firstly, Eskimos live in the North Pole, not the South Pole. Secondly, you'd need so many blocks of ice that you'd be effectively turning the Ross Ice Shelf itself into an ice wall. Thirdly, unlike your good selves, Eskimos eat blubber, they don't talk it."

"But ..." muttered Paht.

"But nothing," said Malachy raising his crackling finger and silencing Paht, "we'll wait for Banbha's plan."

"We will," said Banbha, slightly concerned. "And now I finally have a solution to the Ross Ice Shelf puzzle."

"You do?" asked Malachy with delight.

"But we'll need King Cormac to ok it," she went on.

"Right, so," said Malachy, "I'll arrange a meeting for tomorrow"

"Excellent," said Paht, rising from his chair. "I'll get my kit ready." He walked towards the kitchen door and opened it. "Come on Donn-Dubh, help me up onto that bass powered contraption of yours and we'll visit yer one down at that Technological Shenanigans."

"Sit down you," said Malachy menacingly, a pointed finger following Paht back to the chair. "Sure if we sent you there, as soon as you set foot on her, you'd sink what's left of the Ross Ice Shelf. No you can stay at home in the command bunker."

"Right then," said Donn-Dubh, keen to make his excuses and preserve what dreadlocks he had left, "I'll be on my way, also. Thanks for the tea Banbha."

"Where do you think you're going?" said Malachy, the oul' zapper fired up and sparks bristling on the tip of his finger.

"Home," said Donn-Dubh, "I'm working on a new Daniel O'Donnell re-mix at the moment and ..."

"Congratulations," said Malachy, cutting him off, "you've made it onto the team."

"What team?" asked Donn-Dubh.

"The Ross Ice Shelf team," replied Malachy. "With a hat like that on you head, you could carry half the supplies, never mind anything else."

"With all due respect," said Donn-Dubh, "but are you mad?"

"What do you mean?" asked Malachy, restraining himself in the process. He didn't want to fry any brains this particular recruit might have, not before the journey had started at least.

Donn-Dubh pinched his own face and arms in several places. "Look at me man? Do I look like I do snow?" To emphasise the point he laid the patois on a little thick. "Palm trees, sandy sunny beaches and de oul' rum punch maybe, but snow? Nah man .... Eva-lution nah prepare me for dat weather, dere. Yu ever seen a black man in one of dem cold countries?"

"Penguins are black," said Paht after a few moments reflection.

"Do I look like a penguin bruv?"

"No," said Paht, "but you've a funny 'oul walk all the same. If you just waddled a little more from side to side and kept your arms tight to your body, like one of those yokes from River Dance, sure you'd easily pass for one."

"I don't want to pass for a xx#@@##xx penguin!"

"Mind that language," said Banbha.

"Sorry," said Donn-Dubh, "but funny walk or not, I'm waddling nowhere except home, and I don't mean Jamaica. Not that I waddle you understand."

"Talking about Jamaica," said Malachy, "what about that Jamaican Bobsleigh team?"

"What about the Jamaican Bobsleigh team?" asked Donn-Dubh.

But Malachy didn't get a chance to answer.

"Would you look at that," said Banbha, "sure there's someone outside in the yard with a camera, and he's headed this way."

Chapter 12

The Only Kind Of Moron

William McCoy was sat in the GRABiT's lavish headquarters in Manhattan – a beautiful, slender Swedish masseuse kneading his shoulders. That last call with Ryan had been a little worrying to say the least, and the masseuse was busy unravelling knots of tension.

William brushed the masseuse's hands off his relaxed shoulders, walked over to panoramic window, and looked down at the East River. Smiling to himself, he rubbed his hands together as he considered its soon to be new name, East Lake.

"Just imagine," he said to the masseuse, when he sat back down, "in a month's time or less, I'll be able to step out of my twentieth floor office and straight onto a gondola."

Clueless, the masseuse let out a feigned girlie giggle and asked, "Will that be all, sir?"

"Yes, yes," he said, dismissing her. "For now, just wait outside the office, I may need you again soon."

Five minutes later, he had Ryan back on the phone.

"Ryan," he begged sincerely, "please accept my humblest apologies. I don't know what got into me."

"Sir?" said Ryan, convinced that one too many Manhattan cocktail had gotten into him.

"I mean, how were you to know Paddy Roux would fleece you like that." William said and then he started laughing. "In fact," William looked at the menu again, and struggled to pronounce An Cabáiste agus Bagún Deli, "I'm surprised you didn't end up on the menu at the An K ... a ...bas ...tee ..."

"An Caboysh-teh aa-gus baw-goon deli, sir," interrupted Ryan. "It's Gaelic for 'The Cabbage and Bacon Deli'."

"Whatever," said William dismissively, "why those Micks can't speak English is beyond me."

"What do you mean, sir," asked Ryan, "you're surprised I didn't end upon the menu?"

"Well Paddy Roux fleeced you like a lamb didn't he... get it, fleeced you like a lamb?" then William broke into laughter again.

"Oh yeah," said Ryan, feeling a little relived, and also laughing, "fleeced me like a lamb, that's a good one, sir."

"I tell you something Ryan, you're right about this Irish Craic. They may have a language no one understands, but this Irish Craic ... now that transcends language itself."

"Be careful with that craic, sir, it's contagious." and Ryan found himself laughing even harder, but not for long.

"It certainly is Ryan," said William sternly. "Not as contagious as a bullet to the back of the head, mind, but contagious never the less."

Satisfied that Ryan had got the message, William rolled his shoulders a few times, and told Ryan to hold the line while he explained a few things.

It was nearly time to implement the final phase of GRABiT's audacious expansion plans. William had been hatching what he considered to be a perfect plan to increase the company's profits for several years now. But company intelligence, in the form of recent headlines in The Eirestown Press and elsewhere, had him concerned.

Unfortunately King Cormac of Eirestown had proposed that the people of Eirestown investigate and, if possible, reverse the melting of the Ross Ice Shelf.

It wasn't the first time that wise King Cormac of Eirestown had intervened in global affairs. A few years ago he achieved legendary status when he turned up out of the blue at the Nobel Prize Award ceremony with a jar full of Higgs Boson particles, and was duly awarded the prize for physics.

William McCoy The Third considered King Cormac and his residents a bunch of interfering do-gooders. Especially after relocation contracts from Fermilab and CERN dried up. GRABiT had made a fortune out of previous residential upheavals, caused by the need for high energy particle accelerators, extending over hundreds of miles, and under pristine countryside in most cases. But that jar full of Higgs Boson put the brakes on multimillion dollar scientific experiments which had been set up to search for the God Particle, and had cost GRABiT billions in new housing development contracts.

And now King Cormac was at it again. He would have to be stopped this time.

CORRECTION: HE WOULD BE STOPPED THIS TIME!

"So you see Ryan, we can't afford another Higgs Boson fiasco," concluded William, thumping his desk. "They have to be stopped, at any cost. Even if we have to go to the South Pole to stop them."

Ryan spoke cautiously: "Sir, I'll do my best to sabotage the rescue attempt, but I'm not sure I'm up to going to the South Pole. I really don't do snow."

Blond haired, blue eyed California Dreaming Ryan was originally from Los Angeles, home of the Sun. Just like Donn-Dubh, he didn't do snow, and the only ice he was comfortably with was the one bobbing on top of a glass of Bailey's. However, there was only one thing he feared more than the cold, and that was William McCoy The Third.

"Not to worry," soothed William McCoy. "I'm hoping it won't come to that."

"That a relief sir. But there is another problem."

"Go on."

"As simple as the residents of Eirestown might be, there are a lot of them. I'm not sure I'll be able to stop them on my own."

"Don't worry, I've thought of everything Ryan," said William. "I sent reinforcements earlier this week from DumbHK, one of my recent acquisitions. They should be with you anytime now."

"Reinforcements, sir?"

"Yes, and don't you fret," said William. "They'll do all the dirty work. You just play dumb."

"Dumb?"

"Yes," said William, "you should be good at that. You'll probably get yourself an Oscar at next year's Academy Awards."

"When will I meet these reinforcements?" said Ryan.

"Don't worry," answered William, "they'll find you."

"But how will I recognise them?"

"Love," said William, struggling to hold back laughter.

"Love?"

"Yes," continued William, smiling to himself, and thinking he'll show Ryan a thing or two about the Irish craic, "the reinforcements will contact you with a coded message of love. One of the brutes will make his intentions very clear. You are to respond very carefully with the phrase: '*I never do that on a first date.*' Otherwise he'll blow your head off."

"But sir," said Ryan, making a mental note of the response phrase, "even if we do sabotage the rescue mission ..."

"What is it Ryan?" asked William, "Not having second thoughts I hope. I'd hate to lose you at this late stage of the operation."

"Are you sure this plan will work, sir?" stammered Ryan, hoping that 'lose you at this late stage of the operation' would be a transfer to another GRABiT office and nothing more sinister. "Melting the South Pole ... I mean ... it seems very farfetched."

"Work!?" bellowed William, putting the phone on mute, and calling Freya, the Swedish Masseuse, in from the foyer. She immediately got to work, kneading and undoing knots in his shoulders as fast as they popped up.

A little calmer now, William un-muted the conference phone: "Ryan, I've not spent the best part of the last three years planning something that won't work. We've already implemented the first phase. Why do you think sea levels have been rising these last few years? Do you think I'm some kind of moron?"

"No sir," said Ryan, thinking that William was not some kind of moron, William The Third McCoy was the *only kind* of moron. "But it's such an audacious scheme, sir. And the ramifications are truly global."

"Global?" said William

"Yes," said Ryan, "are you not concerned about any side effects. What happens if the sea levels rise too high, even New York could be threatened. Your offices, your home, your family ..."

"Ryan," snarled William, "do you really think I would flood the USA, my home, my beautiful office; risking the lives of my family, and millions of my fellow American citizens?"

"No," Ryan lied timidly.

"Good," said William, "but just to put your mind at ease. You may or may not be aware of this but the polar ice caps expand and recede over a natural twelve thousand year cycle."

"I've heard something like that sir."

"Well," said William, "we are just speeding up the process. Instead of waiting twelve thousand years, we are increasing the cycle to every twelve months."

"I see," said Ryan, "it sounds fascinating."

"That's one way of putting it Ryan," said William. "The annual melting of the Ross Ice Shelf will be one of the most controlled projects the world has ever known," he boasted. "And once certain uninhabited areas have been irrigated and transformed into arable land, we'll reverse the melting process immediately. GRABiT's intentions are honourable Ryan. We wish to help the world, and feed the starving millions."

"But what about the global migration you mentioned?"

"That's right Ryan," lied William, "when people have access to land which can be farmed, they'll migrate there in their millions. You remember Egypt don't you?"

"Yes, sir."

"And you are aware that there was a time, before the Aswan dam was built that is, when the Nile flooded every year to irrigate the land for farmers."

"How could I forget?" Ryan said, waiting for the penny to drop.

"Oh yes ..." said William, recalling one of Ryan's first million dollar purchases in Egypt as International Acquisitions Executive, "the housing complex with a Nile river view. A knee deep view for three months of the year, if I remember correctly. Despite the Aswan dam, the foundations were quite a mess on that one."

"Sir like I said at the time ..." began Ryan, intent on apologising for the millionth time.

"Not to worry," William said, cutting him off. "How were you to know that the complex had spent most of its life in the flood plains? The point is Ryan that the Nile flooded every year for thousands of years, and this flooding cycle provided nutrients for the land, such that it could be farmed. Why without it, Egyptian civilisation may never have been born."

"Amazing sir," said Ryan.

"So you now understand exactly what we are doing, and why we are melting the Ross Ice Shelf," enthused William, "the only difference is we are stepping the process up a notch."

"A global irrigation scheme?" said Ryan.

"Exactly."

"Ok, sir, thanks for the clarification. I feel a little more comfortable now."

"Not at all Ryan," chirped William. "Can't have my staff worried about their fellow man. We are an ethical company after all, and that is the foundation on which we will propel GRABiT to the top of the Fortune 500."

"Yes, sir!"

"Sorry for any discomfort the confusion may have caused you."

"No problem, sir," said Ryan earnestly. "It's all perfectly clear to me now. We're embarking on a humanitarian project to feed the world, and I'm proud to be part of such an endeavour."

"And we're proud to have you on board, Ryan," said William. Then he said goodbye to Ryan and called his personal assistant Mrs Baxter.

"Mrs Baxter."

"Yes sir?" said his PA.

"A little lower."

"Yes sir?" she whispered.

"Not you Mrs Baxter, I mean the masseuse."

"Oh pardon me sir," said Mrs Baxter, her voice back to normal volume. "Now what can I do for you sir?"

"Get hold of Waste Disposal in Dublin, and tell them to call me immediately."

"Waste disposal sir?" said Mrs Baxter anxiously, fully aware of the implications. It was a clichéd Mafioso euphemism, but William McCoy still used the term when disposing of people.

"Yes," confirmed William McCoy, "Waste Disposal. Unfortunately a little problem may be developing."

"I'm very sad to hear that, sir," said Mrs Baxter.

"Me too," said William, having calculated that Ryan's efforts in Ireland so far amounted to pittance with respect to his debt, "the little problem still owes me eight million, nine hundred and ninety nine thousand, nine hundred and ninety nine dollars." Then he suddenly remembered something. "Actually you can add another $3000 dollars to that."

Chapter 13

A Little Shillelagh History

No matter how hard he tried, QuickMIC couldn't get to sleep, and spent most of his time twisting and turning, his pillow wrapped around his ears like a headset.

PaddySan running up and down the stairs looking for him was bearable, but when he started zealously sharpening his sword outside the bedroom door, it sounded like he was using a heavy duty angle grinder. Sure the noise was bad enough, but when sparks began to fly under QuickMIC's bedroom door, and several sparks landed on the pillow beside him, singing it, he leapt out of bed.

Being hacked to death by a deranged iShillelagh in the form of a samurai warrior was one thing, but the thought of his livelihood going up in flames was another thing altogether. There was no other solution. He couldn't wait any longer for DumbHK's remote updates. He would have to get PaddySan into the laboratory at the back of the shop, open him up, and see if he could find any technical problems himself. His mind made up, he threw a glass of water on the smouldering pillow, and opened his bedroom door to find PaddySan sat on the floor sharpening his katana and smiling up at him.

Half an hour later, QuickMIC had PaddySan's head and shaft under a magnifying glass. The panel on the side of his head was open, revealing some of the technical wizardry.

A pair of Ancient green eyes, covered by bushy twig eyebrows, looked down from the wall, where Eógan took pride of place in a niche, sitting on an oak rocking chair. Eógan was the very first shillelagh to have spoken all those millennia ago.

"Times have changed," said Eógan, in a deep, gentle voice. "What is that creature?"

"'Tis one of the latest technological shillelaghs," replied QuickMIC, "an iShillelagh by the name of PaddySan."

"He's a funny shaped head," said Eógan, his chair creaking, as it gently rolled back and forth, "is he ill?"

PaddySan's angular head tapered elegantly towards the back, violating age old standards of traditional shillelagh design.

"Evolution," said QuickMIC, running his hand across PaddySan's smooth contours, "these lads are much more refined than older models like yourself. You'll find no woody knots or gnarls on these modern day fellas. Most of them aren't even made of wood."

"Not made of wood?" Eógan was bewildered.

"Not at all, many of them are made of modern synthetic materials," replied QuickMIC.

The old ways were being eroded by the youth, and an ancient craft was being lost. Shillelagh whittlers around the world were a dying breed and Eógan was mortified. "Shillelaghs should look like shillelaghs," he complained, preferring the old mallet head look like himself. "And they should be made of wood."

QuickMIC had enough worries without entering into a debate about the nuances of shillelagh whittling, especially with a deranged, samurai pyromaniac, staring up at him.

"Whist," said QuickMIC, poking around inside PaddySan's head, "let me concentrate. One wrong adjustment and he could kill us all."

"They wear dresses now?" asked Eógan after a few minutes silence.

"Not at all," said QuickMIC, "he's Japanese and that's a kimono, not a dress."

"What life-force does this PaddySan use?"

"He uses no life-force," said QuickMIC. "Unlike meself and yourself, these creatures do not have that divine spark." QuickMIC extracted a mini-motherboard from PaddySan's head which was full of electronic components. "Here look-it, they rely on these manmade devices instead. The flow of micro electric currents gives them life."

"Lifeless computers, then," reflected Eógan, "burrowed inside the top of shillelaghs. Devoid of the Light ... It sends a shiver down my shaft."

"Lifeless? ... Hmmm... to a degree," mused QuickMIC, twirling the motherboard around in the shiny tweezers. "They do have some autonomy on account of their Artificial Intelligence and primitive emotional circuits."

"Here," said Eógan, extending one of his arms, "PaddySan may have a sacred splinter, that he might live like you and I, and feel the universal life force flowing through his veins."

"That won't be necessary," snapped QuickMIC.

Ancient Irish mythology has it that Eógan was whittled from the branches of a sacred, eternal Yew Tree which grew on the Hill of Uisneach.

Óengus, the god of youth, love and poetry, and one of the Tuatha Dé Dannan, had become a laughing stock of that mythic Irish tribe of gods because his blackthorn shillelagh sticks kept breaking whenever he went into battle. He lost his first shillelagh at The First Battle of Mag Tuired when he gave one of the Fir Bholg, ancient incumbents which the Tuatha Dé Dannan were trying to run out of Ireland, an almighty belt altogether across the back of his head. The recipient of the deadly blow collapsed on the spot immediately, but the shillelagh paid a high price and split in two. Therefore, no longer able to participate in the battle, Óengus ran off home to compose one of his most famous works called 'Ode To A Broken Shillelagh'.

After that things went from bad to worse for Óengus. He lost his second blackthorn shillelagh stick in the next battle against the Fomorians, known as The Last Battle of Mag Tuired, when he leapt to Lugh's aid. Lugh was struggling to load a sling with which he hoped to remove Balor's poisonous eye. Balor, the king of the Fomorians, always led his army into battle because his large eye, centrally positioned in the middle of his even larger forehead, was what a modern day, technical savant like QuickMIC would call an ancient WMD (Weapon of Mass Destruction). When opened, Balor's eye would wreak havoc, killing and destroying all it looked upon. So, as you can imagine, he wasn't the kind of person you'd want to get the eye from, no matter how pretty you considered yourself to be. And, as for eye tests at the opticians, forget about it.

At the height of the battle, whilst avoiding Balor's cyclopean, deadly stare, Lugh almost had the sling loaded when a goat headed Fomorian assassin pounced on him from behind, dragging him to the ground, intent on wrapping the sling around his neck and choking the bejaysus out of him. Fortunately for Lugh, Óengus saw what was happening and didn't he give the Fomorian assassin an awful hammering altogether with his new shillelagh. After which Lugh jumped back to his feet, re-loaded the sling and flung a well aimed stone, knocking Balor's eye straight through and out of the back of his head. A moment later, the eye popped out the other side of Balor's skull and destroyed the Fomorian army behind him, when his deadly, poisonous pupil looked upon them. The army wiped out, Balor fell to the ground, whereupon his destructive eye burnt a hole into the very earth itself, a hole which eventually filled with water to become the 'Lake of the Eye' in County Sligo.

The battle was won and the hero Lugh became king of Tuatha Dé Dannan; but, sadly, once again, Óengus' shillelagh stick was lost, smashed to smithereens on the head of the Fomorian assassin.

As the Tuatha Dé Dannan celebrated their victory and derided him, he traipsed home to write 'Ode To Another Broken Shillelagh', which, admittedly, was not quite as famous or as well received as his epic 'Ode To A Broken Shillelagh', but helped pay the bills in any event, and secured his position as an eloquent, albeit somewhat repetitive, and increasingly ridiculed, poet to the gods.

All was well in the war free kingdom, Óengus hadn't lost a shillelagh for ages, and the giggles he often heard behind him, mocking his shillelagh fighting skills, as he made his way to and from Tara to give his daily poetic recitals had subsided significantly. Yes all was well ... until, that is, the Milesians, Gaels from Iberia, tired of the Mediterranean sunshine, invaded Ireland for a bit of inclement weather, and Óengus went into battle for a third time, with a newly whittled and ill fated black thorn shillelagh stick. Sadly, this time, he didn't even get as far as the battle field.

Óengus was on his way to the front line to meet the Milesians head on when he bumped into Ériu, a goddess who gives her name to Éire, on top of a mountain. She was livid when, during a brief conversation with our misfortunate bard, she discovered that Óengus had composed a few couplets to honour her younger and much prettier sisters Banbha and Fódla, with an appropriately titled work called 'The Wooing Of Banbha And Fódla', but, he reluctantly admitted, he had never ever mentioned Ériu in verse.

Ériu became enraged altogether when Óengus told her that he was going to rectify this omission by writing another ode to honour herself titled, 'Ode To An Older Sister Who Was Never Wooed'. Well that was to be the first half of the title, anyway. But poor oul' Óengus never got a chance to tell her the second half of the title which was, 'Until I Saw Her Beauty'. For with himself halfway through the title, Ériu grabbed the newly whittled black thorn shillelagh from him and snapped it in two over her knee, after first giving Óengus a few belts across the jaw with it.

Shillelagh-less and writhing in agony, Óengus stumbled home to write one of his last odes. An epic of Homeric proportions which became an instant bestseller titled, 'Ode To Ériu Who Will Never Be Wooed, Another Snapped Shillelagh And A Throbbing Jaw'.

As time went on, no longer able to cope with the loss of black thorn shillelaghs and growing tired of the increasing ridicule from everyone, including the Milesians, who were now sharing power with the Tuatha Dé Dannan, Óengus became determined to craft a shillelagh which would never break, a shillelagh which would be eternal like himself.

It took Óengus thirteen full moons to craft Eógan, a name which means born from a yew tree. However, unbeknown to either party, by a process similar to osmosis, didn't Eógan slowly became endowed with a spark of Óengus' divine essence. Merely a spark, mind, but wasn't it enough to ignite Eógan's passionate intellect and soul; and now, not only was Eógan immortal, he also had his very own personality.

One ancient morning, as the thirteenth full moon waned and Óengus whittled his last few shavings from the yew branch, didn't Eógan, what with the divine essence coursing through every cell of his body replacing his sap, open his eyes for the very first time. Sparkling green eyes opening beneath twig eyebrows was shock enough for Óengus, but, despite his immortality, Eógan's next action nearly scared the eternal life out of him.

For Eógan stared deep into Óengus' eyes, took a deep breath of pristine, unpolluted Irish country air and gave thanks to another member of the Tuatha Dé Dannan. 'Thank Dagda for that,' he yelled, after which proclamation he sprouted arms and legs.

His creation thanking another god was insult enough, but Óengus nearly cut Eógan's immortal life short one evening when, sick to death once and for all with shillelaghs, he reverted to the old ways and took his sword, Moralltach - the Great Fury - to Eógan's neck. For, in an act of blatant plagiarism, Eógan had been visiting the assembly of the Tuatha Dé Dannan in Tara and reciting some of Óengus' love poetry, claiming it as his own.

With Moralltach piercing the bark on his neck, Eógan pleaded with Óengus claiming that they had a symbiotic relationship. "Therefore," Eógan beseeched Óengus, "I am effectively an extension of your personae. Like a twin." It hadn't been plagiarism after all, he tried in vain to convince Óengus, "I just couldn't help myself."

Twins or not, Óengus became enraged by growing rumours of Eógan's amorous recitals, his superior charm and wit, his poetic improvisation skills and his way with the ladies. Worse he couldn't even recite his own poetry in Tara now without being accused of stealing it from Eógan, making him a holy living show altogether.

Frothing at the mouth, with Eógan's terrified green eyes imploring mercy, Óengus drew back his sword to hack off his chattering head.

It was only the last minute intervention of Óengus' wife Caer, who threw herself on top of Eógan, which spared him. Like many a fair and not so fair maiden, she had taken an immediate liking to Eógan's husky, seductive voice, and his passionate recitals. Sure Caer was now so enamoured by Eógan that the thought of life without him became unbearable, even after only hearing one verse.

Since those ancient times, it is claimed that any shillelagh in possession of a splinter of Eógan becomes a 'chip off the old block' and similarly endowed with a divine spark. Not that QuickMIC had any interest in that ancient nonsense as he stared into PaddySan's black eyes.

"Does PaddySan not deserve a spark of life?" Eógan asked QuickMIC again, presenting him the sacred splinter once more.

"This little fella has sparks enough," said QuickMIC, refusing the splinter again. "Sure he nearly burnt the shop down with one of them earlier."

"But life," implored Eógan, "allow him that."

"He's life enough, too," said QuickMIC dismissively. "He's like one of the oul' boys."

"What do you mean?" asked Eógan.

"A pugnacious brawler," answered QuickMIC, turning PaddySan's head around so he could see his face. "Don't let this serene look fool you. He loves a good oul' fight this one. He has enough fighting spirit for all of us. No ... they'll be no need for a splinter here, he's enough life alright."

"But he cheats," scoffed Eógan, "he uses a sword." He strained his neck back and feigned a few flamboyant head butts. "Not like meself in the good oul' days. Sure I knocked many a champion to the ground with this elegant move."

"The days of chivalry and Bataireacht are no more," said QuickMIC. "PaddySan's Japanese anyway, and they used to use swords over there to settle their differences, not shillelaghs."

"The days of Bataireacht are no more," repeated Eógan dolefully, staring into PaddySan's eyes, "they are no more ..."

Chapter 14

Céad Míle Fáilte

Most people are of the opinion that the Irish frequent Irish pubs for the craic, to swear with carefree abandon, share stories, talk a little cod-olody, and spin a bit of exaggerated blarney from the looms of their legendary, overly creative Celtic imaginations.

Others are of the opinion that the Irish frequent such places to swear with carefree abandon, get drunk, sing songs which make them feel miserable about the home towns they left behind, and start fighting to help them forget about why they got drunk in the first place.

However, those opinions, and many like them, are wrong, a fact which was established some time ago now, by an eminent Sociologist from Trinity College, Dublin, named Dr. Sam E. Ágain, in his legendary PhD Thesis: 'Power-dynamics, Integrated Social Stability, Cohesion and Economic Differentials within a confined, communal Irish public space. An examination of John Nash's Equilibrium Dynamics and resource sharing in a non-Pareto Optimal environment.' A thesis that was ten years in the writing because it involved visiting every pub in Ireland, at least three times, to verify the findings of previous observations, which had been obtained while under the influence.

Dr. Sam E. Ágain became internationally renowned when he published his thesis which proved that Irish bars have pioneered the way in the modern age, and are in fact the first distributed office complexes the world has ever known, making the Irish Diaspora not only the largest Corporation on the face of the earth, but also a virtual global industrial complex. And all this in the days before the internet was invented.

In his celebrated thesis, Dr. Sam E. Ágain went on to describe how Irish bars are the hubs around which the Irish do all their business, all their gossiping, all their debating, bartering, haggling and fraternising. Non-Pareto optimal it may be, but it is an environment in which they share all their news, and the place where they all keep an Orwellian eye on one another. Dr. Sam E. Ágain was even shocked, but delighted to report, that every Irish pub is an autonomic cell in a unified global organism, which stretches around the planet like a Celtic skin.

Therefore, Dr. Sam E. Ágain concluded that when they're not enjoying the craic, swearing with carefree abandon, talking cod-ology, spinning blarney, singing, or fighting the Irish are either engaged in deals which would put the combined efforts of NASDAQ, Wall Street and the NYSE to shame, or they are putting the world and each other to right in a host of other ways.

As you can imagine, Dr. Sam E. Ágain's thesis made quite an impression on the world, but it made an even bigger impression on Ryan O'Reilly who once considered a career in Sociology and had spent one year at Cal-Tech where he was fortunate enough to be exposed to Dr. Sam E. Ágain work.

So when Ryan arrived in Eirestown, just as when he arrived in Dublin, he knew instinctively that the best place to begin his infiltration and gather information was Paddy McGinty's Goat.

"Good morning," said Ryan when Banbha opened the kitchen door.

"Well," said everyone in the kitchen, except Paht who said, "*Céad míle fáilte!*"

"I'm sorry," said Ryan apologising to Paht, "I didn't realise that this was a Gaeltacht region. I'm afraid I don't speak Gaelic."

"Neither do I," said Paht smirking, "but the tourists love that one. Kade-me-laa-fall-cha," he added, pronouncing *Céad míle fáilte*, "it means, a hundred thousand welcomes."

""I know what it means," said Ryan smiling. "I'm just saying ... I don't speak Gaelic. And, by the way, just the one welcome will do," he concluded, sincerely.

"I'm sure it will," said Paht. Then, after a brief chuckle, he composed himself, looked sternly at Ryan and added, "*Dún an doris.*"

Ryan blushed, shrugged his shoulders and was about to apologise again.

"*Dún do chlab,*" Fin yelled at Paht, telling him to shut up, and turning to Ryan he said, "Don't worry, he's only saying close the door, here, I'll get it."

"What can we do for you?" said Banbha.

"I was wondering if you could help me?" answered Ryan, after introducing himself. "I'm doing a documentary, and I thought an Irish pub would be as good a place as any to start gathering information."

"A documentary?" said Paht. "Well Ryan you couldn't have arrived at a better time; we've the very subject for you. Pull up a chair now, here you go. Banbha get the Murphy pan back on, and throw in a bite for Ryan, a few rashers, sausages, white pudding and tha'."

"Thanks," said Ryan sitting down at the table, "but I already have a subject."

"Is it about penguins?" asked Paht, nodding in Donn-Dubh's direction.

"No," said Ryan, somewhat bemused. "Why, do you have penguins here in Eirestown?"

"We might have," said Paht, winking at Donn-Dubh. "If we found you one, would you pay us to film it?" Hoping to entice Donn-Dubh into fancy dress costume he added, "Of course I'd split the proceeds 50-50 with the penguin."

"No," Ryan said, becoming even more concerned at the surreal line of questioning, "I'm not here about penguins."

"Then what are you here for?" asked Fin.

"I'm doing a documentary on shillelaghs and the latest iShillelaghs," Ryan said. "Hopefully you guys can get me started?"

"You've an awful funny accent," said Paht, "where are you from?" Ryan said he was from Los Angeles but was actually working out of New York.

"American," Paht sighed.

"Irish American," corrected Ryan, proudly.

"Well that explains it."

"Explains what?" asked Ryan, slightly concerned that Paht was about to say something derogatory about Americans.

"Why you don't speak Irish."

"Oh yes," said Ryan.

"Sure ye only speak American over there."

Actually Ryan wasn't sure if that statement was derogatory, a matter of fact observation or a compliment. He was about to ask Paht what he meant but Fin interrupted him again.

"Dada" said Fin, pouring Ryan a cup of tea, "leave him alone."

Banbha flipped a couple of rashers and said, "if you're looking to do a documentary on iShillelaghs, you've certainly come to the right place."

"You certainly have," agreed Malachy, "but I'm afraid that documentary will have to wait."

Ryan looked down to where the voice was coming from, "You ... you're ... you're a ..."

"An iShillelagh," said Malachy, "but I've more important things to be doing at the moment than discussing my taxonomy."

"What do you mean?" asked Ryan, getting out his notebook.

"My taxonomy," answered Malachy, pointing to himself, "I mean my classification as a species." He pointed to Ryan and the others, "Ye lot are *homo sapiens*, which is Latin for the 'wise man', although why they call ye lot wise is beyond me. Your species is *sapiens*, your genus *homo*, family *homindae*, order *primate*, class *mammalia*, phylum *chordate*, kingdom *animalia* and finally your domain is *eukarya*. And I'm just a ..."

"Look," interrupted Ryan, "I know what taxonomy means, I spent a year at Cal-Tech studying biology and sociology. I meant what's so important that I can't do a documentary about you?"

"The earth is drowning, and we're away to find out why, and hopefully fix it."

"What?"

Banbha placed the plate of breakfast on the table for Ryan, and gave a brief overview about the Ross Ice Shelf melting.

"But it'll not be that bad," said Ryan, remembering details of William's global irrigation scheme, "chances are it will freeze back over when the seas have risen a little. I mean to say," he continued, slicing through a sausage, "it melts and refreezes every twelve thousand years anyway."

"The natural cycle," said Malachy, "takes thousands of years to complete. And the environment has plenty of time to adjust and adapt, along with all the life forms affected."

"So what's different about what's happening now?" asked Ryan.

"I'm afraid," said Malachy, "that the current rate of melt acceleration is unprecedented."

"But surely it will refreeze?"

"Sure you've not considered the domino effect, and the point of no return," said Malachy, taking a sip of tea. "When the Ross Ice Shelf starts melting and crosses a critical threshold, a whole series of planetary weather conditions change, and feed into the process, further increasing the speed of melting. Soon all the ice sheets will be gone, even Greenland's, and the seas will be at least twenty meters higher than they are in all coastal areas. It will be the worse climate catastrophe the world has ever faced. If it isn't stopped, that is."

"Major cities like Dublin, Tokyo, New York, San Francisco, Los Angeles to name a but a few, will be completely submerged, causing mass migration, and untold damage and death," added Banbha.

"And don't forget London," said Paht.

"Oh yes, and London."

"You'd need a diving suit to get on the tube," giggled Paht.

"This is no laughing matter!" said Banbha, berating Paht.

"But," said Ryan, nearly choking on a bit of sausage, "that sounds dreadful, awful ... I mean, are you sure can't just refreeze it?"

"Not at all," Malachy said. "Like I say, once it crosses the point of no return, we're finished. Not since the dinosaurs were wiped out sixty million years ago has the earth faced such a crisis. The very existence of humanity is threatened."

"You mean our existence?" asked Ryan.

"You are human I assume, unlike meself?"

"I am," said Ryan, "and I'm making no assumptions there."

"Who knows what other knock-effects there might be, if the Ross Ice Shelf melts completely," explained Malachy. "Life for humanity may no longer be possible."

"But there must be something that can be done," asserted Ryan. "He's got to be stopped."

"Who has?"

Ryan had to think fast. He couldn't mention William McCoy's plans, so he said, "I mean HE, the Ross Ice Shelf. HE has to be stopped, stopped from melting."

"That's what we're away to find out," repeated Malachy. "So if you'll excuse me, I have no time for documentaries about iShillelaghs. Even handsome, witty, intelligent and charismatic iShillelaghs like me."

"Hey," said Banbha, "you're a reporter looking to make a documentary, why don't you come along with us."

"Where to?" asked Ryan, taking a bite of some soda bread.

"The South Pole, of course," answered Banbha.

Chapter 15

The Dark Side Of The Moon

Captain James Bush had been at McMurdo Research Station on the Antarctica longer than he cared to remember, which was just over three years now. He was told that he'd get used to the cold one day. But three years, thirty days, six hours and forty minutes later, he was still shivering every second of every day, waiting for that glorious sweltering moment to arrive.

As far as he was concerned you would find more heat on the dark side of the moon than you'd find in the Antarctica. He was becoming so desperate for a few scorching rays of sun that he'd even started a petition to open up the Ozone hole again. Sadly, three years later, this petition still only had one signature, his.

Of course Captain James had serious reservations about the transfer order to Antarctica in the first place. Having been born in Houston Texas, he had a natural affinity with heat, and being already based in Miami, all his dreams had come true.

Thirty years old, of medium height, slender frame, blue eyes, chiselled features and a jet black, slicked-back couture hairstyle, he firmly believed he suited a tan and residency in a town which kept it topped it up on a daily basis. Miami even welcomed his entrepreneurial skills with open arms. However, Miami may not have welcomed the body count those nefarious skills left behind. Captain James considered such body count collateral damage when in the battle-zone, or just plain old tax write-offs, bad business decisions, acquisitions or necessary expansion into new territory, when back on Main Street.

Miami! It seemed like another planet. A lush tropical paradise ... Miami! Where Captain James Bush had his own Oceanside condo on South Beach, and part ownership of a bar&grill called Bush Tuckin in the heart of Lincoln Road.

Miami! Not a night went by without him dreaming of waking up back in that paradise, surrounded by bunny playmates on a golden beach – only to find himself back in McMurdo's freezing nightmare each morning, hugging his pillow, surrounded by penguins and seals. Granted the wildlife was naked, but no matter how hard he tried, he just couldn't imagine them in skimpy bathing suits with pouting lips.

But things were about to change for Captain James Bush. William McCoy The Third's debt would soon be paid-off and he could return to sunnier climes. Get himself a cushy job in a US Military Entrance Processing Station somewhere hot, top up his tan and settle back into the dream world he'd left behind all those years ago. Yes ... the nightmare was coming to an end ... or so he thought.

"Is that you Captain James?"

"Yes sir," replied James, gritting his teeth and clenching his free fist, but not from the cold. He was in a conference call, talking to William McCoy The Third, and William's smarmy, patronising attitude always made him angry.

"How's the weather there in sunny Antarctica?" asked William, surveying the Manhattan skyline before him.

"Same as the last time you asked," mumbled James.

It was summer in Antarctica where the sun rose and set once a year, giving its residents six months of daylight in summer and six months of darkness in winter. But even in summer, temperatures stayed well below zero, and the wind chill could take the frozen skin off the end of a polar bear's nose.

"Colder than an ice cube at the bottom of a Manhattan cocktail, perhaps?" giggled William, shaking and swirling his cocktail glass for good measure, close as possible to the microphone.

"Colder," said James, but not as cold as your heart he thought, when he heard the ice tinkling at the bottom of William's glass.

"The latest parts from DumbHK have arrived, then?" William asked, knocking back a swig of his whiskey concoction.

"Yes sir," confirmed Captain James. "The latest parts arrived last week and are being put together as we speak."'

"Great news," said William. "It won't be long now." He swirled the glass several more times, tinkling the ice. "Sunshine beckons, my boy, sunshine beckons."

"Frankly sir, I'm relieved." James said.

"Relived?"

"Yes sir," James went on, "I'm not sure how much longer I can hide or explain these geothermal anomalies the nerds are finding underneath the Ross Ice Shelf. McMurdo is a scientific research centre as you know, and more and more people are wondering what the hell's going on down there. We need to get a move on."

A move on? William was becoming agitated by all this negative rhetoric. Ryan's whimpering was bad enough. It was becoming harder by the day to find people with commitment and vision on a par with his own aspirations.

"James ..."

"Yes sir ..."

"Is that your teeth chattering ...?"

"Yes sir," stammered James, "it's just the cold ... you know ... even wrapped up like a polar bear with a Russian raccoon hat on and all, it still gets me... I swear it's warmer on the dark side of the moon than it is here, sir."

"Oh the cold ... BBBRRR," shivered William, shaking his shoulders for good measure and BBBRRR-ing as loud as possible into the conference phone. "How could I forget? You poor little frozen mite."

Captain James could hear more clicking, tinkling and glugging then William said: "The dark side of the moon, you say?"

"Yes sir," said James, "It's got to be warmer there."

More silence, then: "I was going to wait James, but now that you mention it, we should really discuss your new assignment. I mean if things don't work out for you there in Antarctica."

"What do you mean, sir?" asked James, apprehensively, daring to think that he was about to be relocated to a hot country.

"If you can't," began William, outlining his fiendish plans, "and please do forgive the pun, take a little geothermal heat there in Antarctica. Well there's really only one thing for it."

"What?"

"We'll just have to send you to a place where there's no heat at all."

"The dark side of the moon?" Captain James stammered in a state of disbelief.

"Obvious isn't it, Jamie my boy?" mocked William, determined to motivate James. "We're already in discussions with NASA and a few others."

"NASA?" Surely not James thought.

"Yes, NASA and the Russian Federal Space Agency," William said, struggling to contain his excitement. "All your flying skills will come in very handy on our next space project. After we've finished our little business venture on Ross Island and the sea levels have risen all over the world, there'll be very little space left here on Earth. GRABiT has been thinking of interplanetary expansion for ages now." He paused to savour another sip of whisky. "And where better to start than the moon?"

These comments were met with silence.

"James?? ... Jamie boy ... are you there??"

"GRABiT while you can sir ..." sighed Captain James, affirming his allegiance. "But the geothermal anomalies, sir, how can we expla ..."

William cut him off mid sentence. "Obvious Jamie boy, obvious." James could hear William pouring another glass of Manhattan, the ice tinkling was driving him nuts now. "Mount Terror my dear Jamie ... Mount Terror."

Shortly after arriving in Antarctica, James had been amazed to discover that Mc Murdo was located on the southern tip of Ross Island which was composed of four volcanoes. It seemed bizarre that there could be active volcanoes in such cold, icy extremes

"Intriguing idea sir," said James, "but Mount Terror is not active."

"It will be by the time we're finished," chortled William.

"Mount Erebus," added James, "on the other hand is still active, although we've not had a significant eruption out of her since 2011."

And boy how James looked forward to that next eruption. Every morning he looked out at Erebus praying for a lava flow through McMurdo, in the hope of raising the local temperature a few degrees.

"Erebus it is then," agreed William. "If an active volcano on the South Pole and a few subterranean lava flows can't keep that nerdy lot happy with a suitable explanation for the geothermal anomalies, I'm sure we could arrange for the more inquisitive ones to join you on the next space mission." He chuckled to himself. Here's an idea, you could all huddle together on the dark side of the moon like a group of penguins. Now that would keep you nice and warm, wouldn't it?"

"Probably," whimpered Captain James.

"Or how about my smile?" sniggered William. "I'll be with you on the first mission and, as you know, my teeth light up a room like a supernova. I'm more than sure a smile like that would bring a little warmth to the moon."

"I think I'd rather hug a penguin, sir," whined James.

Captain James Bush had been born into an army family. So when he joined the USAF as expected, James Bush quickly flew up the ranks, and got himself relocated to a comfortable administration position in Miami, courtesy of a friend of his grandfather.

It didn't take James long to feel like he'd never lived anywhere else, and now he never wanted to live anywhere else. But private Oceanside condos didn't come cheap, and no matter how high the body-count grew in the form of tax relief, acquisition or expansion, Captain James was never going to be able to afford one. Until, that is, he came across a once in a life time offer, advertised in the window of one of GRABiT's many covetous arms, a Realtor office on South Beach.

The deal sounded too good to be true, and James spent many a cold night in the Antarctica cursing the fact that he hadn't gone with his initial army training instincts. William McCoy The Third was offering substantial discounts to Military Personnel with certain skills, questionable morals and copious amounts of greed. Unfortunately, Captain James fit all the requirements perfectly.

It was only supposed to be a temporary assignment to Antarctica, to organise and help out with the set up operations for one of GRABiT's more adventurous business ventures.

Selling snow to the Eskimos was to be GRABiT's *pièce de résistance*. "You're going to sell snow to the Eskimos?" James had asked during his interview, convinced that William was a madman.

"Snow blocks actually," William replied. "We're going into the igloo business."

"What?" asked James, letting out a belly laugh. "Selling snow to the Eskimos would be as foolish trying to as sell sand to the Arabs."

Despite his reservations, James' application, interview and processing were successful, and a few days later, William McCoy The Third used his contacts in the military to arrange for Captain James, now the recently appointed International Business Development Strategist for GRABiT, to be transferred to McMurdo.

However, when he arrived in McMurdo, it didn't take long for Captain James Bush to realise two things: firstly, there was no snow block market, since Eskimos live in the North not the South Pole; secondly, William Mc Coy The Third really was a madman.

Once James was secure on McMurdo, and there was absolutely no way he could retransfer back to the USA without William's say so, William phoned him and let him in on the real reason for GRABiT's interest in the Antarctica: "We're going to melt the Ross Ice Shelf."

"What?" James asked, overawed by the scale of this megalomaniac's plans. "Won't that be a little dangerous?"

"Not at all," William clarified, "no ... not at all. It'll be no worse than defrosting your freezer at home."

And when Captain James suddenly realised that defrosting the earth's global freezer would submerge Miami along with his prized condo and his Bush Tuckin' grill, he told William the deal was off.

But William had already thought of everything, and put James' mind at ease immediately.

"You were right in the interview," said William

"About what?" said James.

"Selling sand to the Arabs," mocked William.

Captain James was flabbergasted when William explained that he had actually sold vast quantities of sand to the Arabs. In fact, William revealed, GRABiT had supplied Dubai with trillions upon trillions of tonnes of sand, with which to build the two artificial Palm Islands.

"Jesus, sir!" said James, when it dawned on him that William wasn't joking. "Where did you get all that sand from, the Sahara desert?"

"How did you guess?" replied William.

It turned out that Ryan's time in Egypt had not been completely wasted, and although, as International Acquisitions Executive, Ryan had bought several million acres of barren land, the sand came in handy after all. (Not that William ever thanked Ryan, or wrote off any of his debt against its value.) And GRABiT had transported the sand from the Sahara, across the Red Sea, through the Gulf of Aden, the Gulf of Oman and into the Persian Gulf itself, and on to Dubai where it was dumped tanker by tanker to form palm leaves.

Not only had GRABiT supplied all the sand, they had also taken a poetic leaf out of Dubai's Palm Islands. GRABiT had been spending hundreds of billions of dollars, building state of the art condos in exotic locations, high up across several mountainous coastal regions, anticipating the day the seas and oceans rose to kiss the shores of those pristine, unadulterated beaches.

Of course William promised Captain James his pick of the bunch, if he saw the project through in Antarctica. And being the greedy, gullible fool that he was, Captain James agreed and asked William to send him a New World GRABiT catalogue.

So William had already proved he was capable of anything, and arranging a trip to the moon would be nothing compared to selling sand to the Arabs.

"Huddle like penguins," said James. "Good one sir. But I'm sure they'll be no need for a trip to the moon."

"Great news, Jamie my boy, great news."

"Rest assured I'll handle things here, sir. And if any of those nerds step out of line, I'll frog march them back into it."

"By the way," said William, "you're right. We really do need to get a move on over there in Antarctica."

"Thank you sir," said James grateful for this new impetus.

"And if things go according to plan I'll be arriving there in the next few days by private jet."

"James?? ... Jamie boy ... are you there??"

"GRABiT while you can sir ..." harped Captain James reluctantly.

Chapter 16

Bataireacht And Talking Shillelaghs

Over in QuickMIC's laboratory, Eógan was still reminiscing about the good oul' days, and the loss of the traditional art of shillelagh whittling.

"Shillelaghs not made of wood," he moaned. "And using swords? What next, shillelagh geeks? The days of Bataireacht truly are no more."

The Irish are known for many things, but possessors of an ancient stick based martial art form, which they call Bataireacht, based on ancient laws of chivalry, is not one of them.

"The days of Bataireacht are no more," repeated QuickMIC sarcastically, a little miffed at the shillelagh geek comment. "Sure they never were in your case."

Bataireacht wasn't just a martial art it was a sacred way of life based on a code of moral principles and honour. To imply that Eógan had violated that code was too much for him, "Why I've never been so insulted in my life," he grumbled.

"I find that hard to believe," responded QuickMIC.

"Why?"

"Did you spend most of your life with mutes?"

"No," Eógan bellowed.

"Trappist monks then?"

"I only meant," said Eógan, trying to get the subject changed as quickly as possible, "that a sword might be considered cheating."

"Not to the samurai," said QuickMIC. "But looked at another way," he further surmised, "I suppose you could say a shillelagh stick is a bit like a sword without an edge."

"Like your humour, then?" said Eógan, who still reeling from the fact that his Bataireacht code of honour had been questioned in the first place.

"What do you mean?" asked QuickMIC.

"That has no edge either." Eógan started giggling and rolling manically in his oak rocking chair, so much so that he nearly did a loop-de-loop.

"King Cormac should have left you where he found you," hissed QuickMIC, and he continued to probe and poke around inside PaddySan's head, ignoring further jibes from Eógan.

King Cormac's castle takes pride of place on top of Sí Bheg (The Little Fairy Hill), overlooking Eirestown. And it was under Sí Bheg that Eógan was discovered many, many years ago, following a rumour that a pot of gold had been buried there by a leprechaun; a scurrilous leprechaun with a penchant for gambling, who went by the name of Fíniún. But wasn't Fíniún on the run from the local bookie, and determined to hide his fortune, until he could declare himself legally bankrupt, therefore he buried it beneath Sí Bheg, or so the rumour had it.

The rumour and the size of the pot of gold grew larger by the day in the furtive, Celtic imaginations of the residents of Eirestown; imaginations which were fuelled by a few smackers from the Blarney Stone itself. And it was not long before the whole town went mad to get its hands on it, the pot of gold that is, not the Blarney smackers.

Within a few days Sí Bheg looked like the victim of a mole infestation, and it now had so many tunnels and burrows that some observers became convinced that the residents of Eirestown were creating a tube line to rival the London Underground.

In less than a week it was like a mini Klondike, but King Cormac didn't believe a word of the rumour. So he left the villages to their own devices, if only to keep them out of his hair. Unfortunately it didn't keep them out of his hair for long, a harsh truth he found out to his dismay when a wayward tunneler poked a shovel between the cleft of his buttocks while he was sat on the toilet one pleasant afternoon reading The Eirestown Press.

Bedbound and face down for a week, the King had the wayward tunneler, the very same leprechaun Fíniún, thrown into the dungeons and simultaneously created a Royal Edict banning everyone from further subterranean incursions under Sí Bheg while he investigated the matter for himself, when he could eventually lie the right way up and walk again.

Three weeks later, Sí Bheg resembled a block of Swiss cheese, and King Cormac was about to give up on the gold when his shovel hit a Connemara marble box. He dug in with his hands and brushed ancient soil aside to reveal the lid, on top of which was carved the following words in ancient Gaelic:

EÓGAN SON OF ÓENGUS
A LADIES MAN NO MORE
IF YOU DARE TO OPEN THIS BOX
LOCK UP YOUR DAUGHTERS FOR SURE

Unfortunately, King Cormac could not read ancient Gaelic and there really was no time to get a translation. If re-construction work was not started immediately on Sí Bheg, the whole lot, including the castle, might collapse in on itself at any moment. Therefore King Cormac wasted no more time and opened the box.

No sooner had the lid been lifted than Eógan popped open his green eyes and breathed air for the first time in millennia. Until that moment he had been in a state of deep and eternal hibernation.

"Thank Dagda for that!" Eógan cheered as the bemused King hoisted him from his marble, mausoleum. A talking shillelagh stick was shock enough for the King, but Eógan's next question, 'By the way, how's the missus?' suddenly had him wishing that he'd had the script on top of the marble translated before he'd opened the box after all.

Back in QuickMIC's laboratory, tired of him antagonising him, Eógan was reminding QuickMIC that he owed him his very life: "You should be thankful King Cormac didn't leave me in that Connemara marble box," he pronounced, "or else you and Malachy wouldn't be here either. So show some respect."

"Respect is it now, Mr Lover Lover?" said QuickMIC, raising an eyebrow at him. "Like the chivalrous respect you showed all those years ago?"

"How dare you," complained Eógan.

"Respect my eye," huffed QuickMIC.

"Yes respect," sneered Eógan. "Without me you would have joined your forefathers many years ago, on top of the compost heap."

"If only I had joined them," said QuickMIC, zooming back into PaddySan's circuits, "I wouldn't have been cursed with you then."

"It can easily be arranged," threatened Eógan.

All of the Irish Mythological Cycles confirm that Eógan had indeed been spared Óengus' sword on account of Caer's passionate intercession, but matters only got worse after that. Unfortunately, Eógan had absorbed more of the lover from Óengus than anything else, and his sultry voice combined with his even more provocative, poetic recitals meant that no woman could resist his charms.

Finally, after accusations of several affairs and the ruination of several noble families, the elders of Tuatha Dé Dannan decided that Ancient Irish Mythology had no place for a lothario, and Eógan was banished to an eternity in a specially made marble box, and subsequently buried under a mound.

"I suppose you're right, me and Malachy do owe you our lives," relented QuickMIC, feeling he'd overstepped his own code of chivalry, as he poked further into PaddySan's head, "but don't you forget."

"What?" said Eógan

"Without Fíniún's pot of gold, nothing would have been possible."

Having only just dug him up, King Cormac enjoyed Eógan's company, especially the mythological stories he told of the good-oul' days. However, Eógan was soon up to his old tricks. His daily amorous recitals drew larger and larger female crowds and his way with the women had the men folk of the castle up in arms within a month of his resurrection. So before Eógan fell into the moat, which was a euphemism amongst the castle men folk for someone being assassinated, King Cormac decided to banish him from the castle grounds, if only to spare his life.

But what would he do without Eógan's company. The King had no children of his own, and Eógan had been great company altogether.

Hearing of the King's plight, Fíniún came up with a plan. In exchange for his freedom from the dungeon and with Eógan's help, he would create for the King a talking shillelagh, one based on a combination of ancient and modern technology. A splinter from Eógan would provide the essential life force, and Fíniún's leprechaun know how combined with his technical wizardry would do the rest.

Fíniún, a fanatic gambler with the longest losing streak in history, so long that he had never won anything in his gambling life, had just finished a long distance course in micro and nano-electronics from Trinity College, Dublin. He was certain that he could use such knowledge to build miniature hacking machines. Something to put on the side of a roulette table to force the ball into a certain number pocket, perhaps; or a little device attached to a Fruit Machine to trigger the Triple 7 jackpot; or a stealth nano-machine which could walk around the poker table and report back what cards the other players were holding. But little did he know that this modern technological knowledge would ever be used to create a new walking, talking shillelagh.

The King agreed to Fíniún's deal, with some restrictions placed on him – which you'll read about later - and he set to work on creating the first ever technological shillelagh. Fíniún called his first creation QuickMIC, because the shillelaghs wit was designed to be quick and he used Microprocessor Integrated Circuits (MIC) to get himself about the place.

Unfortunately for poor oul' King Cormac, QuickMIC was more interested in modern technical shenanigans than ancient ones. Sure compared to the flamboyant, charismatic - some might dare say womanising – Eógan, QuickMIC was a bit of a nerd. The King could hardly get a word out of him some nights, never mind a conversation. So the King was only too happy to release him from his duties, when QuickMIC turned up in the King's chambers one day, having just finished inventing his own replacement, Malachy Malarkey.

But that was a long time ago, and QuickMIC had gone on to open up his very own shop, Technological Shenanigans, in the heart of the town, where he was still arguing with Eógan.

"Oh yes," said Eógan, "the buried pot of gold, "how could I forget that."

"Whist, I think I have it," said QuickMIC, his own eyes turning an excited shade of orange. He quickly finished a few adjustments on PaddySan's motherboard, clicked it back into his head, and screwed the shaft into a diagnostic test unit.

QuickMIC switched the diagnostic test unit on and PaddySan's eyes popped open: "Kazuteda inu daze!"

"What did he say?" asked Eógan.

"You really don't want to know," sighed QuickMIC.

"I think I know what riles him so," said Eógan after a few moments.

"What?" asked QuickMIC.

"He has a mother-board, correct?"

"Correct."

"I think PaddySan might be home sick, so," intuited Eógan. "Here I'll sing him an oul' song to remind him of his home and his dear oul' mother. That'll should settle him for sure."

"Go on, so" said QuickMIC, "anything's worth a try at this stage."

Eógan got up from his rocking chair, cleared his throat and in a voice reminiscent of the great tenor Josef Locke, he sang:

"I'll take you home again Kathleen,
Across the ocean wild and wide ..."

At the end of the first verse, tears began forming in PaddySan's eyes.

"But, I will take you back again Kathleen,
To where your heart will feel no pain."

And by the end of the third chorus, which Eógan sang in Japanese, PaddySan couldn't take any more. With tears gushing from his eyes he looked forlornly at QuickMIC and whimpered: "Watashi no kokoro wa ai no kotoba o hanashi te iru!"

"What what that?" asked Eógan.

QuickMIC wiped tears of joy from his own eyes and said, "Good man yerself Eógan, I think you've done it!"

"What did he say, man," repeated Eógan excitedly, "sure I'm no mind reader?"

"But you just sang in Japanese?"

"Sure I only learnt those words from a karaoke machine. I haven't got a clue what PaddySan said."

"My heart speaks the language of love," QuickMIC announced to Eógan, smiling while he wiped more tears from his eyes.

"Steady on now, you," said Eógan lowering his voice an octave and shuffling behind his oak throne, "I might be a lothario, but I'm not that kind of man."

"No you eejit," said QuickMIC. "That's what PaddySan just said ... 'My heart speaks the language of love'."

"Hai, so desu," agreed PaddySan.

Chapter 17

Ye Olde Ross Ice Shelf Committee

It was a beautiful morning and Cormac's Castle, overlooking Eirestown on top of Sí Bheg, shimmered in the morning sun, as the remnants of a blanket of green mist, covering the town, slowly wafted away. In the distance to the West, the King could see the Croagh Patrick coming into view. A few minutes later, the green mist had lifted completely, leaving Eirestown somewhere just outside Claremorris, County Mayo.

A chorus of birds in the branches of a tree outside the castle were whistling a sublime, harmonious rendition of Turlough O'Carolan's tune, 'Sí Bheg, Sí Mhór', The Little Fairy Hill, The Big Fairy Hill. But King Cormac couldn't hear a thing. He was sat in his sound proofed chambers, ear plugs firmly in place. Although it was a firm favourite with tourists, the King was sick to death of that particular lament these many years now, and it nearly had himself and everyone else in the castle driven round the twist. The birds were like modern day Sirens, happily twittering away first thing, every Sunday morning. There was no chance of a lie in with those little feckers chirping away.

The only saving grace was that, as it was Sunday morning, the bells of 'Kells Gothic Monastery', which was perched right next to Sí Bheg on top of Sí Mhór, the Big Fairy Hill, would soon let out an almighty gong, and scare the chirpy little gobshites away. Then the King and everyone else in the castle might be able to get back to bed for a few hours.

Just outside the gates of Cormac's Castle, a round figure, wearing green braces and with one sideburn missing was on his way. As arranged, Malachy met Paht at the gate, to escort him over the drawbridge into the castle, and then into King Cormac's chambers.

"Here he is m'Lord," announced Malachy, entering the chambers, Paht following a few paces behind.

Ignoring them, King Cormac continued staring out of one of the tripled glazed windows in the chambers.

Malachy cleared his throat and announced Paht once more; "Ahem! ... M'Lord as you requested, here's the representative."

King Cormac didn't budge, not one iota, except to scratch his bum through his green, gold trimmed royal robes, and slightly adjust his golden crown.

"He must be awfully t'ick this fella," said Paht, "sure I thought he was the wisest man in all Ireland?"

"Shush," hissed Malachy, nudging Paht in the knee, "carry on now and he'll stick you in the dungeons."

Malachy tried to get the King's attention again, and this time let out an introduction which shook the rafters: "M'Lord ... he is here!"

King Cormac remained motionless for another minute, scratched his bum again, farted extremely loudly and yelled, "Thank Christ for that!"

Which Paht could only assume was an expression of deep relief following the expulsion of what must have been some seriously pent up gases.

"Poo ....was that a Royal fanfare?" asked Paht, nipping his nose and giggling. "To think I waited my whole life for an audience with this smelly eejit."

"Shush," hissed Malachy, pointing a sparkling, blue tinged finger at Paht, the zapper primed.

Malachy was also extremely alarmed by King Cormac's behaviour. Funny it might have been, but the King was getting on a bit. He'd shown no signs of dementia yet, however, Malachy wondered if this bout of deafness was one of the first signs. To be sure, Malachy felt he had no choice but to violate Royal protocol and walk over to tap King Cormac on his shoulder. With that in mind, he had only taken one step forward when King Cormac turned around suddenly, threw up his arms in terror and screamed, "Be the hoh-key." before collapsing on the very spot.

"Is he dead?" asked Paht as Malachy ran over to help him. "I'd not be surprised, he's probably been poisoned by all that noxious gas."

"M'Lord, m'Lord!" Malachy bent down and put his ear to Kind Cormac's chest. "Thank Dian Cécht, he's breathing!"

"Who's that?" asked Paht.

"Jesus Paht," Malachy replied, opening King Cormac's collar. "It's people like you who give the Irish a bad name. Dian Cécht was the Irish God of healing in Irish mythology." He patted King Cormac a few times on each cheek, trying to revive him. "Don't you know anything about your own culture, or are you just a thick eejit?"

"No," Paht said, "not who's Dian Cécht. I know who he was." Malachy turned around to find Paht pointing at the chamber door, where a very odd looking iShillelagh dressed in a white lab coat, and carrying a leather briefcase was standing, "I meant who's that?"

"The Court Surgeon," answered Malachy, when he saw the iShillelagh. "Over here quickly, the King has collapsed!"

Half an hour later, King Cormac was sat on his throne in the great hall. It had been touch and go there for a few moments, though. The surgeon said he was lucky to be alive given the experience he'd just had. Sure it must have a terrible shock altogether to have turned around to discover that two of your subjects, one of them holding his nose, were within ear shot of one of the loudest farts you had ever let rip. That's how the surgeon had put it anyway, almost verbatim. Of course Paht disagreed with the surgeon and said the subjects had suffered the bigger shock.

It didn't take the surgeon long to realise that King Cormac had ear plugs in, and couldn't hear a word Malachy had been saying. And that he had only yelled "Thank Christ for that," when the bells of 'Kell's Monastery' rang out scaring those blasted birds away.

Malachy Malarkey, playing the Court Jester, was wearing his usual green, white and orange harlequin suit, with matching pantaloons and had been skipping around the throne for the last five minutes, bells tickling away on his three tailed hat, annoying the poor recovering King. The previous shock had nearly been enough to kill King Cormac, but Malachy Malarkey seemed hell bent on finishing the job.

Round and round he skipped, stopping every now and then to blow several loud raspberries, which echoed around the great hall. 'Brrrppp! ... Brrrppp! ... Brrrppp!' After each raspberry, laughter grew from the back of the hall, where several courtesans, advisers and various staff were assembled, leaving King Cormac with his head in his hands.

"Guards," commanded King Cormac finally, no longer able to take Malachy's tomfoolery, "prepare the dungeons."

"Beggin' your mercy your Highness," pleaded Malachy, when two guards grabbed him and hoisted him off the ground, "you'll get no more malarkey out of me."

"You'll be the death of me Malachy Malarkey," said King Cormac, commanding the guards to release him and waving them back into line.

"To business then if it pleases m'Lord," said Malachy with some fanfare. "I present to you Paht, proud representative of the team you have requested to investigate the Ross Ice Shelf problem."

"M'Lord," began Paht earnestly, "I am honoured to respond to your call."

"You hear that?" Malachy was up on King Cormac's shoulder, whispering directly into his ear. "Paht responded to you call, your Majesty." Malachy let out another raspberry, straight into the King's ear, brrrppp, and added, "I'm surprised the whole of Ireland didn't respond to that apocalyptic trumpet blast."

"Be quite you grovelling wretch," shouted King Cormac, trying to brush Malachy off his shoulder. "Guards!"

"But your majesty," said Paht, "I was only saying ..."

"No not you, you fool, carry on."

It was at times like this that King Cormac was sorry he ever let Malachy Malarkey replace QuickMIC. After QuickMIC, Malachy Malarkey was the next technological shillelaghs to enter the service of the Royal Court. He was great craic for the first few years, and at least he was not as boring as QuickMIC. He also told the odd joke here and there, usually at the expense of King Cormac's guests, which the King really enjoyed. He was also a little insolent at times, with plenty of irreverent, insightful commentary. Eventually, he became the scourge of the castle, but King Cormac felt Malachy's malarkey kept all his advisers and staff on their toes, since they never knew when Malachy would round on them, ridiculing them with his commentary, or criticising them for not performing their duty very well.

But then one day, Malachy started sailing a little too close to the boundaries of his jester's license. QuickMIC blamed it on bugs and viruses which seemed to infect Malachy every week or so. And no matter how often he updated the anti-virus software it was always playing catch-up.

King Cormac told QuickMIC he had a permanent solution for Malachy's malarkey. He still had the Connemara marble box Eógan had been found in. And it'd be no bother to stick Malachy in it and have it buried again. But QuickMIC, having invented Malachy, had an awful soft spot for him, and always pleaded his case.

Malachy managed to avoid the King's sweeping hand, and hopped down from his shoulder and said, "Come on Paht, get on with it, what have ye got planned?"

But Paht was mortified and remained silent, what with the King shouting at him like that.

The King thought he would ask Paht about Paddy McGinty's Goat, to try and calm him, smooth things over and build some rapport, "Tell me, how's the goat, are you doing ok over there?"

How dare he! He's calling me a goat now, thought Paht. "I don't know why you would call me a goat your highness," replied Paht, furious at the insult, "but would you like to buy a pair of soundproof underpants, by any chance?"

The court was in uproar and some people were laughing so loud that they had to leave the great hall before they broke wind themselves. Four guards rushed towards Paht, but the King raised his hand and dismissed them. He just wanted to get back to his soundproof chambers as quickly as possible to recuperate. After assuring Paht that he was not calling him a goat but merely asking after Paddy McGinty's Goat and making sure his business was flourishing, Paht laid out Banbha's plan.

"Is that it," said King Cormac, sorry that, even though it was a misunderstanding, he'd retracted the goat accusation after all, "a reconnaissance trip?" He looked at Malachy with eyebrows raised, winked and added sarcastically, "That's some gift Banbha has, eh? Perhaps I should ask her for six numbers for next week's lotto?"

"Some gift she has, m'Lord," agreed Malachy, "with a gift like that, I'm not sure she'd be able to give you last week's lotto numbers, never mind next week's numbers."

"Last week's numbers!" King Cormac started clapping, applauding Malachy's wit. "Sure that's great craic altogether Malachy."

"It's a start, m'Lord," shouted Paht in Banbha's defence, cutting the laughter short. "Rome wasn't built in a day, you know."

"And it may never have been built at all," said Malachy dismissively, "if ye lot had been commissioned to build it."

"Beggin' your pardon your Highness," said Paht, suddenly feeling that in such historic surroundings it was only appropriate to start talking like someone who had just stepped out of one of Chaucer's Canterbury Tales, "but me doth resent thou admonition of my granddaughter."

King Cormac wasn't sure why Paht was using such antiquated language. However, having already offended him in the worse possible manner with an outburst of flatulence, and, as far as Paht was concerned, having also called him a goat, he was keen to avoid any more underpants jokes. Therefore King Cormac decided to reply in the same antiquated manner, in the third person: "Sirrah, thou art correct, please accepteth our apologies and speketh thy plans fair … What say ye?"

The court already knew Paht's sanity was in question, but they now wondered if 'King Cormac 'hast finally taken leave of his senses'. Or perhaps he was suffering from some kind of post traumatic stress, brought on by his earlier shock.

"Your Grace," continued Paht in a medievalish manner, "thou art most kindeth and thy sweet words play a most soothing melody in mine ears. We will go tither to 'Ye Olde Ross Ice Shelf', whereupon we shall carry outeth a studye. Knoweth well your highness that if it be possibleth we shall repair thy icy trove."

"'Tis a most beauteous bounty thou spreadeth before us, liketh the wings of heavenly Angels dancing on the head of a pineth," said King Cormac. "We shall title you 'Ye Olde Ross Ice Shelf Committee'. Go yonder with our blessings!"

"Prithee m'Lord," said Paht as King Cormac prepared to leave, "does thou not haveth any more advice for us. After alleth thou is the wisest person in all of Irelandeth."

"Prithee, I shall speaketh for the King," piped up Malachy.

King Cormac nodded his approval if only to get away from this madness as quickly as possible, and return to the bliss of his sound proof chambers and some level of sanity.

"The next time thou sneaketh up on a Royal personage," said Malachy Malarkey, pinching his nose to conclude his advice nasally, "be sure that thou is wearing a nose peg."

And with that King Cormac retired back into his sound proof chambers, Malachy Malarkey in tow, blowing squeaky raspberries behind him every second step.

Chapter 18

I Want To Give You A Kiss

"Ye Olde Ross Ice Shelf Committee," said Ryan, "are you sure?"

"As sure as I'm sitting here," said Paht.

"And we've the King's blessing to go on a reconnaissance trip?" asked Banbha.

"'Deed we have," said Paht. "QuickMIC's preparing supplies as we speak. As soon as we've made the travel arrangements, we'll be on our way."

An hour after his audience with King Cormac, Paht was back in Paddy McGinty's Goat with the rest of the Ye Olde Ross Ice Shelf Committee. They were sat next to the open stone fireplace in the bar, where a blackened kettle hung on an ancient hook, hissing over crackling flames.

"By the way, if that's the wisest man in all of Ireland," said Paht, sipping on a pint of the black stuff, sparks hopping away in the flames, "I think I'll apply for the job me self."

"By the way, if that's the wisest man in all of Ireland," replied Fin, sipping some red lemonade, "I think you've had the job all your life."

"Intriguing," said Ryan, "meeting an Irish King must have been a mind blowing experience, to say the least."

"Mind blowing," said Paht, taking another mouthful, "sure I'm lucky I wasn't blown out of the great hall and half way to America when he let rip."

"Cop yourself on granddad," said Bhanba, "and have some respect. He's still the King, never forget that."

"He's the King alright," said Paht, nudging Ryan, "but I'll wear a parachute next time I meet him. Just in case he lets rip and blows me out of a window."

Banbha was about to remonstrate when a familiar tune interrupted them:

'Now old Paddy McGinty's Goat had a wondrous appetite,
and one day for breakfast he ate some dynamite...'

"Donn-Dubh," groaned Paht, knocking back another mouthful. "I'll take a hurling stick to that bass powered contraption of his one of these days."

Paht had barely swallowed his drink when Donn-Dubh burst into the bar ranting and stammering like a man possessed: "Take cover ... Run for your lives."

Close behind him a group of iShillelaghs tumbled chaotically in through the door, playing a cacophonous rendition of Paddy McGinty's Goat. Having played a few bars they hopped up onto the table and started introducing themselves, running and tumbling all over the place:

"Howya!! we're The Cracker Craics... how's the craic ... are you well? Good man yourself ... and good lady yourself too ... would you like a song ... a jig perhaps … ahh go-on go-on go-on go-on I'll give you a song … The craic was mighty … Ahh be Gawwrrr … How's the craic … Sure we're in grand form altogether … you look grand yourself … Howya … The craic was mighty … Ahh be Gawwrrr …. would you like a jig … Ahh go-on go-on go-on go-on … I'll give you a jig … Howya … how's the craic …"

"Be the hoh-key," said Paht when The Cracker Craics came to a standstill on the table and formed a circle, with the female of the group in the middle, "what have we here?"

Once settled, the fiddle player struck up a familiar tune, and the female Cracker Craic, in fine voice now, started singing serenely the Galway Shawl …

'She wore no jewels, no costly diamonds,
No paint no powder, no none at all …'

"I love this song," said Paht, joining in after the first verse. Banbha quickly followed his lead and hummed along. At the end of the first verse, Paht picked up a fresh pint and started saluting The Cracker Craics: "Go on lads, fair play to ye!"

'And round her shoulder was a Galway shawl,'

"They look harmless enough," said Ryan to Donn-Dubh, tapping his feet and humming along.

"No not them, you idiots" shrieked Donn-Dubh, pointing to the bar door and windows, "them!"

Several iShillelaghs dressed as ninjas came flipping and somersaulting in through the bar door. Some of them held samurai swords, others shuriken ninja throwing stars. One particularly excited ninja threw a shuriken star which took the creamy, white head off of the fresh pint of black stuff Paht was saluting The Cracker Craics with.

Paht turned around to find the shuriken star, with the white head of black stuff still resting on it, embedded in the wall just behind his right ear. He took another few gulps of black stuff, just to calm his nerves.

Along the windows, iShillelagh commandos and iShillelagh special service soldiers pointed guns into the bar, and several more iShillelagh commandos rushed in through the back and front doors to join the assault. Some of the commandos, dressed in silver and gold futuristic suits, wore helmets with mirrored visors, and held what looked like Ray Guns of some kind.

Twenty iShillelagh commandos in the bar held smaller iShillelaghs which were shaped like truncheons with a strap on the end. These smaller truncheons were much more like traditional shillelaghs. They were black and had the original mallet-head design, with shaggy, matted grey heads of hair, and canine faces. Part way down their main trunks, not far below the head, two long, black muscular arms stuck out. And on the end of these muscular battering rams, gnarled fists were bursting to get out of huge, bright red boxing gloves.

These smaller iShillelaghs were known as Irish Wolf Hounds. As well as arms they also had legs which they wound around each other to form a single shaft, when held in battle mode. They were also telescopic, and could shrink or elongate their shafts as circumstances demanded. At the moment they were all about ten centimetres long, but when alone they could grow as high as fifty centimetres. Although they were nowhere near as big as real Irish wolf hounds, their ferocious aggression more than made up for any deficiency in size.

In battle the Irish Wolf Hounds could either be used as basic clubs, in which case they tucked in their muscular arms and were swung around like mallets to bash the opponents into surrender, or, in close range, they would stretch out those arms and get up close and personal, delivering flurry after flurry of punches in numerous combinations, 'polishing their gloves' they called it.

"Look at them lads," said Fin, when he saw the Wolf Hounds.

"They look like fierce little fellas," replied Banbha.

In boxing mode the operator could choose Automatic or Manual, in which case he threw punches using two finger buttons at the bottom of the shaft. Given the choice, the Wolf Hounds preferred Automatic mode, because they could do what the hell they liked, and beat the living daylights out of anything that crossed their paths, including each other.

"Stick em' up!" the Irish Wolf Hounds roared, "I'll fight ye for yer pints!" In between phrases they growled and barked. Some of them wore protective eye goggles, others just didn't care, and although they were strapped to burly wrists, their operators struggled to hold them back, even using both hands.

"Let me at 'em," shouted one Wolf Hounds being held by a commando who looked like he'd rather be holding a lion than one of these virulent fellas, "and I'll polish me oul' gloves on one of their faces."

"No," barked another Wolf Hound dragging back the first iShillelagh, "let me at 'em! Your gloves are polished enough!" This Wolf Hound was a battle hardened southpaw, and was being held by a commando who had veins popping out of his forehead, trying to restrain it.

Unable to get at their intended prey, these two particularly rebellious Wolf Hounds started fighting each other, polishing each other's gloves and punching seven bells out of one another. The commandos holding them ducked for cover, trying to untangle the straps around their wrists, and ohh-ed and ahh-ed as they received a fair share of the stray punches.

With the forces amassing, Paht and Ryan dived for cover beneath the table they'd been drinking at, while Fin and Banbha ran to the fireplace, where Fin picked up a poker and Banbha a log grabber.

You could cut the air with shuriken ... there was complete silence, except for some noise from behind the bar where Donn-Dubh was crouched down, rummaging around in his hat, looking for a suitable weapon. So far he'd pulled out a teddy bear iShillelagh which was a particularly cuddly creature with the cutest face you'd even seen, a tin of beans, a mug, a white pudding he'd promised Paht and an autographed CD of 'Volume 1 of Donn-Dubh's Classic Jiggy-Reggy' which he'd promised to Ryan.

Apart from Donn-Dubh, Ye Olde Ross Ice Shelf Committee were surrounded, outnumbered and all wishing they were somewhere else. Even standing behind King Cormac would be preferable, Paht whispered.

Presently the silence was broken. The bar front door creaked open, and in walked a short haired, leather clad iShillelagh, wearing dark sunglasses.

"Hey," Ryan whispered to Paht underneath the table, "that one looks like a Hells Angel."

'I must get that door oiled,' Paht replied.

"Nobody makes a move and nobody will get hurt," the Angel from Hell commanded in monotonous, dreary tones. Then he scanned the bar with a black .45 gun, a bright red dot from his laser-lock tracing out the gun's path.

Ryan winced when the dot finally came to rest on Paht's forehead. "What is it Ryan," said Paht, "is it the halitosis?" He breathed into a closed palm and sniffed it. "Sure I can't smell a thing."

"Shhhh .... you eejit," said Ryan, "and don't make a move."

"Nobody make a move and nobody will get hurt," the Angel repeated, pointing the laser dot back at Paht's forehead.

As the Angel continued to survey the barroom, a Cantankerous Cabbage rolled out from behind the bar like a tumble weed and stopped at his feet. The Angel pointed his .45 at it and the cabbage opened its leaves, saying in an awfully sombre voice:

"Did you hear about the fella from Tipperary who went into the same bar every night to buy three pints?"

"No," shouted Paht from under the table.

"He'd take the three pints outside," continued the Cantankerous Cabbage, climb up on the highest branch he could find, drink them, and go back to the bar for three more pints.

"One day," the cabbage went on drearily, "the barman asked him why he drank three pints up on the branch like that. The Tipperary fella answered, 'I do everything in t'rees'. "

"I don't get it," said Ryan.

"I do everything in t'rees," said Paht, struggling to hold his laughter in. "That's gas!" he added, holding up three fingers for Ryan, and pronouncing the words, 'threes' and 't'rees'.

Despite Paht's explanation, Ryan still looked blank and the Angel didn't get it either. He shot the cabbage three times, making it the most cantankerous cabbage to have ever come out of Technological Shenanigans. Each time it was hit, the cabbage let out an almighty OWWW.

After the third shot, the cabbage rolled out of the bar, wincing, whirling and whining, and headed for Technological Shenanigans, where it hoped to get some medical assistance. Having despatched of the Cantankerous Cabbage, the Hells Angel said, "Anyone else got a joke they'd like to tell?"

"We've no more jokes," said Ryan. "Just tell us what you want?"

Suddenly the Angel puckered his lips a few times, put his left arm on his hip, blew Ryan a kiss and said: "I want to give you a kiss."

Ryan suddenly realised that these must be the reinforcements William McCoy The Third had sent, and that the request for a kiss was the coded love message.

"I never do that on a first date," answered Ryan. Paht told him not to be shy and get on with it.

"What else do you want?" Ryan asked the Angel, telling Paht to keep out of it.

"You know what we want," answered the Angel.

"What does he want?" asked Paht.

"I haven't a clue," said Ryan.

"Well you better find out fast," replied Paht.

"Why?" said Ryan.

"I've a delivery at twelve," answered Paht.

"I wouldn't worry about that," said Ryan, reaching out to drag Paht back. "Hey where you going?"

"To give him a kiss," said Paht.

Chapter 19

Nobody Move Or The Bear Gets It

You could still cut the air with a shuriken, as the amorous Hells Angel shouted "Get off me," pushing Paht's face away from his, "I really don't want that!"

"Playing hard to get, is it?" said Paht. "Right so, come on now you, pucker up."

Against Ryan's warnings, Paht was on his knees in the middle of Paddy McGinty's bar room, trying to kiss the Hells Angel iShillelagh, but the Angel was having none of it.

"Come on now," repeated Paht puckering his own lips, "I'll give you a juicy one."

"How about I give you a juicy one?" offered the Hells Angel.

"Right so," said Paht closing his eyes, his lips primed. "Give me your best shot."

Without another word, the Angel gave Paht a punch which sent him rolling back under the table.

"Be the hoh-key," exclaimed Paht, "now that's what I call a smacker." He was about to go back for seconds when the Angel pulled out his .45.

"Don't move," commanded the Angel, rubbing his lips, "I really, really, really do not want anymore of that."

The Hells Angel rubbed his lips a few more times, and was about to speak when Paht said, "Are you some kind of t'ick eejit or what? We really don't know what you want."

The Angel nodded at one of the iShillelagh ninjas, and two shuriken stars whizzed across the bar, slicing through the braces on Paht's shoulders. Paht heard two twangs and felt his trousers give.

"So what do you want?" said Ryan, helping Paht with his braces.

"The Ross Ice Shelf," replied the Angel.

"We don't have it here," said Paht, trying to wrap his braces around his waist, "we only serve ice cubes."

"What about it?" said Ryan, prodding Paht to shut up.

"You're not to worry about it," said the Angel. "We're going to fix it."

"I don't trust them," shouted Banbha from across the bar room.

"Let's worry about that later," Ryan said.

Ryan felt the best strategy was appeasement. Just get rid of these thugs and then call the Garda. Even though he knew they had been sent by William McCoy The Third to help him, these iShillelaghs were volatile, and prone to violence which he had no wish to be on the receiving end of.

"Ok," said Ryan, "we'll go nowhere near it."

Satisfied that he'd fulfilled their mission, the iShillelagh Hells Angel placed his gun back in its holster, and signalled to the troops to stand down, immediately several ninjas started flipping towards the door.

The Irish Wolf Hounds were not happy at all though, and a few of them started fighting each other again, until the Angel got his gun back out and also threatened them.

"They're going," said Ryan with a sigh of relief.

They were all glad to be alive and Paht was just getting ready to jump up and lock the door and windows when Donn-Dubh sprang up from behind the bar and opened the gates of hell with an unexpected ultimatum:

"Nobody move or the bear gets it!"

Donn-Dubh had the teddy bear he'd found in his hat in one hand - a cuddly looking iShillelagh holding a bright red heart between its legs with the words I LOVE YOU embroidered in the middle of it.

"I mean it," Donn-Dubh screamed, holding a white pudding menacingly above the teddy bear's head in his other hand, "I'll beat its brains out."

"He means it," said the teddy bear meekly, its eyes wide open in terror.

Donn-Dubh had been oblivious to much of the proceedings on the other side of the bar and in desperation had hatched a plan to save his friends.

He was hoping to do a hostage exchange: the bear for Ryan, Paht, Fin and Banbha. He figured camaraderie amongst iShillelaghs would mean that the Angel would not want to see the bear get hurt. He couldn't have been more wrong.

The bear got it alright, but it wasn't Donn-Dubh who gave it him. The Angel took his .45 out of its holster and blew the bears head clean off its body with one shot.

Donn-Dubh now had the white pudding in one hand and the teddy bear's head in the other

"I told you not to mess with him," the teddy bear said. "Now what are you going to do?"

Donn-Dubh screamed and threw the teddy bear's head on the bar.

"Alas poor Yorick, I knew him well," said the bear, eloquently quoting Shakespeare, as his head rolled across the bar like a bowling ball, knocking a few glasses and bottles over.

The leather clad Angel pointed the gun at Donn-Dubh and was about to pull the trigger when a flurry of shuriken stars sliced through his bulbous hat, chopping the top off, along with a few more green dreadlocks.

Donn-Dubh was furious and about to curse his ninja hairstylists when the Angel let off a few shots, smashing several bottles behind him. He got the message and ducked back down behind the bar.

Satisfied that everything was back under control, and happy that he'd made the point that he was not to be messed with, the Hells Angel was about to order his troops to stand down again, but then the bar room door flew open with a vengeance behind it.

'Ano yarou!'

PaddySan had been stood at the door with QuickMIC, both peering through a crack. Despite being shot three times, the Cantankerous Cabbage had managed to roll to Technological Shenanigans, tell the worse joke it ever told and alert QuickMIC about what was going on over there in Paddy McGinty's Goat. QuickMIC knew at once that it was that shower of AWOL iShillelaghs. He was reluctant to bring PaddySan along, but because Eógan had sang him 'I'll Take You Home Again Kathleen', PaddySan told QuickMIC that love had overpowered his earlier programming, and he wanted nothing more than to protect Eógan, QuickMIC and the people of Eirestown, pledging his allegiance to them.

Himself and QuickMIC had been at the door a few minutes now, but PaddySan became enraged when he saw the Hells Angel blow the teddy bear's head off and flew into the bar to have it out with him.

The Angel spun to shoot PaddySan but he was too slow. PaddySan twirled several times, ducked down, slid under the Angel's extended arm and sliced it off. It fell to the floor still holding the .45, where it let off another shot, taking out two iShillelagh commandos on the windowsill.

Blood was in the air: The Wolf Hounds let out even more ferocious howls, and the ninjas started flipping back into battle positions, along with the remaining commandos, who returned to their positions on the windowsill.

Suddenly a very loud whistle blew and there was complete silence again.

Everyone looked over to the bar where The Cracker Craics had assembled.

"Give us an oul' chance lads," said one of The Cracker Craics, pulling a whistle from his lips.

"This is gas, great craic and all," added Whistler, "but you can't have a bar fight without two things."

"What're they?" shouted Paht.

"A drop of *uisce beatha* and some lively music," replied Whistler.

"Pass me down a drop, so" said Paht, "and strike us up an oul' song."

"What is *uisce beatha*?" Ryan asked Paht.

"Irish fire water," said Paht, adding the word whiskey, because Ryan still looked confused.

"Good man yerself," said Whistler, as one of the Cracker Craics leapt down from the bar with a full short glass and ran over to Paht.

"Goodbye Ryan," said Paht, knocking back the shot in one, "I'll see you on the other side."

"Better get me one of those," Ryan said.

"And I'll have a red lemonade," said Fin.

"Me too," said Banbha.

"A glass of saki for PaddySan," said QuickMIC, "and don't worry about me. I never bother meself this early in the day."

"And hand me down a rum and coke," Donn-Dubh whispered from behind the other side of the bar.

"I'll have a banana milkshake meself," said the head of the iShillelagh teddy bear. "But do us an oul' favour, put an extra long straw in it please, and stick it into the side of my mouth."

A few moments later, everyone was drinking their last requests, even the teddy bear who was drawing his milk shake through an elongated straw.

As the last drinks were savoured, the Cracker Craics' percussionist started beating out a warrior rhythm, *con brio,* on his bodrhán. The oul' spoons, God bless them, fearing for their lives, decided to sit this one out, and tucked themselves firmly into his socks, where they managed to peer out every now and then over the hem.

The female Cracker Craic, still serving behind the bar, threw up Whistler a third glass of *uisce beatha,* and he knocked it back in one gulp.

"Yeee-aaahhh ..." he gasped, letting out another almighty ahhh and licking the last few drops of *uisce beatha* from his lips, "'Tis away we go!" The battle cry initiated, he threw up the fiddle onto his left shoulder and starting playing The Bucks Of Oranmore, *presto bellicoso accelerando*, his fingers a blur as they flew up and down the strings. Sure he could outplay the devil himself after an oul' sup of *uisce beatha*. Within a few bars, the rest of the Cracker Craics had taken up the feisty reel. The piper took up the main theme and led them into battle. He was like Séamus Ennis himself, pumping away on the bellows, his fingers flying up and down the chanter.

Moments later it was like a shoot-'em up scene in a bar from an old cowboy movie. Except this was Eirestown and there were no cowboys drinking in Paddy McGinty's this morning. There were a few Indians in the local Curry House alright, but they didn't count, since they were from Goa in India, not Native Americans.

The gates Donn-Dubh had opened unleashed a plethora of tracers, lasers, bullets and shuriken stars. Ninjas started flipping all over the place. And the Irish Wolf hounds had a field day beating the hell out of each other and their retainers.

PaddySan became a whirlwind and spun around the bar at high speed, taking out 90% of the attack force in his first circuit with cuts, thrusts, slices and deft deflections of lasers and shuriken stars, which turned the salvo back on the attackers, blowing many of them to smithereens.

Fin and Banbha sprang into action, too. Fin used the poker to bat ninjas and commandos towards Banbha and she used the log grabber to catch them and throw them onto the open fire.

Ryan and Paht were terrified and stayed huddled together, hugging each other under the table.

One shuriken star whizzed across the bridge of the Cracker Craics' fiddle and cut through one of the strings. "Not a bother, lads," bragged the fiddle player when the string snapped, and the maelstrom grew around him. "Sure I once out-fiddled Maxim Vengerov with only one string at the *Conservatoire De Paris*," he bragged.

"He did as well," the uilleann piper confirmed. "Sure they said he could play like Paganini himself."

"But they called him Paddynini," said the bodrhán player.

"On account of him being Irish and all," giggled the lady with the Galway shawl.

Now that the compliments were over, Paddynini took a quick bow, and adjusted his fingers to compensate for the loss of the first string, but as he did, a laser burnt through another one.

"'Deed I love a challenge," boasted Paddynini, adjusting for the two lost strings.

Unfortunately, two shuriken stars later, he was string less, and the last sound that particular violin ever made was an almighty thwocking-twang as it shattered on the head of the ninja who'd just cut the last two strings. Paddynini burst into tears as he realised that he had just destroyed his ancient violin, which was a Paddyvarius, a musical masterpiece, crafted by an Irish contemporary of Stradivarius.

The fire was nearly full to the top with ninjas and commandos and PaddySan was whizzing around so fast now that he was actually leaving the floor at times, his kimono filling out as he floated back down to earth.

"Thank God he's not Scottish," said Paht, when he saw PaddySan's kimono rise as high as his waist, revealing a mawashi, similar to a sumo's.

After a few rounds of polishing their gloves, all the Wolf Hounds had black eyes and some had so many bumps and bruises that they looked like they'd been in ten rounds with another Irish Wolf hound, which they had.

Suddenly a very loud whistle blew again, and the maelstrom came to an end.

"We'll call that a wrap, lads," said Paddynini, snivelling and pulling the whistle out of his mouth. "It wasn't a bad oul' fight. Mighty craic and all. But I think we could have done with John Wayne, or Clint Eastwood half way through, to add a bit of glamour to the proceedings, wha'? Now if yis'll excuse me," he sniffed, himself in bits like the oul' fiddle, he bent down to pick up a few pieces of shattered maple, spruce, willow and blackthorn, holding them tenderly in his arms like a fallen soldier, "I'm off to see if I can get the oul' Paddyvarius repaired."

PaddySan was in a crouched position at the feet of the Angel, his katana in held in front of him.

The Hells Angel harrumphed in PaddySan's direction, before he analysed the remnants of the engagement. The fire was full to the brim with iShillelagh commandoes and ninjas, and the floor was littered with the scattered remains of the rest the Angel's men. The Angel bent down to pick his arm up, and attempted to place the gun in his other hand.

"Usero!" PaddySan ordered.

"What?"

"Get lost, he said," translated QuickMIC.

"You win," said the Angel. And with that he gave the retreat signal.

Only six Wolf Hounds were alive to see it, but they had other plans. Slowly they dragged themselves across the floor on their bloodied gloves and propped themselves up on the bar, where they asked for a menu and six pints of Paddy McGinty's finest.

Chapter 20

Gondolas On Canal Street, NYC

William McCoy The Third was in his plush offices, ohhing-and-ahhing as his Swiss masseuse worked his neck, and shoulders.

It was a special occasion and he had awarded himself a treat. He was semi-naked, a white towel covering his lower half, and lying down on a massage table, overlooking the East River. He glanced over at the office wall clock and smiled to himself. Any moment now Ryan would phone with the news he'd waited all day to hear. The Eirestown sabotage mission had been a success, and GRABiT could carry out its audacious expansion plans carte blanche.

Carte blanch? He sipped on a glass of Goût de Diamants, smirked again, before repeating the phrase under his breath, Carte blanch.

Why was he suddenly thinking in French? He assumed that it was probably a side effect of having spent all his spare time salivating over An Cabáiste agus Bagún Deli's menu and Paddy Roux's cuisine, ever since Ryan faxed it over.

Just as soon as New York was flooded, he was going to open his own An Cabáiste agus Bagún Deli on Canal Street, and ship Paddy Roux over to run it. Turn it into the New World's first franchise. And with the cuisine sorted he could focus on transport routes up and down Canal Street. Just imagine he mumbled to himself ... gondolas ...

"What was that sir?" asked the masseuse, kneading his right shoulder.

"Gondolas on Canal Street, NYC," replied William, lost in a daydream. "Just think of the convenience, the romance. Eating at the finest establishments in the world, and arriving there in style on a gondola."

"Yes sir," said the masseuse, chomping on bubble gum and oblivious to William's fantasy.

William dreamily drooled over the Manhattan skyline. "It's hard to believe, but Manhattan will soon be giving Venice a run for her money. And I'll be able to step out of my 20th storey window, straight onto a gondola." William was completely immersed in his fantasy now. "Gold embellished gondolas on Wall Street and 5th Avenue," he declared, unable to control his imagination.

"You mean Venice, sir, Los Angeles?"

"No, my dear," answered William. "Venice Italy, home of the Medici's."

"Oh yeah," said the masseuse, "the Medici's, I go there all the time."

"You do?" said William, impressed by her cultural excursions.

"Yeah," she said, blowing a chewing gum bubble, "they do the best pizza pie on 5th Avenue."

"Oh," said William patronising her, "but you're such a sweetie. No my dear, I'm talking about the great Medici dynasty of Renaissance Venice."

"You are?" she said. "That sounds very interesting."

"I am and it is," said William. "For example, consider Cosimo de' Medici, the father of the modern banking system. Now there was a polymath."

"I get ya," said the masseuse, "I've seen him in that film."

"You have?"

"Yeah, Quasimodo, what a character," she said. "Now there's a guy who could have done with a massage."

"He could?"

"Yeah," she said, blowing another bubble, "to get rid of that awful hump."

William was tickled, genuinely tickled. Her ignorance was sublime, blissful but sublime. He rolled his head back down, and carried on talking, aware that she didn't have a clue, but keen to share his visions in any event.

"And talking about Cosmio de' Medici and the banks," he went on, "what better way to travel to the bank, and the theatre actually, than by gondola? And with Little Italy flooded, and all those people out of work, there'd be no trouble finding an Italian gondolier."

Tired of listening to him gibbering on, the masseuse blew an even bigger chewing gum bubble, hoping to beat her own record.

"What was that?" asked William when the bubble popped.

"A chewing gum bubble, sir."

"Oh you are such a sweetie," purred William. "How wonderful, a bubble. Do you know GRABiT is about to create a bubble that will never pop!"

"What kind of bubble would that be sir?"

William could barely contain his enthusiasm and might pop himself at any minute, "A *global* housing bubble."

The masseuse giggled again, the only thought on her mind the bundle of dollars she'd be getting just as soon as she'd finished greasing this slime ball.

"Perfect isn't it, just perfect," he murmured, the masseuse's fingers rippling up and down his relaxed neck. "With the Ross Ice Shelf gone, millions of people will be looking for new houses to buy, and new land to build on. But GRABiT's thought of everything, haven't we my dear?"

"We have?" asked the masseuse, in a stupor.

"We certainly have," answered William, his megalomania taking over. "It's a good job GRABiT has been investing in so much land and housing way above the new projected sea-levels these past five years. I can't wait for the next AGM, the shareholders will give me the longest standing ovation in GRABiT's history."

"Gee, sir," said the masseuse, taking hold of a mound of flesh on each shoulder, "five years? Now that's what they call forward planning."

William McCoy The Third agreed and said: "Not since Moses parted the Red Sea will so many people be forced to migrate. It will be a global event my dear. Actually," he added, "the parting of the Red Sea will look like a ripple in a wash basin compared to this cataclysmic event."

"Yes sir," said the masseuse, not sure if William was even awake, and convinced that the champagne was taking its toll.

Suddenly the conference phone rang and turned William McCoy's dreams into a nightmare. Unfortunately, there was one thing William McCoy The Third hadn't thought of when outlining GRABiT's five year expansion plans.

"Sir ... sir? ... are you still there?"

"Yes Ryan," said William, struggling to come to terms with the latest update from Eirestown. "I'm still here. Just give me a minute to get my head around all this."

Chapter 21

Call Us When You Are Dead

"Is that customer support?" QuickMIC was back in the laboratory in Technological Shenanigans, glad to be alive, but livid. He'd spent a few hours with the others clearing up the mess at Paddy McGinty's Goat before returning to have it out with DumbHK's customer support.

PaddySan was in the kitchen sharpening his katana, and Eógan was sat in his rocking chair, humming an Irish air, overjoyed that PaddySan had returned in one piece.

QuickMIC's patience was being tested to the limits again, and his LED eyes were flashing bright red. He finally had an DumbHK rep on the line. This time it had taken him nearly an hour to get through to DumbHK's 24/7 IPC (Instant Priority Customer) Support Service, and he was seriously beginning to wonder if they actually knew what the word instant meant, let alone service.

"Hello," said the support rep, serenely, "DumbHK's 24/7 IPC ... How may we be of assistance to you?"

"It might help if you answered the phones instantly as in ... Instant Priority Service," argued QuickMIC, who had the phone on loudspeaker. "It took me over an hour to get through again today."

"Can you hear me now?" asked the service rep, her voice a bouquet of dulcet tones.

"Yes, of course!" huffed QuickMIC.

"Well is that not instant enough?" she asked, her butteresque voice melting down the line.

QuickMIC made a rather rude remark at this point, and asked her if she knew what the word instant actually meant. The service rep made it quite clear that she understood the meaning of the word instant, and made it even clearer that if he spoke to her again with that kind of attitude, she would disconnect him in less than an instant.

"Sorry," squirmed QuickMIC, much to Eógan's glee, before outlining to the service rep some of the earlier events from Paddy McGinty's, including the fact that the iShillelaghs which had gone AWOL had nearly killed everyone in the bar.

"It is impossible," she replied calmly. "The iShillelaghs are programmed to obey Asmiov's laws of robotics and cannot kill humans."

"I said he *nearly* killed us," grumbled QuickMIC.

"Did anyone actually get killed?" asked the service rep, again with the dulcet tones.

"No," hesitated QuickMIC, "but an iShillelagh teddy bear lost its head."

"You'd hardly call that a violation of any of the three laws of robotics," stated the rep, "would you?"

"No," admitted QuickMIC, regretfully. "But it was an awfully cute iShillelagh. And then there's the Cantankerous Cabbage, sure he's awfully cantankerous now, having been shot three times."

"I'm sure," she replied, "that if you take the lead out of the cabbage, you'll still be able to boil it with a piece of bacon."

"What's that?"

"Thinking about it," she said, "with the little added saltpetre, that's potassium nitrate from the gunpowder, it might even improve the flavour."

"It's not that kind of cabbage," snapped QuickMIC. "I said it's a Cantankerous Cabbage."

"Cantankerous?" repeated the rep. "A bit like yourself, then. By the way, who's that in the background, is it Terry Wogan?"

"No," shouted QuickMIC, "that's not Terry Wogan in the background. And you might be a bit cantankerous yourself, if you'd spent half the day dodging bullets."

"Who does she think I am?" asked Eógan.

"Listen," said QuickMIC to the rep, ignoring Eógan, "I don't care if he has a sexy, sultry voice."

"You might not," drooled the rep, "but I think I'll book the next flight over to meet him."

"Look here," asserted QuickMIC, dousing her romantic flames of passion, "the whole town was nearly kilt stone dead today!"

"Did anyone actually get killed?" asked the rep for the umpteenth time.

"No"

"Then," replied the service rep apathetically, "DumbHK really do not understand the nature of your complaint."

Eógan was in stitches as QuickMIC tried his hardest to remonstrate with and simultaneously placate the DumbHK service rep. As well as complain, he needed to keep her on side, if he had any chance at all of securing a refund.

The sound of PaddySan sharpening his katana in the kitchen, and the odd flash of sparks flying down the hallway past the laboratory's open door, didn't help matters much, and QuickMIC's nerves were being slowly frazzled by his AI circuits.

"Fair enough," QuickMIC, relented, "the teddy bear iShillelagh and Cantankerous Cabbage may not be classed as living beings, as in human beings. But, surely, that is not the point."

"What is the point, then?" the service rep asked.

"The point is ..." began QuickMIC, before the rep interrupted him tersely.

"I mean, did anyone actually get killed?"

"Not yet," muttered QuickMIC. "But I'm starting to lose the will to live, does that count?"

"I lost the will to live a decade ago and I'm still here," said the rep monotonously. "So no, that doesn't count."

"Then no," said QuickMIC. "No one got killed."

"Therefore, without wishing to repeat myself," maintained the service rep assertively, "DumbHK really does not know what all the fuss is about."

"Fuss … fuss!" At this point QuickMIC nearly blew a few fuses, never mind *fusses*. "Fuss? Be the lovin' … Sure I nearly lost an arm meself, and a leg … and I've laser scorch marks the size of tyre tracks across my backside. Is that fuss enough for you?"

"Are *you* dead?" asked the service rep, in a tone which suggested she might be.

"Obviously not!"

"Then call us back when you are," said the customer service rep, curtly.

"Are what?" asked QuickMIC.

"Call us back when you are DEAD!" And with that she instantly disconnected the call.

"Hello … hello!" QuickMIC screamed.

"I don't believe it, she's cut me off."

"You were a bit cantankerous with her, weren't you," Eógan teased.

"Cantankerous," huffed QuickMIC, slamming the receiver down. "Cantankerous?"

QuickMIC looked up at the ceiling, asking no one in particular. "Now what are we going to do?"

"I'd forget about the refunds," answered Eógan.

"Not about that."

"Do about what then?"

"Them for starters," said QuickMIC, pointing at the six Irish Wolf Hounds who were on their seventh bowl of Irish rabbit stew.

After the fight in Paddy McGinty's, the iShillelagh Irish Wolf Hounds drank the bar dry. And it was unanimously decided by Ye Olde Ross Ice Shelf Committee that QuickMIC should take care of them, because PaddySan was the only one who could control them.

"In the days of Tuatha Dé Dannan, said Eógan, "the witches would have changed the Wolf Hounds' demons."

"Oh," said QuickMIC, after a few moments, "you mean reprogram them."

"I'll take your word for the modern parlance."

"Sure reprogramming them is a great idea, and all," said QuickMIC, "but I don't think I'd be able to get close enough. As you can see, these lads are a fiery oul' shower."

"I see they also like an oul' sup," said Eógan. The Wolf Hounds were busy washing down their stew with pints of black stuff.

"If you call drinking Paddy McGinty's dry," said QuickMIC, "I'd say they like a sup alright."

"Grand so," said Eógan, handing QuickMIC a small bottle of clear liquid, "give them a sup of this, and they'll be asleep in no time."

"What is it?"

"Poitín from the still of Méadhbh herself."

"Who?"

"Méadhbh," repeated Eógan, "the Goddess of intoxication. Her skills were in high demand amongst the Tuatha Dé Dannan."

QuickMIC took the bottle and poured a few sips into six short glasses. True to their name, the Wolf Hounds wolfed them down, and proceeded to finish the bottle, but not before Eógan also had a few oul' sips himself.

Two hours, and ten empty bottles later, Eógan and the Wolf Hounds were performing a never ending rendition of the Wild Rover, with Eógan strumming away on the banjo. The song was bad enough, but they had the table nearly smashed to bits, repeatedly hammering it four times during the chorus.

It occurred to QuickMIC that Méadhbh's magic potion was having the opposite effect, and the boisterous crowd was getting more lively, rambunctious and louder by the minute.

He was on the verge of phoning the Garda Síochána and having the whole drunken shower, including Eógan, arrested and locked up for the night where they could sleep it off, if only to save his table, when he heard some familiar music approaching.

"Howya," said a ten centimetre high dishevelled, violin player, entering the laboratory and playing the first few bars of an Irish classic.

"Watch now, QuickMIC," said Paddynini, when the uilleann pipes joined him, "they say that music soothes the animal soul, wha'."

As the music started, PaddySan came into the laboratory, his katana held tenderly to his shoulder like a dancing partner, singing I'll Take You Home Again Kathleen, quickly followed by the rest of The Cracker Craics.

Eógan and the Wolf Hounds were mesmerized into silence, as round and round PaddySan waltzed, and by the end of the first verse, the uilleann pipes started to sniffle, straining to hold back the tears.

"He's like yer one," said the uilleann pipe player, handing the uilleann pipes a hanky to blow his nose, "PaddySan. He misses the mother something rotten."

"He's set her off now," said Paddynini, when he saw the fiddle welling up.

By the time they got to the end of the second verse and a darkening shadow was looming over Kathleen's brow, the pipes were in bits, with the fiddle and the accordion not far behind them. A beat later, the fiddle was shedding tears, but Paddynini was a virtuoso, and even though the finger board was slippery wet, what with a torrent of fiddle tears streaming down it, he never missed a note.

PaddySan himself struggled to hold the last note, before he also collapsed into a slobbering wreck.

As QuickMIC mopped tears off the laboratory floor, he wiped a tear or two from his own telescopic eyes. The Cracker Craics were long gone, the pipes and fiddle howling as they were carried away, and PaddySan, Eógan and the Wolf Hounds had cried themselves to sleep.

"The curse of the Irish lament," whispered QuickMIC, wiping another tear from his sad grey eyes.

But at least now he'd have a chance to try and reprogram the six matted, iShillelaghs known as Irish Wolf hounds, if he could only hold back his own tears and see what he was doing.

Chapter 22

That Damned Irish Craic

William McCoy The Third, a white towel wrapped around his waist, was sat upright on his massage table in a state of shock, staring blankly across the Manhattan skyline outside his boardroom window. As hard as he tried, he still couldn't get his head around the news Ryan O'Reilly had just given him.

He'd specifically purchased DumbHK, one of the largest buyouts in the San Jose region since the last tech bubble burst, for their expertise in robotics, military hardware innovation, counter surveillance and other sinister capabilities too numerous and too secret to mention. DumbHK's products were supposed to be invincible, and he was struggling to come to terms with the fact that a crack team of DumbHK iShillelaghs had been defeated on their very first mission.

"All dead, you say?" said William in a state of utter dismay.

"Yes sir," confirmed Ryan. "All except six Irish Wolf Hounds and the Hells Angel."

"But how?"

"A large proportion of the ninjas and commandos went up in flames, thrown on an open fire by children. The others became victims of a crazed samurai iShillelagh by the name of PaddySan."

"All dead? ..." William's voice was bereft, "killed by children you say, and a crazed samurai?"

"All except a few Wolf Hounds and the Hells Angel," repeated Ryan. "The Wolf Hounds drank the bar dry and then took off with QuickMIC. The Angel's in a bad way, sir. I found him slumped outside, a few hours later."

"Bad way?"

"Don't worry, sir, he'll live to see another day," said Ryan. "I can parcel him up and post him home if you'd like."

"No, no ... he's very dangerous and extremely volatile by the sounds of it." said William. "Must be some kind of software problem," he assumed. "A technical glitch in his AI, perhaps?"

"Well," giggled Ryan, picking up the Hells Angel's right arm, "he might have been dangerous once upon a time, but he's 'armless now."

"Anyway," said William, making a note of Ryan's insolence, "I'm not sure he'd get through customs and GRABiT could do without any adverse publicity at this point."

The iShillelaghs had cost William nearly ten million dollars to develop and almost a year in time. The cost and time really didn't bother him. What concerned him most was the fact that DumbHK had told him that these particular iShillelaghs were virtually impossible to destroy. They also had AI which put them on a par with the best that NASA or even the NSA had to offer, so they should have been able to read the signs and avoid such a catastrophe. And yet they had been outwitted by a couple of children and PaddySan, a crazed samurai.

Never mind their sophisticated cuisine over there at An Cabáiste agus Bagún Deli, perhaps Ryan was right, perhaps William had underestimated the residents of Eirestown.

And PaddySan ... how could he have betrayed GRABiT like that? William had asked DumbHK to develop a few iShillelaghs which could perform martial arts. He was fond of Akira Kurosawa samurai films, and when William entered his late teens, he became a huge fan of Bruce Lee. In response to William's request, DumbHK produced PaddySan, who was supposed to be a loyal assassin and personal bodyguard, with specially designed AI which was brainwash proof. However, it appears that either PaddySan had been brainwashed, or some kind of malfunction had developed.

"You get it sir?" Ryan repeated, as if William hadn't got it first time, "'Armless ... you know ... Harmless without the *H*."

"Armless?" bellowed William, nearly popping Ryan's eardrum. "Armless? I got it first time Ryan. But this is no time for that damned Irish craic of yours."

"No sir," Ryan agreed, "it certainly isn't."

"How would you feel about a little *harmless* without the 'less'?" threatened William.

The craic, thought Ryan: that damned Irish craic! I'm infected with it, to hell with my Irish heritage. I'd rather become a miserable recluse of a hermit, and never laugh again, than run the risk of letting the craic get the better of me. Why the craic seems to have a life of its own. It can creep up and out of you at any moment. 'Armless? What a ridiculous thing to have said. What an eejit I am.

"Please forgive me, sir," grovelled Ryan, when he finally worked out that *harmless* without the 'less' was *harm*, something he could really do without, be it a little amount or not. "It must be the shock of the bar room fight. I'm not feeling myself this afternoon."

"Tut-tut-tut ... this puts a whole new spin on things," said William when he'd finally composed himself.

"Me not feeling myself?" asked Ryan.

"No you bumbling buffoon," hissed William, "the loss of so much military personnel."

"Oh," said Ryan.

"They were only meant to scare off the residents of Eirestown," said William. "There was to be no violence."

Ryan felt it necessary to defend the residents, "They drew first blood sir."

"What?"

"They shot an iShillelagh teddy bear, real cute fella as well."

"Never mind that," said William. "I was hoping that you'd bring them all with you to McMurdo, as a little rear guard action."

"Rear guard action?" gulped Ryan.

"Yes," said William. "Despite the fact that it's minus something or the other over there most days, things may get a little bit heated. You understand?"

"Sir ..." said Ryan sheepishly.

"Yes, Ryan?"

"You're not expecting violence, are you, I'm not the violent type and I'm not sure my nerves will be able to cope."

"Not to worry Ryan," said William.

"Really?" Ryan was delighted and let down his own rear guard. "That's a relief, sir, I can tell you. I'm really starting to like these guys over here in Eirestown. They really looked after me during that assault in Paddy McGinty's Goat. And they've already asked me to go to Antarctica, but I'd rather not, I don't do cold."

"You poor thing," said William after a few moments reflection. "Why didn't you say? It must have been traumatic for you, huddled under the table like that in a cosy Irish bar with Armageddon flaring all around you."

"Sir," said Ryan confidently, "I just thought you'd think I was making it all up, a coward or something."

"Not at all, Ryan my boy," said William, with a genuine air of concern. "Why I'll have to phone President and get you the Congressional Medal, the Purple Heart at the very least."

"That won't be necessary sir."

"Thinking about it," William said, ignoring Ryan, "you're probably suffering from Post Traumatic Stress disorder, combat fatigue, or something like that."

"Very kind of you to be so understanding, sir," said Ryan, amazed by this sudden display of compassion.

"Actually ...Ryan..."

"Yes sir?"

"We'll relieve you of duty immediately."

"Fantastic," cried Ryan, struggling to subdue his joy. "I mean ... I'll be sad to go, of course, sir."

"And GRABiT will be even sadder to see you go. Just hold on the line a moment, and I'll get Mrs Baxter to make a call to waste disposal, to arrange your leaving party."

Mrs Baxter? Ryan experienced a sudden rush of adrenaline on hearing the name of William's PA and the ominous phrase *waste disposal*. He was starting to feel perked up already. "Wait a moment sir, did you say Mrs Baxter?"

"Yes, Ryan" said William, "Mrs Baxter. Here at GRABiT we believe in rewarding loyalty, perseverance, grit and determination. And, up until today, you've been a paragon of all those virtues, and more."

"But *waste disposal*, sir? Did I hear you correctly"

"Oh, dear, oh dear," William apologised. "This is a bad line today. I said *haste proposal*. Of course you want to be on your way quickly, no?"

"Haste proposal?"

"Yes," said William, "haste proposal. It sounds like you are hearing what you want to hear. Now what do psychologists call that? Some kind of shock syndrome brought on by operations in the theatre of war, no doubt."

Or paranoia thought Ryan, wishing he'd taped the call so he could play it back and check.

"Now that you mention it sir," Ryan reflected, "and now that you've expressed such confidence in me, perhaps I'll be able to handle the pressure over there in the Antarctica, after all."

"That's my boy Ryan," said William, "that's my boy. But don't you worry, you'll not have to deal with all that pressure on your own."

"Sir?"

"Of course I'm not going to leave such an important mission to an incompetent buffoon like you."

"I'll have help then?" said the buffoon.

"Yes," said William. "You just stay with the committee, keep an eye on their movements, and I'll deal with them when I meet you out there."

"Are you not worried, sir?" said Ryan. "I mean," he mumbled nervously, "they've just trashed your iShillelagh army."

"Ha," scoffed William, "call that an army? I've an army of 5000 out there in Antarctica! Nothing can go wrong."

"Ok, sir," said Ryan, "if you insist."

"You just get yourself out there, my boy," said William confidently, "and stay close to those trouble causers from Eirestown. I'll be with you just as soon as I can. I've got every faith in you Ryan."

"Sir, yes, sir!" shouted Ryan, a fresh recruit in William's five thousand strong army.

"That's my boy!"

William made a few more perfunctory statements, said goodbye to Ryan, switched the conference phone off and called Mrs Baxter into his office.

"Mrs Baxter," he began, tugging his towel tight around his waist and reaching into his drinks cabinet, "call Waste Disposal in Dublin and tell them I'll no longer be requiring their services."

"That's nice to hear sir," she replied, "Ryan is such a considerate young man."

"You think?"

"I do sir," she said, "why I still have that pyramid paperweight he brought back from Egypt for me."

"You do?"

"Yes," she said. "He told me it was the great Pyramid of Khafre and that it had cost him three million dollars. He's a bit of a joker as well, isn't he sir?"

"You could say that," said William. "However, I'm sad to say that I think we are still going to have to say goodbye to Ryan."

"We will?"

"We will," said William. "So cancel one of those return seats from Antarctica."

"Oh dear, sir," Mrs Baxter said, "you won't be requiring the services of Waste Disposal in Antarctica I hope?"

"Not at all Mrs Baxter," said William. "It appears that Ryan O'Reilly has fallen in love with an Eskimo. A pretty little thing met on an internet dating room."

"How sweet," cooed Mrs Baxter.

"Very sweet indeed," agreed William. "Why she even has a Michelin star for her culinary skills with blubber." He poured himself a Manhattan and took a glug, "She's the one alright, Mrs Baxter, she's the one."

"You can't build a good loving home without a hearty kitchen," said Mrs Baxter.

"You're right Mrs Baxter," chuckled William, "and with blubber on the menu they'll have a whale of a time."

"Oh sir," teased Mrs Baxter, "you've such a wicked sense of humour."

"GRABiT's loss is Antarctica's gain," said William. "Ryan plans to settle down and build himself an igloo."

"Aww," purred Mrs Baxter, "how quaint. I'll alter the travel arrangements immediately, sir."

Chapter 23

Great Grammatical Versatility

"Howya Fíniún," Paht and Fin had just stepped into Eirestown's one and only travel agent, called You'd Be Mad To Go Anywhere Else.

"*Céad míle fáilte* Paht agus Fin," Fíniún said, welcoming them into the shop.

"Now you know we don't speak the Irish," said Paht.

"It means *a hundred thousand welcomes*," translated Fíniún.

"We know what it means," said Paht, "but we still don't speak Gaelic."

"Force of habit," apologised Fíniún, shrugging his shoulders, "the tourists love that one."

"Not a bother," said Paht. "How's she cutting?"

"How's she cutting?" Fíniún snapped, "How's she cutting?" repeating it again as if his pointed ears hadn't heard it the first time. "She's cutting like a rubber knife!"

"Is business that bad?" asked Paht.

"Business is trollix, absolute trollix!"

"That sounds bad, alright," said Paht, rubbing his chin.

"Let's just say," Fíniún moaned, "that I welcome them in hundreds of thousands, they t'ank me in millions and say goodbye with fehk alls."

"Not to worry," announced Paht, "she'll be cutting like a razor blade after today."

"Why?"

"The lads want to go to the Antarctic."

"Do they indeed?"

Although they were a little shaken by yesterday's events in Paddy McGinty's, The Ye Olde Ross Ice Shelf Committee had decided that no matter the risks, they would complete their mission on the South Pole. The World, and in particular all the major cities built in ports and coastal regions, depended on it.

So early the next day, as agreed, they split into two teams, one to make travel arrangements and the other to get the necessary supplies together.

However, as early as they started, it had taken the Travel Arrangement Sub-team, Paht and Fin, almost an hour to get to the travel agents, even though it was only a stone's throw from Paddy McGinty's Goat.

The problem was An Cabáiste agus Bagún Deli, The Cabbage And Bacon Deli. Paht couldn't resist running over to see the menu, where he would have loitered all day given the choice. An Cabáiste agus Bagún Deli was one of Paht's favourite haunts when he wasn't eating at Paddy McGinty's, that is.

Today's menu, which covered every centimetre of the glass front, reflected the usual range of internationally renowned fusion food - modern interpretations on Irish classics.

He pointed to the French section of the menu first, "Here Fin, do you remember the time I ordered *Les cuisses de grenouille et Escargots*."

"I do," moaned Fin, like a boy who'd heard the story a thousand times.

"Paddy Roux said I'd have to catch them first, that's gas isn't it, Fin? I'd have to catch the snails first."

"Yes," Fin lied, "that's gas."

Paht pointed at the menu again, nudged Fin and gasped. "Would you look at today's specials, all the way from Mexico, sure the Irish are everywhere, aren't they, Fin?"

A cornucopia of delicacies had Paht frothing at the mouth as his eyes flew up and down the menu, stopping every now and then to savour the latest Mexican range:

Cabbage and Bacon tortilla wraps; Cabbage and Bacon tacos; Cabbage and Bacon quesadillas; Cabbage and Bacon fajitas; Cabbage and Bacon Burrito; Cabbage and Bacon guacamole; Cabbage and Bacon enchiladas; Baja black beans with Bacon and Cabbage rice; Refried Bacon and Cabbage; Chipotle Bacon and Cabbage, Bacon and Cabbage salsa; Chilli Verde con Bacon and Cabbage; Frijoles negroes with Cabbage and Bacon; South-western stuffed bell peppers (stuffed with Bacon and Cabbage)

"Just look at this menu," he whispered again, "Paddy Roux's a genius. Either that or he's an Irish Mexican himself."

Fin was worried he might have to phone the fire brigade to free Paht's tongue from the window, as he tugged him by the back of his braces. But after an almighty heave, there was an explosive PLOP and TWANG, which could be heard on O'Connell Street, and he managed to drag Paht away.

"The tickets granddad," said Fin, "remember?"

Running a little late, they finally made it to the travel agents, where they were trying to book tickets to the Antarctica. But the proprietor of You'd Be Mad To Go Anywhere Else had other ideas. A bitter, twisted excuse of a yoke, who also happened to be a genuine leprechaun, the proprietor went by the name of Fíniún, but the locals preferred to call him TongueSlinger, because he was an awful slandering gossip, with an unholy tongue in his head.

"But before ye book those tickets," said TongueSlinger.

"What?" said Paht.

"Did you hear about yer one?" whispered TongueSlinger, leaning over the counter.

"I did," replied Paht.

"And yer other one," TongueSlinger went on, raising his right eyebrow, "did you hear about him?"

"I did."

"And did you hear about himself?" TongueSlinger winked.

"I did."

"And herself, did you hear about her?"

"I did."

"And herself's self?"

"I did."

"And what about himself, over beyond," said TongueSlinger, folding his arms, "the dirty rotten animal. Did you hear about him?"

"I did."

"Then you know more than me, so," said TongueSlinger. "Sure you must have a few things you could tell me?"

"Come on now," said Paht, "less of this gossiping, we've tickets to book."

"And come on now, you," said TongueSlinger, wagging a finger at Paht, "and cop yourself on." He pointed to a poster on the wall. "Look, sure there's fehk all in the Antarctica except penguins, ice and snow. And even the penguins are booking themselves into more inviting climes in Disney's Animal Kingdom faster that you can say Mickey Mouse."

"Sure never mind all that, now," said Paht. "We're not going there as tourists."

"Sure what are ye doing there then?"

"We're going to save the Ross Ice Shelf!"

"Sure you couldn't save a fehkin' ice cube."

"Mind that language," cautioned Paht, grabbing a handful of TongueSlinger's red beard and lifting him off the ground, "before I drag you over this counter and rip that wicked divil of a tongue out of your mouth!" He tugged on TongueSlinger's beard a few times and nodded in Fin's direction, "Fin has delicate ears, understand?"

"I said 'fehk'," explained TongueSlinger in his defence, stressing the *h* and enunciating the letters out one by one, as he dangled two feet above the ground, " F ... E ... *H* ..." He repeated the 'H' several times for emphasis and Paht released him after the third intonation. TongueSlinger fell to the ground with a thud, "... K!" Rubbing his hairy, swollen chin he cried, "Jesus you've nearly the face ripped off a-me man. Sure don't you know your own culture?"

Paht shrugged, and rubbed his thumb up and down one of his braces, "Please enlighten me."

"FEHK ..." began TongueSlinger. "It's a secret ancient Gaelic word of great grammatical versatility, left to us by the Seanchaí of old. Its true meaning was known only to the High Kings Of Tara."

"Carry on, so," said Paht.

"For example, it can be used as verb," explained TongueSlinger, "either transitive or intransitive now, mind."

"Go on so," said Paht.

"'*Fossil fuel fehked The Ross ice Shelf*', is a fine example of the transitive," said TongueSlinger, "and "'*Paht fehked off to The Ross ice Shelf for some penguin stew*', is a fine example of the intransitive."

"Fascinating," said Paht, "would you say penguin stew is tasty?"

"I fehkin' would," said TongueSlinger, staying with the intransitive.

"I must tell Paddy Roux," said Paht, "I can't wait to see penguin stew on the menu over there in An Cabáiste agus Bagún Deli."

"Fehk can even be used as an adjective," TongueSlinger revealed, getting back to his grammatical lesson.

"Really?" said Paht, "'tis a great little word."

"'Tis a fehking miracle," exclaimed TongueSlinger.

"What is?" asked Paht.

"That?"

"What?"

"That's a classic example of fehk's use as an adjective."

"Oh fehk!" said Paht, keen to demonstrate the intransitive form again. "And to think they say the Irish are forever swearing, if only they knew."

"That's not all," said TongueSlinger, "sure there's a whole book could be written about the many uses of fehk."

"Go on, so," said Paht.

"For example," said TongueSlinger, "you can use it to express ignorance."

"How?" asked Paht.

"Fehked if I know!" answered TongueSlinger.

"But you just said," began Paht "that you could use it to express ignorance."

"I just did," giggled TongueSlinger.

"Fehk," said Paht, using the word's versatility to express *surprise*, "sure I get it now."

"You're in the fehkin saddle now, me boyo!" TongueSlinger cried, praising Paht's newly discovered grammatical versatility.

"You're right," said Paht, "I fehkin' am in the saddle. I'm riding a grammatical horse, and I must admit that this is fehkin' liberating."

"How about hostility?" TongueSlinger asked.

"What do you mean?" said Paht.

"I'm going to knock your fehking head off!" shouted TongueSlinger, waving a fist at Paht, who grabbed him by the beard again, hoisted him off the ground, and pinched and yanked on his tongue.

"How about its use as a *request*?" said Fin, tapping Paht on the shoulder.

"Ohhh K," stuttered TongueSlinger, his tongue firmly wedged between Paht's right thumb and index finger, "gLow oHHHn."

"Let's get these tickets booked and get the fehk out of here," requested Fin.

Paht released TongueSlinger and wiped his thumb and finger on TongueSlinger's green waistcoat.

"Sure t'anks a million for the cultural lesson and all that," said Paht. "But Fin's right, just sort out the booking to the Antarctica and we'll be on our way."

"I hope so, ye miserable fehkers," squealed TongueSlinger. "Sure you've the tongue nearly ripped out of me head!"

Chapter 24

Jian Dao Ni Wo Hen Gao Xing

Over in Technological Shenanigans, QuickMIC was just packing the last of the supplies for the Ye Olde Ross Ice Shelf Committee Supply Sub-team, Banbha, Donn-Dubh and Ryan. He'd also given Donn-Dubh a new bulbous hat, and Donn-Dubh was busy relocating the contents of his old hat, including Snippy, who nearly lost a pincer when the shuriken stars sliced off the top of the old hat.

A few other customers, including Mr Muscles, were also browsing around the shop, rummaging through its many shelves.

Mr Muscles had not long finished playing with a set of dancing and singing shamrocks, known as the Sham-melodies. QuickMIC had them invented a few years now. This particular set was dressed in black leather, wore dark shades and had just finished belting out U2's, All I Want Is You. And now Mr Muscles was having fun with a new range of technological shenanigans known as Oul' Sods. QuickMIC had only just invented these. They were a range of shenanigans, ten to fifteen centimetres high, that took the form of freshly cut sods of turf. They had eyes, ears, arms and legs. The range, not yet complete, currently included The Happy Oul' Sod who never stopped laughing, The Miserable Oul' Sod, who ran around asking to be thrown on the fire as soon as possible because his life was so miserable, and The Crafty Oul' Sod, which had Mr Muscles somewhat intrigued at the moment.

"Repeat that crafty oul' puzzle again," said Mr Muscles.

The Crafty Oul' Sod repeated the puzzle: "If it takes two Irish men thirty minutes to dig a hole, how long will it take one Irish man to dig the same hole?"

"Give us a clue, so," said Mr Muscles, having given the matter another few minutes thought.

"Ahh now, but you have the young fella criss-crossed," complained the Miserable Oul' Sod. "Go on, give him an oul' clue, before I throw myself into the flames."

"He has me criss-crossed alright," agreed Mr Muscles, "that's a tough puzzle. Sure I'm only just starting algebra at school."

"Have you any relatives up in Dublin?" The Crafty Oul' Sod asked Mr Muscles.

"Is that another puzzle?" asked Mr Muscles, scratching his chin. He couldn't see what having relatives in Dublin had to do with digging a hole.

"Not at all," replied The Crafty Oul' Sod, "it's just that you remind me of someone I once met up there."

"I may have a distant cousin in Finglas," he hesitated, "or was it Glasnevin. Would that do?"

"Actually," said the The Crafty Oul' Sod, "I was thinking of Phoenix Park, home of the zoo."

"No relatives there that I know of," said Mr Muscles, pursing this lips in contemplation.

"Are you sure, now?"

"I am."

"Because there's a monkey in Dublin Zoo, and I'd swear he was your cousin."

The Happy Oul' Sod nearly fell off the shelf with laughter when he heard that one.

"I've no relatives in Dublin," Mr Muscles insisted, blushing as The Happy Oul' Sod doubled up again with laughter. Even The Miserable Oul' Sod started to perk up a bit.

"You're right of course," exclaimed The Crafty Oul' Sod, "sure you can't be related to that monkey."

"Why?" asked Mr Muscles.

"He has more brains than you," said The Crafty Oul' Sod.

"Get away will yeh," said The Happy Oul' Sod.

"I'm not codding," said The Crafty Oul' Sod, "the monkey would have solved this crafty puzzle five minutes ago."

"Forget the relatives then," said The Happy Oul' Sod, laughing hysterically at Mr Muscles, "sure I'd say there's a cage in Dublin Zoo with his name on it."

"Five minutes!" Mr Muscles blurted, ignoring The Happy Oul' Sod and assuming that he'd just been given a clue. "It takes one Irish man five minutes to dig the hole."

"Are you codding me?"

"It's five minutes, I'm sure."

"You've Muscles enough young fella," said The Crafty Oul' Sod, tapping the side of his own head. "It's only a shame you never developed that muscle between your ears."

"It's not five minutes, then?"

"Are you sure you're not related to that monkey?"

"An hour and thirty minutes, so," blurted Mr Muscles in desperation.

"He's a head the size of a cabbage," The Crafty Oul' Sod informed The Happy Oul' Sod, who was in stitches now, "but a brain the size of a pea."

"An hour," said Mr Muscles, "it takes one hour. Two men dig twice as fast as one man, so one man will take twice as long."

"So you can dig the *same* hole twice can you?" asked The Crafty Oul' Sod, slyly.

"Maybe the first two Paddys filled the hole back in," cried The Happy Oul' Sod, before he fell off the shelf, laughing uncontrollably.

"Oh," said Mr Muscles, when the penny dropped into the hole he'd been thinking about, "I see what you mean ... how long to dig the *same* hole. Sure you're a crafty little sod alright, that's for sure."

Over at the counter QuickMIC was busy taping up the last box of supplies.

"Do you never get any women in this joint?" asked Banbha, as QuickMIC wrapped the masking tape around the last box.

"Duck!" screamed QuickMIC.

Banbha ducked and a flying technological Shamrock, five centimetres long, and known as a Shamdiver, just missed her head, before landing on the counter, where it stood on its split stalk, flapped its two side leaves like wings, all the while whistling a chirpy Irish jig.

"They're very dangerous," said Banbha, picking the flying shamrock up, and placing it in her palm where it chirped away as she stroked it, "but awfully cute."

"Not at all," said QuickMIC, they're as safe as you like."

"Then why have some of them got crash helmets on?"

"Admittedly, they have a few teething problems," said QuickMIC as a Shamdiver crashed into the counter in front of him head first.

After a few moments the Shamdiver got up, rubbed its head and tried to whistle through broken teeth before it collapsed into a heap.

"See what I mean about the teething problems?" said QuickMIC, smiling.

"I'm surprised they have any teeth at all," said Banbha.

"Oh this cheeky little chap will be alright," said QuickMIC, picking the concussed Shamdiver up and slipping him under counter. "I'll fix him up in the lab later, and give him a new set."

"He came out of the blue that little fella," said Banbha, "are you sure they're safe?"

"They're a new range of Shamdivers," explained QuickMIC. "Fast as bullets when they dive from on high. But you'll soon get used to them. Sure they're better than a work out."

"Why?"

"They keep you on your toes these lads, what with all the ducking and diving. You have to be like yer one. You know, the legendary boxer, what's his name?"

"Mohammed Ali?" said Banbha.

"That's yer man," said QuickMIC, weaving and bobbing up and down, "you have to float like a butterfly, sting like a bee." He threw a few punches at an invisible opponent. "But I'm not sure a human could keep up, though."

"Why not?"

"You have to be alert, fast, or microprocessor controlled like meself, able to respond in a nano-sec. Quick as a flash," he winked at her, ducking and diving rapidly. "That's quick ... as in Quick ... MIC."

"Are you sure they're not dangerous?" Banbha asked again, looking around the store where she could see rakes of Shamdivers, perched all over the place, and numerous others flying around.

"'Deed I am," said QuickMIC. "Just keep your wits about you, you'll be alright."

"Duck ..." Banbha screamed, but it was too late. A Shamdiver hit QuickMIC in the back of his tapered head, knocking him off his toes, and clean off the runner behind the counter.

Slowly QuickMIC climbed back up onto the runner, where he found the Shamdiver perched, nonchalantly whistling Danny Boy.

"Perhaps it's yourself who needs the crash helmet?" said Banbha, ducking out of the way of another Shamdiver.

You were saying," said QuickMIC, ignoring her jibes and rubbing his head, "about women?"

"Have you no women in this joint?" Banbha asked again, smirking. "Or are you worried they'll also keep you on your toes?"

"'Deed we have women enough," said QuickMIC, hoisting another small box up onto the counter, with the large red words PRODUCE OF DumbHK printed on the side. "Hold on there a nano-sec."

He reached into the box and pulled out the head and shaft of this latest iShillelagh. "Here look-it, just in this morning, the latest in feminine role models for the more refined young ladies of Eirestown."

"Wow," said Banbha, when she saw the iShillelagh's caramel skin, "her complexion looks almost human. And look at her elegantly shaped head."

"That would be the bio-silicon polymers, one of the latest innovations in iShillelagh technology" said QuickMIC. "They give her skin that authentic look and feel. Oh and look-it," he reached in for an instruction leaflet in the box, "she has an added iFGM module. "Let me see, now," he continued reading the leaflet, "that stands for Interactive Female Gyration Module, in her Motor units. Not sure what one of them is, but it sounds interesting to a nerd like meself."

QuickMIC ran his fingers through the iShillelagh's huge head of side swept blond hair, which cascaded in luxurious curls over her right shoulder. "Sure she's a fine head of hair, alright."

"She has," agreed Banbha, excitely. "Fire her up so!"

QuickMIC pulled the iShillelagh's body out of the box and almost returned it back immediately. The iShillelagh was wearing a very short, tight fitting skirt, black thigh high boots and he noticed, with some dismay, that she had more curves and bumps than you'd see on the red carpet at an Oscar ceremony.

Ryan, Donn-Dubh and even a few Shamdivers wolf whistled when they saw the body, much to QuickMIC's disdain.

Reluctantly QuickMIC, with some provocation from Banbha, screwed the iShillelagh's head and shaft into the body and placed her on the counter, if only to prove to Banbha that his was a progressive equal opportunities shop. However, he went on, he wasn't sure this iShillelagh was the kind of role model he had in mind for the young ladies. Sure he was having second thoughts about switching her on at all.

But Banbha was persistent, urging him on.

QuickMIC threw the switch on the iShillelagh's back, and she flicked her head to one side. Then she flicked her head to the other side and her blond fringe lifted slightly to reveal deep auburn eyes, with shimmering highlights. Winking provocatively at Ryan and Donn-Dubh, she puckered her glossy skin coloured lips, pointed at Banbha and a few other young girls, her arm bobbing up and down, and said huskily, "Come on ladies, let's show them who's boss."

With her hand still bobbing, she started slowly gyrating to her inbuilt background music and, as the music grew louder, she did a few provocative thigh thrusts, before dropping down.

Banbha cheered with delight. "Look-it … she's doing a spread eagle."

"Go on girl," said Donn-Dubh, clicking his fingers to the beat, "get jiggy with it."

The iShillelagh's heels locked together, and with knees akimbo, she opened and shut her legs, flashing her underwear a few times.

QuickMIC, although somewhat shocked by this brazen move, was relieved to see she was wearing boyshorts and nothing more revealing like, heaven forbid! a thong.

Almost as fast as the iShillelagh dropped she sprang back up into a double stanky leg and started singing ... "All the ladies in the house, are you ready to rock and shock?" To which all the boys replied louder than the girls, "You bet!"

"Hey, did you see that move," shouted Banbha, "that was a stanky leg."

"She's great isn't she," yelled another young girl over the music, knocking her own knobbly knees together and trying a stanky leg herself.

Another young girl shouted, "I think I'll buy one of them meself. Me ma would love one of them yokes dancing around the kitchen while she was putting the breakfast on."

"Considering that your mother plays the organ every Sunday morning in Kells Gothic Monastery young lady," said QuickMIC dismissively, "I doubt very much that she would welcome a stanky leg around the dinner table anytime soon. Let alone a spread eagle over a cup of tea and a plate full of rashers."

The iShillelagh carried on gyrating and grinding, with her adoring audience, nodding, singing and cheering her on. But when she started twerking provocatively, and her shorts started riding up her thighs, QuickMIC had had enough demonstration of her iFGM. With sweat dripping from his anxious brow, he reached around her back, and switched the iShillelagh off. Much to the dismay of one or two of the young male members who started booing and hissing, confirming QuickMIC's suspicions that this iShillelagh was definitely not a suitable role model for anyone, never mind young ladies.

"Sure they're grand, aren't they?" Mr Muscles said, his face flushed with exuberance. "How much for two?"

"Grand or not," apologised QuickMIC, snatching the iShillelagh off the counter, "they're not for sale. DumbHK have sent me the wrong models."

The booing and hissing grew louder. "I ordered Maria from The Sound Of Music," QuickMIC roared above the onslaught of boos and jeers, "not Jezebel from Phoenicia!"

"Listen up now," said QuickMIC, pushing Jezebel back into her box and under the counter as the boos subsided, "would ye all kindly leave the shop, or I'll phone the guards to have ye ejected," he nodded to Ryan, Donn-Dubh and Banbha, "except ye of course."

After a lot of pushing, shoving and further protests, Mr Muscles and the rest of the shoppers were escorted off the premises, and QuickMIC quickly turned the OPEN sign to CLOSED, locking the door behind them.

"Sure they're like a pack of wild dogs," he said, returning to the counter. "You'd think they'd never seen a woman before."

"They've probably never seen a woman like that," said Ryan. "Are you sure you've not got one for sale?"

"Here's the last of your supplies," said QuickMIC, grimacing at Ryan and ignoring his question.

"What about PaddySan," said Banbha, "we want to bring him?"

QuickMIC still had major concerns over PaddySan's erratic behaviour, and he had found a more suitable replacement, also just in this morning.

"Look Banbha," he pulled up another box, "talking of women, meet Mai-Ly. She's a fine looking iShillelagh, eh?" He put Mai-Ly's shaft and body together and placed her down on top of the counter. She had the new shaped iShillelagh head, a bit like PaddySan's, was about his height, and her black hair was tied up in a bun.

"*Mary*," said Banbha, "sure she looks a bit stuffy this one, more like a nun."

"No," corrected QuickMIC, "Mai-Ly, not Mary the mother of God." He reached round her back and switched Mai-Ly on. "And you're right, she is a nun."

"I've never seen a nun dressed like that," said Donn-Dubh, commenting on her yellow Hia Ching robes.

"Ah," said QuickMIC, "that's because she's a Shaolin nun. You can take her instead of PaddySan."

"Jian dao ni," said Mai-Ly serenely, bowing ever so politely and closing her palms together in front of her chest, as if praying, "wo hen gao xing."

"What did she just say?" asked Banbha.

"*I'm glad to meet you*," said QuickMIC.

"A nun will be no good where we're going," said Donn-Dubh. "We wanted a little fierce fella like PaddySan, you know." He raised his fists, bobbed and weaved like a featherweight, and threw a few shadow punches. "Just in case things get rough out there."

"Yeah," said Banbha, "perhaps Mai-Ly should just stay here and say a few prayers for us while we're gone?"

"Fuzakeru na!"

Nobody had seen PaddySan creep into the shop from the kitchen. And now he was up on the counter facing Mai-Ly screaming *Don't mess with me!* his katana drawn.

Everyone, including QuickMIC, took a step back.

"Oh, oh," gulped Donn-Dubh, "looks like it's Mai-Ly who'll be needing the prayers."

QuickMIC looked on in horror. He didn't know which was worse, the thought of phoning DumbHK to ask for a refund for Mai-Ly, or the fact that Mai-Ly, an extremely polite, innocent, harmless, and compassionate iShillelagh, was about to be sliced into a pile of Shaolin fries.

PaddySan began shuffling slowly, one foot in front of the other, his weight distributed perfectly in a cat-stance, circling Mai-Ly. Mai-Ly, her head still bowed, and her palms locked in prayer in front of her, didn't move a muscle.

After a few moments, PaddySan was facing her again, and without saying a word he raised his sword above his head and brought it down at lightning speed, intent on splitting Mai-Ly in two.

QuickMIC cringed and looked away while Ryan, Banbha and Donn-Dubh covered their eyes.

A moment later a thunderous clap had them all wide eyed again, and focussed on what can only be described as one of the most incredulous sights any of them had ever seen.

No one, especially PaddySan, could believe it. Mai-Ly had caught PaddySan's katana between her palms just above the black bun on her head, and as hard as PaddySan pulled and tugged to release it, it wouldn't budge.

"Ok we'll take her," Ryan, Donn-Dubh and Banbha exclaimed in unison.

"Hui tou jian!" Mai-Ly whispered passionately, looking PaddySan directly into his eyes. "Wakarimasu ka?"

"Hui tou jian," QuickMIC's UTU interpreted for everyone, "that's Mandarin Chinese for *See you later*. And *Wakarimasu ka*," he carried on translating, "that's Japanese for *do you understand?*'"

"Hai ... wakarimasu ..." relented PaddySan, releasing his katana and traipsing back towards the kitchen, his head bowed in disgrace.

"Yes said PaddySan," translated QuickMIC, "I understand."

Mai-Li threw the katana up into the air and let it land on her knee, where it balanced precariously for a few moments.

Despite the fact that it was made of the finest ancient Japanese *tamahagane*, steel folded in upon itself repeatedly to produce a million individual layers, the last thing PaddySan heard as he entered the laboratory was a characteristic ping. Mai-Ly had snapped his katana in two like a matchstick.

Himself a soul-less warrior now, PaddySan stumbled into the laboratory, in the hope that Eógan would console him with a song, or an oul' sup of poitín at the very least.

Chapter 25

You're The First Customers I've ever had

"Trollix! But you're one grammatically, illiterate, fehkin', fat, baldy fehker, so you are."

Back in You'd Be Mad To Go Anywhere Else, TongueSlinger was still grunting and groaning, and complaining that he'd nearly had the tongue ripped out of his head.

"Now would that be a transitive or intransitive fehkin', fat, baldy fehker?" inquired Paht

TongueSlinger ignored Paht and fiddled with his tongue a few more times, checking to see if it was still attached, and in one piece.

"Come on now," said Fin, "or we'll finish the job off, just give us the tickets to Antarctica and we'll be on our way."

"Ah, come on now, lads" implored TongueSlinger. "Sure ye'll have a much better time here in Eirestown … why you'd be mad to go anywhere else."

"I think we were mad to have come here, in the first place," said Fin.

"You're right Fin," agreed Paht, "we were mad to have come here. Never mind Antarctica, sure there's even less to do in Eirestown."

"Oh there's plenty enough, all right," said TongueSlinger, handing Paht a magazine called, You'd Be Mad To Go Anywhere Else, Weekend Breaks in Eirestown, "if only you know where to look."

"Such as?" asked Fin.

"What about the Caves of Sí Bheg," said TongueSlinger, pointing to another poster on the wall, which showed a medium sized hill riddled with holes, many of them filled in with cement, "have ye been there, lately?"

"The Caves of Sí Bheg," Paht said, nodding sagely, "sure the whole town's been there."

"That's right they have," tutted TongueSlinger, fidgeting with his false red beard, a gleam in his eye, "I'll tell ye what I'll do, so." He paused for a little dramatic effect, "I'll meet ye half way."

"Grand so," said Paht, "what's the deal?"

"That's it," sniggered TongueSlinger. "I'll meet ye half way to the Antarctica and sell ye bargain tickets back to Eirestown."

"Come on, granddad," said Fin, "I've enough of this nonsense; we'll book the tickets on the Internet."

Fin and Paht were almost out the door.

"'old on a minute now lads," TongueSlinger pleaded. "I've just the deal for ye."

"About time," said Paht.

"'Deed I'm sorry for all the messin' and all," said TongueSlinger. "Sure, you're right, I'm possessed." He heaved a pile of travel magazines out from beneath the counter, brushed his red fringe aside and started flicking through them. "I've a divil in me alright," he continued, fingering his way through the pile, "and I must admit he gets the better of me now and then. He's a right little fehker he is, always getting me into trouble." His fingers stopped and he pulled a magazine out of the pile, placing it on the counter, "Here now lads, just what you're after."

"Antarctica on a *budgie*?" asked Fin when he read the title. "Are you serious? You're going to fly us there on a budgie?"

"Ah look," said TongueSlinger, "an 'oul crumb." He scrubbed at the magazine's cover, removing a moulding crumb of questionable provenance, to reveal the real title: 'Antarctica on a *budget*'.

"Are ye happy now lads?" TongueSlinger asked, flicking the crumb away, "I mean with the travel arrangements, not the menu?"

"We are," said Fin. "Just arrange the bookings now, and we'll be on our way."

"Book us four tickets, so," said Paht.

"Jesus," said TongueSlinger, looking at them like they'd just stepped off a spaceship, and laughing so much that he fell back into his office chair, "but I've never met a bigger pair of fehkin' eejits in all my life."

Fin and Paht looked at each other with raised eyebrows and shrugged.

"What do you mean?" asked Paht.

TongueSlinger took great delight in telling the lads that all travel arrangements had already been arranged by King Cormac, and that there was to be a leaving ceremony in the main square tomorrow afternoon, to see Ye Olde Ross Ice Shelf Committee off.

"Don't you read The Eirestown Press?" TongueSlinger asked, once he finished bringing them up to speed.

"She'd tell us nothing this morning," grumbled Paht.

"I'm not surprised," said TongueSlinger, "sure you've the newspaper scared out her wits every day, dangling her over the open range, like that. The whole town has you down as a newspaper sadist."

"Wait a minute, now," said Paht, reaching behind the counter and hoisting TongueSlinger out of his chair by his beard, "if you knew travel arrangements had already been made, why did you keep us here so long?"

"Sure I was enjoying the company, great craic and all."

"What?" said Paht, tugging harder on his beard.

"Sure I've been open for years and you're the first customers I've ever had. I get lonely something rotten in here all day long with nothing to do."

"What do you mean," said Paht, grabbing an even bigger fistful of red beard, "we're the first customers?"

"Sure the whole town knows," squealed TongueSlinger, repeating the company's mantra, "that you'd be mad to go anywhere else."

"But I see people coming in and out of here all the time," said Paht, somewhat confused.

"Yes, to see me."

"What?"

"Look at the cut of me, man. I'm the biggest tourist attraction in the town!" cried TongueSlinger.

"You've only yourself to blame for that!" huffed Paht.

"Sure how was I to know King Cormac was sat on the toilet seat?" TongueSlinger squealed in his defence.

TongueSlinger had a divil in him alright, a few divils actually. And it was the divil with a penchant for gambling which had got him into trouble all those years ago.

Sure wasn't he the leprechaun who tried to save his fortune from the bookie's creditors by burying it under Sí Bheg, figuring that the King's hill would be the safest place in town. But when the whole of Eirestown started excavating the hill in search of it, things got out of hand.

TongueSlinger had no other choice but to join in the commotion and he started digging like a gang of navvies, desperate to find his priceless pot before anyone else did.

Sadly, just when he thought he'd struck gold, he found himself looking up at the redden clefts of King Cormac's backside, and ten minutes later, he found himself looking up at the ceiling of the castle dungeons.

Later that day, as part of his release contract, he was told he would have to establish the You'd Be Mad To Go Anywhere Else travel agents to promote Eirestown's first tourist attraction, 'The Caves Of Sí Bheg', a fortunate, and hopefully profitable, geological anomaly which came out of the whole digging fiasco.

So now, during office hours, TongueSlinger spent his days dressed in a large black, leather belt, green breeches, red false hair and beard and buckled shoes. As you can imagine, he had slowly grown to resent the company uniform, and it had him nearly half way round the twist, especially with half the town in every day mocking him.

"Just look at the curt of me," TongueSlinger repeated, tears welling up, "sure I'm surprised you've not been in more often yourself to mock me."

"I'll give you two pieces of advice," said Paht, feeling a little sorry for the oul' dressed up eejit.

"Go on, so," said TongueSlinger, nodding his head eagerly in anticipation.

"Stay out of the bookies," Paht said releasing him, "and never bury a pot of gold under Sí Bheg again. Come on Fin, we'll waste no more time in this lunatic asylum."

"Lunatic asylum, oh that's a good one," TongueSlinger screamed after them. "Sure ye're the biggest lunatics I've ever met. In fact," he added, "I'm not sure why the King's sending ye to the Antarctica in the first place. Sure ye couldn't build a snowman out there. A land of snow, and ye couldn't even build a fehkin snowman. Do you hear me?!"

As Paht slammed the door shut behind himself and Fin, TongueSlinger sighed, brushed down his red beard and morosely looked up at the clock: 10.30. He smiled to himself, that had been scandalous craic altogether, but he'd be awfully bored for the rest of the day now; however, in just a few hours time, he'd be transformed into a trendy clubbing VIP, minus the red hair. And that thought kept him going through the most miserable of days.

Free of the company shackles, Fíniún would pin back his pointed ears, comb back his black hair, slip into something sophisticated and modern like jogger cuffed jeans, a Ralph Loren shirt and Louis Vuitton Fuselage sneaker boots. Then he would head out through the green mist into the nearest Irish city, where he would pass himself off as a celebrity who had once performed as one of the Ewoks in Star Wars.

He might call himself Warwick Davis tonight, and hopefully end up somewhere trendy like Lillies Bordello on Grafton Street, where, after a few oul' drinks to drown his sorrows, Eirestown would just be a bad dream he'd left behind, until he woke up tomorrow morning.

For, as part of his penance, King Cormac had an awful curse on him altogether. And no matter where he went to sleep, no matter how far he managed to get away from Eirestown, every morning poor oul' Fíniún, aka TongueSlinger, woke up in the flat above You'd Be Mad To Go Anywhere Else, wishing that he was anywhere else in the world.

Chapter 26

Hyperbolic CRAP

The next day, just like TongueSlinger had told Paht and Fin, the whole town gathered in the Eirestown Town Hall square to wish Ye Olde Ross Ice Shelf Committee good luck, and bid them farewell.

Even King Cormac and his courtesans made an appearance. And stalls had been arranged under the Town Hall clock, where An Cabáiste agus Bagún Deli, courtesy of the culinary genius of Paddy Roux, had laid on a fine Antarctica spread for everyone, which included such delicacies as:

Allatla (baked snowballs) wrapped in Cabbage balls and layered with Bacon icicles.
Muktuk (whale blubber) igloo blocks, comprising blocks of whale blubber heartily filled with Cabbage and Bacon mousse.
Ross Sea cod and chips, comprising fried Antarctica cod with Bacon fries, wrapped in Cabbage leaves.
Ross Sea Seaweed surprise, comprising shredded Cabbage, sprinkled with cured Bacon bits.

And for the more discerning residents, with deeper pockets, a take on one of Paddy Roux's signature dishes:

Beluga rolls, comprising pourpre petits pois à la Française, Bacon and Cabbage crème fraîche with potato shallot croquette.

On another table, Paddy McGinty's Goat provided a range of beverages, which included pots of tea, and that was that.

Ever the opportunist, TongueSlinger took the opportunity to promote Eirestown's latest tourist attraction, nipping in and out of You'd Be Mad To Go Anywhere Else, offering everyone free tickets to Eirestown's bog, recently acquired by *Bord na Móna*.

In the centre of the town hall square, on a newly built platform, a cylindrical orange, green and white capsule, capable of holding up to four travellers, awaited its occupants.

QuickMIC lead the rest of Ye Olde Ross Ice Shelf Committee up the rackety flight steps, leading into his latest invention. Ye Olde Ross Ice Shelf Committee had been whittled down and consisted of QuickMIC, Ryan, Donn-Dubh and Mai-Ly. Fin and Banbha had begged to go, but after the attack at Paddy McGinty's, it was considered too dangerous to allow children. Also, Paht was afraid to be left on his own, just in case the Hells Angel came back with more iShillelagh reinforcements. All the committee, except for QuickMIC, were wearing green parkers, with white fur around the edge of the orange hood, thick green insulated, waterproof trousers, and black waterproof walking boots.

"It looks like an orange cylindrical fish bowl," said Donn-Dubh. The vehicle had a round door in the middle of one side, and a single round window on each end, which had been partitioned into octagonal sections. Along the rim of each viewing widow, it also had a shamrock.

"And look at the size of the balloon," Ryan said, "it must be as high as the clock tower." Even though the balloon was only partially filled, he could see it was going to be very tall.

"Is it safe?" asked Donn-Dubh. "Sure I've never travelled in a party balloon before. In fact, I think I might need the toilet before I go anywhere. Does it have a toilet?"

"Cop yourself on, now," said QuickMIC, who was wearing a white lab-coat, carrying a clipboard under one arm, and donning a monocle, to add a little sophistication to the proceedings, "there's an en-suite bathroom on board. As for safety, do you really think I spent all that time at NASA's Jet Propulsion Laboratory twiddling my thumbs?"

"You spent time at NASA?" asked Ryan.

"'Deed I did," replied QuickMIC, giving them a brief history of Ireland's space aspirations. "Sure we were to colonise the moon herself," explained QuickMIC. "But in the end, the Dáil decided that it would be too far to go for a pint and an oul' bit of craic."

Ryan took another look at the name of the capsule. He was at the top of the rickety wooden entry steps and close enough to the entrance hatch to make sure he wasn't hallucinating. The name written on the hatch definitely read, The Eirestown POP, which Ryan hoped wasn't to be the title of an obituary in the next edition of The Eirestown Press, for the heroic occupants of the capsules first manned flight.

"QuickMIC," said Ryan hesitantly, bending down to tap him on the shoulder.

"Yes Ryan."

"Why would anyone call a capsule dangling on the end of five story high helium balloon, POP?"

"Pressurised Orbital Pioneer," responded QuickMIC resolving the acronym, POP. Ryan looked even more confused than before, so QuickMIC further clarified the acronym for him.

"You see the capsule is *Pressurised* so ye have enough oxygen and don't freeze to death once you're up there. You're flying around the globe and therefore ye have an *Orbital* flight path. And ye really are *Pioneers*, since no one else has ever flown her."

"No one else has flown her," asked Ryan, "will she actually get us there?"

"Please God."

"It's not God who needs pleasing at this moment in time," said Ryan, "are you sure she'll get us there?"

"Sure don't worry yourself," QuickMIC assured him, "she's already been around the world thousands of times, and never failed once."

"At least she's been tested then?" Ryan said, breathing a sigh of relief.

"Around the world thousands of times in computer simulations, I should add," said QuickMIC.

"Ok," said Ryan, "so the POP gets us there, but how will we actually get back?"

"*Ádh na hEireannaigh!*" said QuickMIC proudly.

Ryan didn't have a clue what that meant but once inside the POP, he became more concerned with getting there once again, never mind getting back. Unfortunately, he had been chosen to pilot POP, but only because he once went to Cape Canaveral, home of America's space exploration history, as a tourist.

QuickMIC stressed to him that a day visit to such an esteemed establishment was all the exposure he needed to pilot POP. But the control panel, which was at one end of the POP capsule, looked extremely sophisticated, like something that might be seen on the Space Shuttle, or Star Trek's USS Enterprise even.

"What the hell is all this for?" asked Ryan, perusing the control panel and the jam packed ceiling above it. Both were full of switches, knobs, sliders, dials, LEDs, flashing lights of every colour, computer monitors, and literally hundreds of other devices and instruments he couldn't even name.

"Welcome to the flight deck, Captain Ryan," said QuickMIC, giving him a salute. "Now sit yourself down here in the command chair, and I'll run you through a few things."

Donn-Dubh and Mai-Ly strapped themselves into the executive leather chairs behind Ryan, preparing for launch, while QuickMIC tried to settle the Captain's nerves.

"Look-it," QuickMIC said, "sure I understand that it might be a little daunting, seeing so many bells and whistles for the first time, and all."

"A little daunting," said Ryan, "would that be an example of an Irish understatement?"

"But rest assured," QuickMIC went on, "she's been designed with simplicity and ease of use in mind." He stroked a huge red button that said LIFT-OFF, "Look-it, this is the lift off button, press that when you're ready to ..."

"Lift off?"

"Correct!" said QuickMIC. "You're in the saddle now, boyo. You'll have the hang of her in no time. And you won't even have to bother with the LIFT-OFF button, because the King himself will be releasing the tethers remotely, to launch the POP."

Ryan continued to stare at the numerous controls in a state of bemusement.

"And these yokes which rotate like control sticks on a games console," QuickMIC went on, pointing to a set of four controls labelled JB, "are jet booster controls, to give ye more directional precision, and keep ye on course."

Ryan looked at QuickMIC blankly.

"Remember," said QuickMIC, "you'll be entering the first jet stream at a height of about ten kilometres." He continued to twiddle with the JB sliders. "Now that jet stream will carry ye around the globe ..."

"The first jet stream?" Ryan inquired apprehensively.

"Yes," sighed QuickMIC, who was becoming irate at the fact that he was having to repeat himself, "the first jet stream. As I said earlier, there are four jet streams which you will have to navigate, two in the northern hemisphere, and two in the southern hemisphere."

"Four?"

"Yes," said QuickMIC, "four. And navigating them couldn't be easier. Look here." He pointed to a screen which showed a picture of the earth with four wavy lines meandering around it. "This is the north polar jet stream," his finger ran up and down, along the highest contour on the globe. "You'll enter the first jet stream here," his finger continued to follow the contour, "and when it's close enough to the sub tropical jet stream, like so," his finger hopped over to a wavy line near the equator, "you will cross over. Just as soon as you've navigated through the doldrums that is, after which time you'll be picked up by the southern sub tropical jet stream," his finger jabbed at another contour, "here. Then onto the south polar jet stream, down here. Ok?"

"Yeah," said Ryan, tracing out the lines, "that seems simple enough. Just run my finger along these lines."

"Simplicity itself," said QuickMIC. "As I also explained earlier, the jet streams act like high wind conveyor belts which encircle the earth. However, they're multi-layered and unpredictable, and in case the last one doesn't get you close enough to the landing point in Antarctica, you'll need these little beauties, to guide you in. There's a jet booster on each corner of POP and you increase or decrease their power using these JB yokes." He twiddled with all four controls. "Also there's a chance you might be blown out of a jet stream at any moment, so you can use these little beauties to pop the POP back into the conveyor belt. Comprende?"

"And how will I know where the jet streams are, if we pop put of them?"

"Easy peasy," said QuickMIC addressing another set of complex instruments. The first showed a three dimensional globe with multicoloured paths streaking across it. "Every eight hours," he continued, running his finger along the paths, "you'll receive a real-time update from the Global Forecast Data system, the GFD over there at NOAA, which plots the forward trajectory for the jet stream, on these coloured paths."

"Noah," said Ryan, "the guy with the ark?"

QuickMIC tutted, "Sure didn't you take any notes at all at this morning's briefing in Paddy McGinty's?"

"I tried to," replied Ryan, "but Paht wouldn't shut up long enough to let me hear a word."

"Alright so," snapped QuickMIC, "pay attention now. NOAA, that's the National Oceanic and Atmospheric Administration, and nothing to do with arks, provides tracking information for the jet stream's whereabouts."

"Ok," said Ryan.

"So you'll plug the data from GFD into the JSTA, that's the Jet Stream Tracking Algorithm I've programmed over here," QuickMIC pointed to a small computer monitor, "and read the co-ordinates from JSTA here," he pointed to another monitor, "and the necessary vector propulsion modalities, VPM, for the

JB yokes, will be provided over here. One VPM for each booster, and you'll use both hands simultaneously," he demonstrated, twiddling all four JB yokes, "to apply cross radial acceleration power, that's CRAP," he concluded, pointing to a set of four small monitors, one for each jet booster. "Got it?"

"I think I need to lie down," said Ryan, his head spinning from information overload.

"Look-it," said QuickMIC, his eyes a flustered crimson, "it's real simple. You'll take the TA data from GFD, kindly provided by NOAA. Plug it into the JSTA, get the VPMs over here, and twiddle the four JBs yokes to give you CRAP, ok?"

"Crap's right," said Ryan, overwhelmed by the controls and what QuickMIC was saying.

QuickMIC was pondering the processing steps, and suddenly remembered something else.

"Oh wait a minute now, not that it needs mentioning, but I'll mention it anyway, don't forget that once you have the data from GFD you'll have to do the conversion from Euclidean two dimensional co-ordinates into non-Euclidean four dimensional space co-ordinates, using the Riemann-Minkowski hyperbolic Differential Alignment Function Tensors, that's DAFT. Do you remember I mentioned them briefly this morning in Paddy McGinty's?"

Ryan nodded, but not because he remembered anything.

"Sadly," apologised QuickMIC after a few moments reflection, "I didn't have time to automate DAFT, so you'll have to do the hyperbolic conversions in your head. If you don't do the conversions, the output from JSTA will be crap, not CRAP! sure ye'll probably end up in outer Mongolia, or somewhere. Get it?"

"Do the conversions or else I'll get Hyperbolic CRAP," said Ryan in a stupor, summarising QuickMIC's lengthy technical spiel into a simple mnemonic. "Get it? ... I think I'm already sitting in it."

QuickMIC turned around to make sure Ryan was taking it all in. "Ryan," he waved his hand in front of Ryan's glazed eyes, "Ryan!"

Ryan was in a daze. It was as if he'd been inadvertently hypnotised by the information overload, and his cerebral functions had shut down.

"Ryan!" screamed QuickMIC, his eyes flashing bright red.

"I can't do it," said Ryan panicking and jumping out of the command chair. "Why can't you fly her?"

"I'd love to," sighed QuickMIC, stroking the JBs affectionately, "but I'm afraid of heights."

"Afraid of heights?"

"I am so," asserted QuickMIC. "Sure I can't be looking out of windows after lift-off. If I did I'd have a system shutdown."

"So where will you be," asked Ryan, "if I need any help?"

"In a moment," said QuickMIC, "I'm going to slip into my parka, slip into that seat over there, and put myself into Stand-by mode, until we land."

"I'll be on my own, so?" said Ryan, becoming more anxious now.

"Calm down," said QuickMIC, "sure it's too late to turn back now. Cop yourself on and remember your day out at Cape Canaveral."

"I was only ten at the time," argued Ryan, "and no one expected me to fly the feckin' Shuttle!"

"Ok, ok," said QuickMIC, looking down at his clipboard, where he had a copy of the POP design plans and the flight procedure, "we'll implement plan B, so."

"There's a Plan B?" said Ryan.

"'Deed there is," said QuickMIC. "You see this button over here," QuickMIC ran across the console to a huge button labelled AuPi.

"Yes," said Ryan, not sure if he could take in any more acronyms without his brain exploding at the seams.

"Well this is the Automatic Pilot," said QuickMIC. "So after lift-off, just count to fifty and press this AuPi button."

"That's it?"

"That's it," said QuickMIC, "Lift-off and the oul' AuPi will do the rest."

Ryan slumped into the command chair, having fainted with relief.

"Ryan, Ryan!"

Outside Malachy finally finished pumping helium into the balloon. It was fabricated from individual sections of green, orange and white, and stood five storeys high, with the words: The Eirestown POP printed in huge letters along the middle of one side, using the traditional Gaelic font, with a shamrock underneath the name and a huge shamrock on the other side of the balloon.

With all the preparations complete, and Ye Olde Ice Shelf Committee safely on board The Eirestown POP, King Cormac got up onto a makeshift stage to give a farewell speech. Solemnly he approached the podium, where he intended to give an inspirational speech about the sacrifice the people of Eirestown, and especially the selfless act of bravery Ye Olde Ross Ice Shelf Committee, were about to make, to ensure the safety and prosperity of all mankind. He also hoped to wish them a safe journey. He had four sheets of paper full of inspiration material like that.

"I am honoured to stand before you today ..." King Cormac began his dignified speech, but the whole town started laughing.

King Cormac cleared his throat a few times, tapped the microphone and tried again, "People of Eirestown we are gathered here today ..." But it was no use, his voice was warbling three to five octaves above normal. What the king didn't know is that Malachy Malarkey had left the helium canister open beneath the podium, and wasn't it the gas which had him squealing like a baby pig.

With the King ridiculed and the whole town in bits, didn't Malachy, wearing a gas mask, hop up onto the King's shoulder, jump down onto the podium, grab the microphone and start singing 'The Leaving Of Liverpool' in a baritone, raspy voice reminiscent of The Dubliner's Ronnie Drew, altering the lyrics accordingly for the occasion. He was accompanied for the first verse on a banjo by one of the Cracker Craics:

'Farewell to Paddy McGinty's,
Fare well An Cabáiste agus Bagún,
We are bound for the Antarctica,
a place we don't belong ...'

Sure King Cormac tried to wrestle the microphone back off Malachy at this point, but by now the whole town had joined in the song, and the helium had them all singing in squeaky voices.

'So fare thee well, my own true love,
When I return, united we will be.
It's not the leaving of Eirestown that grieves me so,
But my darling when I think of thee.'

At the end of the second chorus, which sounded like it had been delivered by the largest high-pitched Munchkin choir the world had even known, Malachy pressed a huge red button on the podium. Creaking and groaning, The Eirestown POP left its moorings, and ever so slowly, began its ascent. Donn-Dubh, Ryan and Mai-Ly waved out the open windows of the POP, their eyes welling up. But the poor oul' uilleann pipes could take no more, and didn't they have to be carried off the podium, sniffling into a packet of hankies. "Ahhh, look lads, you'll have to forgive the oul' pipes," Paddynini apologised, "sure he hates goodbyes."

As the uilleann pipes passed Paht he handed them a hanky and then he had a great thought altogether. What with all the celebrations in Paddy McGinty's Goat last night, they were running low on essential supplies, so Paht jumped up onto the podium, grabbed the microphone from Malachy, and shouted up to the lads in the balloon: "Don't forget!"

"Don't forget what?" shouted Donn-Dubh and Ryan, still waving out of the POP's window.

"Bring us back an oul' bucket of ice!"

With the uilleann pipes sobbing uncontrollably and the Munchkin choir's voice rising faster than the POP itself, the crew secured the windows and fastened themselves into their seats. Seat belts secure, Ryan crossed his fingers, pressed the AuPi button, and was relived to get verification from a monitor that the automatic pilot had taken control.

"What's that noise," said Donn-Dubh, "is everything alrigth?"

Ryan turned around to locate the source of the noise and found QuickMIC snoring in a corner, using the hood on his tricoloured parka as a pillow, "Some Standby mode," he smiled, raising his eyebrows. "Yeah, Donn-Dubh we're all set, just sit back and enjoy the ride."

The Eirestown POP steadily gained height through the clouds, the town receding into the distance, and within no time at all, it approached the stratosphere. Higher still it would climb towards the troposphere, until it met with the high altitude conveyor belt known as the Jet Stream, which would carry the pioneers to their icy, desolate destination. Where, it was hoped, they would save the world, or at least find out what was causing the Ross Ice Shelf to melt so quickly. And if all else failed, at least Paht would get a bucket of Ross Ice Shelf ice as a souvenir.

Chapter 27

Welcome To The Hotel California

"How was the flight, sir?"

William McCoy The Third had just landed at a makeshift floating runway, not far from the seasonal Ice Runway on Mc Murdo Sound's icy bay, where Captain James Bush was greeting him.

"Not bad," said William, rubbing his neck, "if you like roller coaster rides."

"A little turbulence, sir?" asked Captain James. "The cold fronts out here can play havoc with air streams."

"Not until we landed!" snapped William.

James cringed at the undulating strip of ice, which passed for a makeshift runway. "Sorry, sir," he said, "we built the runway at the last minute. Given the nature of your visit here, we thought you might like a little privacy."

"I would have preferred a little comfort," said William, taking the last few steps out of his Bombardier BD-700 and rubbing his head. "Talk about bumps!"

"The ice is real tough out here, sir," said James defensively. "We did our best. I told the boys to polish the ice until it was as smooth as a baby's bottom."

"A baby's bottom," said William, "what kind of baby were they thinking about, a hedgehog?"

"Very funny, sir," James grinned, trying to lighten the mood, "we've got no hedgehogs out here, but I do get your point. You get it?"

In no mood for jokes, William just frowned at him, "Get the point, after that landing I think I still have it sticking in my backside." Despite the sudden blizzard white out, he could make out several other silhouettes around the plane. "Who are all these people anyway?"

"Trusted employees of GRABiT sir," said James confidently. "We've managed to infiltrate Mac Town and buy a few people."

"Mac Town?"

"It's the local name for McMurdo Scientific Research Station, sir."

William had enough problems accounting for Ryan's expense claims from An Cabáiste agus Bagún Deli without more hidden costs springing up at him. "And you say you've bought a few people in Mac Town? How much we talking here?"

"Not much, sir," said James, picking up some of William's luggage, "just promised them luxury condos in the new territories, at discounted prices of course."

"I like it Jamie boy," said William, picking up a few bags, "I like it! The New Territories. It's catchy, got a nice ring to it. And discounted sales already."

"This way sir," said James, "I've an EUVx, an Electric Utility Vehicle, waiting to transport you to Mac Town."

"Wow, an EUVx," William repeated with some excitement. "I've seen the Saturn V5 rocket engine in Houston. It was the full length of a soccer pitch. But

I've never even heard of an EUVx. Sounds like one hell of a beast, point me at her." His enthusiasm didn't last long, though. The bright yellow, EUVx mini-truck looked like something a couple of pensioners would be happy driving around a golf course.

James shrugged his shoulders, "Electric, compact, quiet and no pollution sir, much easier on this pristine environment."

"But there won't be a pristine environment to worry about soon," sneered William.

James picked up the rest of Williams bags and loaded them into the cargo hold. "I know that sir, but we have to keep up appearances."

"You really thought of appearances when you decided to pick me up in a golf buggy," William griped, taking his seat. "Thank god the boys from Augusta can't see me now."

"By the way," said James, hoping to placate William as he started the engine, "we've booked you into the Hotel California."

"Hotel California," whooped William, slapping his thigh, as the EUVx rumbled and wobbled from side to side like a tortoise, "now that sounds more like it."

Despite the fact that Mac Town looked like a mining town which had been abandoned when the Klondike opened in 1896, William McCoy The Third became very excited when he saw a name sign on the side of what looked like a two story, mustard coloured, corrugated building, mounted on concrete blocks. Even though he was frozen to the bone, the sign was like a blast of sunshine.

He felt bad enough when they drove past Mac Town's helipad, and wondered why James hadn't picked him up by helicopter, as their EUVx struggled to keep up with someone walking past them. But the mustard coloured sign gave him some hope that civilisation had made it this far south. The sign read 'Bldg. 166, Hotel California', and underneath the sign were painted a huge orange sun, gently rising above a strip of beautiful blue ocean, with two silhouette palm trees on one side of the sun and a yacht on the other. Yes, despite the desolation, he had hoped that Building 166 contained a modern day oasis in the middle of the coldest, moist brutal landscape he had ever had the misfortune to find himself immersed in, and the bright orange sun on the sign gave him every reason to believe that was the case.

It was obvious to him now, having seen this sign, that these geeks, scientists and computer nerds must have built such an oasis, a retreat from temperatures and barren landscapes which would otherwise be unbearable. He imagined a choice of pine lined, Finnish saunas, wo-manned by Swiss masseurs, who would gladly pour ice cold water over red hot coals. As the EXUv trundled along, in his mind's eye he could see corridors lined with hydroponic systems throughout out Building 166 to grow palm trees, and various exotic flora and fauna, so that, even here, they could feast on tropical fruits. And there'd be rooms full of sunbeds and sunlamps, and the latest technological wonders and gadgets everywhere. Curved High Definition televisions, iPlayer docking stations, SONOS wireless sounds systems, robot Vacuum cleaners ... yes these geeks would certainly make the place comfortable for themselves.

"Welcome to Hotel California, sir," said Captain James Bush when they arrived at his room, "the pride and joy of Mac Town."

What William wasn't expecting was a 20 person bunk room in the middle of a two story dormitory, with no windows, and the only link to the outside world, a clapped out thirty year old valve radio.

"It's a bit basic, sir," apologised James, when he saw William's jaw drop as fast as his baggage, "but functional."

William ran his eyes around the bland dormitory, which was almost as barren as outside: "Basic? I'd have gone with living quarters fit for neanderthals, but even they would probably feel more at home in a cave. Is this really how these geeks live out here?"

"'Fraid so, sir," said James. "We have all the mod cons ..."

"Mod cons probably get better facilities," interrupted William.

"Good one sir," said James, finishing his sentence, "but I wasn't talking about modern convicts. What I meant was that we have all the mod cons, that's convinces, but not necessarily all the mod comfs."

"Mod comfs?"

"Modern comforts."

"Any comfort at all would be a bonus here."

"You'll adjust sir, you'll see."

"But what about the name," William asked, "and that sign outside, the palm trees, the sun, the yacht?"

"Oh that," said James, "a little Mac Town humour. They named the building after the song by the Eagles, you know the one." James began singing a few lines, "'Welcome to the Hotel California ....dah de de de dum. As the song says, you can never leave.'"

"Some humour these nerds have, eh? Leave? I wished I'd never arrived," said William miserably, sitting down on a bunk.

"That's why they chose that song sir," sighed James, "for its irony." And believe me," he went on, placing an understanding hand of William's shoulder, "I know how you feel."

"Never did like that song." William quipped, shrugging James' hand off. Looking around the bland room in despair, and tutting every now and then he said, "It's hard to imagine, twenty, sweaty, zit faced scientists horned into this corrugated tin shack. I hope none of them snore?"

"You won't have to worry about that, sir," said James. "It's all yours for the duration. We've created a health scare to keep it empty."

"What kind of health scare," replied William, "acute claustrophobia?"

"Very funny," said Captain James, "glad to see that you're relaxing into it. No, we created Penguin Flu, a virulent flu which can cross species. Well we just created the rumour, not the actual flu, so don't be worried if any penguin approaches you for a cuddle."

"Penguin Flu," huffed William, "surely no one will believe that."

"Why not, sir?"

"Given the choice," said William dejectedly, "even a virus wouldn't live in here. Come to think of it, I'm not sure a penguin would either."

"Stop it," said James, feigning a belly laugh, "you're killing me here."

"Have you any good news for me at all?" asked William, opening one of his suitcases, and impressed by James' intuition, because he might actually be getting killed before the day is out.

"We've made contact with one of the Eirestown saboteurs."

"They've arrived then?"

"Affirmative sir," said James, "and the first fool hired some of my men to be his bodyguards and guide."

"Who would that be?"

"An iShillelagh by the name of Malachy Malarkey."

"And the others?"

James looked at his watch. "Hopefully they'll be getting picked up within the hour."

"Is Ryan with them?"

"Yes sir."

"We may have a problem with him, I think he's become a bit of a sympathiser."

"We always had a problem with that Californian hippy if you ask me sir."

"I think we may have to say goodbye to Ryan."

"Leave that to me sir."

"By the way, where's the pickup happening?"

" Murphy's On The Rocks, sir."

 "Where?"

Captain James Bush told William McCoy The Third about an Irish bar which didn't exist, a snowball's throw from McMurdo.

"So the geeks do have some mod comfs," said William, unpacking case, "but what's wrong with the local facilities?"

"No one knows how to party like the Irish sir," said James. "And the only craic you'll find in the local facilities is the crack on the toilet seats, and they're no fun in this weather."

"I can imagine," said William wincing.

"Of course the upper echelons of McMurdo's deny all knowledge of Murphy's officially, sir." James went on. "But you'll find most of McMurdo's geeks popping in and out of there, day and night. It's the only thing that keeps them sane in this God forsaken place. Why if it wasn't for the craic in Murphy's," concluded James, "some really would crack, as in crack up."

William doubted that and said that you'd have to be cracked to have wanted to come out here in the first place.

"Can we trust these bodyguards?" William asked, changing the subject.

"Never trust a penguin sir," said James, "unless you've got something real good on them. And even then, err on the side of caution."

"Noted," said William, unpacking a few Armani suits. James burst out laughing when William hung the suits inside a rackety old wardrobe.

"What's so funny?" William asked.

"Do you have any white ones in there?"

"Just one, why?"

"Because if you go outside wearing one of those, you'll be frozen solid within minutes," James said, laughing even harder. "And with a white suit on, you'd make a great snowman. Should I call catering and get them to send a carrot over for your nose?"

"But you said it was summer."

"We might have the sun for six months, sir," James said, gritting his teeth and rubbing his hands, "but not the shine. You'll be lucky if it gets above minus 20 most days."

"I think I need to lie down," said William.

"Good idea sir," said James, helping him into the bunk. "Just take a nap," he suggested, tucking him in, "and when you wake it will all have been a bad dream." As William started to doze-off, James thought a little payback was in order. "By the way, sir, how much ice would you like in your morning Manhattan?"

But it was too late, William was dead to the world, and James might not be that far behind him if he carried on winding him up like that.

Chapter 28

Murphy's On The Rocks

"There's no sign of Mai-Ly," Ryan shouted back into the POP capsule, before bending down to get close to the snow, "no footprints either. Looks like she's disappeared into thin air."

"She must have blown a fuse or something," said QuickMIC. "Going crazy like that, sure she could have killed us all."

Ye Old Ross Ice Shelf Committee had arrived HERE wherever here actually was, but not without a few problems. Having been shaken silly in high altitude winds, much like a carbon dioxide bubble in a bottle of fizzy water, they were finally glad to be back on the ground. The AuPi control performed well, but QuickMIC forgot to tell Ryan that a little human intervention would be required when the AuPi automatically released the helium balloon, without warning, while The Eirestown POP was still several thousand meters above its landing site.

With the balloon gone, didn't the POP go into freefall, dropping several hundred meters instantly, scaring the bejaysus out of the pioneers on board, the ones awake at least. The plummeting POP was on course to hit the ground at a mighty speed altogether, where it would surely be smashed to smithereens, killing the occupants on icy rocks below.

Fortunately Ryan and Donn-Dubh's screaming managed to jolt QuickMIC out of stand-by mode. And no sooner had his microprocessors fired back to life than he had the flashing red button, OPEN PARAGLIDE, pressed.

Ryan and Donn-Dubh jumped for joy when the paraglide dispatched from a compartment on the POP roof, filled with cold air, and started slowing the capsule down. But it wasn't enough, and after a brief jolt, it continued plummeting towards the ground.

"Crap, Ryan," yelled QuickMIC.

"Crap is right," Ryan shouted back, clinging onto the sides of his captain's chair, "we're finished!"

"No," QuickMIC yelled again, "CRAP!"

Ryan was terrified and had his eyes closed, so he didn't see QuickMIC pointing to the JB yokes. But Donn-Dubh did. He jumped out of his chair, ran towards the control panel, and twiddled with four JB sticks to generate some cross radial acceleration power, and finally, with the jets pointing down, some much needed vertical lift.

"At least someone was listening," said a very relived QuickMIC, as the vertical lift supported the paraglide, and slowed the POP down to a more comfortable landing speed.

"Like you say," said Donn-Dubh, weaving the POP all over the place with the control sticks, "it's just like playing with a games console."

"Well take it easy there now, Mr Neil Armstrong," said QuickMIC, his face turning green with all the erratic movement, "I think I'm getting sea sick."

As shaken and buffeted as they were by the jet stream and the sudden loss of the helium balloon, they were even more shaken by Mai-Ly's actions. Ten minutes before they actually lost the balloon, didn't they lose Mai-Ly. Sure they couldn't understand a word she said as she grabbed a parachute, opened the front hatch, waved her sword menacingly around threatening to kill them all, screamed hysterically, before throwing herself out the hatch door.

"I wonder where Mai-Ly was going," said QuickMIC, stepping out of the POP and zooming his purple eyes in and out, looking for her footsteps. "Donn-Dubh," he added, with no footsteps to be found, "please repeat what she said again." QuickMIC had been in stand-by mode when Mai-Ly went haywire.

"Well she was waving her sword at us, and saying something like, '*me how ni no toe ping pong poe la no ne nah moe he hoe ni ka mi*'. Something like that."

"Are you sure now?" said QuickMIC. "That doesn't mean anything at all to my UTU app."

"That's because she actually said, '*me how no ni toe pong ping poe la nwo nea nah moohe he hoe ni ka mi ma foe*'," suggested Ryan.

QuickMIC looked even more confused, "Are ye sure? It sounds like ye might be getting yere *pings* and *pongs* mixed up, never mind your *knees* and *knows*."

"I never get my knees mixed up with my *nose*," said Donn-Dubh, adamant that Ryan was wrong. "How would that be even possible? Sure you can only pick one of them, and I've never seen anyone genuflect on their nose in church, have you?"

"Look, let's forget where Mai-Ly is for now," said Ryan, "and worry more about where we actually are, before we starve or freeze to death."

"I can only assume we are in the Antarctica," said QuickMIC his eyes zooming along the horizon, looking for any recognisable landmarks. "However, when the helium balloon detached from the POP and we entered freefall, we may have been blown off course. We could be hundreds of kilometres from where we should be."

"Wherever we are, I think we're lost," said Ryan anxiously. "This terrain is all the same. White everywhere we look, and no landmarks of any significance."

"What about your phone," said Donn-Dubh, "can't you get Google maps up or something?"

"No good, I've already tried," said Ryan. "There's no network coverage out here."

"Don't worry, man," Donn-Dubh reassured them, and he reached into his hat and pulled out a book.

"What's that?" asked Ryan.

"An Irish Pub Guide," said Donn-Dubh, flicking through several pages.

"A what?" said Ryan.

"Yes here it is, Antarctica," continued Donn-Dubh, running his finger under an entry in the large compendium, "'Murphy's On The Rocks.'" He read the description: "'DESCRIPTION: Sure isn't it a fine Irish Pub altogether, fitted out in a quaint Country Cottage style. Typical of many Irish establishments around the world, Murphy's boasts a welcoming staff, and a boisterous, mostly harmless, cliental.'"

"Where is it?" said QuickMIC.

Donn-Dubh continued reading, "'LOCATION:

Murphy's On The Rocks is situated on the remnants of an ancient Antarctica glacier, not far from McMurdo scientific research installation.'"

"Is this some kind of joke," asked Ryan, "an Irish pub in the middle of the Antarctica?"

"You'll find an Irish pub anywhere in the World, Paht told me when he gave me this," said Donn-Dubh, shaking the Irish Pub Guide at him. 'Paht said the Irish are the only nation to have conquered the world without ever having gone to war.'

"You're codding us," inquired QuickMIC cautiously, "aren't you?"

"'CONSPIRACY NAYSAYERS and party poopers,'" answered Donn-Dubh, reading the Irish Pub Guide FAQ on Murphy's. "'Please note that Murphy's existence is controversial to say the least, and denied by many, including senior American Public figures. Only last year during The State of The Union Address, despite the fact that a picture of the American President drinking with a leprechaun in Murphy's On The Rocks had been circulating on social media for the previous six months, the President told congress that if you believed Murphy's existed, you might as well believe in leprechauns. Which, as you can imagine,'" Donn-Dubh went on with a smile, "'didn't go down too well with IALL, the Irish American Leprechaun Lobby, subsequently losing the President 0.00000001% of his vote. In recent years, Murphy's has also been the victim of a heinous CIA disinformation campaign. But it does exist. So if you ever happen to find yourself near the South Pole, sure pop in for an oul' bite and a drink. But take it easy on the Green Avalanche, sure it'll blow your socks off!'"

"And how on earth will we ever find Murphy's, if it actually exists at all?" inquired Ryan dubiously.

"Oh you're not far from it," a strange, warbling high pitched voice announced.

They all turned around to find a rather inebriated penguin hiccupping in their direction. It was so cold that his hiccups formed green ice bubbles which drifted in the air.

"Are you sick?" asked QuickMIC, fanning away a few green bubbles.

"Not at all," the penguin slurred and hiccupped, wobbling from side to side. "One too many Green Avalanches, that's all."

"How far is Murphy's, then?" asked QuickMIC.

The penguin burped, squinted at him and said, "Oh, I'd say about twenty Green Avalanches, thirty with a good thirst on you."

"Avalanches?" said QuickMIC, looking over his shoulder to see if there were mountains of ice and snow cascading towards him.

"He means," said Ryan, having spent enough time in Ireland to understand how a drunken Paddy navigates between bars without modern contraptions like GPS, "that Murphy's is as far away as the time it takes you to drink twenty Green Avalanches."

"And how long does it take to drink twenty Green Avalanches?" QuickMIC asked the penguin, who looked like he drank twenty Green Avalanches every few meters or so.

"That all depends," answered the penguin.

"On what?"

"How fast you drink them," he sniggered, burping and hiccupping again.

"Come on brother," pleaded Donn-Dubh, who was seriously considering taking Paht's advice to walk and wobble like a penguin, if only to keep himself warm, "how do we get there?"

"Brother?" yelled the penguin, giving Donn-Dubh a questionable look up and down. "I've drunk more than I thought did!"

"You know what I mean," said Donn-Dubh. "This cold is killing me!"

"Go north," said the penguin, doing a twirl with his flipper extended, and sniggering again.

"Thanks a lot," said Donn-Dubh. "North it is."

"Sure wait a minute," said QuickMIC, "we're on the South Pole, right?"

All the others nodded their heads in agreement, even the penguin.

"Which means," explained QuickMIC, staring disapprovingly at the penguin, "that any direction you take is north."

Following which the drunken penguin blew a few more icy, green bubbles and fell over laughing, "Nearly had you then, lads."

Donn-Dubh kissed his teeth.

"Sure I'd love to help you brother," said the penguin sadly, "but unfortunately, I'm bipolar."

"Bipolar," asked Ryan sympathetically, "you mean you suffer from depression?" Like most Americans, Ryan was well versed in the latest developments in psychology.

"No, I'm not depressed," laughed the penguin, "I'm only bipolar." Ryan looked at him, clueless. "I mean," continued the laughing penguin, slapping his thighs hysterically and holding his flippers up in alternate directions, "that I can't tell my south from my north pole." Then he wobbled a few times before collapsing in a heap.

"Look-it," insisted QuickMIC, his eyes bordering on agitated orange, "this is a matter of life and death. Will you please give us the directions, man?"

The oul' inebriated penguin got back on his feet and looked sternly into QuickMIC's orange eyes, as if the mention of death had sobered him slightly. "Well," he began solemnly, struggling to maintain his balance, "getting to Murphy's is easy enough, but," he hiccupped.

"But what?" snapped QuickMIC, his eyes an anxious scarlet.

"I wouldn't start from here," the penguin announced, before he hiccupped one more time and fell flat on his face again, where he started snoring, on a pile of snow shaped like a pillow, dead to the world.

"Well that's just great," said QuickMIC derisively, kneeling down to gently slap the penguin's face, trying to revive him. "'I wouldn't start from here'. So where would you start from then? Hey come on, wake up."

"I've got it," said Ryan, pointing at the snow, "this guy has obviously just come from the pub."

"Now that's a safe assumption, I'd say, wouldn't you?" said QuickMIC, getting back on his feet, nearly drunk himself from the smell of the penguin's breath.

"So we just follow his footsteps, or penguin steps," Ryan concluded, tracing out the penguin's first few paces, "or whatever the hell they're called."

"And they'll lead us to Murphy's," whooped QuickMIC. "Sure Ryan you're a genius."

And follow the penguins steps is exactly what they tried to do for the next fifty five very cold minutes. But didn't they lose their way a few times, on account of snow drift which covered most of the penguin's tracks. Worse still, they nearly fell down three crevasses into oblivion, and almost toppled over a cliff edge. Finally, with the lads frozen to their very bones and QuickMIC frozen to his microprocessor core, they saw a welcoming green, hazy light in the distance.

"Over there," shouted a very relived Ryan, "that must be it."

Donn-Dubh said, "Hang on a minute, lads." And he poked around inside the folds of his hat, pulled out some kind of tablet device, pointed it in the direction of the inviting green light and declared, "Yes, you're right Ryan. That's Murphy's over there, exactly fifty meters away, according to this yoke."

"What exactly is that yoke?" asked Ryan, incredulously.

"Sat-Nav," said Donn-Dubh.

"Sat-Nav!" screamed Ryan. "Sat-Nav! You mean to say we've been stumbling around out here lost for the last hour, following snow covered penguin tracks, almost tumbling over cliff edges, and you had Sat-Nav all this time?"

Donn-Dubh shrugged his shoulders and quickly stuffed the Sat-Nav back into his hat, just in case Ryan decided to take it off him and knock some sense into him with it.

"Wow," said QuickMIC, "so Murphy's On The Rocks really does exist!"

Murphy's was an architectural wonder, which would come as no surprise to the accountants over at the National Science Foundation's Office of Polar Programmes in Arlington County Virginia. Ten years ago they received a fax from McMurdo requesting five million dollars to build a Penguin Reserve. The real surprise for the accountants in Arlington, if they were to ever find out, would be the fact that the reserve had since been converted, surreptitiously, due to the declining penguin population, into a non-existent Irish bar. One of the largest and most innovative uses of ice blocks the modern world had ever known, QuickMIC said Murphy's looked like a big igloo, and being an iShillelagh he could be forgiven for his rather immature appraisal, which ignored Murphy's more nostalgic, subtle allure.

Murphy's reminded Ryan of a snow covered cottage from a Christmas card scene. A green coloured snow path, with two green Victorian lanterns either side welcomed you in. The roof was made from millions of slithers of icicles, layered to create the effect of thatching and the main structure was fabricated from green coloured ice blocks. Murphy's boasted an oak framed revolving door – to keep the heat in and the cold out - four Georgian quadrupled, glazed window frames to the front, with hints of snow drift in the lower corners, and two moss covered chimneys.

From one chimney, bellows of Irish turf infused smoke wafted gently, curling and writhing in the air to form fingers which beckoned weary, frozen travellers in. From the other chimney, depending on the day, bellows of cabbage and bacon or Irish stew or Irish breakfast infused smoke wafted. 'Murphy's On the Rocks' was not only a sight for cold, sore eyes, it was also an olfactory oasis for frozen, blue tipped noses.

As Ye Old Ross Ice Shelf Committee approached Murphy's a couple of hefty, menacing penguins were loitering around outside, blocking the revolving door. The others hesitated, but Donn-Dubh carried on and said he'd handle it. He said a few words, gave each penguin a high-five on their flippers and they waddled aside to allow them access.

Nobody noticed them as they entered 'Murphy's On The Rocks'. Even though it was only nine in the morning, Murphy's was packed to its icy rafters.

As remote and as hidden as it was from the base, many of McMurdo's resident scientists and military personnel could be found in Murphy's on many a cold day, all 365 of them actually, 366 in a leap year, drowning their sorrows by an open log fire, with ice cubes coming out of their ears.

A large painting of an Irish scene hung behind the wooden bar, with a small country village in the centre of it. In the painting a few locals danced a jig outside their pastel coloured houses, as a farmer on a pony-and-trap, delivered the morning's milk churns and the village pub's beer casks.

Various country ornaments, including copper jugs and kettles, hung around the walls of Murphy's, along with harnesses full of horse brass. Traditional black thorn shillelaghs hung in several places, and ad hoc shelving and a Welsh Dresser were adorned with Irish delf, including tea sets and floral butter dishes. One wall boasted pictures of famous Irish writers including William Butler Yates, Oscar Wilde, James Joyce and Brian O'Nolan.

Finding the pub had been shock enough, but finding tiny red bearded Eskimos wearing large green, velour hats with buckles on, in one corner of Murphy's playing céilí music had been the icing – if there was any more icing actually needed in the South Pole - on the cake.

"Eskimos are from the North Pole aren't they?" said Ryan, ordering his drink, a Murphy's On The Rock's classic known as a Green Avalanche. The drink sounded exotic enough, but watching the barman prepare it was almost as entertaining as drinking it. First he swirled a tall glass with mint-choc-chip ice-cream, so that waves of green and chocolate covered the inside of the glass. Then he filled it with a combination of white ice-cream, Bailey's Irish Cream, and single malt Irish whiskey. To finish, he added a load of ice cubes and topped the drink with green, dry ice which continued to tumble out of the glass for several minutes. Donn-Dubh ordered a Green Short Back and Sides cocktail which sounded like a haircut, but its preparation was even more entertaining. Sure he nearly fled Murphy's when the barman plonked a green coconut on the bar, and produced a machete to chop the top off it. "Now that's what you call a short back and sides," laughed Ryan, green, dry ice filling his mouth. As soon as

Donn-Dubh had recovered from the shock of the coconut's decapitation, the barman poured some fiery Jamaican white rum into it, followed by three large coloured ice cubes, red, yellow and green. "Yeah man," said Donn-Dubh, sipping on his drink, "Eskimos playing Irish music is strange enough, but Eskimos in the South Pole, now that is weird."

It was only when the Eskimos started playing and singing their next song that suspicions grew, and by the end of the first verse of a rather cacophonous, rowdy, rendition of Mursheen Durkin, QuickMIC said, "They're not Eskimos, it's The Cracker Craics!"

The shock or losing the POP helium balloon was one thing, the shock of Mai-Ly jumping out of the POP, another. And combined with the shock of finding an Irish pub in the middle of the Antarctica, you'd think they'd be all shocked out by now. But the shock they were about to get was something else altogether. For the Cracker Craics weren't the only familiar face waiting for Ye Olde Ross Ice Shelf Committee in Murphy's.

Chapter 29

Hotstuff, She's Hot

William McCoy The Third was sitting on a single bunk in the not so lavish Hotel California, rubbing his tired eyes with one hand, whilst brushing his sandy, brown locks back over his balding head with the other.

It wasn't the best night's sleep he'd ever had, but it wasn't the worse either, although Captain James' snoring had taken some getting used to. He couldn't imagine what it would be like with twenty geeks in here snoring away.

William yawned loudly and took a few deep breaths. He was shattered already, and that was just from making his bed. Back from the bathroom, Captain James had insisted that he make his bed to exacting military standards, so exacting that it had taken him seven attempts. At one point he questioned the sadistic nature of the exercise and the unrealistic demands of the repetitive folding-and-tucking of bed linen which he felt a sufferer of OCD would have given up on. By the sixth attempt, he wondered if James was somehow getting his own back, by punishing him in such a manner, but James assured him that such folding was essential to ensure a draught free bed. If the Hotel heating failed, you could be frozen solid in your sleep within minutes, unless you were tucked in tight, to retain body temperature, until you were rescued or the heating came back on.

At the other end of the bed lay a two foot pile of EWC (Extreme Weather Clothing), which James had only just dumped, telling William they were replacements for his designer collection. At bottom of the pile William could see the distinctive red McMurdo parka, and on top of that there appeared to be enough clothing to kit out a baseball team including mittens, socks, long johns, cold-weather-bibs, face mask, wind pants, goggles, balaclava ... on and on it went.

"You have to dress in layers," James explained. William argued that he was only here for a few days, and it would take him that long to put this lot on. No wonder these geeks never got out, they spent all their time getting dressed and undressed for bed.

William's own coat, a mottled Armani Sabre Tooth Parka, with bright, blonde, fang shaped fur around the rim of the hood, hung in the rackety wardrobe at the end of his bunk. As gruff and ferocious as the name sounded, Captain James scoffed when he picked it up. "It would struggle to keep a flea warm out here, sir," he laughed. It looked like it had been designed with San Francisco winters in mind, not the extremes of Antarctica. "One gust of icy wind and this Armani sabre would be toothless," James said, brushing the fur teeth back. "And you wouldn't be that far behind, sir," James smirked. "Those chattering teeth of yours would be enamel dust in minutes."

The previous evening, James had compromised on one item of clothing, and he let William keep his Prada sable, fur lined pyjamas, which he was just slipping out of. William reached over to the pile of EWC and pulled out the silk long johns. Grunting, he started tugging at one of the legs. These long johns were a fashion faux pas, but at least they were silk, because silk, James informed him, unlike cotton, did not absorb water in the form of sweat.

William continued to struggle with the long johns and stared morosely at the covered windows, which Captain James Bush insisted were necessary to ensure privacy, and to also add weight to the Penguin Flu epidemic. Although there was not much to look at in Mac Town, the covered windows coupled with the enclosed space gave William the creeps, it was almost like a prison dorm, except a prison would definitely have better facilities.

"Goooodddddd morning happy campers," the Radio Mac Town DJ yelled, "hope ya'll are chillin' out on this fine summer's morning."

"Chilling out," said James, who'd just switch on the radio, "get it, sir?"

William stood up and wriggled his hips into the long johns. He got it alright, and James might get it soon if he carried on.

The chirpy Tennessee DJ continued getting chirpier as William slowly acquired more and more layers: "It's going to be a lovely day, ya'll. Only minus 15 with wind chill chillin' ya'll down to minus 20 in the shade. Ya'll be some seriously cool campers by the end of the day. So why not meet me down in Gallagher's pub or the Erebus Club, and I'll do my best to warm ya'll up with a little Tennessee moonshine. And by the way ladies, I'll throw in a little body warmth ... Touch me baby I'm on fire! But seriously campers, wrap up well ya'll and get back indoors this afternoon if possible. We're expecting another Herbie Mc, and chances are he'll blow your little cotton socks off before he takes ya'll down to minus 50."

"A herbie what?" asked William, slipping his feet into a pair of white bunny boots.

"A hurricane blizzard, sir," said James. "We call them herbies sir. But it's only a Condition 2, nothing to worry about."

"Hey these boots are too big," complained William.

James pointed at the EWC pile, "You forgot your thermals socks, and fleece booties, sir. Your boots are one size bigger to compensate."

"Finally," said the DJ, "you'll be relieved to know that the Penguin Flu epidemic over at the Hotel California is under control, so all ya'll can chill even more. But remember ... if you run into a coughing penguin, don't offer him a hanky, run for Mount Erebus! .... And here's a classic one from The Mama's And Papa's, for those happy campers missing their bunks over there in Building 155."

"Now you look the part, sir," James beamed, as California Dreamin' blared out of the radio. William had finally managed to get his huge mittens on, and looked like something from a 1950's B Horror movie. Two black goggled eyes stared out of a black balaclava, bright yellow mittens hung on the end of a bright red body, and black thermal pants sat on top of bright white bunny boots.

"I woook widikulosu," said William, standing in front of a full length mirror, his voice muffled by the balaclava.

"You look real cool to me, sir," lied James, bobbing up and down to the music with his arms open, "kinda like a Rap star. Just like 50 cent."

William ignored him and continued to turn in the mirror.

"Hey, I got it," James giggled, "instead of 50 cent, we could call you 50 D, as in 50 Degrees below, get it homey?"

"Wvery vunny," said William, making a mental note to rename James 50 F, as in 50 Feet below if he carries on ridiculing him like this, "I'm wooassting ... it's more liwke 50 abowve!"

"Nice one homey," said James, clicking his fingers to the beat. "Don't worry, you'll get used to the heat." He stopped bopping as William took his balaclava off and gave him a hard stare. "As soon as we get outside, you'll be glad of the heat, trust me sir."

"And I hope there'll be no more surprises over at Frosty's place?" said William. "There's nothing you need to tell me now, no more hotel nightmares, for example?"

James gulped, "No sir," and crossed his fingers behind his back, "everything is running smoothly over there at Frosty's.

"And the industrial boiler?"

"We've just installed the last shipment from DumbHK, and Hotstuff will be firing on all pistons when you're ready to go."

"Who?"

James smiled again, letting out a wolf whistle, "Hotstuff, sir, the team gave the boiler a new name recently"

William nodded his approval. "Yes I can see why. Hotstuff ... well she certainly is hot, or she soon will be."

"No doubt about it sir," said James. "With the new equipment fitted, she's so hot now she's even twerking."

"Twerking?"

"It's that new dance craze sir," explained James. "You must have seen the youngsters wriggly from side to side provocatively, sticking out their butts."

"She's got that wriggly dancing thing going on as well?"

"Yes sir," said James, "even though she's not been fully powered up, Hotstuff twerks from side to side when the heat really gets going. The whole boiler room shakes with her."

William turned his back to the mirror and tried to twerk, checking the swing of his backside.

Captain James walked over to him, "That's not quite right sir," he bent forward and started gyrating his hips, his backside extended until it was nearly polishing the mirror, and used his knees to bounce up and down gently, "this is it sir, nice circular motions, with backward pelvic thrusts," he let out a primordial harrumph as his backside shot out, "in time with the main beat ."

William put his balaclava and goggles back on so that he could lift his Red Parka, to focus more on his bum's movements. Minutes later they were both twerking, bumping bums every few seconds.

"That's it sir!" shouted James.

"It fweeells gwreeat," William said. "Just like a good workout, I couwd wreeely get into disss!"

Suddenly the dorm door opened. Neither of them noticed at first, but one of James' underlings had come in to tell them that their transport was ready. "Sir!" the underling cleared his throat and shouted even louder, as their bums kissed repeatedly, "Sir!"

It was no use, William and James were twerking for America, whooping and yelling to their hearts content. Then the radio went off, and a goggled eyed monster and Captain James turned around to be greeted by a bespectacled, blushing minion, who whispered awkwardly, avoiding eye contact, be it goggled eyed or not: "The transport's ready sir."

Without saying a word, Captain James pointed at the door, and the minion nearly fell over his two left feet, clambering to get out.

William took his balaclava off. His face was flush and his blond locks dangled scraggily down one side of his face. "And how's Hotstuff doing down there?"

"As you know, sir," James said, his voice dropping an octave to assert his manliness, "the tunnelling under the Ross Ice Shelf has been going very well, and preliminary tests have already started the melting process. But with this new equipment installed, Hotstuff will cut through the rest like a knife through a slab of continental butter."

"That good?"

"Put it this way sir," said James with a wry grin, "by the time we're finished with the Ross Ice Shelf, you'll never run out of ice cubes again."

"Great work," said William, putting his balaclava back on, "the pictures and videos you've been sending me look great, but I can't wait to see it for real. Come on, let's get a move on."

Chapter 30

Another Change Of Plans

"Sure who was you expecting," said Paddynini, "U2?"

"No it's just that ..." Ryan stammered trying to explain that he was amazed to see them here. But Paddynini interrupted him, raised his glass and said, "Well lads, you took your time, but you finally made it, how's the craic?" A few of the other Cracker Craics joined in, "Howya!! We're The Cracker Craics... how's the craic? ... are ye well?" While everyone else in the bar raised their glass to welcome the lads from Eirestown.

"'Deed they took their time alright," someone shouted from a booth near the open log fire, on top of which a few sods of turf had been freshly laid. "Anyone would think Eirestown is on the other side of the world."

"It is," a drunken reveller shouted, before he fell off his barstool. Fortunately his bulbous, green, velour hat broke his fall, and he was back on the stool in minutes.

"Sure, I don't believe it," said QuickMIC, looking over at the booth, "it's another talking penguin, a small one at that." He raised a finger to scratch his chin, in deep thought. "It must be a Fairy penguin."

"A Fairy penguin?" said Ryan, "You just made that name up."

"Not at all," said QuickMIC, "the species *eudyptula minor* is the Little Blue Penguin, also known as the Fairy Penguin."

"Rubbish, what kind of penguin smokes a pipe?" Donn-Dubh asked, nodding in the penguin's direction, "Look-it."

"That's no penguin," said QuickMIC, zooming his telescopic eyes for a close-up, when the penguin finally turned around and blew a raspberry at them, "that's Malachy Malarkey."

"Three cheers for Malachy Malarkey," Paddynini shouted into the microphone, raising his glass to start the first cheer, "HIP HIP BRRRRRPPPPPP!!!!!!" The whole pub joined in for next two cheers and the last raspberry nearly ripped the roof off.

"How do like the disguise lads?" Malachy asked when they joined him in the booth.

"I think the three tailed hat with the bells on the end," answered Ryan, "kind of gives it away. Don't you?"

"Do you think I'm as daft as you look?" teased Malachy, pulling up a black oval shaped hood to cover the hat and his shillelagh shaped, elongated head, leaving his face exposed.

"That's grand," said Donn-Dubh, Malachy's rosy cheeks and ebullient smile on full display. "Just do us all a favour, now."

"What's that?" asked Malachy.

"Cover your face," chuckled Donn-Dubh.

"Are you on your own?" asked Ryan.

"I am now," said Malachy, frowning at Donn-Dubh.

"Now," said QuickMIC, "what do you mean by, *I am now*?

"I did have those six iShillelagh Irish Wolf Hounds with me," Malachy continued. "But you wouldn't believe it."

"Believe what?"

"As soon as we landed, didn't they run off shouting something about rabbits."

"No I don't believe it," said QuickMIC, his eyes flashing bright red. "You brought those crazy Wolf Hounds, out here."

"I did."

"Why on God's earth would anyone bring them wild savages anywhere?"

Malachy told QuickMIC to calm down, and waited for his eyes to return to a more relaxed blue. Then he explained that Eógan had managed to reprogram the Wolf Hounds – or change their demons as Eógan described it - and suggested he bring them to the Antarctica as back up, just in case things got out of hand.

"Look-it," said QuickMIC, struggling to take it all in. "Never mind all that, what are you actually doing here in the first place?" he paused to take a sip of Ryan's Green Avalanche, his nerves getting the better of his emotional control circuits again. "And more importantly, how did you get here so fast? We left you in the town hall square. And why are you smoking a pipe? "

"Now let me see," Malachy said, holding up a closed hand and counting out his fingers, starting with his thumb. "One: King Cormac sent me as an advanced scout; two, to do a bit of digging; three, to make the necessary preparations and establish contacts for ye; and four, the pipe is empty, it's part of the disguise." He hesitated and looked around, even glancing under the table. Then he placed a finger to his lips, and shushed. "As for the travel details," his voice went even fainter, "they must remain secret."

"What?" said QuickMIC, straining to hear him. "Speak up man!"

"I said," boomed Malachy, nearly knocking QuickMIC off his bar stool, "the travels plans must remain secret." Then he lowered his voice again, "Suffice to say that the King has a vehicle which is powered by Higgs Boson particles."

"Higgs Boson particles?" said QuickMIC, sceptically.

"The very same," said Malachy. "Remember now, he won the Nobel Prize for having jars full of them lying around the place."

"Sure I'm King Cormac's Chief Technical Adviser," QuickMIC complained, "and I know nothing about this."

"Don't worry yourself," said Malachy, looking over his shoulder to make sure no one was listening in, "sure the vehicle's so secret that the King himself knows nothing about it either."

"But why Higgs Boson particles?" repeated QuickMIC, genuinely intrigued.

"They allow us to travel at 99% of the speed of light," said Malachy.

"Get outta here," said Ryan, taking a sip of Green Avalanche. "You can travel at the speed of light?"

"No," corrected Malachy, "you can't travel at the speed of light."

"Why not?" asked Ryan.

"That would be a violation of Einstein's theory of Special Relativity," said QuickMIC authoritatively.

"Einstein's theory of Special Relativity?" scoffed Malachy, taking a sip of a Green Avalanche. "Sure that's not the reason why you can't travel at the speed of light."

"Then what is?" said Ryan.

"If you travelled at the speed of light, you wouldn't be able to see where you were going," answered Malachy. "And that's why The Eirestown Flash travels at 99% of the speed of light. We leave the other 1% ahead of us like a headlamp."

"The Eirestown Flash?" said Ryan

"The very same," said Malachy. "That's the name of our almost as fast as light ship," he added. "And before know it all here asks," he sneered at QuickMIC and went on, "the Flash exploits the decay of the Higgs Boson particle, giving us almost unlimited energy supply, and propulsion that packs a real feisty punch. Like one of them country fellas from the bogs."

Malachy looked around again, reached into a satchel, and pulled out some detailed plans, along with a few sheets of mathematical equations. "Look-it, here's the complete design." With the group huddled in, he pointed to one corner, "Over here's the unit which controls the decay process. Sure we call that the Decay Processing Unit, DPU for short. See how it uses certain types of electromagnetic energy, creating standing wave harmonics which control the Higgs Boson decay, thereby providing the necessary particles," he reached for his drink, took a gulp and pointed to a few other areas of the design, "for the propulsion unit over here, and the energy matter converter over here. And here's a head full of quantum mechanical, special and general relativity equations which prove the concept. But like I say," concluded Malachy, wrapping up the plans and equations and stuffing them back into his satchel, "at the moment it's all top secret."

"If the King has that kind of advanced technology at his disposal," asked QuickMIC, "then I repeat, why did we have to risk our lives flying here in The Eirestown Pop?"

"Are you a t'ick eejit or what?" said Malachy, also repeating himself. "I just told you: The Eirestown Flash is secret. So secret in fact, that even King Cormac doesn't know about it. Sure it's so advanced it even uses stealth technology, to hide itself, when it's empty."

"Stealth technology," said Ryan, "she's invisible then, just like that plane, the F-117?"

"She's invisible alright," fretted Malachy, "which presents me with a little problem."

"What?"

"I've forgotten where I parked her," he sighed.

"Are you not worried you'll lose all the documents, or they'll be taken off you?" asked Ryan.

"Not at all," said Malachy, "all the information's printed on the same sort of paper as The Eirestown Press. It will be blank if anyone else gets hold of it."

"And why are you wearing that silly hat?" said Donn-Dubh.

"I could ask you the same question," smiled Malachy. "I brought the hat with me for someone out here. You'll find out who soon enough."

"Well?" interrupted QuickMIC, annoyed that Malachy appeared to know more about technology than he did.

"Well what?"

"Have you made any contacts and what have you found out?"

"I've contacts enough," replied Malachy, "and I've found out more than you'll ever know."

"So?" said QuickMIC.

"So?" replied Malachy.

"What's going on?"

"Erebus," whispered Malachy.

"The volcano?" whispered QuickMIC.

"The very same."

"What about it?" whispered Ryan.

"I'm not sure," whispered Malachy, "but there are rumours."

"And the contacts?" whispered Donn-Dubh.

Malachy stuck two fingers in his mouth and let out three sharp whistles, leaving the huddled group with ringing ears. The whole bar came to a standstill and there was complete silence. A few moments later the front door creaked and started to revolve slowly. One by one, two large muscular Emperor penguins waddled into Murphy's. They wore white Advanced Combat Helmets and carried Mini-M249 US machine guns, which were smaller versions of the original M249, and had bandoliers slung across their shoulders sash style, the ammunition criss-crossed down to their waist. They took up positions either side of the revolving door, and one of them shouted, "Clear!"

The door slowly revolved again and another penguin sashayed in. Dwarfed by the other two, this was a rockhopper penguin. However, because of a genetic mutation, he had pink plumage, instead of blue. He wore a US Military style ECWCS parka, with subtle pink and white camouflage motifs, and a pink shoulder bag. A bright pink fur ruff ran around the parka's neckline, the ends of which were sticking out of a tightly fitting cobra hood.

"Ohhh myyy cooollld!" the rockhopper shrieked in a nasally, Brooklyn accent, stepping out of the revolving door. Because of his accent, when he spoke he didn't walk or talk, he *wawked* and *tawked*. Rubbing his hands together briskly, he pulled his hood down to reveal a spiked white and pink hair style. "Let me tell ya! Tawk about the cold." He stroked his beak a few times and nudged one of the large penguins, "Is it still there?" then he nudged the other, "Can you see it ... huh, can you? My beak's numb," and stamping his feet he carried on moaning, "and I can't remember the last time I felt my feet. This cold is breaking my shoes."

The two large penguins, standing either side of him, nodded up at the ceiling in despair shaking their heads, glanced down at his pink UGG boots and remained silent.

"To think I left a life of luxury in Central Pawk Zoo for this, pleassseee!" the little pink penguin yelled. "Somebody call me a cab, or get me a drink or somethin'."

He stamped and huffed a few more times and then blurted, "Hey there," waving in the direction of the bar, "hey! CUUU-EEEE, CUUU-EEEE," he shrieked, "what's a boy gotta do to get a drink round here?" As soon as he had the bartender's attention he blew a kiss and said, "Be a dear and prepare me a flamin'sambuca ... take it easy on the ice though," he fanned himself at this point, "but don't spare the flames, I got to get me some heat." Then he spoke to one of the large penguins, "What are you doing?"

"Who me?" said the large penguin, pointing a flipper at himself.

"Ohhh myyy gaaawwwddd," said the little penguin, arms akimbo. "No your mothaaa."

"Why my mother's doing swell, thank you," said the big penguin. "How's yours?"

"I'm surrounded by imbeciles," said the little penguin. "Forget your mothaaa, I meant you." He jabbed an aggressive, pink flipper in the large penguins lower stomach several times, "YOU," jab, "YOU," jab, "YOU," jab, "YOU," jab, "What are you doing?"

As confused as he was, before the large penguin had a chance to answer, the little penguin pointed to the bar and screamed, "Well don't just stand there: fetch!"

Groaning and rubbing his stomach, the emperor reluctantly waddled over to the bar, with several condescending remarks ringing in his ears and returned a moment later with the flamin'sambuca.

"God help his mothaaa," said the little penguin, taking the drink off him, "that's all I can say. God help his mothaaa."

"Meet the team," said Malachy, when the penguins finally waddled over to the booth to join them. Well the two large ones waddled, the small one sashayed, the flipper holding the sambuca extended, and the other flipper on his hip.

"Talking penguins?" said Ryan. "I can't believe it, they're everywhere."

"You're in the Antarctica honey, get over it," said the rockhopper. "And anyway, you're sat next to a couple of wawking, tawking iShillelaghs," the little penguin added, "and you're surprised by tawking penguins?"

"But penguins," Ryan stammered, "it's just like that film, Happy Feet."

"Well I can tell you one thing, honey," said the pink rockhopper, "you can forget all that Hollywood fantasy stuff about glamorous, happy-clappy penguins out here in the Antarctica, shuckin' and jiving' for the man, because," he took a gulp of his flamin'sambuca, dejectedly glanced down at his UGG boots, and sighed, "trust me darling, these ice blocks on the end of my legs may be glamorous, but they are certainly not happy."

"Sorry," said Ryan.

"And less of that penguin tawk, darling," the pink rockhopper went on, "if you really don't mind. No one calls you homo sapien sapien, now do they?"

Ryan apologised again.

"You kidding me with that hat, or what?" said Squawky, commenting on Donn-Dubh's hat. "I've seen some hats in my time honey, but that one I'll need therapy for."

Donn-Dubh kissed his teeth, and Malachy made the introductions. He introduced the two large penguins first, "This is Orky and Dorky," and then the pink rockhopper, "and this is Squawky. These guys are like my brothers from another mother. They've been looking after me since I got here."

"And I'm afraid, leaving our mothaaas outta of this, we're going to look after all of you now," said Squawky ominously.

"What do you mean?" said Malachy warily.

"Honey," said Squawky, sipping on his flamin'sambuca, "I'm afraid there's been a change of plans."

"A change of plans?" Malachy gasped. "I'm not sure I like the sound of that."

"I wouldn't like the sound of it either," said Squawky. And before Malachy had a chance to ask why not, he clicked a flipper and issued the command, "Boys!"

"On your feet," ordered Dorky, pointing his mini-M249 at Malachy. "And you lot, too," said Orky pointing his mini-M249 at Ryan, Donn-Dubh and QuickMIC. "We're going for a ride."

Chapter 31

Open Sesame

For two people who didn't do cold, Ryan and Donn-Dubh couldn't believe they were actually in Antarctica, snow and sleet lashing at their faces as they flew across crevasse and ravine. For a brief moment, in their excitement, they had forgotten that they'd been kidnapped, or penguin-napped as their captors preferred to call it, and they were currently huddled together, strapped to the back of a sledge, where Malachy and QuickMIC were also tied together. However, Malachy was gagged as well, because he wouldn't stop protesting and calling Squawky *a back-stabbin'-good-for-nothing-son-of-a-mothaaa* when he was escorted out of Murphy's On The Rocks at gunpoint.

Their cargo secured and silenced, the penguin-nappers headed north east for several hours, away from McMurdo, along the Hut Peninsula. Orky and Dorky took turns at the helm, cracking the whip above the head of thirty two Little Blue penguins. The oul' terrified, little mites hopped up and down from the back of the sledge-gang to the front, taking small leaps forward in a synchronised, rhythmic, caterpillar motion, hauling the sledge, with many a MUSH-MUSH between cracked whips.

"Be careful boys, be careful," squealed Squawky, jumping down from the sledge when it came to an abrupt standstill, flinging the unprepared penguin-napped passengers face first onto the ground. "The Boss wants them all in one piece, kapish?"

"Kapish," Orky and Dorky replied, wondering why Squawky had recently started to use Mafia speak.

They had come to a halt under a large rock shelter, which was roofed by thirty meters of snow covered basalt, on the side of a mountain. The edge of the overhang was lined with different sized icicles, which sparkled and glittered in the sun. Ryan struggled to breath, crushed by Donn-Dubh and QuickMIC, who were flung on top of him when the sledge stopped without warning. Malachy was like an ostrich with his head in the sand, except his head was embedded deep in a pile of snow.

"Come on," commanded Orky, waving his mini-M249, as Dorky dragged them off the pile one-by-one, "get a move on."

Malachy didn't move, in fact he couldn't move, what with his head buried and his hands tied behind his back. Dorky struggled to pull him out of the snow, his head leaving on the last tug with an almighty plop.

"Hmmm," screamed Malachy through his gag, "mmmwhhttt thhheee mmm, hhhmmm." Dorky pulled his gag down to hear what he was saying. Malachy took a deep breath of air and let rip, "*You-back-stabbin'-good-for-nothing-son-of-a-mothaaa.*" Satisfied that Malachy was not hurt, Dorky replaced the gag.

"Hhhmmm ... hhhmmm!" and gave him a flipper across the back of his head, knocking him back into the snow.

"Where are we?" asked Ryan, getting another flipper in his face as an answer from Dorky. "Ooowww!"

"Oh do be careful, you brute," said Squawky, jumping up onto Dorky's shoulder, and giving him a flipper across the side of his face. "Your face might be fit for radio," he sneered at Dorky, while gently stroking Ryan's face, "but this is such a handsome, delicate face." He continued to rub Ryan's cheeks with both flippers and answered, "If you must know handsome, we're half way up Mount Erebus."

"You're not taking us up there are you?" asked QuickMIC, worried that they might be on their way to the active crater on top of Mount Erebus. "Sure that's an active volcano."

"Move it," shouted Orky.

"But Mount Erebus," protested QuickMIC, "she could be about to blow."

"Move it," Dorky repeated, digging his mini-M249 into QuickMIC's ribs, "or my little friend here will blow a hole into the side of your stomach."

"Please," QuickMIC pleaded with Squawky, "she could erupt at any moment."

"Really?" said Squawky, jumping back down into the snow, where he stamped his pink UGG boots a few times. "How quaint, an active volcano. Just what I need, a lava foot spa, my feet are freezing."

"Are you serious ..." began QuickMIC, but Dorky silenced him with a poke of his M249.

Squawky sashayed over to the thirty two Little Blue penguins, officially known as the sledge-gang, intent on congratulating them on a job well done. "Whoa, wait a minute, now that's what you call my kinda blue."

Except for their harnesses, the Little Blue penguins were commando, and cooling down rapidly had altered their colour slightly. "You know I could really do with that colour in my boudoir," Squawky carried on, pulling a magazine from a pocket inside his pink ECWCS parka. It was a New York Times supplement, dedicated to interior design. "You kidding me, or what?" He placed the centre spread next to the darkened plumage of one of the frozen little penguins in the middle of the sledge-gang. "This shade would match my curtains perfectly."

"Glad you like it," said the freezing cold, chattering penguin, "I'm a few shades darker than normal. You should see me just after a bath in one of Erebus' heated springs. You might prefer that shade in your bathroom."

Squawky put the magazine away immediately, and pulled out a paper bag from another pocket. "Here, please take a few, you've earned it," and he gave the chattering penguin some petite chocolate penguins, filled with Crème brûlée, which had been purchased from L.A. Burdick NYC. "Oh you poor little mites, you must be starving, here, here," he handed a few chocolate penguins around to enthusiastic thanks you and a little cold, flipper applause. "I know, I know, call me a martyr already, but what you gonna do?"

"A martyr," said the sledge-gang lead, gasping for air, sweat dripping off him in buckets, "you kidding me?"

A few of the others behind the lead gulped.

"You tawking to me?" said Squawky, putting the bag back in his pocket, and sashaying rapidly to the front of the sledge-gang.

The lead penguin looked around as if to say, there's no one else here, and said, "No I'm talking to your mothaaa."

A moment later the lead penguin was dangling in the air, a mini-M249 embedded in one of his temples, and a Swiss Army knife resting on his throat.

"You want we should kill him boss?" said Orky, his finger poised on the mini-M249's trigger.

"Yeah," said Dorky, pushing the Swiss Army knife into his throat a little, "you want we should kill him, boss?"

"I may have a refined palate," said Squawky, "but château de manchot might be too sophisticated, even for my liking."

"Huh?" said Dorky.

"Château de penguin."

"Huh?"

"You've got the corkscrew on his neck," snarled Squawky, "you imbecile!"

"Gee, sorry, boss," said Dorky, pushing the cork screw back into the handle of the Swizz Army Knife, and pulling out a razor sharp blade. "Well do you want us to kill him or not? After all he insulted your mothaaa."

"Hmmm," said Squawky, placing a finger on his pursed lips, "just look at all this lovely white snow. It would be such a shame to stain it with bright red blood, don't you think?"

"Yes it would," gurgled the lead penguin, appealing to Squawky's interior design sensibilities, "and it's probably blue blood by now, it'll be a garish contrast to say the least."

"You know what," said Squawky, ignoring the penguin's colour blend critique, "I've a better idea. Un-harness him," he waved his hand as if fanning away a bad smell, "and put him at the back of the line"

"No," screamed the lead penguin, bouncing his neck on-and-off the blade a couple of times, "kill me already, and just get it over with."

It had taken him five years to work his way up the gang line. The thought of been downwind of thirty other penguins was almost too much too bear, especially after they'd had a night on baby octopus, which played havoc with their gastrointestinal tracts.

"Oh," added Squawky, "one more thing, they can forget the chocolates." Turning to Dorky, he said, "Let them eat their fill of octopus."

While the lead was unharnessed and plonked in his new position, Squawky made his way to the other end of the rock shelter, where he found a large vertical slab of basalt. Having fed the sledge-gang enough baby octopus to sink a whale, Dorky and Orky caught up with him, pushing and prodding the Eirestown captives in front of them.

"We're here boss," announced Dorky.

"You don't say," said Squawky, his flippers stretched across the vertical slab, and one UGG boot wedged into a knee high crack, "and here's me thinking it was the Yetti creeping up behind me."

"What you doing boss," asked Orky, "you gonna climb it?"

"I'm looking for the entrance," said Squawky, shaking one of his pink UGG boots, "you think I could climb anything in these things? It takes me all my time to get up the stairs."

"Entrance?" said Dorky.

"Yes," said Squawky, running his flippers along several more cracks on the basalt slab's surface, "the switch is in here somewhere." He carried on fiddling in numerous nooks, cracks and crannies, stopping every now and then, plunging his flippers deeper inside. "It's been a while, but I'm sure it's in here," he grunted, pushing even deeper into one moss encased hole, "somewhere!"

After another thirty minutes of fumbling with the rock, including a few higher incursions from the shoulders of Dorky, Squawky was exasperated and exhausted. "That's it, I give up!" he screamed, flopping to the floor.

"Why don't you just use the voice activated password?" said Orky,

"Yeah," agreed Dorky, "why don't you use the voice activated password, that's what we do."

Squawky gave them the kind of look a wife gives a husband after he's opened a screw-capped bottle of wine with a corkscrew, "What password?"

"Open Sesame," said Dorky and Orky in unison, giving each other a high-five.

Squawky jumped to his feet and was about to berate them both, with a few slaps around their heads, when the ten foot high slab of basalt creaked, groaned and slowly slid to one side, revealing a cavernous entrance into Mount Erebus.

"Welcome to The Erebus Hilton," said Dorky, when the slab had fully opened. "Now move it," he commanded, prodding the captives in.

Squawky looked at his dirty flippers with repulsion. Some of those nooks had been disgusting. Taking a few wipes out of his shoulder bag, he looked up at the clear blue sky in a state of incredulity, "God help their mothaaas," he sighed deeply, brushing and wiping moss and slime from his pink parka and flippers. Then he followed them into the cavern, scrubbing the end of his manicured flippers, and grumbling under his breath, "That's all I can say. God help their mothaaas."

Chapter 32

Welcome To The Lava Suite

"Pooh it stinks, is that you?" said Donn-Dubh pinching his nose. He recalled one time in Eirestown on a farm, when he stepped into a cow-pat. But this smell was much worse. "Well is it?"

"Not me," said Orky, giving Dorky a questioning glance.

"Do ye have King Cormac here by any chance?" asked Malachy. "He's a right smell on him when he's trumping."

"No," answered Orky, "never heard of him."

"Then what the hell is that smell?" asked Donn-Dubh again. "Has someone dropped a rotten egg?"

"Hydrogen sulphide honey, if you must know," said Squawky, spraying a few squirts of DKNY Golden Delicious in front of him, "an unfortunate by-product of an active volcano."

"Any chance the lads can get a peg?" asked Malachy.

Dorky twiddled with the peg on the end of his own nose and said in a nasally tone, "There are to be no prisoner privileges."

Despite their reservations, Ye Olde Ross Ice Shelf Committee had been pleasantly surprised when they entered the basalt doorway, halfway up Mount Erebus. For a start, despite the smell, it was lovely and warm, and they found themselves in a ceiling lit corridor. At the end of the corridor they could see a glass elevator which moved in one of six directions, forward, backward, left, right, up and down. Their first direction was backwards.

The basalt door way became a point of receding light in the distance, as the elevator quickly reversed away from it, with safety lights flying past them on either side. After twenty minutes or so, the elevator slowed down, came to a standstill and changed direction.

Leaving their stomachs behind, it soon became clear that they were going down, way down ... deeper than that even ... the elevator seemed to penetrate to the very foundations of Mount Erebus. For the first few hundred meters all they could see was the dimly lit rock face accelerate past them, then suddenly a blast of light hit them as the elevator entered a vast open chasm. After another five minutes the elevator stopped, and they were prodded out into an underground foyer.

"The heat is unbearable," said Ryan, unzipping his coat, "any chance we can take our parkas off?"

"Keep it down there," said Dorky, digging Ryan in the ribs with his mini-M249, "or you'll get some real heat!"

QuickMIC was amazed at the size and shape of the foyer, which represented only a very small section of the map on the elevator wall. That map had been impressive, and outlined a vast multileveled, subterranean complex, covering an enormous area. Included on the map were shopping malls, cinema complexes, health suits, gymnasiums, restaurant complexes, living quarters, everything and anything which an army would need to survive down here. The foyer itself was no less impressive. Dome shaped, like Donn-Dubh's hat, it extended at least twenty five stories high, with glass encased corridors and floors, and numerous passage ways. It was definitely man made, and must have taken years to carve out. It had a glass ceiling part way up, through which you could see a spot of daylight in the distance, which he assumed was the surface. Much of the floor was also fabricated from glass sheets, underneath which QuickMIC could see numerous lava streams approximately fifty meters below, and, if he wasn't wrong, some of those appeared to be running through manmade trenches. Large cast iron pipes ran around the upper levels of the cavernous dome, and bursts of steam could be heard and seen where many sections of piping connected.

Throughout the foyer, there were huge plasma screens, dotted here and there. One, the size of a house, took prime position on the wall directly opposite the elevator. Leading off the foyer in every direction were doors and corridors, too many to count. And there were penguins everywhere, a whole city full, many with different coloured construction hats on, all waddling about their business without even noticing Ye Olde Ross Ice Shelf Committee's arrival.

"Wawk this way," said Squawky, exiting the elevator. Holding his left flipper on his hip, his right flipper aloft, palm side up, he sashayed towards a door on the right hand side of the foyer.

"I'm not walking like that," said Malachy, "sure I'll be the laughing stock of Eirestown."

Ryan couldn't help himself and broke into fits of giggles. "He didn't mean ..." began Ryan, but Malachy winked at him, placed his hands on his hips and sashayed, with elegant panache, as close behind Squawky as was possible.

Squawky opened the door flamboyantly and said, "Welcome to the Lava Suite boys, the best room in The Erebus Hilton."

"What was that hissing noise?" asked Ryan.

"Airlock honey," said Squawky, "keeps that dreadful smell out." Then he waved his flipper, directing the committee in one-by-one. "In you go, come on now, make yourselves comfortable," he looked up as Ryan passed him, "especially you dear. You've got a long day ahead of you tomorrow."

The Lava Suite may have been the best room in the Erebus Hilton, but it was effectively a prison cell, albeit a very comfortable one. Someone had been expecting them and had done their best to ensure their stay was comfortable. In one corner of the suite, there was a pan of freshly prepared Irish stew, gently bubbling on a range. In the middle of the room there was an oak table and several chairs. On top of the table Ryan could see a few empty bowls and a plate full of soda bread. "Thank God for that," he said, running over to take a seat at the table, "I'm starving."

"Hands!" yelled Squawky.

"What?"

Squawky didn't even speak, he just grimaced at Ryan, rubbed his flippers together and pointed at another door, which led to an en-suite bathroom.

"And when you're done in there," said Squawky, opening another door to reveal a small stock room with a single mattress, bedding and white pyjamas, "prepare your bed before you eat."

After they'd all washed, to save some time, Donn-Dubh served the stew while the others put mattresses on the floor, and prepared the bed.

They were starving and exhausted. Malachy was so tired that he fell asleep at the table with a spoon hanging out of his mouth. Ryan quickly finished his own bowl and carried him to the mattress, where he tucked him in. Not long after, they were all in bed, where they hoped to get at least ten hours sleep.

Unfortunately it felt like they'd literally only had one wink of sleep when they were rudely awakened.

"Did you guys sleep ok?"

"The mattress was a bit small," said Ryan, rubbing his eyes.

"Really?"

"Yes," said Malachy, "when one of us turned all the others had to."

"I'll have you all strapped in next time," said Squawky, smiling. "Ohhh myyy follicles ... Honey, now please do something with that hair."

Squawky, dressed in a tight fitting, pink DKNY onesie, and sporting a Ralph Laruen white baseball cap - which had cut-outs either side to let his spiked hair through, had just entered the Lava Suite and was standing over Ryan's sleepy head. "Here let me help you," he said, pulling a pink brush out of his shoulder bag, and running it through Ryan's blond mop, trying to restore some order, after a night of tossing and turning.

"Give me that," Ryan snapped, snatching the brush off Squawky.

"You kiddin' me'?" gasped Squawky. "You look like Donald Trump with that hay stack on your head." He tried to snatch the brush back, "Now give that back to me, and I'll have you ready for the cat wawk in no time."

Ryan pushed Squawky away, jumped up and walked into the en-suite, where he brushed his hair in the mirror above the sink.

"You've an awful big nose," said Malachy, who was just beneath Ryan, brushing his teeth, "and I can see a few bogies up there."

In no mood for jokes, Ryan picked Malachy out of the sink, and dropped him into an empty waste paper basket underneath it, "There you go Malachy, your very own bogie free zone."

"Now, now, boys," said Squawky, who was standing at the en-suite door, "we'll have less squabbling."

Malachy popped his head out of the basket first, and then scrambled out of it. "Ryan's very touchy this morning," he said to Squawky, "sure I was only giving him a little grooming advice, to sharpen up his appearance. Sure you never know who's going to look up your nose next."

"Funny you should mention appearance Malachy," said Squawky, "since we're almost the same size, I thought ..."

"Thought what?" said Malachy.

"That we can't have you wawking around in that abysmal penguin disguise any longer," he replied. "I've brought you a change of clothes."

"Right," said Ryan, patting down his fringe and admiring himself in the mirror, "that's it."

"You with hair," said Squawky, "you kiddin' me?"

Ryan stepped over Squawky, in two minds about stamping on his head, and out of the en-suite.

"Where's my old clothes?" said Malachy.

"Incinerated," said Squawky, handing him a shoulder bag, "I couldn't take the chance."

"What chance?"

"Who knows," surmised Squawky, "with a penguin suit on, you might have slipped away in a penguin crowd. And honey, having only just met, I'd hate to lose you so soon."

"I wouldn't dream of it," argued Malachy, taking the shoulder back from Squawky, "even if you had given me enough time to dream last night."

"Don't worry," said Squawky, sashaying out of the en-suite. "There'll be plenty of time to sleep. Now get dressed quickly, the boss is waiting. Oh and Ryan ..."

"Yes?" groaned Ryan, hanging his head in his hands.

"On second thoughts, honey, I absolutely love that hipster hairstyle!" And then he wawked outside the Lava Suite, where he said he would wait for them.

Ten minutes later they were all dressed and ready to go, all except for Malachy.

"Come on now Malachy," shouted QuickMIC through the en-suite door, "sure everyone's waiting."

"Ye promise ye won't laugh?" Malachy shouted back through the door.

"Cop yourself on now Malachy," said QuickMIC earnestly, "sure this is no time for laughing."

Assurances in place, Malachy opened the door and slowly exited the en-suite in his new change of clothes.

"Would you look at the cut of that?" QuickMIC hollered, nearly laughing the head off himself, when Malachy finally appeared wearing a pink DKNY sarong, and a yellow Ralph Lauren baker boy hat on the end of his head, tilted to the side, in the Jennifer Lopez style.

"Jesus," QuickMIC went on, himself in bits and his eyes an ecstatic yellow, "sure you must be Malachy's twin sister." Composing himself a little, he zoomed his eyes in and out the full length of Malachy, extended his hand and introduced himself, "I'm QuickMIC an oul' friend of your brother, and I'm very pleased to meet you."

Malachy turned his head defiantly, brushed QuickMIC's hand away and strolled confidently passed him, determined to ignore him. But when QuickMIC saw the pair of Christian Louboutin multi-coloured spikes on the end of Malachy's feet, sure didn't the laughter take him away altogether, and didn't he have to be carried out of the Lava Suite by Ryan and Donn-Dubh, the two of them also shaking with the laugher.

Chapter 33

Now Where Are Those Brakes?

"Welcome to the world's highest desert, sir!"

"A desert?" said William, "what about all this snow and ice?"

"Only 2% precipitation per year, sir," answered Captain James, "that's a desert in my book. A paradoxical one perhaps, but a desert none-the-less."

"Fascinating," said William, gliding through the snow, "a desert of frozen water."

"The Icicle is some beast, eh?" said James, throwing them in and out of a few tight turns, through invisible hairpins.

William and James were literally flying up the Hut Peninsula at times, towards Erebus, in a two man Ice Vehicle called the Icicle, which looked like a three-way cross between a plane, a sledge and a large bluish, translucent bullet. Captain James had only driven the Icicle once before on a short test run, but after the EUVx golf buggy fiasco, he was taking no chances, and had pulled out all the stops to impress William. Fortunately, William was thoroughly impressed, and said that the ice blue, truncated, cone shaped cockpit, enclosed by a large panoramic window, reminded him of an Apollo Command Module.

Sleek and stylish, Captain James said that the Icicle was fabricated primarily out of light weight aluminium. "And the four skis," he continued, pointing underneath the cockpit, where four skis, two oversized ones at the back which stuck out like wings on the end of girders, and two central ones in front, supporting and transporting the cone, "are Teflon coated. She literally flies along the ice and snow on these." Patting one affectionately, he added that the skis had been designed to provide a frictionless contact path. "And notice how each ski is mounted independently on these hefty shock absorbers."

"Why's that?" asked William.

"Oh you'll find out soon enough," teased James.

"That's some size," said William, commenting on the jet engine mounted behind the cockpit, "is she fast?"

"That's a jet engine with hyper-speed capability, provided by solid fuel jet boosters, sir," replied James. Adding that, although the average top speed was 150 kilometres per hour, the boosters could propel them forward at speeds of up to 300 kilometres per hour, when necessary.

"That fast?"

"Fast enough to actually leave the ground at times sir," said James. "And if we have to outrun a Herbie Mc, you'll be glad of those boosters. So please make sure you're firmly strapped in."

"What about those wings sticking out on top?" asked William, pointing to two slim line structures which stuck out on either side of the cockpit.

"Stabilising fins, sir. When she does leave the ground they provide downward force, similar to a Formula 1's aerofoils, and they also help control her as she glides though the air."

They'd been travelling along the Hut Peninsula towards Mount Erebus for over thirty minutes now, and taking their time. Within a few miles of leaving McMurdo, William kept asking James to pull over, so he could get out and admire the breathtaking views. Fortunately, the Herbie Mc the Tennessee DJ forecast did not arrive, and it was a brilliantly clear day, with a crystal blue sky. On their first stop, a few miles outside McMurdo, William got a clear view of the summit of Mount Erebus in the distance to his left, spindrift being whipped all around it. "Are we going to the top?" he asked James, worried that he might succumb to altitude sickness. James answered no. They were going to carry on along the Hut Peninsula for a few more miles, as far as a landmark known as Sultans Head Rock. Here they would turn left and pass the top of The Erebus Glacier Tongue, which terminated in Erebus Bay on the edge of McMurdo Sound. Shortly after, they would pass the Turk's Head Ridge and head towards their destination near the Three Sisters Cones.

Shortly after their first stop, William asked James to pull over again, not far from the Sultans Head Rock. Captain James was delighted and jumped out of the Icicle, pointed into the distance and exclaimed with some passion, "Behold your nemesis, Captain Ahab!"

"What?" said William, concerned that James was already succumbing to altitude sickness.

"The Ross Ice Shelf, sir," said Captain James, pointing out over the Windless Bight and further into the distance, where they could see the white leviathan he was comparing to a whale, "it's your Moby Dick."

"Well let's just hope I don't end up like Ahab," growled William, indicating that James could have thought of a more appropriate metaphor.

Having turned left, they stopped once again at the top of the Erebus Glacier Tongue, so that William could take in the view of McMurdo Sound, an ice clogged region which formed a barrier between the Ross Sea and his nemesis.

"I said the Icicle's some beast?" James repeated. It had been fifteen minutes since their last stop, and William was looking out of the panoramic cockpit, absorbed in the surroundings. He had no idea of the scale of things out here. The pictures and videos James had sent him just didn't convey the immensity of it all, and the pristine condition of this unpolluted white wilderness.

"She's some beast," agreed William.

"Slides over the snow and ice like a seal's belly," said James, tugging on the steering wheel to perform another sharp slalom manoeuvre.

"Great shocks and all," said William, "you can hardly feel a thing. I see why the skis are independently mounted."

"The independent mountings are absolutely essential sir, but they're not for going over general terrain."

"They're not?"

"No, we need them just in case we hit any ice boulder fields or sastrugi ...."

"Sas what .... whoooaaa," the Icicle left the ground and William's stomach behind, as it hit an array of sastrugi, which looked like a field of roughly ploughed ice and snow.

"Sastrugi," yelled James, struggling to control the Icicle in mid air. "They're compacted ripples in the snow and ice, formed by the wind."

"Ripples? ....whoooaaa," shrieked William.

"Ripple-ish," shouted Captain James, as they landed with a dampened thud. "Most are very small, but they can be a few meters high, just think of them as snow dunes," he continued, "hold on there, sir, here comes a dune tsunami."

The Icicle undulated aggressively across tens of meters of extreme sastrugi, left the ground one last time and landed with a muted thud, leaving a cloud of snow, twisting in ribbons behind the jet engine.

"Wow," said William, "that was some tsunami!"

"Should be plain sailing from here on in, sir," said James, "almost there now."

As the Icicle zipped along, William inspected the dashboard, "By the way, what are all these instruments? Looks like something out of Star Trek."

"She's got all the latest gadgets and applications, sir," said James, gingerly. He wasn't too sure about all the controls, having only driven her once before, but he was determined, as ever, to impress William.

"Gadgets and applications, sounds like an iPhone on skis?"

"Yes sir," said James, "she's got more gadgets than an iPhone, I can tell you." He took one hand off the steering wheel and gave a quick tour, pointing to buttons, dials, and luminous coloured, gridded screens, all labelled with acronyms.

"iceRAD, ice penetrating radar, sir. Helps us search for underground anomalies, things to avoid falling into. Then there's SatNav and RadMac, that's Radio McTown," James giggled, nudging William, "just in case you should fancy another twerk, eh?" William sighed and cut his eye at him. James coughed apologetically, and his finger flew to the right hand side of the dashboard, where it ran up and down another array of buttons. "Here's the WAP, Wireless Application, Protocol, for wireless communication; DAP, Digital Audio Patrol, to listen out for distress signals, distant animals, penguins, seals, things like that; then there's SAP, BAP, MAP and..."

"Ok, ok, enough already," said William, aware of the huge mound of snow they were rapidly approaching. "WAP, SAP, DAP, BAP, MAP, I get the message.... but how do you actually stop this thing?"

"Oh craaappp!" screamed James, fumbling over the dashboard apprehensively, looking for a BRAKE or STOP button. "Now where are those brakes?"

A few moments later, the Icicle slammed into a ten meter high pile of snow drift, underneath an overhanging basalt rock formation, half way up the side of Mount Erebus.

"I suppose you don't know where reverse is either," said William angrily, rubbing a large bump on his head.

"Affirmative sir."

Chapter 34

Frosty Oighear

"ENTER!"

There really was no need to shout. Squawky had been standing in front of Frosty Oighear for several minutes. However, Frosty was in a foul mood this morning, real foul. The heat in some parts of The Erebus Hilton was becoming unbearable, and the cold in other parts enough to freeze the blood in your veins. Even worse, now that they'd altered the lava flow so much, was the growing stench, which wafted and waned, becoming overwhelming at times. Fortunately the main living areas were all protected with air locks and filtration systems; but still, that smell lingered, and once it got on your clothes, there was no getting rid of it.

Frosty was sorry that he'd ever let Captain James Bush blackmail him into this nonsense in the first place. But that was one of the risks you took when you played poker in Murphy's On The Rocks. Forfeits were big, legendary actually. Only last year, one loser had to re-enact Jonah from The Old Testament, and live inside a blue whale's stomach for three days, or pay up the $10,000 IOU. Jonah's first day went fine, but when he lit a fire to cook some fish the whale had just swallowed, the whale developed a smoker's cough, and subsequently hoicked him out. Whereupon he was scrubbed until blubber-less, and hoicked to the Mac Town ATM, and spent the next ten days drawing the IOU out in batches of $100 bills.

So Frosty's forfeit really wasn't that bad, and it came with a few perks. As often as possible, Frosty Oighear tried to remind himself that Antarctica, with the Ross Ice Shelf gone, would soon be sweltering desert, its edges gently lapped by a brand new ocean named, somewhat unimaginatively, in his honour. His new mansion, built on a lavish promenade full of casinos, eateries and bars with one pier for Las Vegas style entertainment and one for Frosty's theme park, would take pride of place facing Frosty's Ocean. Yes, Mac Town would soon be no more, and Frosty would be the first Mayor of Frosty Town.

"Hello, hello, Frosty," squealed Squawky for the umpteenth time, "I'm already in heaaarrr! Down here!"

Frosty looked down at his brogued feet, where Squawky was busy inspecting his pink, freshly manicured flippers. "So you are," bellowed Frosty, "and where are the saboteurs?"

"Outside, boss," said Squawky, blowing on one end of a freshly painted flipper.

"Well don't just stand there you little pip-squawk, bring them in!"

Having to build Hotstuff these last few years was bad enough, but now Frosty had been asked to kidnap saboteurs and, if necessary, kill them. And not just any old saboteurs, these saboteurs were Irish, and from Eirestown of all places.

"Howya Frosty," Malachy Malarkey was the first to speak when they entered the room. "I'm Malachy Malarkey." Introductions over, he hopped up onto a large table. "Sure it's a nice office you have here." The others remained silent, overawed on one level, but terrified on another. Frosty was a giant of a man, with snarled features which would scare the devil himself.

"It's a boardroom," said Frosty, correcting Malachy.

"Well given the size of it," said Malachy, hopping down onto a chair, "I'd say you must be awfully bored, altogether."

"And what kind of creature are you?" asked Frosty.

"I could ask you the same question meself," said Malachy, removing the yellow Ralph Loren baker boy hat, to reveal his elongated head and a three tailed hat which he had hidden underneath.

"An iShillelagh," exclaimed Frosty.

"Technically," interrupted QuickMIC, "we're not iShillelaghs, but what with all the software updates and all, and the addition of apps, sure we're as good as."

"As good as what?" said Frosty.

"iShillelaghs," answered QuickMIC. "So you might as well call us iShillelaghs."

"I just did," said Frosty.

"So you did," said QuickMIC, blushing. "And how come you know so much about iShillelaghs?"

"Oh," said Frosty, "I read about them in an edition of Your Ireland recently, and anyway," Frosty turned back to Malachy, "you're a long way from home, and a bit of a clown I see."

Malachy shook his head, skipped from side to side, his bells tinkling away, "Sure it takes one to know one."

"I'm not an iShillelagh," growled Frosty.

"I never said you were," said Malachy, taking off his three tailed hat, and offering it to Frosty. "Sure I've heard the rumours ... take it please, for heavy lies the heart of a clown."

Frosty flexed to jump out of his chair. He was going to wrap that crown around Malachy's neck and pull on all three bells.

"Control this insolent creature," commanded Squawky.

Dorky gestured to Orky and they both started waddling towards Frosty, Orky pointing his Mini-M249 at him, and Dorky extending the corkscrew out of his Swiss Army knife.

"Sit back down and stick 'em up!" said Orky.

"Yeah stick 'em up," repeated Dorky, "you insolent creature."

"Their mothaaas," said Squawky, shaking his head in disbelief at Ye Olde Ross Ice Shelf committee, "it's their mothaaas you gotta feel sorry for."

Dorky and Orky looked at him, clueless.

"Not Frosty you imbeciles," screamed Squawky, pointing them at Malachy, "that insolent creature!"

Malachy was right, Frosty's boardroom was very large, and it had been dug out of the finest basalt. It was just off the main foyer, and had to be big, because he held monthly project planning meetings there, which were attended by over a hundred penguins.

The boardroom desk, on top of which Malachy was about to be accosted by Dorky and Orky, was oval shaped and made of finest Irish pine, shipped in from the hill side of Bearnán Éile. It could accommodate sixty penguins, forty Emperors and twenty Little Blue penguins. Frosty was sat at the head of the table, the tricolour hanging on the wall behind him. To his right, an open fire place blazed, and a brass coal bucket, in the shape of a Notre Dame Fighting Leprechaun, was overflowing with sweet smelling, Tipperary Turf.

"Ahhh," said Malachy, sniffing at the air a few times, ignoring the Mini-249 at the side of his head, and the corkscrew under his chin, "if I'm not mistaken, that turf would be from the ancient bogs of *Teampall Tuaithe* or Templetuohy if you prefer the English translation, correct?"

Frosty jumped out of his executive's chair, again. A behemoth of man, it looked like he would never stop rising as his shadow sped down the length of the oval table. Six foot six, and half as wide, his hands looked like the end of two shovels. He wore a black jacket with a green velvet collar, white ruffled shirt, green waistcoat and black pantaloons. His unkempt, scraggily, jet back hair reached down to his shoulders, and his piercing blue eyes were filling with tears as they homed in on Malachy. "Don't mention that name again," he ordered, thumping one of his shovels on the table, nearly splitting the pine in two.

"Which name," said Malachy, "Templetuohy?"

Frosty collapsed back into the chair, tears flooding from his eyes, "*Teampall Tuaithe*," he whispered, biting on his trembling lips as he called his home by its Irish name.

"Now look," said QuickMIC, "could someone please explain what we're doing here?"

"You know why you're here," said Squawky, filling in for Frosty, who looked like he might start gibbering at any moment, "you've been asking too many questions about the Ross Ice Shelf, and snoopin' around."

"What about the Ross Ice Shelf?" said QuickMIC, snooping further.

"We have plans," said Frosty, hammering down a fist onto the table, and scaring everyone into silence, "and we can't afford to let you, or anyone else, get in the way of them. The little clown over there," he scowled at Malachy, "seems to know too much already."

"There, there," an elderly lady shouted from across the room. She was stood next to the fireplace, cooking breakfast in a huge frying pan on top of a black range, "Sure breakfast is nearly ready." She flipped a few of the contents over. "It won't be long now, Frosty. Some of your favourites are in here, too," she stabbed at a few more sizzling items, "Clonakilty sausages and an oul' white pudding from *Teampall Tuaithe*."

But Frosty was temporarily inconsolable. Mention of his hometown had him drowning in waves of nostalgia again. It had already occurred to him that with the Ross Ice Shelf melted, Templetuohy, and the rest of Ireland actually, would soon be history, submerged forever, a few hundred feet below sea level.

Like many an Irish man and woman, in search of fame, fortune and love, Frosty left Templetuohy decades ago, but he'd never forgotten his home town. Following in the footsteps of his ancestors, he worked as a Navvy, literally digging and shovelling his way around the globe. Sadly, love gave him a wide berth. He was handsome alright, in a wild, roguish way, with warm blue eyes and plush lips above a dimpled chin. But his temperament was enough to drive away any woman, especially after a few drops of *uisce beatha* had passed those lush, plump lips. Love may have eluded him, but fortune and fame were now knocking on Frosty's door, and would soon be his. But at what cost? Could he really sacrifice his home town, his culture even?

His tunnelling skills had come in very handy when he lost at poker that fateful night in Murphy's, and accepted his forfeit. Diverting lava flows from Erebus to create hundreds of kilometres of channels under the Ross Ice shelf, to begin the melting process, had been a stroke of genius, doing away with the need to excavate millions of tonnes of rock and ice. Instead they could just melt the ice and put in place huge drains. It had saved decades of tunnelling. But Hotstuff had been an idea of such creative audacity that even Captain James Bush doubted its feasibility.

Although he knew Frosty was Irish and that the Irish were mad, the creation of Hotstuff catapulted Frosty into the Hall of Fame of the most demented scientists history had even known. To build along those lava channels, once the lava had cooled to form rock hard platforms as wide as a highway, an industrial radiator heating system, nay a continental radiator heating system, four stories high and running in sections hundreds of kilometres long, with which to increase the melt speed of the Ross Ice Shelf, had seemed preposterous. But Hotstuff was nearing completion, and she would soon be fired up to full capacity.

Frosty's tear filled eyes caught the copper plaque, hung on the boardroom wall to honour and commemorate his ancestors. On it a nineteenth century quote from David Brooke was etched, "Only the ubiquitous Irish can be regarded as a truly international force in railway construction." And now skills which were once used to build and construct whole cities, countries and continents even, were being employed to destroy them. Oh the shame!

"Come on now *a stór*," said the elderly lady, who happened to be Frosty's grandmother, calling him *uh storh, her treasure* in Gaelic. Frosty wiped away the tears from his eyes, as his grandmother placed his Irish breakfast before him, accompanied by a freshly cooked white soda pan, and a lovely cup of tea, which she pronounced taayyyy.

"Leave Malachy be, now," she said. Dorky and Orky looked at Squawky for confirmation, before standing down.

"Sit down now lads," she went on, gesturing to Malachy, Ryan, Donn-Dubh and QuickMIC. "Here," she added, pulling over a specially adapted high chair for Malachy, "you'll be needing one of these, young lady." The high chairs were used by the Little Blue Penguins when they attended project meetings.

"Thank you kindly, ma'am," said Malachy, donning his tinkling hat and hopping down into the high chair, "but I'm male not female. And furthermore, I'm an iShillelagh."

"Sure I can't keep up with this modern-day fashion," she said, walking over to Donn-Dubh, "they're all wearing each other's cloths these days." She gave Donn-Dubh a good oul' once over, head to toe, "My but we don't see many fellas like you around here."

"Black you mean?" huffed Donn-Dubh.

"Oh no," she smirked, "we've plenty of black fellas. Sure we've five thousand penguins out there, and most of them are black."

Here we go again, thought Donn-Dubh, and he kissed his teeth. "Do I look like a penguin, sis?"

"Not at all," she said. "But now that you mention it, you've a funny oul' walk on you. Sure if you just held your arms to your sides a little bit tighter. I dare say that you'd pass for a penguin."

"Look," insisted Donn-Dubh, addressing the table, "and would you all please take note. I have never, and neither will I ever, wish to pass for a penguin. Is that clear?"

"Calm down," she said, and she poured him a cup of taayyyy. "It's just that ... you're from the Caribbean I assume."

"Steady on now missus, are you racially profiling me," complained Donn-Dubh, "because if you are ..."

"Not at all," she assured him. "It was just that, sure you've an awful fiery temper, altogether."

"What do you mean that?" snapped Donn-Dubh.

"Ahhh now that'll be the oul' Irish rubbing off on you I suppose," she said politely. "Sure we're an awful fiery race ourselves."

"There's nothing rubbing off on me," said Donn-Dubh, checking his hands to make sure.

"Is that so," she said, a smile developing on her gentile face. "So would it be that fiery stuff from Jamaica, giving you the oul' fiery temper, by any remote chance?"

"It might," said Donn-Dubh with a wink.

"I was wondering," she said, straightening up with a creak and rubbing her back a little, her poor oul' face distorting with the strain, "did you bring any of that oul' liquid sunshine with you? Sure me bones are frozen solid these last few months, and I can barely bend down to tie me oul' laces."

"Why didn't you say, ma'am," smiled Donn-Dubh, reaching into his hat for a bottle of Jamaica's finest, over-proof white rum, and he poured some into her taayyyy.

"Jaysis!" she gasped, after she'd downed the cup in one gulp. "That's mighty fiery stuff altogether. Sure I've the makings of a nuclear furnace in my belly now." And off she waltzed, wrapping her shawl around her in a spin, with a little Caribbean skip in her step, *one-two-three*, humming Margo's I'm At Home In Any Tipperary Town, *one-two-three*, to fetch the others a plate. The table set and her joints and bones lubricated with Jamaican fission fuel, she returned, *one-two-*

three, from the range with an extra large platter, *one-two-three* , which was overflowing, *one-two-three*, with fried eggs, rashers, white pudding, sausages, *one-two-three*, mushrooms and tomatoes, which she placed in the middle of the table, "Go on so," she urged, *one-two-three*, "tuck in."

Squawky licked his lips and jumped up onto a chair, "Not you *deahman*," she shouted, "be off with ye!"

Music was in the air, but not any old music. It was the kind of music which had Irish men and women demented all these years, nearly driven round the twist, pining after the homes and childhoods they left behind. As Frosty tucked into his breakfast, a fiddle from another corner of the boardroom gave out a beautiful, nostalgic, melody. Everyone stopped eating and looked over to find a small dishevelled fiddle player stepping into view from behind a silver decanter, placed on top of a small round oak table. Such was the grief the oul' fiddle conveyed, it was as if someone had his hands around its neck and was strangling the very life out of it. Before the singing had even started, the oul' uilleann pipes, along with the rest of the group, decided to sit it out, overcome with emotion already.

"You'll have to excuse him, lads," whispered Paddynini, talking about the violin, "he's a new Paddyvarius," he winked, and then he bowed a few more heart wrenching notes. "Wasn't he brought up on Bach, Mozart and Paganini, those kind of fellas. These oul' Irish tunes have him in bits. Sure I think he misses the oul' mother something rotten, back there in Itlay."

With the song hardly started and the fiddle already close to shedding tears, Paddynini decided to stop playing the Paddyvarius. Cupping his left hand to his ear, he sang When I Mowed Pat Murphy's Meadow in the ornate Gaelic *sean-nós* style, instead. His voice a deep, soft richness, tempered by a vibrant and at times almost nasally, upper register, Paddynini sang with such pathos and longing that Frosty, unable to swallow on account of a lump in his throat, coughed out a half eaten piece of Clonakilty white pudding:

"The autumn days are here again, and the night winds chilly blow."

"Hey look-it," QuickMIC said, taking a sip of taayyyy, "you know who that is, don't you?"

"Jesus," said Ryan, "it's The Cracker Craics; sure they'll have me crying into my rashers if they don't stop."

"Howya lads," whispered the lady in the Galway shawl, winking at them, "glad you could make it, how's the craic, is she mighty?"

By now everyone, including Frosty and his grandmother, were softly singing or gently humming along, many close to tears, including Paddynini himself:

"The woodland turns to golden hue, and the harvest moons aglow;
To hear again of days long past, to come no more I know.
When I mowed Pat Murphy's meadow in the sunny long ago."

Paddynini managed to compose himself for the last verse, but it was all too much for Frosty, "Make him stop *máthair chríonna*, make him stop!" he pleaded, pushing his breakfast away, and calling his granny *maw her khree un na, wise mother*, in Gaelic.

"Whist, now child, whist," *wise mother* said, stroking his head, as he laid it down onto his folded arms, where he sobbed himself to sleep.

Paddynini started the last verse, and with Frosty dead to the world on folded arms, no longer able to engage in business matters, máthair chríonna suggested that Squawky take Ye Olde Ross Ice Shelf Committee back to the Lava Suite until they could reconvene at a more appropriate time.

As they left the boardroom, with the flames of the open fire gently hopping and dancing over bright red, glowing turf, and a pan of bacon and cabbage bubbling on the range, Malachy, Ryan, Donn-Dubh and QuickMIC all hid their faces, wiping tears from their own eyes, with Eirestown in their hearts, as Paddynini's ethereal, forlorn voice followed them out the door ...

"Those days are but a memory like the snows of yesteryear,
And when evening shades are falling, all alone I'll shed a tear;
On my cheek I feel the soft touch of the winds that whispered low,
When I mowed Pat Murphy's meadow in the sunny long ago."

Chapter 35

Go Wax A Gazza, Like

"Get off me," screamed Malachy, "I want to go home!"

"Less of the drama, honey," said Squawky, ordering Dorky to restrain him, "you'll be home soon enough," he lied.

Ye Olde Ross Ice Shelf committee were walking along a corridor, off the main foyer, heading back to the Lava Suite, but they were becoming a little rebellious. Orky had gone on ahead to open the cell door and Dorky was providing armed escort.

The haunting words from the song, When I Mowed Pat Murphy's Meadow, were still ringing in their ears, and making them more and more homesick with every step they took. It didn't help that Donn-Dubh and Ryan were still humming the tune, their eyes full of tears.

"Get off me," Malachy screamed again, with such ferocity this time that Dorky released his grip.

"Just cool, Malachy," said Donn-Dubh, winking. Then he made Squawky an offer, "How about if we paid you to let us go?"

"With what," demanded Squawky, "that silly hat?"

"It's funny you should mention that," said Donn-Dubh, "I've got ten thousand dollars tucked away in there."

Squawky looked down at his pink UGG boots. What with all the traipsing about in such cold conditions, they were showing signs of wear and tear and he'd dearly love a new pair. "How much?" he probed again, and Donn-Dubh repeated the amount.

"Ohhh myyy dollars," squealed Squawky in delight, "are you kidding me? What's to stop me from just taking it off you?"

Ryan looked at Donn-Dubh and shrugged his shoulders, as if to say nice idea, shame about the execution.

"Well," said Donn-Dubh, trying to buy some time, "you're not tall enough for a start."

"True," admitted Squawky, "there are times when height has its advantages. Dorky, take a look in that sack and see if you can find anything."

Dorky waddled over to Donn-Dubh and started rummaging around in his hat, sticking his flipper rapidly in and of out of several folds. "There's nothing in here, boss."

"Keep trying," commanded Squawky, "search every fold. It could be anywhere in that duvet."

Dorky jabbed his enthusiastic flippers even deeper into the folds, "Wait, I think I've got it boss."

"What is it?"

"Ahhhggghhh!!!" Dorky let out a good oul' fashioned blood curdling scream and dropped his Mini-249. He was writhing around on the ground, screaming in agony, and trying in vain to shake off Snippy, who had two claws deeply embedded into his flipper.

"Run!" Donn-Dubh yelled, and Ryan and QuickMIC darted off down another corridor, away from the boardroom and the foyer, leaving Squawky wide eyed and confused.

Ignoring Dorky's screams for help, Squawky picked up the Mini-249 but Malachy jumped on him, trying to wrestle the rifle out of his grip. Dorky saw what was happening and rolled into position behind Malachy, and Squawky managed to wriggle, heave and push Malachy so that he tripped over Dorky.

Malachy was on the floor now, lying next to Dorky, about to jump back onto his feet ... but he froze, and flopped back down, his arms surrendering in the air. Squawky was aiming the Mini-249 at him, grimacing like a lunatic, and then he pulled the trigger, letting off a burst of bullets.

QuickMIC, who'd ran back down the escape corridor to find Malachy, let out a harrowing scream as the shots rang out, and then everything went into slow motion ...

With his hands still over his mouth, and his eyes almost ultra violet with shock, QuickMIC couldn't believe it when PaddySan jumped out of Donn-Dubh's hat, triple somersaulted through the air faster than a speeding bullet and landed in front of Malachy, where he drew his katana. QuickMIC cheered for joy as PaddySan's blade flashed through the air and stopped all ten bullets dead. Their momentum spent, the bullets dropped to the ground, where they came to rest at PaddySan's feet.

Squawky, determined not to be outdone by an iShillelagh, pulled on the trigger again, but PaddySan was under the Mini-249 faster than you could say *ohhh myyy God*, and sliced it into three pieces, rendering it useless. PaddySan twirled and spun again a few times, slicing the arms off Squawky's pink onesie, the beak off his baseball cap, and finally the toes off his UGG boots. Mortified, Squawky ran away as fast as he could

"Come on Snippy," yelled Donn-Dubh, "time to go."

Snippy released his grip on Dorky and scampered off into the tunnel, with QuickMIC, Malachy and PaddySan right behind him.

"This way," yelled Ryan, diverting them into another corridor, where he was hiding. Twenty minutes and ten corridors later, they reached what looked like an ice tunnel, hidden behind some black drapes. "This way," Ryan advised, "they'll think we stuck to the main corridors."

Without a second thought, they all followed Ryan into the ice tunnel, closed the black drapes, breathed a sigh of relief, and screamed to high heaven when the floor gave way.

"It's not a tunnel," screamed Donn-Dubh, trying in vain to cling on to the sides, as they rumbled, tumbled and slid further down, "it's some kind of ice chute."

"Let's hope it's not for rubbish!" shouted Malachy. "And there's not an incinerator waiting for us."

After what felt like hours they finally exited the ice chute into another ice corridor, which had many other chutes feeding into it. Fortunately, the chute's gradient was minimal, so they exited with a soft, pleasant thud, rolling out and piling one on top of the other.

"Like ehhh, come off a me, ye langers! ... I said come off a me, ye mebs. Can ye hear me, like?"

Nobody recognised the irritating, high pitched voice, until they all rolled off the pile.

PaddySan was at the bottom of the pile, "Ye've made a holy mortifying show of me, so ye have. Have a deko, like." He pulled on his new luminous blue kimono, which had a white shamrock motif running through it, and pointed at several fresh, deeply ingrained creases, "I'll not be shapin' in this rig-out tonight. Ye'd have to be a spur to miss this lot, like, or guzz eyed, like."

"What's he saying," said Ryan, "and why isn't he speaking Japanese anymore? Is that really you PaddySan?"

"I was all gillete and now I look like oul' Tom Shehawdy. Me a gildy and all, like," PaddySan continued, trying to brush the creases out of his kimono. "Of course it 'tis meself, Ryan," he said. "Sure who else were you expecting, Atty Hayes' Goat?"

"I can only understand a few words," said Malachy, "he's lost me."

"Don't make me throw a rabie, like, Malachy," said PaddySan. "Go wax a gazza, like!"

"That's because he's speaking in a Cork dialect," explained QuickMIC.

"He's me daza, like," said PaddySan to QuickMIC. "Sure I'd give him a rake of rasa. And talking of drink, mi tongue feels like a pair of bare-as after a ten mile walk in the Sahara, I could drink the cape off Saint Paul himself, like."

"And people used to say they couldn't understand me," said Donn-Dubh, scratching his temple.

"Some of us still can't," said Malachy.

"Can you translate for us QuickMIC?" asked Donn-Dubh.

"As ye know," began QuickMIC, "I have a UTU app."

They looked at him questioningly.

"That's a Universal Translation Unit app which can translate almost every language and dialect, known to man."

"So," said Ryan, "can you translate this Cork dialect?"

"Don't be a baytur, like," said PaddySan to Ryan, "carry on now and ye'll break me melt and get a lowry followed by a dawk."

"Not really," said QuickMIC somewhat embarrassed, "this particular Cork dialect is hard work, and what with the colloquialisms ...my UTU is struggling."

"You can understand nothing at all?" asked Ryan.

"Oh I'm getting a few words and phrases alright," said QuickMIC, intent on demonstrating the accuracy of his UTU. "Like 'carry on now' and 'and' and 'break' and 'melt' and 'lowry' and lots of 'like', but all together in a sentence, they make no sense to me whatsoever."

"Like, I'm away for slates, with this accent, like," said PaddySan, laughing.

"Away with the fairies, more like ... like," said Malachy.

"I preferred the Japanese," said Ryan.

"You're allergic to me are ye, like? Hold on, so," said PaddySan, reaching up to his head, where he pulled down a side panel and started fidgeting around with the electronics inside his elongated skull.

Seconds later he repeated the phrase, 'Is this any better, like?', twisting a micro-dial, to tune his own UTU like a radio, flying through every dialect in Ireland. Eventually they all agreed on a soft, buoyant Tipperary accent.

"That's grand now, PaddySan," Malachy said, "but don't forget the *h*, it's three, not *t'ree*."

QuickMIC was shocked. "You have a UTU yourself, now?"

"'Deed I do," said PaddySan. Then he sealed the panel on the side of his head, and now that everyone could understand him, he told them that Eógan had fitted him with a UTU, so he could effectively speak and understand every language under the sun. "And he thought he'd give me an Irish accent to begin with," continued PaddySan, "to make it easier for ye lot to understand me." He giggled a little, and added, "Not that ye did."

"And how did you get inside my hat?" asked Donn-Dubh.

"Oh that was easy enough," said PaddySan, explaining that after Mai-Ly had caught him off guard in Technological Shenanigans, defeated him and snapped his katana, Eógan replaced the blade with an unbreakable, diamond edged titanium one. Then he installed a UTU and told him to stowaway with the team to keep an eye on them.

"I wondered where you'd disappeared to," said QuickMIC.

"Mai-Ly caught you off guard?" said Malachy, raising an eyebrow, "that's not what I heard."

"She beguiled me with her looks," said PaddySan.

"Would that be her good looks?" asked QuickMIC.

"No," PaddySan protested, "she gave me the evil eye. I think that oul' one's a witch, a banshee or something. She put a spell on me."

"Not a love spell, by any chance," said Malachy, sarcastically. "Is she your daza, like?" he teased.

"Anyway later on that day," said PaddySan to Donn-Dubh, ignoring Malachy, "I waited until t'ree minutes past t'ree, just after you put on your t'ird Jiggy-Reggy track and went into the shower, and then I sneaked into the t'ird fold of your hat."

"And I never felt a thing," said Donn-Dubh.

"I'm surprised at tha'," said PaddySan. "Me and Snippy had a rare oul' time, altogether. Sure we were often up 'till t'ree in the mornin', drinkin' that fiery stuff of yours, singin' and carryin' on. And one of our favourite songs was that Bob Marley classic T'ree Little Birds."

"So that's what all that itching was, I thought I had nits," said Donn-Dubh. "And that explains why my rum supplies were dwindling so quickly."

"By the way," said PaddySan, "how's the oul' hero?"

"I'm grand," said Donn-Dubh, "a little shaken by the gun fire, but grand all the same."

"Not you, you eejit," said PaddySan, "I mean how's Snippy?"

"Oh," said Donn-Dubh, rolling his eyes up, "that hero. Sure Snippy's grand himself and probably up there having another oul' sup to steady his nerves. If you left any at all that is."

"And where is Mai-Ly?" asked PaddySan, having apologised for drinking so much rum.

"We don't know," said Malachy.

"You could be right about her, though," said Ryan, "before she ran away, she tried to kill us all."

"I told you," said PaddySan, folding his arms resolutely and nodding his head at Malachy. "She's trouble that one."

"I don't believe it," said Donn-Dubh. "We don't know what she was saying before she jumped out of the Eirestown POP."

"Listen fellas," said Ryan, "I hate to break up the debate, but look," he was pointing towards the end of the corridor, where there was a large riveted steel door, with a sign above it, 'Industrial Boiler Hall', with huge red words: DANGER: RISK OF DEATH, written beneath it.

"Industrial Boiler Hall," said QuickMIC, hopping up onto Ryan's shoulders and peering through a window in the middle of the door, "wonder what that is?" But no matter how hard he rubbed, he couldn't see a thing; the window was steamed up from the other side.

"Never mind what it is," said Donn-Dubh. "Risk of death suggests to me that we find another way out of here."

As they continued to struggle, hoping to see what was behind the door, there was a loud rumbling noise, followed by some hollering and screaming behind them. They turned around to see what was going on, and a green ball flew out of an ice chute at the other end of the corridor, rolled rapidly towards them and stopped at their feet, where it appeared to be breathing heavily.

"Whooo ... hoo hoo me boyo!" the green ball blurted. "Now tha's wha' yeh call an entrance, wha'!"

"PaddySan, come back," QuickMIC shouted when PaddySan flew up the very same chute the green ball had just come out of, "where are you going?"

"To find Mai-Ly," PaddySan shouted back, and then he was gone.

QuickMIC was in two minds about whether to follow him, but was intrigued when the green ball unravelled and jumped up to become a green penguin.

"Hiyis," the penguin said, "welcome to the engine room o' The Erebus Hilton. Yis must be the oul' Inspection Committee?"

"The what?" said Ryan, getting a nudge off Donn-Dubh. "Oh, yes," Ryan stammered, rubbing his ribs, "we're the Inspection Committee."

"And what better way to find out what's really going on around here," said Donn-Dubh with a knowing nod of his bulbous hat.

"Yis're roight about tha'," said the green penguin. "Sure I'll tell yis everything you need to know, wha'."

"Great," said Ryan, extending his hand, "I'm Ryan, pleased to meet you. And this," he added, introducing the others, "as you've already guessed, is the Inspection Team."

"Frosty told me to expect yis," the green penguin replied, taking Ryan's hand in his flipper and shaking it, "Séamus O'Mally's the name. I'm Frosty's Chief Engineer, please to meet yis all. Now which one of yis is William The Third?"

"Oh," said Ryan, who nearly collapsed when he heard the name, "we left William back with Frosty, discussing some business or the other."

"Not a bother," said Séamus.

"Séamus," said Ryan, "so you're Irish?"

"Not at all," said Séamus, "I'm a green penguin speakin' with an Irish accent, but I'm actually from Russia."

"Russia," Ryan was amazed, "which part?"

"Did you ever hear tell of a place called Leningrad?"

"Yeah."

"Well I came from the place next door, called Paddygrad."

"You did? Paddygrad ... can't say I've ever heard of it."

"Jaysis," said Séamus to the rest of the Inspection Committee. "And they say the Irish are t'ick."

"I'm Irish descent," blurted Ryan, "so part of me is Irish!"

"It must be the other part of you which is t'ick, so," said Séamus, giggling.

"He's only messing with you Ryan, he's Irish alright," said Malachy. "Dublin by the sounds of it, although," he went on flippantly, "we might have to ask QuickMIC to use his UTU to confirm the accent for us."

"Not a problem," said QuickMIC, keen to unleash the technical prowess of his UTU app, and make up for the fact that it had just failed miserably with the Cork dialect. So didn't he run through his memory banks and muster up a Dublin accent, a Barrytown accent at that, which even Roddy Dolye would have been proud of: "Yas as rite ov curse," began QuickMIC, in his so called Dublin accent. "He's spaakin', an' Is maens spaakin', not speakin' wit a Dublan, that's Dubana, wha', akkzant, alritee, wa'. Rrr shud Is say alrite, roiyt!" and he winked at Séamus, as if to say, I've got you now me boyo.

"Roight lads, to tell yis the truth," Séamus said, raising his eyebrows in alarm and nodding at QuickMIC, "I haven't a clue what yer man just said, and I suggest you take him to see a doctor, just as soon as yis get home. Because he could be sufferin' from hypa't'ermia or somethin' more serious. But yer other man," and he nodded at Malachy, "is roight, Dublin it is."

"By the way," Malachy asked Séamus, just after he smirked at QuickMIC, "where does the chute you've just come out of lead?"

"All the way back up to the surface, wha'," said Séamus. "Isn't it a quick entry point for when I'm runnin' late, saves me messin' about with the elevator, wha'. Or when that fierce cold is biting," he rubbed himself with his flippers, "and you want to be down in this heat and no messin', roight."

"Roight," said Malachy, winking at QuickMIC.

Séamus pulled out a key from his jacket and put it in the lock of the steel door, "A green Irish penguin from Russia," he giggled, "get's them every time, wha'," he turned the key and said, "Come on so, lads, she's waiting for yis."

Chapter 36

Shin O'Beef: A Living Irish Myth

"Kidnapping's bad enough, but murder? You can't go through with it *a stór*, sure two of them are iShillelaghs as well. And as for yer man from the Caribbean."

"What about him?"

"Well he put a skip in my step, that's for sure. I've not stopped waltzing like Matilda since I had a drop of that fiery, over proof Jamaican rum."

"Sure I know máthair chríonna, they're fine lads and all, but what choice do I have? Captain James and William have me between a glacier and a hard place."

"As big as you are Frosty, you've an even bigger heart. If you harm a hair on their heads, sure you'll only be killing yourself."

"How?"

"The guilt would eat you alive, dear child, and torment you in the grave."

Frosty and his grandmother were in the living room, just off the main boardroom in The Erebus Hilton, discussing the future of the Eirestown saboteurs. An open fire was burning a few oul' logs, and the aroma of Templetuohy turf pervaded the air. His grandmother was in her favourite rocking chair, next to a Welsh Dresser loaded with delf, and Frosty was sipping on a cup of medicinal taayyyy.

"Sometimes we have to fight," said his grandmother.

"Just like Shin O'Beef," asked Frosty, "against all the odds?"

Yes, she nodded.

"Tell me of Shin again, máthair chríonna," pleaded Frosty hoping to draw some inspiration from her stories. Ever since he'd been a child, bouncing up and down on her knee, Frosty's grandmother had told him stories of the legendary Shin O'Beef, a modern day Irish myth. If she wasn't telling him stories, she was reading them from Your Ireland magazine, a sister magazine of Ireland's Own, where, she claimed, she first read about Shin.

"Shin O'Beef, the Irish Shinobi," said wise mother, reminiscing herself now, "now there was a fighter!"

As young as he was then, Frosty could still remember the first article she'd ever read him from Your Ireland, circa 1970, about Ireland's only official Shinobi. "Shinobi," she read, her finger running under the word, "that's the Japanese word for ninja." Then she told him what a ninja was. Your Ireland stated that this particular Shinobi came to prominence in the 1960s, working undercover for *Stiúrthóireacht na Faisnéise*, Ireland's Intelligence Agency, also known as G2.

But, Your Ireland reckoned, making the story even more mysterious, juicy and riveting for its readers, the Shinobi working for G2 was just a cover story. The truth was that the Shinobi actually worked for a branch of Irish Intelligence so secret, that no one in Leinster House, home of the Dáil, or the upper echelons of the military, knew if it actually existed at all, not even the Irish President. No one, that is, except the Your Ireland reporter, who had infiltrated this clandestine organisation in order to bring their readers another exclusive.

"Minus 1," máthair chríonna whispered, rocking gently, and staring into the flames. She could still see the Your Ireland title in her mind's eye, like she'd only read the article yesterday.

"Minus 1," Frosty repeated, drawing on a sup of taayyyy. "Shin nearly fell at that first intelligence hurdle, eh?"

"Not a truer word spoken," said wise mother. "Sure everyone nearly fell at that hurdle."

Your Ireland of course knew the reason why Ireland's most secretive intelligence agency was actually called Minus 1. And they also knew that the first hurdle in the recruitment interview was the question, "Why do you think we are called Minus 1?"

Your Ireland even tried to answer it, but admitted they were no match for those oul' mathematicians up there in G2. Irish Intelligence, continued Your Ireland, is I squared, or I^2, if you take the first letter of each word Irish and Intelligence. Further, the imaginary number i is the square root of minus one. So $I^2 = -1$, that's Minus 1 to ordinary people like the ones reading the article, they said.

"Irish Intelligence squared, the 007s of Ireland," Frosty smiled, recalling what she had told him. "Licence to kill, full diplomatic privileges and everything."

"And just like their namesake," máthair chríonna giggled, "everyone thought Minus 1 was imaginary."

"As imaginary as Shin O'Beef, even," added Frosty.

"Minus 1," máthair chríonna went on, complimenting Frosty on his memory. "Honour bound to look after Ireland and all her people no matter where they were in the world. Can you imagine an Irish ninja with a tricoloured suit and all," said wise mother, "and all this in the 60s?" she smiled again. "Sure the whole country couldn't get enough of the Your Ireland reports."

Frosty never forgot. The idea of an Irish ninja, wearing a tricoloured outfit, on exotic secret missions in the Far East, was as exciting then, as it was now.

Your Ireland magazine claimed that the Dáil's explanation for why they needed a Shinobi was almost as farfetched as the story itself. The Dáil claimed - what with certain portions of the Irish population beating each other senseless in pubs up-and-down the country, when they weren't singing, telling jokes or spinning blarney, that is - that it made perfect sense to train the security forces in deadly arm-to-arm Ninjitsu combat. If only to keep the drunken hoards out of Leinster House, where they kept the really hard stuff tucked away for themselves.

"But, as you found out yourself, the real reasons for the Shinobi's commission were even more unbelievable," said wise mother.

"I remember," said Frosty, drawing strength from the Shinobi's story, "ever since childhood, Shin had been a regular in the local Chinese chipper and had learnt to speak fluent Cantonese ordering food there."

"Yes," said his grandmother.

And it was this linguistic skill, Your Ireland were proud to report, unheard of in most of Western Europe at the time, never mind Ireland, that first attracted the attention of Minus 1. The Shinobi was subsequently handpicked and trained to protect the Honorary Consul Of Ireland to Hong Kong and other Embassy staff.

Your Ireland claimed that the Dáil had established an Embassy out in Hong Kong because 700 million Chinese, that was approximately 99% of the total Chinese population at the time, were claiming they were Irish descent. The Department Of Foreign Affairs in Dublin was inundated, and just couldn't keep up with the passport applications. That this might be a ploy to escape Chairman Mao and Communism couldn't be ruled out, Your Ireland admitted. But because the 700 million had hand written Gaelic birth certificates, most from obscure parishes in the bog lands of Ireland, where no official of the Department Of Foreign Affairs would be caught dead, the applicants got the benefit of doubt.

However the Dáil had a growing problem at its fledgling Embassy in Hong Kong, which might soon end up in a war with China, if it wasn't resolved as quickly as possible.

"Just imagine if we had gone to war with China, and lost," said Frosty, pouring himself and his grandmother another cup of taayyyy in the living room, next to the main boardroom of The Erebus Hilton. "There'd have been a Chinese chipper in every town up and down Ireland."

"Sure there is a Chinese chipper in every town up and down Ireland," replied his grandmother.

"Then there'd have been two Chinese chippers in every town," and they both started laughing.

The Dáil's problem, all those years ago, came about because their Consular staff, over there in Hong Kong, all spoke the official language of China, Mandarin. However, when they landed in Hong Kong, the Mandarin speaking staff may well have been speaking Gaelic, because 99% of the population there spoke Cantonese, an incomprehensible dialect for a Mandarin speaker. And vice-versa: the Cantonese didn't have a clue what these Irish, red haired, pale skinned, gibbering idiots were saying, and just assumed that they were drunk. And though the Irish Mandarin speaking staff gave it their best shot, the indigenous population of Hong Kong thought the Irish's language so bizarre that it confirmed the popular, and by now world held belief, that the Irish were in fact mad, or away with *Tian Xian Pei* (the legendary Chinese fairy couple) at the very least.

"*Tian Xian Pei*," said Frosty's grandmother overjoyed, "you remembered."

"Sure how could I forget," Frosty laughed, nibbling on a Kimberly biscuit, "I thought you were away with the fairies yourself, telling me stories like that."

Slowly, the Your Ireland exclusive reported, the Consular staff's pronunciations developed in an ever more exaggerated manner, as they tried to match the local Cantonese inflexions – inflexions and tongue twists which

TongueSlinger himself would have been proud of. However, unbeknownst to themselves, via these guttural distortions, the Irish Embassy staff had now started to insult everyone they spoke to in the most condescending and heinous of manners, insulting government officials, wives, husbands, children, extended family members, and even pets. Another feat TongueSlinger would have been even more proud of.

But do not be alarmed! For eight weeks later, with war between China and Ireland looming, Your Ireland's front page boasted to the world that, following a six week intensive Ninjitsu course, the Cantonese speaking Shinobi had been finally dispatched by Minus 1, under a secretly guarded code name, to Hong Kong. The Shinobi's remit was simple and threefold - protect the Honorary Consul Of Ireland and the Irish staff at the newly established Embassy; smooth out any linguistic problems; and iron out any creases in the local social fabric. A fabric in tatters and nearly ripped to bits, where, on a daily basis, the Embassy staff were being insulted, threatened, harassed, beaten and worse, by most of the Cantonese speaking residents of Hong Kong Island.

Sadly that wasn't the end of the Dáil's linguistic misfortune. Unfortunately, the Consular staff were as fluent in Japanese as they were in Cantonese. So when the receptionist received a telephone call from Dublin, over a rather crackly communication line, informing her that they were dispatching a "Shin O'bi to beef up security,", she could not understand why the Irish Intelligence Agency was sending out a *Shin of beef*, and neither could anyone else in the Embassy. "Perhaps they want it returned to Dublin," another linguistically challenged staff member guessed, "after we have it sliced and cooked Cantonese style, in black bean sauce?"

"Can you imagine, black bean sauce," Frosty laughed even louder, a little more relaxed after hearing some of the story. "That must have been great craic, máthair chríonna, reading stories like that back then."

"It was," she agreed, "gas and all. Sure the whole country went mad altogether," she added. "And when Your Ireland ran a recipe piece on An Cabáiste agus Bagún Deli's stir fried Cabbage and Bacon with bean sprouts, Dún Laoghaire itself couldn't import woks fast enough."

All was going well for Shin O'Beef, the Cantonese speaking Ninjitsu out there in Hong Kong in 1955, Your Ireland was pleased to report in a special edition to wrap up the series. Tensions in the social fabric had been ironed out, and Shin O'Beef had performed linguistic miracles, placating most of the insulted residents of Hong Kong Island by clarifying some of the more dubious Mandarin phrases.

Indeed the Taoiseach, the Irish President himself, was thinking of honoring Shin O'Beef in some manner. Especially when the Department Of Foreign Affairs reported that Chinese passport applications had dropped by 99.99%. Because, in a Classic case of Chinese whispers, most people in China now feared the crazy, gibbering Irish more that they feared Mao Tse-tung, who wasn't such a bad lad after all, and at least they could understand him. But because Shin didn't officially exist, the Taoiseach's hands were tied.

All was going well, until Shin O'Beef's brother got himself into a little bother with some local Triads in Paddy's Town, a corner of an infamous destination for outlaws in Kowloon Walled City, which was way beyond the pale over there in 1950s Hong Kong. But Your Ireland was saving that series for a Christmas special.

"Stir fried cabbage and bacon," said Frosty, "it sounds delicious."

"It is, and as soon as we're back home in Templetuohy, I'll make it for you."

Frosty's mood changed immediately, máthair chríonna wasn't in possession of all the facts. Soon there would be no home, no Templetuohy, no Ireland even. When Hotstuff had finished melting the Ross Ice Shelf, who knows what shape the world would be in. But one thing was for sure, the Emerald Isle would be no more ...

"What's wrong," said his grandmother, when Frosty closed his eyes and hung his head despondently.

"Nothing máthair chríonna ," he lied, " just a little tired."

She threw a shawl over him, and he went to sleep beside the fire, the crackling of wood and sweet smell turf, soothing him.

"Shin ..." he mumbled, before he finally fell under, lost in dreams of childhood memories, "Shin help us, please, where are you now."

"You're right Frosty," his grandmother sighed. "We really could do with Shin O'Beef's help now." And she took her frail body off to her bedroom, where she too, despite the 24 hour daylight, would soon be asleep in her own childhood dreams.

Chapter 37

You Name It, We've Seen Crazy

"What is that smell?" asked William The Third for the umpteenth time, fumbling to cover his nose with his goggles. "It stinks. Is that hydrogen sulphide from the volcano or something?"

"'Fraid not sir," said Captain James, "it's the penguins. They been eating octopus again, lots of it by the looks of things." He wafted his hand under his own nose a few times, trying to get rid of the pervasive smell. "It plays havoc with their intestines."

"It's playing havoc with mine at the moment," said William, holding his own nose and struggling to stop his guts from retching.

"Not to worry, we'll be inside soon, sir," said James, groping between a few moss-infested cracks and crannies, "just as soon as I can find this blasted secret switch."

Just after they crashed into the pile of snow, and after several intricate searches of the Icicle's dashboard, and a thorough reading of the Icicle's User Manual, Captain James gave up.

"There's no reverse sir."

"Messerschmitt!" William said.

"Yes, sir," James answered, "You're right, I've made a mess of it."

William was too annoyed to explain to James that he'd actually said Messerschmitt, the famed car which had no reverse gear. James assured William that they would soon be rescued by the supply team, which was not far behind, probably only an hour or so. But William was worried that the Icicle might be completely encased in snow, and no one would know they were even under it.

Luckily, he didn't have to worry for long.

After only ten minutes, they could hear voices, and the sound of digging, and then the sound of scraping as snow was removed from the Icicle's panoramic window. And then a little blue penguin appeared in the cockpit window, waving and smiling at them; and then another one appeared, and then another. Soon the cockpit window was crawling with blue penguins, using their flippers to scrape and carry snow away. And then the stench hit them.

"You making out with that thing," said William.

"Very funny, sir," said James.

Twenty chilly, smelly minutes later, Captain James was still groping around a basalt slab, half way up Mount Erebus, fiddling for the entrance switch of The Erebus Hilton. "It's in here somewhere, sir," he grunted, straining a little higher, along an edge, "in here somewhere."

"Are you sure there is a door?" said William, pinching his nose. "It just looks like rock face to me."

"It's the door alright sir," said James, slipping his hand in and out of a few more crevices. "Now where is that blasted switch?" He felt something snap, a twig perhaps, or, "Ah-ha, I think I have it," and then he stepped back as if he were expecting something to happen.

"Darn it," he said, somewhat exasperated when the slab of basalt remained motionless. "Let me go and get some tools from the CIV."

Fifteen minutes later, William had been all over the slab, hammering away ferociously with a jack hammer, having worked his way through nine drill bits. "It's no use," he said, wiping sweat from his brow, "it's as tough as granite."

James had to agree. He was walking back and forth across one thousand and twenty three spent rifle cartridges, inspecting the impervious basalt slab, which hadn't even been scratched by the onslaught.

William couldn't take it anymore and ran at the slab, hammering on it with his clenched fists, "Please, let us in! Please!!!" Then he dropped to the base of the slab, sobbing uncontrollably.

One of the penguin rescue team, who had recently been demoted by Squawky to the back of the sledge-gang, waddled along the rock shelter towards James and William. "You know," the penguin said, nervously, "me and the guys are starting to get worried."

"Why's that?" asked James, looking down at the concerned, little blue penguin.

"Please understand," the penguin continued hesitantly, licking a piece of octopus from his lower beak, because James was still holding the rifle and had a somewhat deranged look in his eyes, "it's not often that we have to rescue someone who's just driven into a snow pile..." he paused as if afraid to say any more.

"Oh yeah," said James, "thanks again for that."

"No need to thanks us again," said the penguin, "it's just that ..."

"Go on," said James.

"I mean driving into a snow pile without a reverse gear might seem like a crazy idea ..."

"Go on," said James.

"To some people, that is," said the penguin apologetically, "but not us," he stammered. "We've seen it all out here."

"Go on," said James.

"Talking panserbjørns, hairless Yetis, UFO's, honest bankers, honest politicians, the Irish; you name it, we've seen crazy out here." He shrugged and continued. "So if two men want to bury themselves deep into a snow drift, hey, that's just fine with us."

"Go on," said James.

"It's just that your activities this last hour or so," the penguin started over, hunching his shoulders questioningly and wriggling his flipper on the side of his temple in the '¿estás loco' style, "have me and the boys wandering if you're both suffering from the effects of a bang-to-the-head."

James pursed his lips, and raised the rifle slightly, with William rolling around on the floor, gesticulating and hollering like a baby in the background.

"Which would be completely understandable," added the penguin, in a conciliatory manner, "on account of the nasty knock you both endured when you crashed."

"Go on," said James, as William rolled onto his back, screaming and gibbering.

"So," said the penguin, seriously regretting his curiosity, but in too deep now, "we were wondering ... me and the boys that is ..."

"Get on with it," said James, raising the rifle.

"Why have you been groping, hammering and shooting this basalt slab for the last hour or so?" Glad to have the question out in the open, the penguin breathed a sigh of relief, and glanced worryingly over at William to see if there was any froth forming at the corners of his mouth.

"Firstly, since you ask," began James, "we drove into the snow pile because we couldn't find the brakes."

"Ah-ahhh. That explains everything," exclaimed the penguin jubilantly, lifting his flippers as if to praise a penguin god.

"What?" said James.

"You're flying around the Antarctica at 150 kilometres per hour," declared the penguin, "strapped to a jet engine, in an enclosed bathtub on skis, without any brakes." He clapped his flippers together in a Eureka moment. "That's it ... thanks ..." and started to waddle away from these raving lunatics, as fast as his webbed feet could possibly waddle him, "...that explains everything," he clapped his flippers a few more times, "yes sirreee ... flying in a bathtub at 150 kilometres per hour without any brakes ... I mean you're bound to hit something sooner or later."

"Get back here," snarled James, "I never said we didn't have any brakes ... I said we ... I mean ... I ... I couldn't find them."

The penguin gulped when he heard James cock the rifle, and waddled backwards, moon-waddling slowly in the snow. "Sorry," he said, spinning around with a plastic smile, "must have misheard you." He cleared his throat, raised an eyebrow and said, "Anyway, thanks for the heads up ... It's as plain as the beak on the end of my face, now. So if you don't mind, I'll be on my wa ..."

"Secondly," James said, interrupting him, as William rolled onto his back again howling, cursing the cold, cursing the smell, cursing just about everything under the sun, a cursed sun which would not set for at least another four months, and finally cursing the day he ever came to cursed Antarctica, "since you asked ..."

Of course the curious penguin had recognised their attire when he first saw them through the cockpit window, the distinctive red McMurdo parkas gave them away immediately. And now, more than ever, he was convinced that Mc Murdo was some kind of Lunatic Asylum, and these two cuckoos had literally flown the nest in a jet powered bathtub.

"Secondly," James repeated, shaking his head and grinding his teeth, "as you note, we've been groping, hammering and shooting this basalt slab for the last hour," he raised his automatic rifle, pointed it at the slab, and fired another ten rounds, which ricocheted off the slab in every direction, causing the penguin to dive for cover, "because we simply want to get in."

The penguin looked up from underneath snow covered flippers, "Say that again."

James repeated himself word for word, letting off another ten rounds at the slab.

This was it, final confirmation that Mc Murdo was a Lunatic Asylum. The penguins had often wondered what kind of deranged humans would want to live in this barren, desolate environment anyway. But now it all made sense. The rest of humanity only sent the crazies out here, to keep them as far away from civilisation as possible.

"Get in?" said the penguin, getting back on his feet, and brushing some snow off, his ears still ringing from the shooting. "Get in?"

"Get in," said James, despondently, and he aimed at the slab and pulled on the trigger again, but the rifle was empty. He threw the rifle at the slab in desperation, fell to the floor, and huddled up to William, who had his head held in his oversized mittens, where he was still sobbing.

"Why don't you just use the password," said the penguin nervously, "that's what we do?"

"The what ..." James and William shrieked together.

"Open Sesame," shouted the penguin at the wall, through flippers which had been joined to form a megaphone. James and William watched in disbelieve as the ten foot high slab of basalt creaked, groaned and slowly slid to one side, revealing a cavernous entrance into Mount Erebus.

"Welcome to The Erebus Hilton," said the penguin, when the slab had fully opened, one flipper providing an inviting this-way gesture. "Enjoy your stay."

James and William threw their arms around each other and hugged and patted and slobbered, and in between bouts of manic laughter let out primordial whoops and screams of joy.

"Mad ... M ... A ... D .... MAD," whispered the penguin under his breath, as he moon-waddled away across the snow, afraid to even take his eyes off them. "Absolutely stark raving bonkers."

Chapter 38

Dublin's Most Popular VIP

"You're Irish, too? Go 'way will yeh," said Séamus O'Mally.

"'Deed I am," said Malachy.

"I'm American actually," said Ryan, "of Irish descent, of course."

"Yeah," said Séamus, "I recognise tha' accen'. California, right?"

"Right," said Ryan, "or should I say *roight*?"

"Thought I recognised it," said Séamus, winking at Ryan. "Sure I spen' a few years in Los Angeles Zoo meself. Haven't they a lovely oul' penguin enclosure over there."

Séamus turned back to Malachy: "Jaysis but the Irish are everywhere, aren't they?"

"'Deed we are," said Malachy.

"Eirestown?" said Séamus, tapping the side of his white beak inquisitively. "Can't say I've ever been there. But one t'ing's for sure, no matter which part of Ireland yis are from, we're takin' over the world."

"True that," said Ryan, "even the American President, Barack Obama, is proud to be Irish."

"I'm not sure why," said Séamus, "sure he can't even spell his own name. It's 'O'," and here he looked at Ryan like a green goldfish in a bowl, repeating the letter O a few more times, "apostro'fee Baaamaaa, wha'." He started sniggering. "Sure he must be another Irish descen' genius, wha'." He winked at Ryan again, "We must have sent all the intelligent ones over to America when we ran out o' spuds, wha'."

"You must have," said Ryan, not sure if Séamus was being sarcastic, eccentric or just plain stupid.

"An' you an iShillelagh, an' all, a funnily dressed one mind," said Séamus to Malachy, as he opened a locker. "I always wanted to meet one o' you fellas."

"Malachy Malarkey's the name Séamus, pleased to meet you."

"Malachy Malarkey," repeated Séamus smiling, "sure I hope there'll be no malarkey out of yeh today, wha'."

"Technically, Séamus," said QuickMIC, we're not iShillelaghs, "but what with all the software updates, and the addition of apps, sure we're as good as."

"As good as what?" asked Séamus.

"iShillelaghs, Séamus," answered QuickMIC. "So you might as well call us iShillelaghs."

"I just did," said Séamus, wondering if QuickMIC had missed a few of those software updates.

"By the way I'm QuickMIC, and pleased to meet you, too."

"Quick is it?"

"Yes."

"Sure you're quick alroight," said Séamus, "about as quick as a cabbage rolling up a very steep hill."

Ye Olde Ross Ice Shelf Committee, playing the part of the Erebus Inspection Committee and Séamus were inside a dressing room, just outside the main Industrial Boiler Hall. Having concluded the formal introductions, Séamus was pulling some protective clothing out of a locker, and placing it on a bench. He pulled out a black and white striped railroad hat first, a grey grandfather shirt with no collar next, a black waistcoat, a red bandana for his neck, and finally a pair of black steel toe-capped boots.

"Here yis are," Séamus said, passing the committee white boiler suits from another locker, "yis'll be needin' these."

"Malachy needs one alright," said QuickMIC. And wasn't Malachy finally glad to be shot of Squawky's outfit, because he'd nearly killed himself five times, tripping over that blasted sarong.

"So how does an Irish penguin end up in the Antarctica?" asked Ryan, stepping into the boiler suit, tugging on the legs and feigning an Irish accent: "You wouldn't be tha' t'ick yourself now, would yeh?"

"Freck off you," Séamus snapped, tucking green flippers into his grandfather shirt. "Sure we had to leave Dublin zoo just after that last economic downturn."

"That's sad," said Malachy, throwing the pink sarong down.

"It was sad alright," Séamus complained, "having to leave me home town, meself Dublin's most famous VIP and all, wha'."

"A VIP?" said QuickMIC,

"I was the talk of *Baile Átha Cliath* and had the key to the city itself," declared Séamus proudly. He nudged Malachy, and then translated the words slowly for QuickMIC, "Blaahh-Kleee-ahhh that's the Gaelic name for Dublin, or Dubana, as you seem to prefer to call it."

"I find this hard to believe, sure I've never heard tell of you," said QuickMIC, keen to show him how quick he could be. "And I'm sure that a green penguin wondering around the streets of Dublin, would have made headline news."

"Walking ... are ye joking me?" scoffed Séamus. "Sure I spen' every nigh' in the Temple Bar, knocking back kegs of the oul' black stuff, singin' karaoke and eatin' bucket loads of my favourite tapas, Calamares a la Romana."

"What?"

"Is that UTU playin' up again," sniggered Séamus. I said Calamares a la Romana ... that's fried rings of battered squid. A delicacy, wha'. And anyway ..."

"Hold on a minute now," huffed QuickMIC, who knew perfectly well what Calamares a la Romana was, explaining that what he was really amazed to hear was that a green penguin drinking kegs of black stuff in the Temple Bar would actually go unnoticed. That's what he found so hard to believe.

"It's as true as I'm standing here, wha'," said Séamus empathically. "Sure a small green penguin walkin' round *An Lar*, or O'Connell Street, or climbin' the O'Connell Monument itself for tha' matter, can easily go unnoticed these days in Dublin."

"It can?" QuickMIC's eyes became a curious purple mixed with a disbelieving orange hue.

"It certainly can," said Séamus in his defence. "What with immigration at an all time high, an' all sorts of different sized, weirdly shaped yokes coming into Ireland every day. Never mind tha' half th' town dresses as leprechauns every night, and the other half paints itself green."

"Half the town is dressed as leprechauns, and the other half painted green?"

"I can testify to that, QuickMIC," said Donn-Dubh, pulling down a green dreadlock as evidence. "I had my face painted green on a stag party there once."

"There you go," Séamus nodded confidently. "I'm not coddin' yis. You should see some of the oul' tourist stag and hen parties. If you weren't green already, sure they'd turn you green with the frigh' wha'."

"What do you mean," asked QuickMIC, "how would green people scare you?"

"I'm tellin' yis," Séamus went on, "there's nothin' worse than the sight of two leprechauns smooching and gropin' each other, after they've had a few pints. And when a few of them get a little excited and start pinching your backside ... never mind a packet of plasters, sure you'll need a few drinks yourself, if only to numb the pain."

"Gross," said Malachy.

"Sure the Archbishop of Dublin himself came out one night to sprinkle holy water on them, trying to douse their flames of passion."

"And how did they take that?" said QuickMIC.

"They were delighted, of course," said Séamus, "and started going mad altogether."

"They sound like a right holy shower, alright," said QuickMIC.

"They were a holy shower alroight," replied Séamus. "By the time the Archbishop had finished blessing them, at least."

"Did it work?" asked QuickMIC.

"Not at all," said Séamus sadly. "Most of them just assumed the oul' lad was in fancy dress himself. And before the night was out, they were sprinkling him with bucket loads of whiskey, vodka, poitín and anything else they could get their hands on."

"Whiskey, vodka and poitín," said Ryan, "that sounds like a powerful concoction?"

"Powerful is one word for it, alroight," Séamus continued. "Sure the poor oul' Archbishop staggered home half cut, and wasn't he nearly excommunicated by the Pope the very next day.

"Get away," said QuickMIC.

"I'm not coddin' yis," said Séamus. "Himself an awful thumping hangover and all, and the Pontiff ranting and raving down the phone at him."

"Go 'way will yeh," said Malachy.

"As true as I'm stood here, greener than a head of cabbage," asserted Séamus. "Not only that," he continued, "but the holy shower pinched his backside so much, he couldn't sit down for a week."

"So Séamus," said Ryan, zipping up his boiler suit, "you say you had to eventually leave Dublin?"

"You with the key itself to *Ballet Cleaat*, as well," said QuickMIC, mispronouncing *Baile Átha Cliath*.

"Yis're roight, o' course," said Séamus, buttoning up his shirt. "Me and the boys had spent years in Dublin Zoo, and didn't we think we were we were set up for life, wha'."

"What happened?"

"Didn't they take us to the vets one day, without warning," moaned Séamus, "me a picture of health and all. And when we got home, hadn't they rented the place out, wha'."

"That's outrageous," said Malachy, "but why had they rented it out?"

"Outrageous ... yis're roight, o' course," said Séamus, fiddling with a few more buttons. "They said they needed to cover the costs o' the new penguin enclosure which had cost millions, wha'." Right cuff button, left cuff button. "It was such a lovely place as well, I can tell yis." He paused at the neck button, reminiscing. "The finest Donegal sandstone rocks, and tonnes o' the finest sand from Bettystown's beach. Me an' the boys would frolic and sunbathe for hours on tha' sand, waiting for the oul' tourists to throw us in a few bob. Then we were away down the town at night to spend it all. They were the good oul' days, wha'."

"Who did they rent the enclosure to?" asked Ryan.

"Sadly the Irish aren't the only ones on the move, wha'," said Séamus, slipping into his steel toe capped boots.

"They're not?"

"No, they're freckin' not," snapped Séamus. "Didn't they rent the oul' penguin enclosure to two freckin' Chinese panda bears!"

"Chinese," said Ryan dubiously, "panda bears?"

"Yeah," said Séamus, stamping his feet until they were snugly inside his boots. "Chine-freckin'-nese panda bears" He kicked the bench twice to settle his feet in further. "A fertility drive they called it, wha'."

"Like there's not enough Chinese, already," said Malachy, slipping his arms into his boiler suit, one by one.

"Yis're roight, o' course," said Séamus bending down to tie one of his laces. "There's a freckin' billion o' them freckers, they've a country the size o' a freckin' planet, wha'." He grunted and tugged on the laces, pulling them even tighter. "But that's not enough for them. Oh no smoky Joe, send your lovesick pandas over to Ireland ..." He grunted one last time and gave the laces an almighty jerk altogether, "... because if there's one t'ing the Irish know how to do best it's ..."

"What?" asked QuickMIC.

"Get pregnant," said Séamus, finishing the lace with a neat double bow. "Sure the Irish even breed faster than them oul' Chinese."

"And how do you work that out?" said QuickMIC.

"Easy," said Séamus, "it's a well known fact, over there in their Irish bars, that there's more Irish in Beijing than there are Chinese."

"You were homeless, so?" said Malachy, zipping up his own boiler suit.

"Yis're roight, o' course," said Séamus, getting to work on his other lace. "Homeless on account of two freckin', frisky, freckin' Chine-freckin'-nese, freckin' pandas. So we had no other choice but to do the other t'ing the Irish do best."

"Fight, drink and sing," speculated Ryan, adding, "or swear?"

"Emigrate, yeh freckin' eejit!" snapped Séamus, plonking the striped railway cap on his head, and tilting it to one side. "Sure it's ignorant people like you who perpetuate the freckin' myth that all we do is fight, drink, sing an' swear. I'll interrupt the lad's bare knuckle charity fight when I get down the pub later, and let them know tha' we've an ignoramus in town. You should be freckin' ashamed of yourself."

"Sorry," said Ryan. "Go on, so, what happened after you left the zoo?"

"So where was I? Oh yes," Séamus repeated, "after they kicked us out of the penguin enclosure, we did what the Irish do best, when they're not getting pregnant that is, wha', we emigrated."

"And you ended up here?"

"We had distant cousins out here, an' landed a job almost as soon as we swam out o' the Ross Sea."

"But why are you green?" said QuickMIC, zipping up his own boiler suit.

"Yis'll never believe this," began Séamus sombrely, wrapping the red bandana round his neck. "Some t'ick studen' eejit studyin' genetics an' food colouring at Trinity College, Dublin," he twisted the ends of the bandana into an elaborate plait, "thought one year, that it'd be a grand idea to have green penguins for Paddy's day."

"Green penguins," repeated Ryan "for Paddy's day?"

"Green freckin' penguins, wha'," Séamus affirmed, outlining Trinity's plans. "We were to be a novel attraction, to get those tourists floodin' into Dublin Zoo." Finally he put his waistcoat on and extended his flippers through the arms, displaying their bright, green plumage. "Unfortunately," he sighed, "the student eeijt used an experimental drug, and there was no goin' back." He spun around a few times in the full-length locker mirror. "Didn't he make a holy, green, livin' show of me."

"You poor thing," said Malachy.

"Animal cruelty," said Séamus, "that's wha' it is. And tha's not th' worse of it."

"There's more?" said Malachy.

"'Deed there is," said Séamus miserably. "Sure didn't the freckers think it'd be great craic to dress us up as leprechauns as well on Paddy's Day."

"Now that was cruel," concurred QuickMIC. "What with half the town running around dressed as leprechauns, as well. Sure you must have fitted roight in. No wonder I never heard tell of you."

"But not to worry," said Séamus, ignoring QuickMIC's jibes, "I've a compensation lawsuit served on Trinity College, and I'm only waiting to hear back from me solicitor."

As Séamus admired himself in the mirror, he reminded Ryan of a green Victorian Chimney Sweep, except for the railway cap.

Séamus spun away from the mirror, swung his cap around so that the beak pointed to his roight, threw the bandana over his roight shoulder and said: "Roight, that's enough history lesson for one day," and he started walking towards another door at the end of the locker room, which had steam seeping in underneath it. "If yis are all ready .... yis can come an' take a luke-a' the beaut."

Chapter 39

William The Turd

William's elation at having finally gained entry into the Erebus Hilton, quickly turned to dismay, when he read the flashing welcome sign, written in red letters as high as a house, on a plasma screen at the end of a voluminous foyer, opposite the glass elevator him and James were descending in.

"WELCOME WILLIAM THE TURD!"

James stepped out of the glass panelled elevator first. The flashing welcome sign was bad enough, but five thousand penguins, applauding, cheering and shouting, "William The Turd' repeatedly, almost had William in fits of tears again, and looking for the ascend button. But the reception committee, standing in front of the five thousand penguins and consisting of Frosty, Squawky, Dorky, his flipper in a sling, and Orky, was beckoning.

"Ohhh myyy tuuurrrddds," hailed Squawky, waddling towards James and William to meet-and-greet them. Squawky was dressed to impress in a yellow DKNY sarong, a Ralph Loren cream crocheted-yoke peasant top, a Marc Jacobs' plaid pink and white stripped newsboy hat, and a pair of bright, red Jimmy Choo Doodle sandals, to compliment his newly manicured red flippers and toe nails. He had also arranged for a step ladder just outside the elevator, so he could waddle up it and kiss the visitors on both cheeks.

Mmmaaa .... mmmaaa. Squawky hugged and kissed James on both cheeks, then William, mmmaaa .... mmmaaa. Raising his flipper to silence the throng of penguins, Squawky introduced the dignitary, "I give you ....William," he turned flamboyantly to point both flippers at the illustrious guest, "The Turd!" The announcement had the penguins hysterical again, nudging each other and screaming the phrase, 'William The Turd' repeatedly, punching the air with their flippers.

"Third," Captain James shouted once again into Squawky's ear, "it's third not turd."

"Third what?" said Squawky, wondering if James meant that two cheek pecks had not been enough on such a formal occasion.

"It's William The Third," said James, fending off a few more of Squawky's chin pecks. "Turd is a ... well you know ..." he gestured, grimacing and pinching his nose.

Squawky looked up at the flashing neon sign, and recalled a line from his Brooklyn youth, 'pretty little burdies picking in the turdies'. Immediately, he raised his flippers in horror, silencing the rowdy crowd once again. The penguin army silenced, he quickly pulled out a pink, gold encased walkie-talkie from inside his Louis Vuitton shoulder satchel, tapped on the screen and hollered, "Switch it off immediately you Irish imbecile!"

The flashing sign went out, and a hushed murmur slowly gained momentum through the crowd of penguins. The game was up. Sadly there would be no more fun this morning. Of course most of the penguins were in on the joke, and that's why they'd been so especially welcoming, encouraging others in their furore. As the news spread, some started giggling, and many held swollen bellies, struggling to contain their laughter.

"Out," screamed Squawky, "the lot of you .... Out now!"

In fits and bouts of paralytic laughter the penguins streamed out of the foyer. Some were laughing so much that they had to be carried out by others. Many fell to the floor, and unable to get to their feet decided to roll out, whispering every few turns, "William the turd ... the turd," hammering on the floor with ecstatic flippers.

Frosty approached an extremely embarrassed, uncomfortable and blushing William The Third, and extended his shovel sized palm, "I'm very sorry about that William, hmm, how can I put it ... little misunderstanding?" Without looking at him directly, William reluctantly shook his hand. "We've a new penguin from an aqua-farm in Tipperary operating the neon sign today," explained Frosty, "and unfortunately, he has a problem pronouncing and spelling threes and thirds. They're lost in translation you could say."

William looked puzzled, so Frosty clarified it for him, "You see, Tipp boys pronounce three as t'ree dropping the h, and third as .... well ... now ....," he patted William on the shoulder, "the less said the better. This way, please," and he escorted him to the boardroom, trying to smooth out his embarrassment with pleasantries. "Did you enjoy your trip up the Hut peninsula; the views are breathtaking, aren't they?"

With Frosty's arm wrapped around William's shoulder, they stepped over rolling, giggling penguins, who were intermittently whispering the word 'turd' in between further bouts of laughter. Having stepped over their fifth penguin, Frosty could swear he felt William collapse into the arm he held around him, where he started blubbering.

With a little support from Frosty, William The Third made it to the boardroom, Captain James, Squawky, Dorky and Orky trailing behind them. Now they were all sat at the boardroom table, Squawky on a specially adapted high chair, and Frosty's grandmother was serving some tea and ham sandwiches.

"Here y'are Liam, have a nice sup of taayyyy, and take that big coat of a-ya, sure you must be roasting."

It sounded like she was saying, 'here yare Liam' to William, and even though she was placing the cup, saucer and plate of sandwiches in front of him, he wasn't really sure who she was talking to. "Are you t'ick or deaf," she said, rattling the cup on the saucer under William's nose, "here's a sup of taayyyy. Now drink up Liam, it'll put a bit of life back into ye after that awful shock you've just had."

William thought he was actually getting tea not taayyyy, and he still didn't have a clue who Liam was, but already the laughing stock of Erebus, he felt it best to do what the old biddy was suggesting, so he grabbed a sandwich and took a bite.

"Grand, so" said Frosty's grandmother, turning to address Frosty himself, "and you a stór, will ye be having a sup of taayyyy or would you prefer some cabáiste agus bagún, she's on the boil and won't be long now?"

William became even more concerned, perhaps the bang on the head he received when the Icicle hit the snow pile had caused some brain damage after all. He could have swore he just heard the old biddy call Frosty *uh stohr*. Also, if in fact he had not suffered any neural damage in the aural region of his brain, an Eskimo girl by the name of Kabashteh Ahgussbagun was being boiled alive. Once again, though, for fear of further ridicule, he just carried on eating his sandwich, and sipping his drink, not even sure what taayyyy was, rather than ask for clarification.

"T'anks, all the same but I'm grand, *seanmháthair*," said Frosty.

Sean Water thought William completely misunderstanding the Gaelic term, a strange name for a woman, but he was coming to realise that nothing could be taken for granted here in Erebus.

"Now please leave us a while seanmháthair, said Frosty, "we've business to attend to."

Frosty's grandmother left the room and he wasted no time in getting down to that very business, "Right William," he said cautiously, "do you want the bad news or the good news?"

Not sure how much more worse things could get, William opted for the good news first.

"The final parts have been fitted, and Hotstuff's ready and waiting for you to press the genesis button, get her all hot and bothered," Frosty grinned, winking at him, and trying to soften him up for the bad news.

"And the bad news?" asked William.

"The Eirestown saboteurs have escaped."

Chapter 40

She's A Beaut' Wha'?

"She's a beaut', wha'?" announced Séamus O'Mally, who was proudly showing the Inspection Committee around the Industrial Boiler Room.

"She's enormous," said Ryan, "how many stories high?"

"Hotstuff's ten stories high, five stories wide" answered Séamus enthusiastically. "She's the largest boiler ever built in the Southern hemisphere, any hemisphere actually. 100,000 MegaWatts o' energy, wha', at the flip of a switch."

"Why do you call it Hotstuff?" asked Malachy.

"The lads thought it was a great name, because when she's fired up, she's feisty, real hot stuff," said Séamus, pulling a lever on the control panel to release a few blasts of noisy steam, several stories up.

They were on a five meter wide, steel platform which led from the door they'd just stepped in through and right across to the other side of the enormous underground cavern they were in. On the other side of the chasm, to their right, where the platform apparently terminated, they could see two huge tunnels which ran deep into crystal, blue ice.

The Industrial Boiler itself was making all kinds of strange and wonderful noises - plops, plonks, blops, bonks, boinks, oinks, clinks and hisses to name but a few. Ryan thought Hotstuff looked like a cross between some giant skeletal creature, clinging onto the side of rock face and a musical instrument, and the noises reminded him of chemistry lessons back at school. The huge pipes running up and down Hotstuff, twisting and curling in every direction, also reminded QuickMIC of the huge organ pipes in Kell's Gothic Monastery back on Sí Mhór, although the organ pipes were much straighter.

"That must be Erebus," said Ryan, pointing to the rock face on his left.

"Yis're roight, o' course," said Séamus, waving his flipper to guide them, "we're at the interface here, rock on one side, ice on the other."

"What's that?" asked Donn-Dubh, pointing to an enormous red brick, cylindrical wall on the left hand side of Hotstuff, which curved like a huge snake, growing thinner as it meandered up, before it finally truncated into the rock face.

"That's a chimney," said Séamus. "She actually enters Erebus and joins her vents, to release Hotstuff's' flue gasses safely, clever, wha'?"

"And this ice above Hotstuff," said Malachy, pointing up and away to his right, and off as far as the eye could see, "with all the pipes running through it?"

"Oh that's the start of the Ross Ice Shelf," said Séamus, "for now at least."

"You mean the McMurdo Ice Shelf?" said QuickMIC.

"Not at all," said Séamus. "Sure the McMurdo Ice Shelf is only an insignificant part of the Ross Ice Shelf."

"Insignificant?" said QuickMIC.

"Yis," said Séamus, "sure I've seen bigger ice cubes in a Green Avalanche."

Séamus carried on tinkering with Hotstuff's control panel, which consisted of numerous levers, wheels, circuit-breakers, dials and gauges, measuring things like amps, volts, mega watts, humidity, main steam pressure, auxiliary steam pressure, vacuum pressure and temperature. He tapped at a few dials, turned a few wheels, pulled on a few more levers, and said, "She's a beaut, wha'?" whenever a lever produced another cloud of hissing steam.

"Given her size," said Donn-Dubh, "she's very quiet."

"Yis're roight, o' course," said Séamus. "She's in stand-by mode for now. Gently hummin' away, like a sleeping dragon. We've to keep her runnin' on account of the cold. We don't want nothin' freezin' up." He stroked a few brass wheels affectionately. "But when she fires up and starts twerkin' yis'll know all about it. She even registers on the Richter scale over there in Mac Town."

"Don't they get suspicious?"

"Not at all, sure they t'ink it's only Erebus grumbling. Mind you, we've not had her at full capacity yet. But the new parts are fitted an' she's raring to go."

One floor beneath the platform, Ryan caught a glimpse of some penguins wearing black baker boy caps and denim dungarees, singing and shovelling coal, "What they up to?"

"Coal-stokers," said Séamus, "country boys from the bog. Look a' the size of them bi-ceps. They get them from cuttin' turf all day and night. Yis wouldn' wan' a be messin' with them lads."

Even though they were one floor down, the coal-stoker's muscles popped out of their flippers like 3D holograms.

"What's that song their singing?"

"Goodbye Muirsheen Durkin," said Séamus, singing a few bars, "sure they're awful homesick, and it helps them to pass the time."

"So how does Hotstuff work? What does she actually do?" asked Malachy excitedly, climbing up onto the control panel, next to Séamus, "Sure she looks very complicated."

"Go away with yis," said Séamus O'Malley entering into a long spiel about Hotstuff being nothing more than a continental sized power station, converting water to steam, to power turbines which generated electrical power for the Erebus Hilton.

"100,000 Mega Watts," said QuickMIC, hopping up to join them, "according to my calculations, that's a lot of power."

"Yis're roight, o' course," said Séamus, "enough power for one hundred million homes."

"You really need all that energy for the hotel?" asked Ryan.

"Not at all," said Séamus, "not even a fraction of it. But you'll see what we do with rest later."

"And you get all that energy from the coal," said Malachy.

"Not at all," said Séamus, pointing to some open channels, way beneath the coal-stokers, "look-it."

"Lava!" gasped the Inspection Team. They were overwhelmed at the sight of bright, red, boiling liquid flowing through a vast network of open conduits.

"Lava," said Séamus proudly. "Geot'ermal energy, from the very bowls of Satan himself, wha."

"Geothermal?" said Ryan.

"Geot'ermal," repeated Séamus, smugly.

"Lava and coal," said Ryan, "that's a novel combination."

"To tell yis the truth," whispered Séamus, "we could do without the coal, but then the bog-boys would be out of a job, getting drunk and goin' mad over there in Murphy's all day an' night, what with them a little prone to the oul' Irish nostalgia. And," he added, flexing a minute green, bicep, and squeezing it with his other flipper, "as you can see, no one could control tha' shower, wha'. So we give them the oul' shovels an' a pay check to keep them occupied."

"What do you do with all the lava?" asked Ryan.

"It all flows into there," said Séamus, pointing at another vast open conduit, where many smaller tributaries carrying lava met to form a river, "and then into the boiler herself, over there, where it super heats the water. Then ..." they followed the path of his flipper to another distant conduit, fifty meters wide, which dropped vertically, "there, look-it, that's where the lava comes out ... there she flows."

"I'd hardly call it flowing," said QuickMIC, "it looks very viscous to me, a bit like a black treacle water fall, wha'."

"Black treacle, I like it," said Séamus, impressed by QuickMIC's analogy. "The lava's flowing very slow alroight, a bit like yourself, wha'." Séamus and Malachy started laughing, but QuickMIC didn't get it. "Sure there's been a little heat exchange," explained Séamus. "The lava has heated the water in Hotstuff's furnace, cooled roight down, and it's off back down to the magma chamber under Erebus, where she gets reheated and rises, through one o' several vents, and is tapped off along the conduits, to feed the furnace again. And the cycle continues."

"Genius," said Ryan, "why you could solve all the world's energy problems over night."

"Yis're roight, o' course," said Séamus, "Frosty designed it all, and he is an Irish gene-e-yis."

"Vast," said Ryan, "she's vast! That's the only word which sums it all up; a modern day miracle of engineering. "

"Sure why are yis so surprised," said Séamus, "didn't us Paddys build the rest of the world, wha'?"

"But this is something else, something on another scale altogether, it's bigger than the Hoover Dam," said Ryan, rotating his head to admire the vastness again. "She must have taken decades to build, and tens of thousands of men."

"Less of tha' men-talk," said Séamus, "us Paddys come in all shapes and sizes."

"Sorry," said Ryan, mimicking Séamus "yis're roight, o' course."

"And we didn't have to do much diggin' or buildin' for tha' matter," added Séamus.

"Why was that?" asked Ryan.

"For a start," said Séamus, nodding his head back towards the base of the mountain, "there was a huge natural underground recess in Erebus, which we exploited, look-it?" They all followed his flipper as he traced out the contour in the rock face, "See how big it is, and how most of Hotstuff fits snugly inside it?"

"And the ice," said Ryan, "we must be hundreds of meters below the surface here. How did you dig that out?"

"Sure that was a cinch," said Séamus, "as soon as we started divertin' lava flow and superheated water into her, the Ross Ice Shelf gave way in buckets. Most of the piping you see overhead is for drainage. We drain off all the melt water into the magma chamber, where she is blown off as steam up the Erebus vent."

"Ingenious," said Ryan, "absolutely ingenious."

"Yis're roight, o' course, but you'd expect nothing less than genius from the Irish."

"An'," said Séamus on a roll, "most of those flues and vents you see in the ceiling, and on the side ice walls, are as wide as a bus, and some go to the very surface itself, to allow steam out, and cut down on the condensation. Before we added them you could hardly see yourself for steam down here some mornings."

"Genius," said Ryan in stupor, overwhelmed by the scale and ingenuity of it all, "absolute genius."

"Come on, so," said Séamus, "let's get a move on. There's plenty more to see."

Half an hour later, they were on the other side of the immense chasm, completely encased in crystal, clear ice, having traversed the steel platform on an ice buggy. Malachy was sat up front with Séamus, and the other three were in the back.

"This is the inlet tunnel, we call her T1," said Séamus.

"Wow," said Ryan, "this tunnel is immense."

"All the pipin' you see up there on the ceilin' is pressurised with super, hot steam, wha'."

"There's so much light," said Ryan, astonished that they could be so far below the ice shelf and still see clearly, as if it they were outside on a summer's day.

"The Ross Ice Shelf is pure and unpolluted," said Séamus. "Just like glass, she lets the sun ligh' through perfectly."

"How far does the tunnel stretch?" asked Malachy.

"The lava highway stretches for four hundred kilometres, along the edge of the Ross Ice Shelf, maybe more," said Séamus. "Then the piping and highway turns around and comes back down the outlet tunnel, T2, over there. It's almost frozen water by the time it gets back to the condensing unit in Hotstuff, so it's not a big job to turn her back into actual water again, ready to be super boiled once more. The t'ermodynamic efficiency of Hotstuff is almost 100%."

"That's impressive," said QuickMIC.

"It is," said Séamus, stepping on the accelerator to take them into T1, "but it just keeps getting better."

"How on earth did you make this lava highway," asked QuickMIC as they trundled along, "without it melting through the ice?"

"Multiple layers of cooling lava," said Séamus, "It was made before I arrived, but some of the lads explained the process to me. It's all about controlling the heat and lava flow. They used a template to build the highway in sections, look we're about to cross a join now." The buggy wobbled slightly as they crossed the seamless join. "The sections were fabricated back at the opening to T1 and then slotted into place, further and further into the ice shelf, using hydraulics systems."

"Incredible," said QuickMIC.

"Genius," added Ryan

"Now will yis please sit back and we'll loop-de-loop, wha'," said Séamus, stepping even harder on the peddle, and accelerating them further into T1.

"Absolutely ingenious," said Ryan in awe, looking up at the three story high, glassy, iced ceiling of T1, and beyond into the sunlit surface, several hundred meters above them. "Absolutely ingenious!"

Chapter 41

Spancil Hill

"Escaped," said William, nearly choking on a ham sandwich, "they've escaped, but how is that even possible? I mean, you've a five thousand strong army guarding them?"

"Escaped," repeated Frosty, hanging his head in shame, "in fact you just missed them by a couple of hours."

"Gee thanks," said William, "that's nice to know. I'll get here a bit earlier next time, shall I?"

After all the talk about Shin O'Beef, Frosty's conscience was stirring. He was staring into the open fire, where freshly laid sods of Templetuohy turf were starting to smoulder, oblivious of William's complaints. Slowly, with William droning on, Frosty placed his hands on the boardroom table, thumbs wrapped around one another. A moment later the glowing embers and the turf had him hypnotised. In his mind's eye he was back with his grandmother, back in their cottage, a pan bubbling on the range, a pot of taayyyy on the kitchen table, the fresh country air outside, gently blown over green lush fields.

"Last night as I lay dreaming of pleasant days gone by.
My mind been bent on rambling to Ireland I did fly.
I stepped on board a vision, and I followed with a will,
Till next I came to anchor, at the cross of Spancil Hill."

William looked over to where the singing had just started. On top of a small round, antique oak table with three elegantly curved legs, a small man appeared with a cat under his arms, which he appeared to be strangling. But it was only a uilleann piper, accompanying a small, peasant looking women with an awfully, mournful voice altogether. No sooner had she started singing Spancill Hill than a few other dishevelled band members appeared from behind a silver decanter to accompany her.

"It being on the 23rd of June, the day before the fair,
When Ireland's sons and daughters, and friends assemble there ..."

Perhaps there are drugs in the sandwiches, William thought, sniffing at them. Or perhaps, like the oracle of Delphi, he was under the influence of toxic, hallucinogenic gases from Erebus. But no one else batted an eyelid when the music started. Therefore, once again, having already made a holy living show of himself, and not wishing to do anything out of the ordinary, whatever ordinary might actually mean in these parts, he did his best to ignore the miniature group and their lament.

"Frosty!" William snapped repeatedly, trying to coax him out of his musically induced reverie, "Frosty!"

"Ohhh myyy days, William," Squawky had decided he'd better do the explaining, since the saboteurs had escaped under his watch, "please let me explain."

*"I went to see my neighbours, to see what they might say.
The old ones were all dead and gone, the young ones turning grey ...."*

As the song developed, and emotions heightened, such was the passion of the lament that the uilleann pipes themselves shed tears, as the uilleann player continued to squeeze the bejaysus out of them.

"You want to know how the Eirestown posse escaped?" Squawky said. "Stand up Dorky, come on show him."

Dorky stood up to model a silk, pink sling with a red cross motif, personally designed and fitted by Squawky, and a huge pink bandage on the end of his flipper. "They were like savages," he said, waving his bandaged, battle scars around. "One minute, tame as babies, the next minute, ripping and tearing at us like animals. Plus they had the help of iShillelaghs."

"iShillelaghs?" said William.

"Yeah," said Squawky, "one was a real tough cookie by the name of Malachy Malarkey. He took a chunk out of Dorky's flipper. He was all teeth just like something outta the Twilight Saga."

"A real tough cookie, that one," said Dorky, holding up his swollen flipper again. "Teeth like a sabre tooth tiger - lock jaw as well. Oh the agony when he sunk his teeth in and started shakin' and twistin' and turnin' and sinkin' and turnin' and twistin', and I'm tellin' ya ... I'm surprised ..."

"Enough already," said Squawky. Although they had agreed not to mention the fact that a lobster actually attacked them, poetic license Squawky called it, Dorky was giving the bard a run for his money, and out running him. "Less of the theatrics, pluuuuueeeaaassse, I get worse bites off my hamster. You hear me complainin'?"

"She's was a farmer's daughter and the pride of Spancill Hill ..."

The violin player had to take up the melody here, because the Uilleann pipes were sobbing mercilessly into a handkerchief, held in the piper's arms like a baby.

"Sorry, Boss," said Dorky, "hamsters are vicious aren't they. I remember this one time when I was helping one onto his wheel and he nipped me on ..."

"Oh do be quite you gibbering imbecile," yelled Squawky, "and get back to the story."

Dorky was now in two minds, one said 'be quite', and the other said, 'get back to the story'. The latter seemed the most sensible one to listen to, given the aggressive stare Squawky had on his face, and the fact that he was rolling his flippers in the hurry-on-and-get-on-with-it manner: "Don't forget that kung fu dude, boss."

"Not that he did any kung fu," corrected Squawky, "but he was an oriental looking iShillelagh who could actually stop bullets with his sword. Just like Neo out of the film The Matrix, except Neo didn't use a sword. Paddy something or the other they called him. And I lost a wardrobe 'cos of that dude."

"A wardrobe?" said William.

"Yeah," said Squawky sadly, "he even sliced the top of my UGG boots off."

"PaddySan," said Dorky, "that was his name, PaddySan."

"Yeah PaddySan," repeated Squawky. "Now he just appeared from nowhere. Literally outta thin air."

"PaddySan, you say?" said William.

"Yeah," said Squawky, "the very same. You know the cat?"

"Then the cock he crew in the morning, he crew both loud and shrill.
I awoke in the Antarctica many miles from Spancill Hill."

"T'anks a million," said the violin player, taking centre stage. "We played that request especially for an oul' friend of ours, Frosty. How's the craic Frosty? But we hope yis all enjoyed that classic. If yis have anymore requests, The Cracker Craics will be back here behind this oul' decanter. We've ran out of handkerchiefs for the oul' pipes, so we'll have to take a rest, now. Anyway, good night and god bless."

Cats and crying uilleann pipes that sounded like cats and old biddies named Sean, and taayyyy, and iShillelaghs and miniature folk groups popping out from behind silver decanters, and iShillelaghs appearing from and disappearing back into thin air ... William was having second thoughts about ever having come out to Antarctica in the first place. He thought they were a wacky lot over in Mac Town, living like some kind of nerdy, medieval monks out in the wilderness; but the crazies in Mac Town had nothing on the residents here in the Erebus Hilton.

"Well do you know the cat?" repeated Squawky.

William did a double take, just to make sure that no one sat around the boardroom table actually had whiskers. The oul' biddy may have had more sandwiches up her sleeve than Subway, and a few chin whiskers alright, but she was no cat. Luckily, William was old enough to know what a 'cat' was in dated vernacular, and with no whiskers on display, he opted for the obvious. "Yes," said William, "I know the cat ... I mean PaddySan. I actually sent him out here ... well not here ... I sent him to Eirestown."

"You sent him here," squealed Squawky, jumping up onto the boardroom table and running across to where William was sat. "Are you outta your mind or what?"

"Yeah," said Dorky, "you outta your mind or something?"

Under normal circumstances, after a display of such disrespect, Squawky and Dorky would have been digging their own graves in the snow, with William grimacing over them. But these were not normal circumstances, although

William made a mental note to kill them just as soon as any semblance of normality returned.

William took in the room again: Frosty was still deep in his reverie, lost in the beguiling flames of the open fire, Captain James was munching away on another pile of ham sandwiches, the uilleann pipes could still be heard sniffling behind the silver decanter, letting out hellish squeaks every now and then, Dorky was still parading his sling, and Squawky had his flippers on his hips, staring him down, infuriated that he was actually responsible for sending PaddySan out to the Antarctica.

"You sent him here," repeated Squawky, waving a belligerent flipper in William's face, "your mothaaa ... it's your mothaaa ..."

William interrupted him: "Please let me explain." Then he did just that. PaddySan had actually been sent by DumbHK, under William's instructions, to Eirestown as a spy. He was also acting as reconnaissance, to prepare the way for another platoon of iShillelaghs, who were going to ensure that the interfering do-gooder, King Cormac, along with his Eirestown minions, would stay out of the Antarctica altogether, and if they didn't ... well they would all be sent to waste disposal. Which, he explained, was Mafioso code for getting assassinated.

"So what went wrong?" asked Squawky.

"Yeah," said Dorky, what went wrong?" Turing to Squawky he said, "It's his mothaaa .... you gotta feel .... ooowww!" Squawky twisted Dorky's bandaged flipper, and told the imbecile that if he didn't keep his beak shut, he'd find another set of teeth in there.

"I can only assume," said William sincerely shaking his head, "that PaddySan developed some kind of technical glitch. Or else he was somehow reprogrammed. He's a new class of iShillelagh, and, unfortunately, there have been a few teething issues."

"Teething's right," said Dorky, holding up his flipper. "I think one of them left a pair in here."

"You have no idea what happened to PaddySan then?" said Squawky, twisting Dorky's flipper again.

"No," admitted William reluctantly. "I sent another assassin to Eirestown to kill PaddySan, after he helped destroy the full platoon of iShillelaghs in a bar called Paddy McGinty's Goat."

"Another assassin?"

"Yeah," said William. "She was also an iShillelagh by the name of Mai-Ly, but she's disappeared as well."

"Quite a talent you have for making things disappear," said Squawky. "Have you considered a spot in Las Vegas?"

"Las Vegas," said William, a bemused look crossing his face, "whatever do you mean?"

"They're crying out for magicians over there."

"But why are you guys not out searching for them?" said William, promising to himself that, magician or not, he'd make Squawky disappear just as soon as he could.

"We are," answered Squawky. "We have a penguin samurai hit squad tracking them down as we speak, and a few other surveillance teams. But as you can imagine, Erebus is huge."

"Can't you just announce their escape over some system or something?" said William.

"Communication is hit and miss this far below Erebus," said Frosty, back in the present now. "Unless we have a direct line of site, then we can use walkie-talkies over a reasonable distance. The iron magma below us plays havoc with electromagnetic fields. So it's word of mouth for the most part."

"But we'll find them," said Squawky, stamping a determined Jimmy Choo Doodle sandal on the boardroom table. "We'll find them alright."

Chapter 42

The Garden Of Eden

"She's some beaut', alright," said Séamus O'Mally, as the Ice Buggy trundled deeper into T1.

The ice tunnel inside the Ross Ice Shelf creaked and moaned all around them, and every now and then they could hear the sound of ice cracking deep beneath them, or the odd rumble, like thunder, way above them.

"Don't worry about the oul' noises," Séamus assured the intrepid ice buggy passengers, who'd all turned as white as the snow, "sure the Ross Ice Shelf is on the move," he added, "constantly twistin' an' distortin' an' readjustin' as it melts. And don't forget, McMurdo Sound is just a slush puppy, anyway."

"McMurdo what?" asked Ryan.

"McMurdo Sound," said Séamus, "it's a vast region of water clogged ice, connecting the Ross Sea to the Ross Ice Shelf. But like I say, it's just like a huge slush puppy, creaking and groaning all the time."

T1 was shaped such that it amplified these sounds, and for the first kilometre, the Inspection Committee thought T1 might be about to cave in, making it the last thing they would ever inspect. But Séamus put their minds at ease, when he explained that it was all perfectly natural.

If the eerie, terrifying sounds weren't bad enough, every few minutes or so, one of the large drainage chutes on the ice wall became a waterfall, and torrents of melted Ross Ice Shelf raged through it, cascading into wide flood trenches along the side of the lava highway, and flowing down through huge drainpipes into even bigger underground channels, where the melt water was carried to be steamed off in Erebus' main magma chamber.

"Yis'll get used to that too," said Séamus, when another five meter wide torrent came gushing down beside them, although, he admitted, he had often been caught off guard when inspecting the flood trenches, and soaked by such a downpour.

"You're right, she's a real beauty," said Ryan. "But what will Hotstuff be used for?"

"Eh?" said Séamus. "Are yis havin' a laff, pullin' mi flipper, or wha'?"

"No," said Malachy, "we've had a brief explanation from Frosty, but we'd like to hear it from the horse's mouth."

Séamus look around himself a few times and said, "Do yis see any horses 'round here? I can see a few donkeys meself, wha'," he nodded in QuickMIC, Donn-Dubh and Ryan's direction, "but no horses."

"Sorry," said Malachy, "I meant ..."

"I'm only messin' with yis," said Séamus, giving him a nudge, "'deed I know wha' yis meant. Unlike yer one," he nodded in Ryan's direction, "not all us Irish are t'ick."

"Ok," said Malachy, smiling at him, "you're roight, not all of us are t'ick."

"Yis're roight, o' course," said Séamus, "to get it from the horse's mouth, I mean, not that I'm a horse, yis understan'."

"So what is Hotstuff for," said Ryan, "and what's the overall plan?"

"Basically, if yis must know, we're goin' to perform a little global cosmetic surgery," said Séamus, looking up through the ice, "give the earth a face lift, wha', a few nips and tucks."

"Nips and tucks?" said QuickMIC.

"The earth's getting on a bit yis know, she's four and a half billion years old," said Séamus.

"That old?" said Donn-Dubh, with a muted whistle.

"That old," repeated Séamus. "An' despite her obvious beauty, for a vintage model at least, hasn't she developed a few wrinkles here and there."

"Wrinkles?" said Ryan.

"Yis, wrinkles," said Séamus, tugging at his waist line, "and she's a little flabby around the edges, wha'. But by the time we're finished with her, she'll be like the Garden Of Eden once more."

"The Garden Of Eden," asked QuickMIC, "as in Genesis?"

"Yis," said Séamus, "sure she'll be a garden to rival the Emerald Isle herself. And she won't even feel a thing, once she goes under the knife."

"Under?" said Ryan.

"Do yis see all those pipes way up there."

They all looked up, "Yes."

"Meet SAM, Hotstuff's other half."

"SAM?"

"Another example of Frosty's genius, SAM is an hydraulic Self Adjusting Matrix," enunciated Séamus. "Like I said before, those main pipes you can see up there, running into T1 and back out of T2, carry pressurised steam for hundreds of kilometres across the Ross Ice Shelf like a radiator system. Up and down her in fact, feeding a vast pipe grid," he added, with a flipper moving in a circular motion above his head.

"What do you mean by self adjusting?" asked Ryan.

"'Tis a miracle of modern day engineering, I'm tellin' yis, Frosty's a freckin' Irish genius, no doubt about it," Séamus went on. "As the Ross Ice Shelf melts and adjusts so does SAM, the matrix of pipes."

"If the Ross Ice is constantly twistin' an' distortin' an' readjustin' as it melts," said QuickMIC, his UTU mimicking Séamus perfectly, "what happens when some of it disappears? Do yis lose sections of the pipe grid, or wha', wha'?"

"Oh, he's fast this one eh, Malachy," said Séamus, nudging Malachy, "a real geek this one I bet."

"He's a geek alright," said Malachy, "a real nerd."

"Did you say nerd?" asked Séamus, giggling.

"I did," replied Malachy. "But if you change one consonant of the word nerd, you'll find a word that rhymes with it, and I'd say meself that it's a much better description."

"Jaysis, Malachy," said Séamus, nearly doubling up when he worked out the replacement Malachy was suggesting, "but you're gas, scandalous altogether, but gas all the same."

"I think I've worked it out," said QuickMIC, oblivious to the banter, "it's a bit like the internet. If a section of piping goes down, SAM readjusts valves, pumps and God knows what else, and the pressurised steam flow continues through other sections of the pipe matrix."

"You were right, Malachy," said Séamus.

"That he's a nerd?"

"No, about changing the consonant!"

"Here," said Séamus to QuickMIC, "take the wheel, you might as well have the job."

"Just look at all the pipe work, the conduits, trenches, everything. The sheer scale of the project is mindboggling. It must have taken thousands of men to construct this," said QuickMIC.

"Jaysis," said Séamus, "didn't you notice all the penguins on the way in?"

"We did."

"And did yis t'ink they were on a busman's holiday or somthin'?"

"Oh," said QuickMIC, slightly abashed, "I see what you mean."

"But where did you get all the material to make the pipes?" asked QuickMIC. "It must have cost a fortune. And how did you transport it all here?"

"Not at all," said Séamus smiling, "the vast majority of the pipe work you can see is made of lava, using the same process as the fabrication of the highway. Lava from Erebus was cooled around an enormous pipe template, and sections slotted into place. It was an exercise in precise thermal engineering, the pipe sections were hot enough to melt further into the ice shelf, and cooled fast enough not to drop through it."

QuickMIC gave an appreciative whistle, "Who'd have thought? Sure I'll never look at an ice cube in the same way again."

"What will happen when Hotstuff fires up to full capacity?" asked Ryan, recalling that Séamus had yet to carry out such a test.

"When that matrix is fired to full power me boyo, it'll be like a hot knife through a slab of continental butter."

"What will happen, then?" asked Malachy.

"Not much," said Séamus, "we'll just melt the Ross Ice Shelf and start a chain of events which will flood the world."

"Melt the Ross Ice Shelf, you mean all of it?"

"Not all of it," said Séamus, "according to Frosty's calculations, we just have to melt a critical ice mass. That will be enough to start a chain reaction. We expect the other Antarctica ice shelves to follow suit first, Filcher-Ronne, Amery, Larsen. It'll be a fresh start."

"A fresh start," asked QuickMIC, "are you sure it won't be the end?"

"A fresh start," Séamus answered. "Sure we're doing the earth a great service, humanity as well. Like I say, t'ink of it as a little cosmetic surgery procedure, a little nip-and-tuck, nothin' to worry about, wha'."

"What exactly do you mean," asked Ryan, "by cosmetic surgery?"

"Well," said Séamus, "it's very simple, Hotstuff will melt the Ross Ice Shelf and initiate a world flood. Sure even Noah himself wouldn't be able to cope."

"Noah?"

"Yis, freckin' Noah from the Old Testament. Even if he had an Ark big enough for a pair of every freckin' eejit under the sun, the flooding would be too much for him. It's going to be a global catastro'fee."

"Let me get this right," said Malachy, "you're going to flood the world?"

"Just the bad stuff, wha'," said Séamus.

"The bad stuff?" said QuickMIC. "What do you mean?"

"The bad stuff, yis know," said Séamus nonchalantly, pausing for a moment to think of a few places. "The bad stuff," he repeated, "like New York, London, Tokyo, San Francisco, Paris, Milan, Venice."

"Sure Venice has major flooding problems already," QuickMIC stated, adding that matters couldn't get much worse for her, stranded out there on the Venetian Lagoon, where's she's already sinking. The victim of seasonal floods, known as acqua alta, which are caused by Adriatic tide peaks.

"You're roight," said Séamus casually, nudging Malachy again. "Venice has been struggling against the tide for years. Sure we'll be doing her a favour, sending her under."

"Anywhere else?" asked QuickMIC.

"Oh there'll be a few other places, alroight," nodded Séamus, "most of the populated world in fact."

"And Jamaica?" inquired Donn-Dubh, worried for his home land.

"Jamaica!" scoffed Séamus sarcastically. "Sure a ten foot high island the size of a football pitch in the middle of an ocean will have no problems, at all."

"T'anks man," said Donn-Dubh, "that's a relief."

"Jaysis," Séamus guffawed, "but they must have been glad to see the back of a simpleton like you."

"Huh?" Donn-Dubh grunted.

"The Jamaicans must be like the Irish, wha'," he said to Malachy beside him, "they kick all the t'ick ones out first."

Donn-Dubh didn't know where to put his face. He pretended not to hear Séamus' scathing remarks, and asked QuickMIC a question about SAM and T1's construction, if only to prove he wasn't a simpleton.

"Ahhh now," continued Séamus, reeling Donn-Dubh back in, "don't yeh worry yourself abou' them oul' Jamaicans, wha'. Sure the Jamaicans are as bad as the freckin' Irish."

"Huh?" hollered Donn-Dubh again, back on the end of the hook, concerned that he was about to be racially profiled again.

"When them lot emigrate, they're just like us," Séamus said, racially profiling the Irish.

"What do you mean, man," said Donn-Dubh, "are you dissin' my peaps?"

"Those Jamaicans don't just emigrate on their own when they leave their homeland, me boyo," Séamus carried on, slapping the steering wheel once for emphasis. "Oh no, when them Jamaicans leave, they take the whole freckin' village with them. Sure Jamaica's nearly empty already. There'll be no one left to miss her when she goes under."

Donn-Dubh kissed his teeth, disapprovingly, and carried on talking with QuickMIC.

"By the way," said Séamus, "do yeh know what the best thing that ever came out of good oul' Jamaica happens to be," he turned around to smile at Donn-Dubh, "apart from your good self of course?"

"Bob Marley?" said Donn-Dubh.

"No."

"Ackee and salt fish?"

"I was thinking more along the lines of lubrication, wha'," hinted Séamus, clearing his throat a few times. "Sure I've an awful t'roat on me this morning." He rubbed it slightly with a green flipper and added, "'Deed it's as dry as one of Mother Teresa's flip-flops." He quickly blessed himself and concluded, "May the Lord have mercy on her dear oul' soul."

"Over-proof white rum, you mean?" asked Donn-Dubh.

"Be Jaysis!" said Séamus, becoming so excited that he momentarily lost control of the ice buggy, scaring the life out of his passengers, and almost ending up in one of the huge flood trenches running along the edge of the lava highway. "That's the stuff, me boyo. That's the devil's own unholy water, and no doubt about it."

Donn-Dubh, clinging onto the ice buggy for dear life, agreed with Séamus, "That's the stuff, me boyo. And if you carry on driving like this, I t'ink I'll be needin' a bottle of it meself."

"Slow down Séamus for God's sake," said Ryan, making sure he was firmly strapped into his seat, "or we won't be long in joining poor oul' Mother Teresa, ourselves."

"Sorry about tha' lads," said Séamus, back on track and the ice buggy under control. "It's just tha'," and he looked into the rear view mirror to catch Donn-Dubh's eyes, his voice imbued with a deep melancholy, "talking of bottles," he said, the very words themselves taking on a t'irst for the devil's unholy water, "you wouldn't happen to have an oul' sup of that unholy stuff on you by any chance?" He dropped his head in shame and added, "Sure I'm awful shook meself, what with all this talk of the world flooding and all, wha'."

"I might have an oul' sup," teased Donn-Dubh, "but after what you said about Jamaicans."

Séamus' eyes became a picture of sympathy, and he spun around to speak directly to Donn-Dubh.

"Ahhh sure, now but I'm sorry about all that Jamaican stuf, wha'," he apologised sincerely. "Doesn't the oul' mouth have a mind of its own." Distorting his beak, he spoke with a feigned voice out of one corner, as if it really did have a mind of its own: "I do!" his mouth's mind agreed.

Donn-Dubh couldn't help but smile.

A smile, sure he's a simpleton alrigth, thought Séamus. Keeping one flipper on the steering wheel, and holding the other shaking green flipper under Donn-Dubh's nose, he carried on his supplication, "Sure I could do wit' a little oul' sup to steady meself, yeh know. Look at this poor oul' flipper, flappin' away wit' the nerves."

"That looks bad, alright," said Donn-Dubh.

"Bad," said Séamus, shaking the flipper even harder. "I know it's aerodynamically impossible, but if this flappin' gets any worse, sure I'll be able to fly, never mind drive."

It's working thought Séamus, when Donn-Dubh looked even more concerned for Séamus' flipper, the flappin' flipper gets them every time. Oh he's a real simpleton, alright. A sup? Sure he's probably got J.Wray and Nephew's distillery hidden away in that hat, somewhere, the size of it and all. A real simpleton alrigth, walking around with a freckin' pagoda on his head. Reverently, Séamus lowered his pleading eyes, and moved in for the kill. "Could you spare an oul' sup of that liquid sunshine, so, brother? If only to bring a little light into the darkened soul of a poor oul' penguin's miserable, godforsaken life."

"No," scowled Donn-Dubh, checking his hat to make sure his own supply was still there, "I've left it all back in Jamaica, so you better change your global flooding plans, if you really want to get your hands on it."

"Ah now," said Séamus, licking his lips, and turning back to the wheel, "more's the pity, wha'. Sure I'll have to stick with the oul' poitín then." He reached into his waist coat, pulled out a small hip flask, drank a gulp, and offered a sup to Donn-Dubh. "She's not as fiery as that stuff you're used to mind, but she'll have the steam coming out of your ears in no time. Sure," he giggled, holding out the flask, "there'll be so much steam coming out of your ears that you'll be able to pump up that oul' duvet on your head."

"It's the size of a duvet, I'll give you that," said Malachy, ridiculing Donn-Dubh's hat.

"I don't know why he's so worried about his peaps, anyway," said Séamus to Malachy. "Never mind half the village, sure he probably brought over half the country in that hat."

"What about Dublin?" said Ryan, as Donn-Dubh snatched the hip flask from Séamus, and kissed his teeth for the umpteenth time.

"What about Dubana?" repeated Séamus, nudging Malachy again.

"Will she be flooded?"

"Yis're roight, o' course," said Séamus, "she'll be going under the knife, too."

"Even Dublin?" gasped Malachy.

"Sure we should have sank her a long time ago," said Séamus. "The Paddys have been a strain on world population for years, now. Don't they breed faster that the freckin' Chinese Pandas!"

"You mean you'll actually be glad to see the Ireland flooded?" said Ryan.

"Look-it," explained Séamus earnestly, "it was bad enough after 1845 when we ran out o' spuds. But if you're t'ick enough to still be livin' there after the banks robbed yis blind, then you're a t'ick eejit who deserves to go down with the ship. And hopefully, when you do go down, yis'll take a few of those robbin' greedy freckers with yis."

"And when is all this due to happen?" said Ryan.

Séamus looked at his watch in dismay, slammed on the brakes, pulled on the wheel, and spun the Ice Buggy around 180 degrees, "For the love of Mary, Jesus, Joseph and Padre Pio himself."

"What's wrong?" asked Ryan,

"We're going to be late for the switch on!"

"Is that bad?"

"It is if you're under the Ross Ice Shelf, and it's about to completely melt," Séamus hollered, pumping the accelerator to the ground, and heading back to the control room as fast as he could.

Chapter 43

Hell Hath No Fury Like A Woman Sean-ed

"Yeah," said Dorky, back in the boardroom, stamping his own feet in sympathy with Squawky's determined Jimmy Choo Doodle sandal, "we'll find the Eirestown saboteurs, alright."

"The sooner the better," said William. "I can't afford any mistakes at this late stage. GRABiT has invested hundreds of millions of dollars in our expansion plans. Admittedly, William The Fourth may only be in kindergarten, but he is poised to inherit his new kingdom, any day now."

"Don't worry," said Frosty, hoping to allay William's fear, "we'll begin Operation Genesis in a few hours, whether we find the Eirestown saboteurs or not. And you will have the privilege of switching Hotstuff up to full capacity. In less than a week, perhaps a few days, the earth will be flooded beyond all recognition."

"And reborn," said William ebulliently. "Operation Genesis, a new dawn on a new day," and he couldn't help but quote the bible. "And the earth was without form, and void; and darkness was upon the face of the deep."

"Would anyone like more taayyyy?" Frosty's grandmother was back in the boardroom, carrying a tray with more taayyyy, and another mountain of sandwiches, her hair tied up in a neat bun, and her face full of fresh blusher.

"No thanks," said Frosty.

"Yourself?" she asked William.

"No thank you Sean," joked William patting his stomach, a bit more relaxed now that Frosty had giving him assurance that Operation Genesis would go ahead no matter what, "I'm stuffed after the last wheel barrel load."

"What did you call me?" asked Frosty's grandmother, her face stone cold.

"Sean," winked William, flirting with her now. Despite her frown, he carried on smiling at her while patting his rotund belly, more than delighted to be on first name terms at last.

But hell hath no fury like a woman scorned, and as for a woman Sean-ed, Jaysis, even hell doesn't have that much fury. Somewhere in the deep recesses of his genetic line, William was of Irish descent, like virtually everybody else in America, but he still had a lot to learn about Irish culture. For example, there are three things which you should never ask an Irish woman:

1) Are you pregnant,

2) Would you like to get pregnant? and

3) How old are you?

Last but not least, age is a sensitive issue for a female in any culture, but in Ireland, the home of Bataireacht, a land fabled for its strong, feisty women, such an insult takes on a level of gargantuan proportions, and many a man has met with a rash of blows to the head for less. Sure you can say virtually anything else to an Irish woman, and you'll be forgiven. For example, if she asks you does her bum look big in her new dress, and you answer that you've seen the back of smaller Double Decker buses on O'Connell Street, you'll be forgiven for telling her the truth, and not letting her go out looking like an Irish hippopotamus. But anything to do with age should be avoided at all costs, if you know what's good for you. And if you don't know what's good for you, then the Irish have a saying: '*Is minic a bhris béal duine a shorn*', which translates as 'Many a time a man's mouth broke his nose', or just about every other bone in his body on this particular occasion.

So when William called Frosty's grandmother 'Sean', which is the Irish Gaelic word for 'old', and not 'Sean Water', spelt seanmháthair, which is a Gaelic term of endearment for 'grandmother', he may as well have been calling her an oul' washed up banshee. Sure hadn't he even noticed that she'd been up half the night doing her hair and makeup for him; himself a corporate executive and probably a bachelor. Not that she had much chance in that department, but he could have paid her an oul' compliment in any case, instead of that dreadful, desperate insult. As for the face peels, hadn't she spent all night, one exfoliation after the other, peeling and scraping the very decades off a-herself? Sure when she looked in the mirror this morning, she saw a sprite, bubbly, taut young face looking back at her, not the wrinkly monster about to be unleashed on William.

If only Frosty had inherited his grandfather's characteristics. His grandfather was a hopeless romantic. A gentle soul ... a poet and pacifist, of such a refined spirit that he wouldn't even hurt a fly on your head. His grandmother, on the other hand, many of whose characteristics Frosty did inherit, had the maternal instincts of Badb, one of the trio of Irish war goddesses, collectively known as the Morrígan. And since Badb took the form of a battled hardened crow, she was known as Badb Catha, the battle-crow.

Now in Badb Catha's case, if there was a fly on your head, never mind the fly, you were going to lose the head, or suffer some form of cerebral trauma at the very least.

"Say that again, Liam," seanmháthair wailed, slamming the tray of taayyyy and sandwiches onto the boardroom table, where the taayyyy itself jumped out of the cup, and grew a pair of legs so that it could run out of the room, scared half to death by the venom in her voice.

William looked around, wondering if anyone else was about to answer to the name of Liam, but because she was obviously talking to him, he thought it best to repeat what he had just said, just in case the crazy old bat jumped on him. "Sean," he muttered hesitantly, finding himself back in the Twilight Zone.

"Why you're a turd alright, a real big turd at that!" screamed seanmháthair, with the energy and passion of a rejuvenated oul' washed up banshee.

Grabbing hold of a handful of ham sandwiches, she proceeded to launch them at William. "Come out ye shower of gobshites, come out!" Grabbing another handful, she proceeded to scatter them around the boardroom, "all of ye." The onslaught was merciless, and became even more intense when she picked up the tray in one hand, and let off salvo after salvo, "Ye've made a holy living show of me, ye shower of blaggards, come out!"

"What shall we do boss?" asked Dorky, as several ham sandwiches bounced off his head.

"Run," screamed Squawky, tripping over his yellow sarong, "run for your life.... run ..."

Frosty knew better than to question máthair chríonna, the wise mother, who wasn't acting very wise at the moment, especially in such a rage.

Máthair chríonna never wanted to leave Templetuohy in the first place, but with all the family gone, she told Frosty she was fierce lonely rattling around in that oul' cottage on her own, day and night. So one day she contacted Frosty and said she'd rather be cold than lonely. Winters were bad enough in Ireland, so how much colder could it be in Antarctica, she wondered. And anyway, Frosty knew he wasn't going to leave her behind forever, to sink with the rest of Ireland. She was the only family he had left, and she'd brought him up after his own mother died at a very young age. So he was glad when she decided she wanted to join him. It saved him having to lie to her at some point, to persuade her to leave Éireann for safety. But it wasn't until she landed in the Antarctica that she truly understood what Frosty meant by fierce cold. Not only that, she had swapped the green, lush, arable land of her ancestors for this frozen, desolate, inhospitable, barren, God forsaken whiteout. And all because Frosty lost at a poker game one night and was now in debt to a Turd.

No, Frosty wasn't about to try and reason with her in this mood, especially now that the turd who had forced her from her home in the first place, had also just insulted her in such a heinous manner. The time was fast approaching for him to make an exit from the boardroom, the more sandwiches she threw, the better her aim was getting. The size of that last ham sandwich nearly took the head off his shoulders. Sure Jesus himself could have fed the five thousand with it - a leg of ham between two loaves of brown soda bread. Ducking one last time, to avoid an even bigger sandwich, Frosty flew out of the boardroom door, grabbing William and James as he passed them.

Just in time, they manage to slam the door behind them, and heard the tray clatter off it on the other side, accompanied by a harrowing wail which sent shivers down their spines. Despite the thickness of the door, they could hear seanmháthair's last sentence, before the cups and saucers smashed off it, "And don't you ever t'ink about coming back in here, you good for nothing smelly oul' turd!"

Chapter 44

Grey Rabbits

After an awful lot of scrabbling and numerous false starts, which resulted in him slipping down more times than he pulled himself up, and having avoided a few penguins flying past him in the opposite direction, PaddySan finally made it to the surface of the chute Séamus O'Malley had tumbled out of earlier. Where, for the last few hours, he'd been running around Antarctica, looking for Mai-Ly. And didn't he have himself nearly gone round the twist looking for her, having been all over the local terrain.

Finally, exhausted, hungry and thirsty he applied Occam's razor, which basically suggests that when faced with a problem, you always look for the simplest solution. Therefore, even though he'd only been immersed in Irish culture for a few weeks now, while hidden away in his hat, he remembered the spiel Donn-Dubh gave from The Irish Pub Guide when they first landed in the Antarctica, and decided that he would head for Murphy's On The Rocks. Even from his brief exposure, he knew that Irish pubs were the hub around which the Irish distributed office carried out its daily business and the medium through which the Irish Diaspora maintained contact with itself.

He had no doubt whatsoever that there was a 100% probability that someone would know something about someone in Murphy's On The Rocks. Sure if not, they would at least buy him a drink and an oul' bite, sing him a song, or beat the living daylights out of him. Or, if he was really lucky, give him a generous helping of all four.

And, as providence would have it at such desperate times, as soon as PaddySan made the decision to find Murphy's, a penguin, who looked like he may have actually drank Murphy's dry, jumped up from a pillow of snow, and blew a few green hiccups. After a brief interchange, during which PaddySan drew his katana to pop numerous green bubbles, the penguin hiccupped directions to Murphy's before waddling off, meandering from side to side, in the direction of home, or so he hoped.

Thirty minutes later, PaddySan pushed the revolving doors and stepped into Murphy's On The Rocks, which was bustling and bursting with the craic as usual. In one corner, a table full of Mac Town scientists and nerds, with tricoloured flags for scarves and large green coloured, velour hats, were discussing environmental issues, and comparing apps on their tablets, taking selfies, and drinking pints of Mac Town stout. This was fine, creamy White Stuff with a black head, which was just as tasty as the Black Stuff back in Ireland, but dyed white with a black head, to blend in with the environment.

The Irish Rover was blaring from the Duke Box, a feisty, full-on duet by The Pogues and The Dubliners. And weren't a couple of bog-boys whopping it up, linking arms, jigging and dancing around, flinging each other silly all over the place. Sure the faster they swung, the tighter the circles became, until they were going so fast that some end links actually left the floor, their legs sweeping high over the bar and the dance floor, as they clung onto to their partners for dear life itself.

Over in another corner, a rowdy group of penguins were downing glasses of Green Avalanche faster than the waiter could refill them, heckling him to get a move on, a stream of green dry ice, trailing behind him.

Admittedly, PaddySan had limited exposure to Irish culture, a week or so by now, but even a decade's worth could not have prepared him for this level of controlled pandemonium. No, you had to be born into this, and even then …

On one end of the bar, standing on bar stools, six iShillelagh Irish Wolf hounds were sweeping back their matted hair, drinking pints of White Stuff, clinking glasses together, saluting one another, and tucking into food like their namesake. They'd not long been in Murphy's themselves, having spent days looking for rabbits with no luck whatsoever.

Rabbit-less, hungry and thirsty, they eventually stumbled upon an inebriated penguin who told them about Murphy's. And as soon as they entered the pub, they got chatting to a few local penguins in a booth, explaining their predicament.

"Ye were looking for rabbits?" said a particularly sarcastic penguin, who grew up on the coast of Kerry, called Frank.

"Sure we couldn't find them anywhere," said one of the Irish Wolf Hounds, licking his lips with the thought of a freshly stewed one on the end of his tongue. "Didn't we search everywhere for the little grey freckers."

"The hunger pains are killing me," said another Irish Wolf Hound, rubbing his hollow belly. "We were told there were thousands of rabbits around here. But could we catch one?"

"Now let me get this right," said Frank, winking at a few of the other penguins in the booth. "Ye were out here in the Antarctica looking for grey rabbits?" He picked up his Green Avalanche, fanned away a cloud of green, dry ice, and took a glug, wiped his mouth and repeated, "Grey rabbits?"

"Yes," confirmed another one of the Irish Wolf Hounds, who'd almost licked the lips off his face thinking about a slowly baked one with all the trimmings. "Sure we looked everywhere," he sighed despondently, patting his empty stomach, "and we found nay the one."

"Be Jeeeeeess lads …" began Frank, picking up the glass of Green Avalanche again, and sniggering with the other penguins, "would ye be havin' the believing' of that?"

"Ye freckin' eejits," another penguin blurted at the Wolf Hounds, "there's thousands of rabbits around here, alright."

"Hundreds of thousands probably," screamed another penguin, in hysterics now.

"What?" asked one of the Irish Wolf Hounds, somewhat confused by the penguins' hilarity.

Another penguin could barley restrain himself and blurted, "Sure there's millions of rabbits around here."

"I'm telling you," we searched everywhere, and found nay the one," repeated the Wolf Hound.

"That's because rabbits are white out here!" all the penguins chorused. Then they clinked there glasses and went mad altogether, with the laughter taking hold of them and shaking them to their core.

The Irish Wolfhounds looked at each other aghast, and Frank handed them embossed pamphlets. "Here," he said, away with the laughter, "I can recommend the Irish White Rabbit Stew, if ye can find it on the menu, wha'." Then he laughed so much that he fell off his chair, and rolled around under the table hammering on the floor, repeating the phrase 'they were looking for grey rabbits, grey rabbits, mind'.

PaddySan ducked to avoid another pair of flying legs, as one of the dancing boys flew past him horizontally. Upright, he looked again to where the iShillelagh Wolf Hounds were still eating and drinking. He hadn't forgotten their treachery back in Paddy McGinty's Goat. And even though QuickMIC had brought them back to Technological Shenanigans, he didn't trust them. So what if they'd shared a drink and an oul' sing song back in QuickMIC's? There were people in Murphy's tonight sharing a pint and a bit of craic who wouldn't even give each other the time of day tomorrow. And anyway, perhaps the Wolf Hounds were only biding their time, until they could catch PaddySan unaware. PaddySan was taking no chances. He approached them stealthy, reached under his kimono for his katana and drew it slowly ...

The music stopped, the lights went up, the dancers froze, some in mid-air, and the whole bar came to a standstill. You could cut the air with an icicle. All eyes were on PaddySan, including those of the Irish Wolf Hounds. One penguin hiccupped, and a green bubble floated menacingly towards PaddySan.

Without even looking, PaddySan sliced the air around the green bubble to his right, cutting it into hundreds of little green droplets, and the silence in Murphy's was interrupted momentarily as the audience gave muted applause.

The Irish Wolf Hounds growled and snarled, but were too interested in the Irish White Rabbit Stew to be worried about PaddySan's histrionics. Sure weren't they driving the bar tender mad altogether, what with them leaving teeth marks in the bowls. 'Deed it was a fine stew alrigth.

Actually, PaddySan thought the Irish White Rabbit Stew smelt delicious. Frozen, and not having eaten for several hours, he contemplated forgetting the past and joining the Wolf Hounds in a hearty bowl. But his Bushido discipline kicked in, and he subdued his hunger pains, adopting a fighting stance instead.

Slowly PaddySan moved towards the Wolf Hounds, who were paying him no attention whatsoever and were busy licking their bowls clean. No, he was taking no chances, none! With the words of Sun Tzu from the Art of War, one of the books he'd read during his apprenticeship, spinning around his circuits, he drew his katana back over his head and prepared to deliver six lethal blows: "Let your plans be dark and impenetrable as night, and when you move, fall like a thunderbolt."

Chapter 45

The Phuk Mee Gang

After Frosty's grandmother had them all nearly beaten to death, with flying ham sandwiches the size of double bed mattresses, Frosty told Squawky to take William The Third and Captain James Bush to their quarters. Where, he said, they could freshen up, get changed and settle their nerves, after what must have been a very harrowing experience.

His grandmother safely in her own quarters, tucked up in bed after an oul' sup of Jamaican over-proof rum she'd managed to wangle from Donn-Dubh earlier, Frosty went to his own room and pulled out one of his all time favourite copies of Your Ireland. The previous chat with seanmháthair about Shin O'Beef had him fired up a little, and the way she'd ran the boys out of the boardroom might have been a little over the top, but it was inspiring none-the-less. Ok, perhaps that feisty outburst was just a side effect of that fiery rum the Jamaican lad had given her. But still, she had Frosty fired up alright, and he was looking for further inspiration.

Here it is, Frosty muttered to himself, pulling a vintage copy of Your Ireland from a storage box. It was a highly sought after special edition, about the demise of a legendary Triad gang. The international linguistic spate at the Irish Embassy resolved, the Your Ireland reporter had hung around in Hong Kong, hoping for another Shin O'Beef exclusive, and they weren't long in the waiting.

Frosty turned the first page, and immersed himself in fantasy. The year was 1965 Your Ireland began, the place Hong Kong, and Shin O'Beef was about to settle a score with more than a few Triads, in a raucous corner of an infamous destination for outlaws in Kowloon Walled City, which was truly beyond the pale in those days.

Only three types of people entered Paddy's Town back then, reported Your Ireland: those looking for a good time, those looking to kill, and those looking to get killed. Oh, and in an addendum at the bottom of the first page, the article mentioned a fourth type of person to be found in Paddy's Town at the time: Your Ireland reporters, without which this exclusive could not have been brought to their avid readers.

Frosty turned the pages and continued to read about Shin's brother, Patrick, a popular landlord in Paddy's Town. Sure poor oul' Patrick had arrived in Hong Kong with mixed blessings. Six months prior to his disembarkation, under the influence of a dark cloud of misfortune, and following a day poaching cabbages to accompany his dear oul' mother's Sunday joint of bacon, hadn't he been arrested.

Unfortunately, the very next day in court, the dark cloud became even darker, and rained a thunder storm on Patrick, the like of which hasn't been seen since. The octogenarian judge, whose brain had been pickling for the last fifty years in illegally distilled poitín, vast quantities of which were paid as bribes to keep various town officials out of prison, had got it into his head, during sentencing, that he was back in the days when anyone caught doing anything at all in Ireland was sent as far away as possible, never to return. That last batch of poitín had been mighty, fierce stuff altogether, and had mangled the judge's mind beyond repair. It always tickled Frosty that Your Ireland carried an advert on the opposite page, just in case any of it readers would like to purchase a bottle or two of that mind bending tipple.

So poor misfortunate Patrick Frosty read on, turning to the next page, with Exhibit A for the prosecution, the stolen cabbage - well half of it anyway, because himself and the mother had eaten the other half before the guards came knocking - tucked firmly under his arm, and what was left of the black cloud still hanging over him, was driven to Dublin port and given a one way ticket to Van Diemen's Land.

Fortunately, Your Ireland was happy to report, Patrick's luck improved, not for the first time, when blessings of another kind intervened. Would you believe that the ship's Captain, running low on essential supplies, decided to pull into Hong Kong harbour to restock. It just so happened that the ship always ran out of essential supplies when it passed Hong Kong, whether it had actually ran out of them or not, due to the fact that the happily married Irish Captain, a devoted husband and a regular church goer back in his home town, had a rake of children to six concubines from Macau.

No sooner had he landed in Hong Kong than the Captain found out that in less than one week, his newest arrival, Paddy O'Lee, the first son of his of latest concubine, was to be baptised by the local Irish priest. So excited was the Captain upon hearing the news of Paddy O'Lee's arrival that, in act of clemency rarely seen since, he let all the prisoners on board go.

But you wouldn't believe it, Your Ireland sadly reported, cursed by the black cloud that had followed him from the courtroom, didn't Patrick's luck turn sour again. A few months later, he found himself in a bit of a fix when, as a complete novice to the game, he ran up more than a few gambling debts playing mahjong with newly arrived Triads from China's mainland. And weren't these good for nothing scoundrels using a marked set of mahjong tiles.

This particular group of Mandarin speaking Triads, known ironically, on account of a transliteration error in the local Cantonese press, as the Phuk Mee gang, were a group who took to Kowloon Walled City like a group of rabid iShillelagh Irish Wolf Hounds might take to a boxing ring.

The Phuk Mee gang not only enjoyed a good time, but they also seemed to enjoy getting killed; or, at the very least, they welcomed the kudos which came from the most unsavoury demise they could find themselves embroiled in. However, much more worrying for Shin O'Beef's brother, Patrick, was the fact that they took a particular delight in killing anything and anyone who got in their way, or dared to disrespect them. At the very least, such disrespect earned a good hiding.

Sure weren't the Phuk Mee gang holy, living terrors, Your Ireland reported, cursing them into the ground. Even the slightest infraction was met with swift and deadly retribution, as a seventy year old rickshaw owner found out one day. Although he knew he shouldn't, Frosty always smiled when he read the next few paragraphs. Having pulled his load half way up Victoria Peak, Your Ireland continued, the highest mountain on Hong Kong Island, the poor oul' bag-of-bones could take no more, and, sweating profusely, he paused, barely able to pull a breath, never mind pull his god forsaken load any further.

Normally the frail old gentleman struggled to pull one person along Connaught Road, which was a relatively flat surface Your Ireland's surveyor stated. But the steep incline of Victoria Peak was fast draining the very life out of him. Sure an empty rickshaw would have been bad enough, but having to run like a twenty year old, pulling such a heavy load, was taking its toll, and he desperately needed this breather.

He'd read the article so many times, Frosty knew what was coming up, and couldn't help laughing a little as he read on. The eight Phuk Mee occupants of the two-seater rickshaw, already running late for a very important meeting with their Mountain Master in The Peak Tower, situated on top of Victoria Peak, were not impressed by such insolence, and showed the breathless septuagenarian no sympathy whatsoever. Didn't they jump out of the rickshaw one-by-one, find a rice barrel, make the poor oul' bag-of-bones hop into it, seal the lid, then roll him down the side of the mountain. The holy terrors!

The rickshaw owner, after meandering down the rockiest part of the mountain, and bouncing almost five meters off the ground at times, ended up in Waterfall Bay thirty minutes later, where he would have drowned had he not been rescued by a junk sailor.

Your Ireland was thrilled to report that the oul' lad survived the tumble, but he sustained numerous bumps and bruises, and, because of several dislocated discs in his back, he couldn't pull a rickshaw for the next three months. However, despite the fact that he would walk with a limp for the rest of his life, the oul' lad later claimed that rolling down the mountain in a barrel had been the best ride of his life. Even better than the roller coaster ride he went on a decade earlier in Coney Island, New York, whilst visiting family in Manhattan's China Town.

Rice barrels or not, Phuk Mee proved they were not to be messed with, Your Ireland warned. Having only just been run out of main land China by the Communist Party, they were spreading like a virus through Kowloon Walled City, carving out patches, and planting illicit seeds which would one day blossom into healthy, illegal income streams.

Fortunately, Your Ireland were ecstatic to report, the Triad's budding expansion plans came to an abrupt halt when they decided to have a drink, and swindle a certain landlord in a bent game of mahjong in Paddy's Town one fateful night, in a pub known as 'Finnegans Wake'. A pub where Finnegan himself wouldn't be caught dead! Sure you couldn't write it Your Ireland went on, but they did, wasn't the landlord of Finnegans Wake Patrick himself, Shin O'Beef's very same cabbage poaching brother.

On hearing of Phuk Mee's mahjong swindle, a prelude to a sustained extortion racket, Shin O'Beef got Patrick to arrange a meeting with them in Finnegans Wake the very next night.

Thirty members of Phuk Mee attended that historic meeting, oblivious of the fact that they were about to be well and truly phuked.

Frosty took a long look at his hero, before he read the last few paragraphs. Your Ireland had drawn a full page picture of a ninja wearing a tricolored outfit. Even though you could only see the hard staring eyes, the ninja looked mighty fierce, and was stood in a cat stance, ready for action, with some kind of knives, just visible over each shoulder, strapped on the back. The image firmly planted in his mind again, Frosty read on.

Patrick did not know the real name of the tricolored ninja who entered Finnegans Wake that night, because Shin O'Beef, under a Minus 1 oath of secrecy, kept their real identify secret, even from the brother. But Patrick was thankful in any event, and watched in amazement as Shin O'Beef tore members of the Phuk Mee gang limb from limb. Shin O'Beef revelled in the onslaught and took so long to dispatch the Phuk Mee members, that Patrick even had time to phone the Your Ireland reporter to give them a blow by blow account of Shin O'Beef's heroics. The poor oul' Phuk Mee gang got an awful hammering altogether, Your Ireland concluded, and that was the last of them. But, thankfully, it was not the last of Shin O'Beef.

Frosty put the Your Ireland magazine down, stood up, and walked over to a full length mirror at one end of his quarters. The size of him, sure there wasn't enough mirror to hold him, and himself worried about two skinny looking articles altogether, William and James. He looked down at his hands. Sure they were as big as the excavator buckets on the end of a JCB. Why he could pick William and James up, one in each hand, and crush the very life out of them. But what fun would that be? He sneered at himself in the mirror, and whispered, "Make them suffer! As yourself and seanmháthair have suffered all these years."

In a flash he tried on Shin O'Beef's cat stance from the magazine. Sweeping back his buccaneering black hair, and adjusting his reflection, he shifted his centre of gravity and settled into his hips, to match Shin O'Beef's picture. He shuffled his left foot, extending it slightly, his right foot behind, taking most of the weight, and the JCB buckets held shoulder high, left in front of right, ready to slice or pummel anything that got in his way.

He sliced through the air twice, his hands quick as lightning bolts, taking the imaginary heads off William McCoy The Third and Captain James Bush. He'd show them alright. "Do you really think I'm going to let you sink Templetuohy," he shouted at his reflection, giving William a dig in the ribs, and taking the wind out of Captain James, with a bucket blow to the solar plexus. "Did ye really think that I'd let ye sink Ireland?" Jab, slice, duck, bob, parry, weave. "Is it mad, ye are, or what?" he roared.

He spent the next hour screaming at the mirror and perfecting his moves, cutting, slicing, jabbing and strangling William and James over and over again.

Ha! Who needed Shin O'Beef? Frosty would show them himself. Oh he'd show them alright. The fight was on!

Chapter 46

Operation Genesis

"Well," said William The Third, overjoyed at the sight of Hotstuff, "your grandmother might be as crazy as a drunken leprechaun on Saint Paddy's day, but Frosty, you sir," he paused to nod his appreciation and silently applaud him, "you are a genius!"

Although fully rested, William and James were still a little shaken after their run in with Frosty's grandmother. But, as arrange, a few hours later, they were in the control room of the Industrial Boiler Hall, having just been escorted there by Squawky.

"Hotstuff, eh?" said William with a glint in his eye. "My, my, she's certainly worthy of that name. She's hot stuff alright."

"Yes," said Frosty, taking a glance over his shoulder every now and then, to make sure Badb Catha, the battle-crow, wasn't in pursuit, her talons extended, ready to rip the heads off them all, "very hot." Wasn't he all fired up himself, having beaten the living daylights out of his own reflection, and he was biding his time, waiting for an opportunity to pounce. Sure the last thing he needed now was the oul' grandmother showing up and ruining his plans, also, he wasn't sure if he'd be able to protect her.

William looked down, where numerous lava tributaries met to form a river. "And that's the power source ... lava?" said William, in awe, seeking further confirmation, after Frosty's brief overview. "The river of lava enters the boiler over there, and away we go."

"Yes, sir," said Frosty, gesturing towards another feature, "and then, after some high pressure thermodynamic heat exchange, the lava exits over there, approximately thirty minutes later. William missed it at first, and looked in the wrong direction. "No sir, over there that black waterfall, that's super-cooled lava."

"Yes I see," said William, laughing a little. "I like it, a tarmac river for the paddys."

"And then the lava slowly flows back down, deep ... deep ... down ..." William followed Frosty's finger, "into the magma chamber, way down below us, where it gets reheated, rises through one of several vents, is siphoned off into one of the tributaries, and the cycle begins again."

"I'm telling, you, Frosty," said William gleefully, "not only are you a genius, but GRABiT shareholders are not going to be believe that you only spent ten million dollars building Hotstuff."

"Ohhh myyy new world," interrupted Squawky, "I can't wait to see Frosty Town, and you a mayor, Frosty."

"Won't be long now," said William, patting Frosty on his back. "I assume this is the button here?" William was talking about a big glass covered, green button with the word GENESIS written across it.

"Yes, sir," said Frosty reluctantly, a lump forming in his throat. "Press that button and Hotstuff leaves stand-by mode and twerks into action ... she'll then establish a self-sustaining, positive, thermodynamic feedback loop ... and it's goodbye ..." It was all too much for Frosty, the tears were welling up, and he was losing control.

".... Ross Ice Shelf," hollered William, rubbing his hands together and laughing fiendishly, "and Hello Garden of Eden! I know why you've got tears of joy in your eyes, Frosty," he shrieked, patting and rubbing Frosty's back again. "It'll be just like a new birth. You're going to be a daddy."

"A new birth," bleated Frosty, "I get it, sir."

"How long will she be in labour, Daddy?"

"It could be over in days," Frosty said gloomily, melancholy taking hold of him. "The World won't know what's hit it, one minute land, the next ocean."

"Days ...." laughed William, joyfully, megalomania taking hold of him. "Do you hear that Jamie boy, days ..." Unable to contain his excitement, he flipped the glass cover off the button, and held his hand over it patiently. "Days Jamie boy .... and it's goodbye Old World ... hello New ..."

"And farewell Éireann," Frosty whispered, tears filling his eyes again, "and Templetuohy, where I mowed Pat Murphy's meadow ... *Tá brón orm* ..."

"You going to press that thing, sir, or fondle it all day?" Captain James was waiting for William The Third to press the GENISIS button, if only so he could get away from this freezing, desolate landscape, and back to a luxury condo on a sun drenched beach, anywhere else in The New World.

"Just savouring the moment, Jamie boy," said William, his finger poised, "just savouring the moment. All those years of hard work, and here we are."

To mark the occasion, all the coal-stokers had joined them in front of the control panel, and some were singing Muirsheen Durkin, others humming and whistling the melody. An armed samurai penguin hit squad had also been summoned as security, just in case that daft old dangerous crow, Frosty's grandmother, decided to follow them after all.

"Goodbye Muirsheen Durkin, sure I'm sick and tired of working,"

Frosty had taken a step back from proceedings; and as the coal-stokers sang, he was starting to crumble.

"No more I'll dig the praties and no longer I'll be fooled ..."

Frosty felt a fool alright, an enormous fool that had not long spilled out of a mirror. Never mind all that hype back there in front of his reflection, chopping and prodding thin air, sure he couldn't punch a hole in a slice of soda bread at the moment, the awful state he was in.

And now the bog-boys with that song ... tormenting him further, reminding him of the crime he was complicit in, the destruction of his home town, his country Ireland, and his Irish culture. And what for? To satisfy a greedy, megalomaniac's fantasy?

"As sure's me name is Carney I'll be off to California ..."

The reality and enormity of what he was involved in was becoming overwhelming. Frosty clasped his hands to his head. And the coal stokers shifted up a gear:

"Where instead of diggin' praties I'll be diggin' lumps of gold ..."

Never mind gold, the only lump he had was the one growing in his throat. Round and round the words went, like banshees wailing and tormenting his mind: Éireann, Templetuohy, Éireann, Templetuohy, Éireann, Templetuohy ... He screamed out and pressed his hands to his ears even harder, shaking his head manically, "Stop it máthair chríonna ... please tell them to stop it ..."

William and James couldn't believe it, the size of him and all, but Frosty was a gibbering wreck, rolling around like a baby, curled up into the foetal position on the floor, his head firmly clasped between shovel sized palms. They looked at Squawky for an answer, but he looked back at them blankly, shrugging his shoulders.

"Restrain him," said William, "sedate him or something. We can't take any chances at this late stage. He might be as mad as that old bat of a grandmother of his."

"Days away Jamey boy, nothing can stop us now," said William The Third, "....days away," and then he pressed the GENESIS button, and took a few steps back.

Sure Hotstuff wasted no time. Didn't she fire out of stand-by mode with a noise that sounded like the shuttle itself taking off from The Kennedy Space Centre. Within moments the lava streams grew bright red as they merged to join the river. William couldn't believe his eyes when hundreds of other sluices opened one-by-one, revealing even more lava streams, and adding to Hotstuff's gargantuan power.

The scene reminded James of a Tibetan mandala he'd once seen on a Discovery Channel documentary. Lava streams fed the base of Hotstuff like spokes in a wheel, meeting in the hub just below her, where they formed a colossal, incandescent circular lake, feeding the boiler unit.

Overhead, myriad pipes came to life, creaking and hissing, clanging and banging as super heated water was forced through them, heading deep into T1. Such was the immense boiler pressure that the steam accelerated through the T1 pipes in no time, filling the several hundred kilometres of SAM in the click of a finger, before returning back down T2 just as fast, to become freezing cold water again in Hotstuff's condensation unit.

"What's that noise?" William whispered cautiously, when he heard a deep rumbling coming out of T1and T2.

"That'll be waterfalls forming," said Squawky, "nothing to worry about. The computer simulator has predicted them, and we're safe here."

Squawky was right about the waterfalls, but wrong about their safety.

Frosty, strapped to a chair now, had not dared to dream that Hotstuff would be so efficient. Already the thunderous rumbles indicated that only fifteen minutes after coming out of stand-by, it was starting. The Ross Ice Shelf was imploding under its own weight, as melt waters formed waterfalls kilometres wide underneath the surface.

He had his chance and missed it, overpowered by his own grief and guilt. Now Frosty would have to sit it out as a prisoner, wretched witness to his own monstrous creation.

Chapter 47

You had me at, hǎo jiǔ bú jiàn

Back in Murphy's On The Rocks, PaddySan slowly shuffled towards the iShillelagh Irish Wolf Hounds, his katana held high over his head, still intent on delivering six lethal blows. But the Wolf Hounds never flinched, and carried on licking away at their stew bowls, because they knew something PaddySan didn't.

"*Hǎo jiǔ bú jiàn.*"

Startled, PaddySan recognised Mai-Ly's voice at once, and looked around Murphy's to see where it was coming from.

On the other side of the silent bar, Mai-Ly was sat in a lotus position, holding a glass of Jinuiang, a non-alcoholic rice wine, best served hot, especially in this part of the world.

The whole pub took a deep breath and gasped as Mai-Ly flipped up out of the lotus position, and across the bar, using a combination of summersaults, back flips and cartwheels, landing squarely between the iShillelagh Irish Wolf Hounds and PaddySan.

PaddySan and Mai-Ly stared into each other's eyes for what seemed like an eternity, but was in fact the exact amount of time needed for the Wolf Hounds to polish off another spoonful of stew from a freshly delivered bowl, their slurps the only sound breaking the silence.

"Hǎojiǔ bújiàn!"

"What's tha'?" asked PaddySan, in a jaunty Tipperary accent, convinced that if Mai-Ly repeated the phrase a few times, his UTU would be able to translate it.

"Hǎojiǔ bújiàn!" repeated Mai-Li.

PaddySan scratched his oul' confused head and said, "One more time, please."

"Hǎojiǔ bújiàn!"

"Sorry," PaddySan apologized humbly. "Sure you've said it t'ree times now, and it still means nothing to me." He tapped the side of his head and added, "The oul' UTU must be banjaxed, on the blink or something."

"Long time no see," shouted Frank, the sarcastic penguin from Kerry, who was sat in his regular booth not far from PaddySan. "She said … 'Long time no see.'"

Several of The Mac Town geeks had just joined Frank in his booth, and were busy whispering to each other. Fresh out of the huddle, one of them tapped Frank on his shoulder, and bent down to his ear, to divulge another translation. Frank cupped his flippers and shouted over to PaddySan, "*Knee how!*"

"Me knee's well, t'anks all the same," said PaddySan, looking down at each knee to make sure he wasn't missing anything. "By the way, the names PaddySan, pleased to meet ye."

"No, you eejit," said Frank, introducing himself. "Say that to yer one. Say *knee how*. It means *hello* in Mandarin."

"*Knee how*," PaddySan repeated to Mai-Ly, bowing politely.

"*Nǐ hǎo ma?*" replied Mai-Ly, bowing herself.

Frantically, some of them giggling, the Mac Town geeks whispered amongst themselves again, then one of them whispered to Frank and he shouted at PaddySan, "How are you?"

"I'm grand," PaddySan shouted back.

"Not you, you freckin' eejit," shouted Frank back at him, "that's what she just said, 'how are you?'." Then Frank got another whisper in his ear, "Tell her, 'wo hen how knee nay'."

It transpired that several of the geeks were of Irish descent. And wasn't it only shame that the sociologist from Trinity College, Dr. Sam E. Again, couldn't have been in Murphy's to see the results of his thesis in action. For in a classic example of efficiency, and a demonstration of the organic, responsive nature of the Global Irish Distributed Office, resource sharing in a non-pareto optimal environment, the geeks came together as one arm of that planetary, wide global Irish organism, to perform a much needed translation service.

Wing Wang Wiley, a geophysicist, who was really a Riley, the pronunciation of the R having been lost in translation, came from Beijing originally, and spoke fluent Mandarin and Russian, but not English. Therefore Wing Wang Wiley translated for Vladimir Fitzgerald, a glaciologist, originally from Vladivostok, who spoke fluent Russian, Mandarin and German, but not English. And Vladimir Fitzgerald translated for Helmut O'Connor, an astrophysicist, originally from Berlin, who spoke fluent German, Russian and French, but once again, not English. Helmut O'Connor translated for Paddy de Gaulle, originally from Paris, and head chef over there in Mac Town. He also later claimed to be a distant cousin of Paddy Roux of Eirestown. Culinary skills aside, Paddy de Gaulle spoke fluent French, German, Italian and Gaelic, but not English. However, Gaelic proved to be the missing linguistic jigsaw piece, enabling Paddy de Gaulle to translate for Frank, the sarcastic penguin from Kerry, who also spoke Gaelic and, more importantly, English.

"Wo hen how knee nay," PaddySan repeated.

Mai-Ly blushed and giggled, covering her mouth with her hand, and entered directly into a lengthy conversation with the translation team.

"She's something to tell you," Frank told PaddySan.

PaddySan glanced at Frank then fell back into Mai-Ly's inviting eyes.

"Wǒ" began Mai-Ly. Frank huddled with the translation team, coming back a few seconds later, and shouting across the bar:

"I" ...

"Ai," continued Mai-Ly, nodding her approval at Frank's translation service. Frank went into another huddle, and shouted back across the bar:

"Love ..."

"Nǐ," concluded Mai-Ly. Off Frank went again, into another huddle with the translation team, who spoke the one word common to all languages, "Awww," Frank said to the lads, before he announced:

"You! ... I LOVE YOU PaddySan!"

"I'm awfully flattered Frank," said PaddySan, shyly, "and I've nothing against same-sex relationships, you understand. But to be honest Frank, you're just not my type. Sure you've a funny oul' walk on you, and the way you hold your flippers ..."

"Jesus," said Frank to the others in the booth, "he's something else altogether, isn't he?" He turned back to face PaddySan and shouted, "I've met some awful t'ick eejits in my life, but you must be one of the biggest eejits I've ever met."

"Do you think so?" said PaddySan.

"Why," said Frank, "do you know a bigger eejit?"

"Sure I might," said PaddySan looking a little confused, "give me an oul' moment to think about it. I've known some awfully big eejits in my time, alright."

"It's you!" yelled Frank. "You, you freckin' eejit ...Mai-Ly said she loves you."

At which point two iShillelaghs looked into each other's eyes and blushed. Everyone in the bar cheered, and some of the women and bog-boys wiped tears from their eyes. Even a few of the Irish Wolf Hounds could be seen surreptitiously wiping their eyes, although they later swore that they were only wiping splashes of stew off their faces.

It wasn't the first time Murphy's On The Rocks had played cupid. A few years ago, didn't The Rose Of Tralee herself walk in one day, and order half a Green Avalanche. Sure the eyes popped out of every bog-boy in the place, when she flicked her flowing red hair to reveal those sparkling green eyes. And when they found out The Rose was stationed at Mac Town, and had spent the previous year looking for love in Lisdoonvarna, without any success whatsoever, didn't they go mad altogether, each determined to win her affections. Of course, The Rose was delighted to hear that the bog-boys were competing amongst themselves, and one night, while she was on the dance floor, she noticed, from either side of her eyes, two suitors shimmying with the nerves towards her. Quickly, to check that everything was in place, she pulled out her makeup mirror. But didn't she drop one of her false eyelashes, trying to adjust it.

Not a bother, she bent down in a flash to retrieve the wayward eyelash, but never got up again. Sadly, when she looked up to see where the suitors were, she found them directly above her head, their eyes firmly shut and lip-locked. Hadn't they both moved in for a peck, one on either cheek, and hadn't she disappeared at the very moment their lips should have been caressing her rosy flesh. Well that night, and you don't need me to tell you, the bog-boys ripped each other and Murphy's to bits, and the blushing, hapless, romantic Rose was never seen, nor heard of again.

So they were used to love in Murphy's, alright. A wild love at times, but love none the less.

But love between two iShillelaghs, now that was a new one. Elated, PaddySan put his sword back in its scabbard and took hold of Mai-Ly's hands, which were frozen to the bone. Sure not even the oul' Jinuiang hot rice wine had been able to warm them.

Mai-Ly grabbed PaddySan's hands firmly, and took to the air in the martial art style, dragging PaddySan with her. A moment later, they landed on the bar, and one of the waiters fetched a black, adjustable desk lamp, plugged it in, and tilted it so that they were illuminated under their very own spot light.

The waiter dimmed all the other lights in Murphy's and, with the crowd cheering and clapping, a disheveled looking fiddle player appeared on the bar next to the Wolf Hounds. Paddynini was in rare oul' form altogether. He threw up the Paddyvarius onto his shoulder, and didn't he open the gates of heaven itself, with the first few bars of *Che Geilda Manina*, from Puccini's classic, La Boehme.

"*What a frozen little hand*," Frank whispered above the heavenly violin, translating the song title for everyone. The crowd became silent again, motionless.

"Hold on a moment, lads," said PaddySan, raising a hand to stop the music, "does anyone have a USB to USB cable?"

One of the geeks opened a briefcase, reached in and threw a Universal Serial Bus cable over to PaddySan.

PaddySan caught the cable, lifted up the back of his hair, plugged one end of the cable into the USB port on the side of his head, and offered the other end to Mai-Ly.

The crowd gasped.

"Jesus," said Frank, "they've only just met, and he's after having his wicked way with her already."

"It's not like that," Paddy de Gaulle explained with Helmut O'Connor, the astrophysicist, whispering into his ear. "It's intimacy Helmut says, but not like human intimacy. The iShillelaghs are going to have a tender moment, during which they'll share their bits and bites."

"Be the lovin' Jaysis," exclaimed Frank, giving himself the sign of the cross. "Share their bits and their bites, you say, like vampires?" He crossed himself again, pulled a rosary out of his pocket, and took a few gulps of his Green Avalanche. Poor oul' Frank, sure wasn't he terrified to death that as soon as PaddySan and May-Ly had finished biting and sucking the blood out of each other, they'd pounce on him, and suck out what little penguin life he had flowing through his veins.

Paddy de Gaulle leaned back in, to hear what Helmut had to say.

"What did Helmut just say?" asked Frank.

"I don't know how to tell you this, Frank," said Paddy de Gaulle in Gaelic, "it's a bit rude, and I'm not sure about the translation."

"Sweet mother of God," Frank said, blessing himself again, "sure I can imagine it'll be a bit rude alrigth, what with them sharing their bits in public. Just brace yourself Paddy and tell me man, what did Helmut say?"

Paddy de Gaulle took a deep breath and relayed Helmut's message, "Cop yourself on Frank, you feckin' eejit. They're only going to share their bits and *bytes*, as in computer bits and bytes. A bit is either one or zero, and a byte is eight bits."

"Thanks be to God," said Frank, the sweat dripping off a-him. "Sure I think I'd need counselling if they were about to share any other kind of bits and bites." He wiped his brow, took another gulp of drink and added, "Or at least a week in the confessional box, wha'."

Mai-Ly hesitated, but eventually, stirred by the Paddyvarius starting up again, she plugged the other end of the USB cable into the USB port on the side of her own head.

PaddySan's UTU switched to the language of universal love, and he burst into song:

"Che gelida manina, se la lasci riscaldar."

Inspired by his new found love, PaddySan was in fine voice. Sure they'd not even heard the likes of such a sublime performance over there in La Scala Opera House, Milan, where oul' Caruso himself used to do a turn. As PaddySan's golden notes spilled forth and oozed into every corner of Murphy's, the whole place was transported to another heavenly dimension altogether.

But it was all too much for the poor oul' uilleann pipes. And when PaddySan sang about his care free poverty, the love songs of a lord and his millionaire's soul, the pipes collapsed into a love stricken heap. Didn't they have to be carried away on a stretcher in fits of tears, leaving the rest of the Cracker Craics to accompany PaddySan, as he continued to warm Mai-Ly's hands, and melt her heart.

Finally PaddySan hit the high C, and held it until light filled himself and Mai-Ly's eyes, at which point two microelectronic hearts fused and became one. Sure the light was so bright that it outshone the desk lamp and momentarily peaked in intensity, dazzling everyone in the bar. Then the USB cable started smouldering, sizzled with a flash and melted.

The oul' romantic wasted no time at all. He swept up Mai-Ly into his arms, pulled out the USB connectors at both ends, kissed her, and they twirled away together, under the light of the desk lamp, the whole place cheering and hollering, going mad altogether.

Wasting no time themselves, The Cracker Craics got right back into the swing of things, the pipes joining in and crying for joy, when they struck up a lively rendition of I'll Tell Me Ma.:

"I'll tell me ma when I go home, the boys won't leave the girls alone ..."

But they had to play on without part of the percussion section. The spoons were too busy smooching in yer ones socks, their hearts ablaze with amour.

In less than a beat, the bog-boys were whopping it up again, flying around the floor, even The Irish Wolf Hounds jumped down for an oul' jig, flinging each other silly all over the place.

With Murphy's hopping again, Mai-Ly whispered into PaddySan's ear, *"Kěyǐ yuánliàng wǒ ma? Gěi wǒ gè jīhuì ba."*

And, following another huddle, Frank was about to translate, but PaddySan told him to hold on a moment.

"Tell her to place her head on the bar," PaddySan told Frank.

Frank gave the instructions, and Mai-Ly dutifully obliged. In another act of intimacy between two iShillelaghs, rarely seen in public, PaddySan pulled out a screwdriver, opened up the access panel on the side of her head, tuned her UTU to English, and sealed the panel again.

"Go wax a gazza, like," Mai-Ly said, giggling with a strange Irish accent, as soon as PaddySan had the panel screwed back on.

"What did she say?" Frank asked PaddySan. "I've asked the translation team but they haven't a clue this time."

"Hold on a moment, so," said PaddySan, "I'll switch her from that Cork dialect, to ..." PaddySan quickly opened Mai-Ly's access panel and tuned her UTU again.

"Be off with you, Frank," Mai-Ly shouted, in a dulcet Kilkenny accent, which would warm the heart of any Irish man.

Frank giggled himself, saluting her with his glass, "She's a fine oul' colleen that one. Sure you've landed on your feet there alright. Fair play to you, PaddySan."

"Sure now hold on a minute," Mai-Ly said, "but I never had a UTU before."

"I just shared it with you," explained PaddySan, "through the USB cable."

"Sweet Jaysis," said Mai-Ly, rubbing her stomach, "I hope you didn't share anything else with me?"

"What do you mean?"

"Should I be expecting a little PaddySan in nine months time?" she giggled.

"What was that noise?" PaddySan shouted over to the translation booth, after hearing a loud thud.

"It's nothing to worry about," said another penguin, "Frank's just feinted."

"Ok," said PaddySan, and then he answered Mai-Ly. "A little PaddySan, sure what kind of iShillelagh do you take me for?"

"Oh," she murmured, "it's just that ..."

"You'll be having triplets at least," PaddySan said, and himself and herself fell around the place, laughing hysterically.

Composing herself, Mai-Ly stared into PaddySan's eyes again, and whispered, "*Kěyǐ yuánliàng wǒ ma?*" before pausing to apologise and add, "Sweet Jaysis, this Chinese will be the undoing of me."

"It takes a few moments to adapt to the oul' UTU change," PaddySan said reassuringly. "Go on so, but take your time," he added, taking hold of her freshly warmed hand again.

"Can you forgive me," she pleaded, "and give me a second chance?"

"You had me at, *hǎo jiǔ bú jiàn*," laughed PaddySan with a glint in his eye. And didn't the oul' romantic move in for another smooch and kiss.

"She is handsome, she is pretty, she is the belle of Beijing City."

Chapter 48

Drinks Are On Leinster House!

It was a beautiful morning in Eirestown, and the mysterious green mist was slowly wafting away to reveal *Sliabh an Airgid*, the Silvermine Mountains, to one side of the town. Over to the north-west of the town, *Bearnán Éile*, The Devil's Bit, was just coming into view, as the green mist continued to dissolve into the morning air above it. A few minutes later, the green haze had lifted completely, leaving Eirestown somewhere just outside *An Teampall Mór*, Templemore, Tipperary.

Legend has it that the famed gap on top of the mountain, known as The Devil's Bit, was created by the devil himself. One morning, feeling particularly hungry, what with the missus refusing to fry him a few oul' rashers, didn't he take an almighty bite altogether out of Bearnán Éile. "Be Jaysis!" the horned mountain eater cried, when it suddenly dawned on him that he'd bitten off more than he could chew. But didn't he crack one of his teeth, trying to masticate the mouthful of rock, hoping to ease the burden on his digestive tract. And wasn't it an awfully delicate tract altogether. Sure it was only used to digesting such delicacies as scaly dragon meat and demons, and, when he was on good terms with the missus, the rare oul' Clonakilty rasher, and not at all in the habit of digesting large chunks from the mountains of Tipperary.

Now didn't the gap from the mountain, having slipped through the freshly formed gap in the Devil's broken teeth, roll down the mountain side of Bearnán Éile, and come to rest many miles away in Cashel, where it became known as Carraig Phádraig, The Rock of Cashel. And still, to this very day, King Cormac's very own Cormac's Chapel takes pride of place on top of it.

However, we are not here to discuss myths and legends. We are here to discuss hard facts, and reality. And the basic facts are that only three hours after being fired up to full capacity, Hotstuff had everyone in the world hot under the collar. More so in the voluminous foyer of The Erebus Hilton, where thousands of penguins, shareholders in GRABiT, were cheering, as headline news from all over the planet, filled huge plasma screens.

Hotstuff had surprised everyone, even Frosty, when her self-sustaining, positive, thermodynamic feedback loop went into overdrive within a few minutes of her coming out of stand-by. Sure no sooner had she come out of stand-by than she took a quantum leap, surpassing all computer model predictions. The innovative lava conveyor mechanism churned the magma chamber below Mount Erebus, taking the volcano into a higher gear, and taking the lava temperature with it. Soon the lava flowing through the system, became as hot as the core of the earth itself. In turn, this super-heated lava made short shrift of the water in Hotstuff's boilers and pipes, taking it beyond a critical super-steam pressure point. Not even the computer models had foreseen the consequences of water raised to that kind of temperature. A jet of plasma steam formed and coursed through the full length of the SAM pipe matrix. And it was this unexpected steam-plasma which melted the Ross Ice Shelf even faster than Séamus O'Malley's hot knife analogy through a slab of continental butter.

Frosty's prediction of the Ross Ice Shelf disappearing in days, was turning into hours, as even more unforeseen effects kicked in. Antarctic amplification triggered an unprecedented global domino effect on the planetary weather systems. As expected, all the Antarctica ice sheets, including Filcher-Ronne, Amery and Larsen melted very quickly. However, the first external victim, beyond Antarctica was the polar jet stream, which normally formed a protective ring, high in the atmosphere above and around the continent of Antarctica. Over in NOAA, the National Oceanic and Atmospheric Administration, they watched in horror as satellites relayed to their computer screens confirmation that the polar jet stream had come to a complete standstill, allowing searing equatorial weather systems to push up over the Southern polar cap, increasing the Ross Ice Shelf melt rate significantly, and increasing local air temperature.

The next domino in the weather chain to fall was El Niño. Thermohaline circulation, the oceanic conveyor belt, became disrupted, when the cold Ross Ice melt waters, a hidden sea within the Southern Ocean, altered the path of El Niño's Southern Oscillation, further increasing air temperature and surface sea temperature along the Ross Ice Shelf, and around the rest of Antarctica.

Domino after domino fell in an environmental chain of disaster. It soon became clear that it was no longer just the Ross Ice Shelf which was melting, the whole of Antarctica, which accounts for 90% of the world's ice, was starting to defrost and melt at an alarming rate. And then reports came in that the second largest ice sheet in the world after Antarctica, Greenland, was also melting at an almighty rate altogether. With the world still recovering from the shock of Greenland, Russia reported that the tundra permafrost was turning into mush, fast becoming the biggest bowl of kasha porridge they'd even seen. Even the North Pole and the Arctic Circle was on its way out.

Domino after domino continued to fall, triggering tornados, hurricanes, typhoons, tsunamis, landslides, blizzards, cyclones, micro heat waves, super cell thunderstorms, forest fires and just about anything else you might expect during such an apocalyptic event. It was clear that Hotstuff had triggered a catastrophe of such proportions which even GRABiT's CEO, William McCoy The Third, had not dared to wish for.

On one plasma screen in the foyer, a screen dedicated to live share feeds from the New York Stock Exchange via Reuters and Bloomberg, thousands of penguins cheered with glee as GRABiT's share price starting rising almost as fast as the Ross Ice Shelf was melting. With every extra inch of water floor traders found themselves standing in, another 2% was added to GRABiT's share price. And GRABiT's price went through the roof of the NSYE, which was already leaking, having been ripped off by a tornado earlier in the day, when it announced its response to the catastrophe. GRABiT had hundreds of millions of empty new builds, built way above projected water levels, whole cities and countries in fact, waiting to populate climate refugees. Next to the financial screen, another screen showed an emergency meeting of the United Nations getting underway at its headquarters in New York, where the East River waterfront was already forming a lake, engulfing lower Manhattan. Most of the UN delegates were wearing wellingtons, and they were tripping over each other to get to their places.

From the Oval Office in Washington, D.C., the President of the United States, himself of Irish extraction, was sitting solemnly in front of a camera, with some of the Joint Chiefs of Staff nodding sagely and gesticulating authoritatively behind him, whispering into his ears. The briefing complete, the President looked back into the camera and pleaded with the world to calm down, to come together, and to get to the bottom of what was going on out there in Antarctica.

Following another ear full of information and advice, the President continued to look relaxed, but full of resolve, as he stated that the world was facing the biggest refugee crisis the planet had ever seen. Adding that there would be unprecedented human and animal migration, as flood waters submerged vast areas of low lying land. Then he sincerely pledged the assistance of the US Army and Navy, which were already moving into action, and any other help or aid the US could give the world.

No sooner had the President delivered his address than he jumped to attention, a little too fast for the camera man, who pulled up the camera to catch the saluting hand bouncing off his temple. The world saluted with a reassuring wink, the President said, "God Bless the United States of America," promising that he was off to the White House Situation Room, to meet with National Security Staff and Watch Teams - including the National Security Advisor, The Deputy For Homeland Security, The Council Of Environmental Quality and anyone else who had a vested interest in saving the planet.

His speech and salute over, the President began to walk regally across the Whitehouse lawn, waving to the world, with the dignified composure of a great leader who was confident that the crisis would be met head on, and further, resolved. However, one or two of the security guards had other ideas.

Two burly secret service agents hoisted the President off the ground and, putting Usain Bolt's 9.58 second 100 meter world record to shame, carried him across the Whitehouse lawn, where a helicopter was waiting to take him and his family to a five star, ultra-secure, water tight facility high up in the Appellation Mountains. A facility way beyond the predicated flood levels, which were not long in from Cray Super Computers, over there in NSA's headquarters, Fort Meade. And the Irish Prime minister wasn't that far behind him.

Several other screens in the foyer showed news helicopters flying up and down the Ross Ice Shelf with camera crews hanging out of them, all around the polar cap actually. Icebergs the size of islands were falling off, and huge depressions were forming on the ice mass, some as large as cities, with cumulus steam clouds bellowing out from them, and stretching miles into the atmosphere. Huge melt lakes were also forming on the surface, creating Amazonian sized rivulets which cascaded as waterfalls over the ice shelf edge.

Beneath one screen, a rambunctious group of green hiccupping penguins, wearing green construction hard hats with shamrocks on, and sipping Green

Avalanches booed and cheered when the Irish Prime minister, the Taoiseach, came into view. He was addressing the Irish public in Dublin, with the rest of the Oireachtas behind him, and the Liffey already lapping at the doors of Leinster House.

The whole of Ireland, and millions of expatriates along with a hundred million claiming Irish descent around the world, were watching RTÉ, praying for news of a solution from the Taoiseach. Or some kind of inspiration: a speech, or phrase of historical import. Sure anything of historical significance at all would do at this moment in time. Something on a par with Martin Luther King's 'I have a dream' speech perhaps; or Neil Armstrong's 'One small step'; or Agnes Brown's – Mrs. Brown, that is - "I used to say fehk off but now I say, that's nice".

With a solemn, concerned eyebrow raised, the Taoiseach glanced around a room full of anticipation, looked squarely into the RTÉ camera, lowered his solemn eyebrow and declared with some aplomb that:

"The Antarctica is banjaxed, lads," adding, as the crowd drew their breath and struggled to calm their nerves, "and so is the rest of the planet."

Agnes Brown had won the day.

The Taoiseach's advice was received with mixed sentiment, and with riots about to engulf Dublin, the throng noticed a glint in the Taoiseach's angelic green eyes. Sweeping back a fringe of strawberry blond hair, he smiled like a cherub, looked back into the RTÉ camera with piercing eyes, and gave them all the hope they could ever wish for, and a solution which would follow him into the annals of brewery history:

"But rather than run for the hills lads," the Taoiseach began, his teeth twinkling under the RTÉ makeshift studio lighting, "ye are to set an example to the rest of the world and stroll leisurely to the highest pubs in the land, where you'll hopefully be safe from the flood waters. What's more," his smile opened up to fill the camera lens itself, "you'll find that drinks are on the house."

The Irish viewers looked at one another quizzically, then back to the Taoiseach. No words passed their lips, but the Taoiseach understood completely, so in tune was he, following the recent economic collapse, with the Irish zeitgeist. Clearing his throat, the Taoiseach made them an offer they couldn't refuse, "When I say drinks are on the house lads, I mean of course that the drinks are on Leinster House," and he subsequently promised to pick up the nation's tab.

Not since The Irish Free State was established in 1922 had the people of Ireland known such joy. The biggest party the World had ever known, and perhaps its last, started immediately, when almost two thirds of the Irish population broke the World Marathon Record -uphill at that - in an effort to secure their first free pint.

Unfortunately, when a bespectacled minion from *An Roinn Airgeadais*, The Department of Finance, with mossy brown hair, and a twitching mousey, nose, which had a penchant for smelling trouble, whispered into the Taoiseach's ear that, following his offer of free alcohol, which was to be found only in the highest pubs in the country, the OSI, Ireland's National Mapping Agency, had been immediately inundated with calls.

The lads called the mouse Nibbler, and didn't he continued to nibble away at the Taoiseach's reddening ear. The Taoiseach was astonished to learn that virtually every pub landlord in Ireland - the majority of which were not on mountains, hills, hillocks, mounds, knolls, ridges or any other kind of protuberance which might qualify them for free drinks - had contacted Ireland's National Mapping Agency to apologise profusely for the previous erroneous measurements of their pub's altitude. Apologies accepted, they then proceeded to update the Mapping Agency with the correct coordinates, all of which were several hundred meters above previous estimates. That alone was shock enough for the Taoiseach, but when Nibbler confirmed that all the new coordinates had been verified with the highest degree of accuracy with respect to the countries datum for such measurements - the mean sea level of the tide gauge at Malin Head, County Donegal – he felt like scrambling for the nearest pub himself.

"Are we rising or sinking?" the Taoiseach asked Nibbler in dismay, when he learned that his favourite pub, just outside Dublin, which boasted spectacular sea-level views, had also just been remapped by OSI, and now sat at an altitude somewhere on a par with the top of the Wicklow mountains.

"I suppose," said Nibbler, trying to make light of the matter, his nose twitching nervously, "that if the rest of the world is sinking, then surely we must be rising. After all, we are Irish."

With Nibbler relaying the predicted costs, the Taoiseach wished the RTÉ camera would open up and swallow him whole. The writing was on the wall of every pub in his fabled land, or at least their accumulated tabs, Nibbler warned him, and the final drinks bill was going to be so huge that no superlatives had yet been invented to describe such sums. Sure the whole economy was threatened from a most unlikely source, Nibbler concluded.

"What national debt, sure we're a part of Europe?" the Taoiseach lamented.

"That might be true," said Nibbler, "but given the size of the debt, the ECB will wash its hands of us." Nibbler winked, "And won't they have plenty of water to do it with."

"Why's that?" asked the Taoiseach, who'd built the country and his administration on handouts from the European Central Bank.

"Global flooding," explained Nibbler, "sure don't you get it. They'll have enough water to wash their hands of us?"

"Look here you, you feckin' eejit," roared the Taoiseach, "this is no time for jokes. I was talking about the size of the debt."

"Oh," twitched Nibbler, "I see. Well the fact of the matter is that we'll have a national debt bigger than America." Which the Taoiseach thought wasn't that bad, until, after another almighty twitch altogether, Nibbler added, "That's the national debt of America combined with the UK, Russia and Zimbabwe."

"How much?" the Taoiseach stammered, when Nibbler told him that he may well kiss goodbye to the next few decades worth of GDP, should Ireland, by any slither of a chance, survive the impending flood. His nose twitching, Nibbler repeated the figures a third time, for the stupefied prime minister.

"Be the lovin' Jaysis, not again," cried the Taoiseach, having spent far too long during the last election campaigning in Barrytown. "Sure I thought the feckin' Ross Ice Shelf was melting, not the feckin' Irish economy!"

With the nation ordering three drinks at a time, the Taoiseach quickly made his excuses and darted out of Leinster House, escorted on all sides by lads from Stiúrthóireacht na Faisnéise, the Directorate Of Intelligence. Excuses which were of a National Security nature, Nibbler assured RTÉ onlookers, before he scurried out after the Taoiseach, his tail trailing behind him. Seconds later, Nibbler hopped in beside the Taoiseach who was waiting in a helicopter outside the Kildare entrance to Leinster House, with both their families already onboard. Its occupants secure, the helicopter took them off to meet with the other Irish man and his family, high and dry on the top of the Appellation Mountains, where their new accommodation awaited them.

Chapter 49

Bend It Like Pythagoras

Over in Eirestown, Paht, the landlord of Paddy McGinty's Goat, was just finishing his telephone conversation with an administrator from OSI, the National Mapping Agency, having updated him on the pub's new altitude coordinates.

"'Deed, I'm awful sorry for the misunderstanding, and all," he said sincerely

"You're not the first," said the administrator, referring to the recent upsurge in ACAs, Altitude Correction Applications, "and I doubt you'll be the last. We've processed thousands of revisions, in the last hour alone."

"All the same," said Paht, "it's very kind of you to be so understanding."

"Not at all," said the administrator, "it must be a terrible affliction for you."

"It's been an unholy curse."

"Worse I'd dare say," the administrator sympathised, "it must have been desperate altogether."

"I blame the Christian Brothers meself," snapped Paht.

"Didn't you get any schooling at all?"

"I don't think so," said Paht.

"Why do you say that?"

"The oul' father said I entered school stupid and came out the same way twelve years later," Paht sighed. "I'm ashamed to admit it, but you'll not meet a t'icker Paddy than me. I can barely read and write, never mind measure the height of the oul' pub with respect to the mean sea level of the tide gauge at Malin Head, County Donegal. "

"'Tis a crying shame," commiserated the administrator, tapping a pen in anger on his desk. "A crying shame that our great Irish education system failed you like this."

"'Tis and all," said Paht. "Sure didn't the oul' lad used to say," he elaborated further, referring to his late father's merciless scoldings, "may the Lord have mercy on his dear oul' soul, that there were monkeys up in Dublin zoo who could read and write better than me. And as for numbers and mathematics, didn't they have a whiz of a chimpanzee named Pythagoras, doing the books for them."

"Jesus," the administrator exclaimed, "sure you've had an awful upbringing altogether."

"I have," agreed Paht solemnly, "and more's the pity."

"But thinking about it now," the administrator came back, "sure I never heard tell of that chimpanzee, and I'm in Dublin all my life."

"'Deed I'm very surprised to hear that," said Paht.

"It must have been a clever chimp," speculated the administrator, "he almost sounds human?"

"Actually, the oul' lad said that there was only a 5% difference between a chimpanzee's DNA and a human's."

"Really?"

"Although, in my case," moaned Paht, "he said there was probably no difference whatsoever, and didn't the chimp have a bigger brain than me."

"Sorry to hear that Paht, but you were scandalised altogether," said the administrator. A few moments later, after racking his brains, he came back again, "But like I say Paht, sure I never heard tell of this Pythagoras."

"I find that very hard to believe."

"You do?"

"I do," stated Paht emphatically. "Sure the oul' lad said Pythagoras was the talk of the town, solving equations all day and night for that shower of animal rights abusers over there in Trinity College. They even sent poor oul' Pythagoras out to NASA in America, where he was to train as an Irish astronaut."

"They did?"

"'Deed they did," Paht claimed. "Sure if the Russians could get a dog into space, said the Provost of Trinity College, the Irish could get a mathematical genius of a chimpanzee up there as well, and not a bother on them."

"Well," said the administrator, finding himself somewhere between flabbergasted and flummoxed, "I've heard some tall stories in my life, Paht." He rubbed his chin in frustration, and went on, "Ahh sure, come on now Paht, you're codding me aren't you, or have you been at the bar all morning?"

"As true as I'm stood, here," said Paht, "talking to your good self on this phone. Or may the Lord strike me down on the spot."

"So what happened to Pythagoras then?" said the administrator, becoming more embroiled in the tall tale. "One thing's for sure, an Irish chimpanzee in space would have made world headlines, and I'd know all about him."

"Well," hissed Paht, "according to the oul' lad, those good for nothing animal abusers over there in Trinity cancelled the Irish space programme, sending Pythagoras mad altogether, himself in training all those years, and it all gone to waste."

"Jesus," yelped the administrator, "Aren't they an awful shower. Go on so, did Pythagoras come back to the zoo?"

"Pythagoras came back to the zoo alright," said Paht, "and carried on solving equations like some kind of mathematical fiend. But didn't he become more and more like that other famous Irish mathematician ... what's yer ones name?"

"Sir William Rowan Hamilton, inventor of quaternion algebra?" proposed the administrator.

"Not at all," said Paht, "sure he was only dabbling. No yer man in the film... what's his name, Russell Crowe played him?"

"Oh," said the administrator, "you mean John Nash?"

"Him very self!"

"I don't think he's Irish, though, Paht."

"Sure he must be," insisted Paht. "Aren't there more Irish Americans in America than there are Americans?"

Scratching his head, and coming to the conclusion that even Pythagoras wouldn't be able to answer that question, the administrator admitted he wasn't sure.

"Never mind," said Paht, "John Nash sounds like an Irish name, and that'll do for me."

"Grand so," said the administrator, intrigued by these latest revelations of Ireland's untold mathematical history, and keen to get on, "what about John Nash?"

"Well didn't Pythagoras become an oul' eccentric like himself."

"Jaysis, Paht."

"Jaysis is right," said Paht. "The oul' lad said Pythagoras would solve equations all day long, nice as pie, and that's not a pun. But at night, wasn't he a wreck."

"A wreck?"

"'Deed he was," affirmed Paht. "The oul lad was in bits himself, may the Lord have mercy on his soul, when he told me. Pythagoras would sit there all night in a dark corner, scratching incomprehensible mathematical equations onto the walls and windows of his bedroom, gibbering to himself like a monkey, him a chimpanzee and all. In the end they had no other choice, but to ..." Paht tutted, reprimanded himself and became silent, he'd gone one step too far.

"What did they do?" demanded the administrator on the edge of his seat, the phone glued to his ear.

"Sadly, the rest is a secret said Paht."

"A secret?"

"A matter of National Security, in fact," Paht added, having just heard the phrase on the television, from the financial mouse over there in Leinster House.

"National Security?" repeated the administrator, pleading with Paht not to leave him hanging on the end of the phone and the end of a story like this.

"Sure I'll tell you what I'll do," said the administrator, hoping to bribe Paht, "I'll put Paddy McGinty's Goat up ten meters higher, just in case anyone comes snooping. The auditors never look above one thousand and thirty eight meters, that's the cut off point for *Corrán Tuathail* the highest mountain in Ireland, down below in Kerry."

"Will yeh now?" said Paht. "we'll be up in the clouds, so."

"Ye will."

"Sure never mind Pythagoras going into orbit, if we don't stop rising in altitude, we'll be the first Irish pub in space."

They both laughed and Paht agreed to tell the administrator what happened.

"Keep it under your hat, mind," Paht whispered down the phone, "but just before he died, the oul' lad assured me that he's still over there in Trinity College, in a basement below The Department of Mathematics. He's their best kept secret."

"Who, the oul' lad?"

"No, Pythagoras himself," said Paht. "They have him locked up over there, feeding him nuts and bananas all day and night, himself doing all the complicated mathematical calculations and applied mathematical research for them these last few years."

"Stop will yeh!"

"As true as I'm the landlord here," promised Paht. "Sure the oul' lad swore Pythagoras is a dab hand at Lattice Quantum Chromodynamics, Symplectic Geometry and Lie Group actions, to name but a few of his specialised fields. And with a bucket of bananas in front of him, sure there's no problem he couldn't solve."

"Get away, will ya."

"I'm not codding yeh, man," said Paht. "Didn't Pythagoras nearly get himself two million dollars the other year."

"How on earth did he manage that?"

"'Deed it was a cinch."

"Go on, so."

"Didn't he prove Fermat's last theorem before that English yoke, Andrew Wiles from Oxford did, to win himself the first million dollars."

"He never did?"

"He did, I'm telling yeh," Paht maintained. "That prize money alone would have kept himself in bananas and nuts for the rest of his life. But Trinity had to recall his paper, titled 'Modular Elliptic Curves: Bent Bananas and a solution of Fermat's last theorem', because they daren't reveal the hairy oul' source of all their mathematical, creative genius these last few decades. And anyway ..."

"What?" asked the administrator.

"The oul' lad said they'd have a hell of time trying to explain to the world how Pythagoras got the idea for modular elliptic curves from the shape of his banana."

After a few moments silence, the administrator howled with laughter. "Jaysis, but they must be all playing with their bananas over there in Trinity as we speak, trying to solve the next great mathematical puzzle."

"They can play with their bananas all they want," laughed Paht, "but they'll never be able to bend it like Pythagoras."

"And how did Pythagoras nearly get the second million?" the administrator asked, still sniggering to himself.

"Oh that was even easier," announced Paht. "Sure wasn't there also a million dollars on offer for the first solution to *disprove* Fermat's last theorem."

"It's fehkin' unreal!"

"Unreal as it might be, didn't Pythagoras also submit a disproof of the very same theorem. And once again, them robbin' animal abusers recalled that paper, if only to protect themselves."

"A million dollars for a proof and a million dollars for a disproof of the same theorem?" said the administrator.

"The very same!"

"Jaysis, but Pythagoras must be a rare oul' mathematical genius altogether. No wonder you could never live up to your oul' lad's expectations."

"It was a torturous cross to bear, I can tell you."

"I'm not codding you Paht," said the OSI administrator, composing himself, "isn't it a crying shame you were never educated yourself, sure it would have been you running rings round that shower over there in Trinity, not Pythagoras."

"A crying shame," agreed Paht sadly. "Sure I'd love nothing more than to be able to spend my days eating nuts and playing with me oul' banana."

"Well thanks all the same for the history lesson Paht, you've given me a lot to think about, and thanks for the new altitude measurements," said the OSI administrator, struggling to hold back more laughter. "With the little leg up I just gave ye, sure Paddy McGinty's Goat is the highest pub in Ireland now, the world perhaps. I may phone the Guinness Book of Records, and get you registered. I might even mention Pythagoras while I have them on the phone, not that anyone would believe me."

"T'anks all the same for the publicity offer," said Paht, "but we're busy enough without it."

"Good luck, so."

"Good luck yourself," said Paht, "and, once again, t'anks a million for all your help."

There were no international cameras in Eirestown, no news teams, but had there been, they would have seen Paht put the phone down, rub his hands together in glee, and walk back into the bar, where a hushed crowd had gathered, waiting for an update.

"How did you play it, Paht?" asked King Cormac

"Nice and thick, just like you said," answered Paht. "He thought I was a real eejit, altogether."

"Good man yerself," said the King, congratulating Paht.

"I wouldn't think much of that," said TongueSlinger, "sure he's forever playing the eejit."

"Did you mention poor oul' Pythagoras?" asked the King, putting a finger to his lips to silence TongueSlinger.

"'Deed I did," replied Paht, "but as usual, he thought I was making it all up."

"And where's Pythagoras now?" asked the King.

"Back in the kitchen with his oul' abacus," replied Paht, "cooking the books for me."

"Sure isn't it awfully kind of Trinity to let you have him once a month like that."

"It's the only way they can buy my silence," said Paht. "And anyway, I couldn't afford another accountant."

"Why's that?"

"Sure I'm only paying oul' Pythagoras peanuts."

"Will we get a chance to meet him?"

"I'm afraid not," said Paht. "Pythagoras is away to Trinity College Dublin later today, to finalise his proof of Riemann's Hypothesis, and win himself another million dollars from the Clay Mathematics Institute. He trying to get it published before the world ends."

"He's written a proof of the Riemann Hypothesis?" the King was amazed.

"He has," said Paht. "Sure didn't he put his banana out of shape altogether proving that one."

"He did?" said the King, wincing a little.

"He did," said Paht. "But not to worry, he bent the oul' banana back into shape writing a disproof of Riemann's Hypothesis, which he'll present at a later date, if we survive the global flood."

"Sure he's a rare oul' genius, altogether" said King Cormac, eagerly, "but back to business. Did the OSI buy it?"

"Buy it," said Paht, punching the air, "sure they nearly took the hands off a-me. It's official lads," and he punched the air again, "we're the highest pub in Ireland, in the whole world in fact."

"Get away will yeh," said the King.

"I'm not coddin' ye, sure I think we're high enough to claim back altitude tax, never mind free drinks."

"Drinks are on the house," shouted the King, to rapturous applause, "Leinster House, that is!"

Paht wasn't sure if he had enough roll in the till to cover the onslaught of orders, but he fired away, running up the national debt faster than the Federal Reserve of America could, given the chance.

TongueSlinger, along with a rake of other residents, had gathered in Paddy McGinty's Goat to drown their sorrows, say their last goodbyes to one another, and drink one last farewell to their fair Emerald Isle. In one corner, a few residents were tucking into *Assiette de selection de lard et chou*, a courtesy platter of bacon and cabbage dips from Paddy Roux over in An Cabáiste agus Bagún Deli, as Antarctica melted before them, clouds the size of Everest bellowing out of the ice shelf, on the plasma screen Paht had ordered in specially for the occasion.

"Say goodbye to the Croagh Patrick," said Paht, raising a free pint of the Black Stuff, having joined a few other residents around a table full of drinks. "And join me in a drink to toast the safety of the lads out there in Antarctica."

"Trollix," said TongueSlinger, venomously. "Sure I'll not be raising my glass to that shower of layabouts. Didn't I tell you not to send that shower to the Antarctica, in the first place?" Relishing another gulp of Black Stuff, he wiped his lips and went on, "They couldn't stop a fridge defrosting, never mind the fehkin' Ross Ice Shelf melting, the dirty good for nothin' fehkers." He took another quick gulp, and continued his diatribe. "And if I had my way sure wouldn't I ...."

"Ahhhggg!"

Paht had TongueSlinger's tongue firmly gripped between his fingers and thumb, and was stretching it across the table, leaving him with his legs dangling in mid air. "The lads are out there risking their lives for the likes of you," Paht yelled, "you dirty good for nothing..." He yanked on the Divil's tongue several more times, causing the Divil to let out an almighty gurgling, scream altogether. "Now you little fehker, come on, I dare you to say that again, either transitively or," he tugged again, "intransitively."

That a tongue could be stretched so far proved somewhat of a miracle. Sure cartoon animators, who were used to drawing such anatomical exaggerations, would be hard pushed to stretch a tongue that close to snapping point. A few Eirestown residents took pictures with their mobile phones, while others crossed themselves, muttered 'Jesus Mary and Joseph, would ye look at the length of that yoke', and said a few prayers over it.

Such a miracle would surely have made headline news across the world, if only it wasn't about to flooded on a Biblical scale, by the melting of the Ross Ice Shelf.

Another person warned Paht that if he didn't stop yanking on the Devil's tongue, it might soon be a holy relic, never mind a miracle. "If you stretch it any further," agreed another fella, "it'll be detached from the Divil's head altogether." Meanwhile, the pictures of the miracle-cum-holy relic uploaded, Facebook, Instagram and various other social media sites went mad to get hold of the stretched tongue, sending the Internet the way of the Ross Ice Shelf, into meltdown.

His eyes full of another round of camera flashes, TongueSlinger could only manage a few apologetic shrugs and grunts before King Cormac commanded Paht to let go of his tongue. The tongue released by royal decree, it snapped back like a rubber band, giving the Divil an almighty whiplash several times across his face, before it finally recoiled into its unholy lair.

The Divil fell back onto his chair, lashed by his own tongue, "You baldy, fat fehker. You've the tongue nearly ripped out of me head again!" he squealed, dipping his tongue repeatedly in and out, for medicinal purposes he claimed, of a pint of Black Stuff, lapping like a cat licking its wounds, until he'd emptied the glass.

"Come on now lads," a voice from over near the bar said, "come on now and we'll sing a last song together." Then the small dishevelled fiddle player threw up the Paddyvarius onto his left shoulder, where he waited for the uilleann pipes to start playing the Cliffs Of Dooneen, in the style of Planxty.

"Be the hoh-key," said Paht, "would you look-it, it's the Cracker Craics." Paht had a fine voice on him, his throat as velvety smooth as the pints he was downing, and he started singing in such a manner that if you closed your eyes, you'd swear Christy Moore himself was singing beside you ...

You may travel far, far, from your own native home,
Far away o'er the mountains, far away o'er the foam,
But of all the fine places that I've ever been,
Oh, there's none can compare with the Cliffs of Dooneen.

By the time he reached the last verse the whole town joined in, even King Cormac and his courtesans. Word had flown around Eirestown, and everyone had gathered in and around Paddy McGinty's Goat to join in the song. Those who couldn't sing, hummed, or gently whistled and swayed together. And they all joined hands, forming an Eirestown chain of support for Irish men, women and children all over the world, all humanity in fact. Especially their own Malachy Malarkey and QuickMIC, and their newly adopted sons and daughter, Donn-Dub, Ryan, PaddySan and Mai-Ly, sacrificing their lives out in the depths of the perilous Antarctica. Their voices strained with grief as the imminent collapse gathered pace before their eyes on the plasma TV.

During an emotional solo, the pipes nearly buckled once or twice. But the oul' fiddle, Paddyvarius, whispered 'cop yourself on, and stay strong for the lads', and the pipes recovered, fought back tears, and had the town in bits, such was the passion it unleashed. As the plaintive uilleann pipe solo came to an end, everyone repeated the first verse for the very last time, some of them waving back at the plasma TV, where, although he couldn't see them, the Taoiseach waved back energetically from a helicopter, courtesy of the Whitehouse, which was just taking off for the Appellation Mountains:

'You may travel far, far, from your own native home,
Far away o'er the mountains, far away o'er the foam,
But of all the fine places that I've ever been,
Oh, there's none can compare with the Cliffs of Dooneen.

Chapter 50

More Beef Than A Herd Of Heifers

With the Antarctica and the rest of the world crashing down around Shin O'Beef's ears, the Irish living myth smirked, opened the curtains and looked out from the Erebus Hilton, onto the cold, desolate, despondent landscape beyond. In the very far distance, Shin could already see signs of the damage that Hotstuff was inflicting on the Ross Ice Shelf. Huge depressions were opening up everywhere, and large sections were forming ice lakes. Above the shelf, cumulus clouds filled the sky, like herds of white elephants. This Frozen Hell was melting and this was the signal Shin had been waiting for. Now it was time to go into action.

Not that Shin was actually looking at the real surface. By wonders of modern technology, the surface was displayed on a window sized plasma screen, behind which, at this depth below Erebus, there was only rock face. If it hadn't been for this plasma though, on which Shin mostly displayed the Irish countryside, wouldn't Shin have gone stir crazy months ago.

Shin smiled again, and switched the plasma to a news channel. To have been reactivated by Minus 1 almost 50 years after having being decommissioned, was something else altogether – a story of mythic proportions in itself. And all for the glory of Ireland herself, for the glory of the world in fact.

Back home in Ireland a few years ago, Minus 1 had been aware for some time that there were problems in the Antarctica, such was Minus 1's global reach. Not only that, rumours were starting to circulate that some Irish descent megalomaniac from America was going to try and melt the Ross Ice Shelf, and flood the rest of the world. Of course Minus 1 informed America first, hoping they'd go out there to investigate and arrest the lunatic. But didn't the American president himself get on the line to speak with the head of Minus 1 saying that, "If we were to worry about the antics of every crazy Irish person living here, which is probably all forty million of those either claiming to be Irish or of Irish descent, sure we'd never get anything else done."

That was a bit of a setback for Minus 1 alrigth, but their Chief of Operations responded, "We sympathise completely Mr President."

"Really?" said the President, who was expecting them to give him an awful scolding for his reluctance to become involved.

"'Deed we do," the Chief replied. "Sure we have exactly the same problem here in Ireland, but we've only four million of the crazy feckers on our hands."

The setback didn't last long though. And when they found out that they already had a sleeper agent out there in Antarctica, Minus 1's luck turned.

Sadly, following Shin's reactivation, it meant a couple of extra years out here in this barren place, but that period was nearly over now, and Shin O'Beef could soon return back home to Ireland. However, there would be no hero's welcome, not even an oul' handshake from the Taoiseach, such was the secrecy which, to this very day, still surrounds Minus 1's existence.

The Erebus Hilton may have been a hell hole, but the living quarters had a few oul' comforts. Air locks to keep out that eggy smell, and a wardrobe being another one of them.

Shin pulled down a suitcase and opened it on the bed. Shin couldn't help but look with admiration on the tricoloured attire, provided by Minus 1 all those years ago. It had been many years since it had seen the light of day, alrigth. But the ninja warrior outfit, wrapped in paper and tucked away in a dark, air tight box all those years ago, was still in perfect condition. Next to the uniform, lay several copies of Your Ireland. Shin picked one up, and flicked through it, reminiscing.

The first copy was an edition dedicated to the demise of the Phuk Mee gang. That was some craic the brother had got himself involved in out there in Hong Kong in the 1960s, alright, Shin laughed. It was rare craic altogether. With some embarrassment, Shin picked up the next follow up edition. A Royal Special, this one even had a picture of Queen Elizabeth II on the front cover. You couldn't write it, Your Ireland wrote underneath the picture, but they did.

With the Antarctica continuing to melt before Shin on the plasma television, and the odd seismic tremor rippling through Erebus, Shin opened the first page of the special royal Edition, and started reading. After dispatching of the Phuk Mee triad gang, Your Ireland boasted, Shin O'Beef was fast becoming a legend in Hong Kong, and even more of a legend back home in Ireland. A status, Your Ireland was proud to admit, which was boosted significantly by their meticulous research and determination to report Shin's exploits out there. And it was that determination, following another tip off from Patrick, the landlord of Finnegans Wake over there in Kowloon, which had given birth to the latest chapter in Shin O'Beef escapades. And this latest exploit catapulted Shin into the all time Irish Hall Of Fame. For hadn't Shin given every Double O secret agent in Her Majesty's Secret Service the beating of their lives. Including the infamous 007, who received an awful hammering altogether, after the Double Os wondered into Finnegans Wake one night for a drink, and started telling Irish jokes to each other.

The fact that all the Double Os were of Irish extraction and that 007's grandfather was Jimmy O'Bond, a farmer from Eirestown, was no help at all when Shin O'Beef, having slipped home to get into ninja costume, came back and rounded on them for telling Irish jokes. Jokes which Shin felt ridiculed the Irish in a most offensive and derogatory manner, especially when told with an Etonian English accent.

All these years later, Shin stilled cringed reading that. Had Shin known they were Irish, never mind beat them black and blue, Shin would have joined the Double Os in drinking Finnegans Wake dry.

A week later, over there in London, Queen Elizabeth II herself was livid, reported Your Ireland. And following a brief visit to the King Edward VII hospital, she phoned Leinster House and demanded that they immediately recall Shin O'Beef back to Ireland from Hong Kong, to spare Her Majesty's government any further embarrassment. It was bad enough that poor oul' 007 would be in King Edward VII hospital for at least a year, Your Ireland went on, relaying Her Majesty's grief, the first six months in traction, undergoing all manner of treatment and surgery. But after an almighty kick in an area Her Majesty would rather not discuss, and Your Ireland was under orders from the Holy Father himself not to print, 007's days with the ladies were open to surgical debate, and Jimmy O'Bond's lineage was surely at an end.

Her Majesty was not so worried about the question of 007's ability to pass on his genes, Your Ireland clarified, because, without female distractions, he would be able to focus on the more important job of protecting the Empire. But poor oul' Miss Moneypenny was beside herself with grief, knowing that her romantic liaisons with 007 were well and truly numbered.

And anyway, Her Majesty went on, with a rash of hungry corgis barking menacingly in the background, the English had enough problems trying to maintain law and order in a land where no one spoke English, let alone a land full of crazy Irish expatriates, who seemed hell bent on beating anyone up for any reason whatsoever. That's if they weren't singing, Her Majesty bemoaned, or roaming the streets of Kowloon playing those infernal fiddles and uilleann pipes, and keeping the residents of Hong Kong awake until all hours of the morning.

With the corgi's nipping at her ankles, Your Ireland were adamant that Her Majesty's nerves were on edge, and this just wasn't cricket old boy, or hurling for that matter oul' lad! Her Majesty thought that the Phuk Mee gang had been quite a violent handful of lads until Shin O'Beef saw them off. But there wasn't a hand in the Empire big enough to hold oul' Shin O'Beef.

Never mind, wrote Your Ireland, personally commenting on Shin O'Beef's reckless actions out there in Hong Kong, that they were Double Os, English accents or not, if you couldn't tell an Irish joke in an Irish pub, what would it be next? No singing? Or Jesus, Mary and Joseph forbid, no fighting? Or, three Hail Mary's, fifty rosaries and one hundred Our Father's forbid, No Drinking? Sure you may as well close down every Irish pub in the world, including Her Majesty's favourite Irish pub, only a stone's throw from Buckingham Palace, Paddy McGinty's Corgi, over there on Bond Street.

With the Irish joke under threat of extinction, what choice did Minus 1 have? Shin O'Beef was recalled from Hong Kong immediately and decommissioned.

Having finished that paragraph, Shin glanced over to the plasma television, where reports were coming in from all over the world. Hotstuff had triggered an almighty domino effect, and it was looking bad altogether. If Shin didn't get a move on, there may be no Ireland left to go home to. With a deep sigh, Shin put the Your Ireland special Royal edition back in the suitcase. They were rare oul' times alright.

No one had seen hide nor hair, nor shin of Shin O'Beef for the last several decades But the phoenix was back from the oul' ashes, Shin O'Beef had been reactivated. Of course, every child in Ireland had heard of this modern day myth, but thought that it was just the Irish imagination on overdrive. Instead of stories about Banshees to scare the life out of children and get them home before it went dark, parents had long ago started telling stories about Shin O'Beef, and how Shin would give you a good hiding if you were caught roaming the streets, when you should have been in bed.

Shin O'Beef looked in the mirror: Green panse, white top with orange sleeves, green balaclava mask, with a slit for the eyes, and patted the rotund belly. Still firm, but the oul' cabbage diet hadn't worked out. Perhaps, thought Shin, you were meant to take the spuds and bacon off the plate, and just eat cabbage for a few months? Fortunately, the oul' green panse were elasticated, so the slightly protruding belly would be well tucked away.

The tricolored ninja flexed and stretched old but supple muscles; muscles which had retained memory of past Ninjitsu training, even if Shin hadn't. Blood surging through the veins, Shin reached up and pulled down another suitcase, which was full of weapons.

It was time to pay Frosty a visit. Anyone who thought they could sink Ireland and get away with it had another thing coming, let alone sinking the rest of the world. Frosty was a gentleman alright, a gentle giant for the most part, when he wasn't shouting and screaming at everyone that is, but no matter, he'd overstepped the mark. As for William McCoy The Third and Captain James Bush, they wouldn't know what had hit them.

If they wanted a little beef, and didn't surrender quietly, sure wasn't oul' Shin O'Beef about to give them more beef than a heard of heifers.

Chapter 51

Séamus O'Malley, The Ice Rat

"Yis're roight, o' course," said Séamus, struggling to control the ice buggy, as himself and the Inspection Committee headed back down T1 towards Hotstuff's control room, "there's an awful lo' o' slush about, wha'. Sure they must have started without us."

"What's causing it?" asked Malachy, hanging onto the buggy.

Ice was giving way to slush, and Séamus was throwing the buggy all over the lava highway, trying to keep it from sliding into the huge trenches on either side, which were almost overflowing, like torrential rivers.

"It looks like she's going already," said Séamus, meaning that the Ross Ice Shelf had gone into serious meltdown mode. "But don't worry yerselves, we're nearly there now." He tugged sharply on the driving wheel, right then left, then right again and alternately stepped on the accelerator and brakes. "Just hol' onto yere horses," then he winked in the rear view mirror at Donn-Dubh, Ryan and QuickMIC, "or yis donkeys ears, wha'. Won't be long now," he said, "one last spurt, wha'," and then buggy got some traction on a relatively slush free part of the highway, accelerating them with a jolt.

William McCoy The Third was standing in front of Hotstuff's control panel, mesmerised by all the levers, wheels, circuit-breakers, dials, gauges and flashing lights, enchanted also by all the creaks, groans, hissing, rhythmic clanking, and the odd thunderous rumble from deep within T1 and T2. He rubbed his hands together in joy. Most of the dials and gauges were struggling to measure amps, volts, mega watts, humidity, main steam pressure and many other variables which were mostly off the scale now.

The day had come, and the hour was not far away. GRABiT would soon be the only Realtor in the world, with desres condos, houses, skyscrapers and any other living accommodation you care to mention on offer. And rents would rocket, not unlike Hotstuff who was starting to rock herself. Only an hour ago, a penguin had come in from the foyer, screaming that GRABiT had just sold billions of dollars worth of real estate, a fact which had just been reported from the NYSE, sending their share prices stratospheric.

"What was that?" asked William, shaken out of his day dreams by the rocking platform.

"Nothing to worry about," said Squawky, tightening the gag on Frosty, who was mortified that his creation would soon destroy his homeland, "a little volcanic and seismic activity, it's to be expected."

The ground shook again, and William clung onto a rail, until it subsided.

Frosty stared in disbelief at the efficiency of Hotstuff, every metric on the control panel was off the charts. When he heard that the whole of the Antarctica ice shelf was on its way out, he shed a tear, and they removed his gag for a moment, allowing him to beg William to switch Hotstuff off. But his supplications fell on deaf and greedy ears, and he was gagged again.

And when the other dominos started to fall, creating havoc with the planetary weather systems, Frosty just couldn't understand how Hotstuff was causing so much damage so quickly. He guessed correctly that the weather systems had been on a delicate knife edge already, what with all the damage humanity had been inflicting on them since they discovered fossil fuels. So, he surmised, Hotstuff had been the catalyst to send the weather systems over the edge, and trigger Armageddon. Not that this analysis made him feel any better. However, because Hotstuff was the key, it gave him a feint glimmer of hope. He thought that if he could somehow get Hotstuff switched off, he might be able to reverse the process. But there was little chance of that, what with himself tied to a chair, gagged and under constant surveillance.

"Here yis go," said Séamus thirty minutes later, stopping the buggy on the entrance platform to T1. "Now be careful of the slush puddles when yis get ou'."

The Inspection Committee breathed a communal sigh of relief, glad to be alive, having spent the last few hundred meters dodging blocks of ice as big as houses, the Ross Ice Shelf falling down all around them.

"That was a close shave, wha'?" said Ryan winking at Séamus and emulating his wha'. He looked up to make sure nothing else was about to land on, or near them and added, "A real close shave."

"I'll tell ye this, and I'll tell ye no more," said Séamus, "your roight!"

"I know I'm right," said Ryan,

"No your right," said Malachy pointing to Ryan's right.

"Welcome home boys," said a familiar voice. "And to think I only came out here to see how T1 was doing. What a pleasant surprise," Squawky snorted, "the rats have been flushed out of the sewer."

Ye Old Ross Ice Shelf Committee thought about running again, but several mean looking, muscular coal stokers, swinging baseball bats, looked like they were in no mood for a chase. And anyway, they couldn't go into T1 that would be a death sentence, if ever there was one.

"Ryan is back," Squawky cheered, clapping his flippers together, "and he's brought his friends along with him. Glad you could make it boys, you're just in time for the party."

"What party?" asked Malachy.

"The End of the World Party," squealed Squawky, pointing a mini-M249 at him. "Wanna try your luck again?"

"Yeah," said Dorky, pointing a pistol at them, his right arm still in a sling, "the End of the World Party."

"You there," snarled Squawky in his nasally accent, pointing the mini-M249 at Donn-Dubh, "with that duvet on your head." He nodded to one of the coal stokers who was holding open a titanium brief case, "Put the hat in there, and no funny business."

Donn-Dubh kissed his teeth, took his hat off, revealing green dreadlocks, and placed it in the briefcase. "But my ears will be freeing without my hat," he complained, rubbing them

"Don't worry about that," said Squawky, "you ain't gonna be needing ears where you're going. Now get back in the buggy, and like my DKNY crocodile handbag once said ..."

"What?"

"Make it snappy."

Ye Olde Ross Ice Shelf did as they were told, and Séamus drove them back across the platform. Dorky and Squawky followed in an ice buggy behind, and in front of them, a buggy full of coal-stokers led the way.

"Good news William, look who I found," Squawky said, arriving at the control panel.

Hotstuff's tremors and shudders had subsided, but despite Squawky's glad tidings, William continued to cling to a brass rail for dear life. Now he really knew what Captain James meant when he said Hotstuff twerked.

"Well, well, well," said William, "we meet at last Ryan."

Everyone jumped out of the ice buggies and Squawky said, "Oh you know pretty boy, then?"

"Know him," said William smiling, "why he's working for me!"

"Sir," said Ryan gratefully, "thank God you're here! I thought these lunatics were going to kill me."

"Ryan," said Malachy "is this true?"

"Yes," said Ryan, "I really thought these deranged penguins were going to kill me sooner or later."

"No," said QuickMIC, "he means do you work for them?"

"Sorry," said Ryan, walking towards William and shaking his hand.

"By the way," said Squawky, "I hate to break up the reunion, but we caught another double agent, sir."

"Another one?" said William.

"This one was fraternising with the enemy, sir." He prodded Séamus, pushing him forward with the mini-M249.

"Yis're wrong, o' course, now come on lads," pleaded Séamus. "Ah come on now, have a heart will yis. Sure they tol' me they were the Inspection Committee."

"Ignore him sir," said Squawky, "He's already shown the saboteurs everything they need to know. It's a good job we caught them when we did, before they had a chance to do any damage."

"Saba wha', wha'?" asked Séamus. "Come on lads, sure I'm due to retire next year, and yis have had the best years o' me life."

"A double agent, eh?" said William.

"Meet Séamus O'Malley, William," scowled Squawky, prodding Séamus again and sneering venomously into his ear, "we call him ... the Ice Rat."

"An Ice wha'?" cried Séamus.

"There's only one thing worse than a Manhattan Hilton rat," said William, who happened to have bitter memories of a night back in New York, when a rat entered the Manhattan Hilton and went on the run, ruining a GRABiT Corporate Event he'd spent a million dollars on to entertain some of their biggest clients.

"What's that sir?" asked Squawky.

"An Erebus Hilton ice rat!" William yelled.

"Ahh, Jaysis, come on now lads," Séamus, implored, "cop yourselves on, wha'." He held up his flippers and waved them around, "Yis're wrong, o' course ... Look-it lads, flippers." He opened his mouth, "No incisors in 'ere wha'," then closed it again, and patted his head on both sides, "an' no floppy ears ..."

"I said Ice Rat," said Squawky, prodding Séamus again, "not Ice Rabbit."

"Aww come on now," said Séamus. "Yis see, can't yis, I'm no ice rat, or rabbit for that matter." Séamus pleaded with the Inspection Committee, "Sure I'm no rat at all. Please, yis have t' tell them the truth. Come on now Donn-Dubh."

"Now what would I know about Ice Rats?" said Donn-Dubh, winking at Séamus. "Sure, after all, I'm only an oul' simpleton from Jamaica."

Dorky gave Séamus a pistol whip across the back of his head.

"Hey, take it easy, man," said Donn-Dubh, "I was only joking. Séamus is not working with us. We tricked him into believing we were the inspection team."

"T'anks Donn-Dubh," said Séamus, rubbing the back of his head. "Now do yis believe me."

"He would say that," snarled Squawky, "he's trying to protect his double crossing contact."

"Wha'?"

"Get back into line ... Ice Rat ... before we melt you," said Dorky, poking him in the ribs with his pistol.

"Melt him?" sighed Squawky, shaking his head in disgust. "Melt him?" Placing one flipper on his left hip, he raised a right waggling flipper in Dorky's face, "You wanna play gangasta, you wanna be a Wise Guy, huh? Then you gotta get your *lingua franca* down. Put some fear into them."

"I'll pull them down boss," said Dorky, reaching for his waist, and wondering what underpants had to do with being a gangster, "but I think they're Kelvin Kline, not Lingua Franca." Without another word, he whipped his underwear off with a flourish, and stood upright, naked as the day he was born, dangling them on the end of his good flipper, "And I'm not sure how they will put fear into anyone, Boss."

"Put them back on you imbecile, have you no shame man!" shouted Squawky making his apologies to Ye Old Ross Ice Shelf. "His mothaaa," he screamed, "it's his mothaaa you gotta feel sorry for her."

"What do you want us to do with the Ice Rat, sir?" Squawky asked William, while Dorky slipped back into his Lingua Franca.

"Liquidate the rat," hissed William, who considered treachery the worse kind of villainy. Talk about the five New York Mafia Families thought William, they had nothing on these treacherous, vicious penguins. James was right about these double crossers, they were not to be trusted, none of them.

Squawky poked Dorky in his stomach. "You hear that," and he repeated William's terrifying order, enunciating each letter menacingly, "L... I... Q... U... I... D... A... T... E."

Smugly, looking Dorky straight in the face, Squawky concluded his complimentary appraisal of William's command of criminal argot. "Now that's what you call *lingua franca,* you hear. You don't just *melt* an Ice Rat. Oh no ... you *liquidate* him. That's hardcore, that's what you call ... real gangsta."

"Sir?" said Dorky.

"What is it?" said Squawky, hoping that he'd finally got his message across.

"Ain't it the case," Dorky inquired warily, "that if you *liquidate* an Ice Rat ..." he paused here, some inkling of self-preservation informing him that perhaps this line of inquiry was not such a good idea after all.

"Get on with it man!" demanded Squawky.

"Ok, ok" said Dorky, shaken into action. "Ain't it the case," he repeated, "that if you *liquidate* an Ice Rat, you are in fact melting him. So when I said, get back into line ... Ice Rat ... before we melt you ... oww!"

Squawky had hold of Dorky's pink bandaged flipper, and dragged it down, so that they were face to face, where Dorky could smell freshly chewed petite chocolate penguins from L.A. Burdick NYC filled with Crème brûlée. "You wanna talk semantics, eh, you wanna talk semantics? You smart now? Huh, huh ... You a Wise Guy all of a sudden, huh? A semantic Wise Guy, now? Huh, huh?"

Semantics? Dorky had enough trouble understanding the meaning of normal words, let alone the meaning of a word which was the name of a subject all about the meaning of words. "What do you mean by semantic and semantics, Boss, I don't know what that means?" He raised his eyebrows apologetically when he saw a red rage come over Squawky's face, and fumbled for a few more words,

"I mean ... I think I know what you mean ... but not what the word semantic means ... if you get my meaning, Boss. Do you know what I mean?"

Dorky screamed even louder when Squawky twisted his swollen flipper again. "Oh, you're getting cute now, eh? How about we liquidate this flipper eh? Know what I mean? Yeah ..." he looked over at William, who had concluded that it must be the toxic fumes of Mount Erebus which made everyone crazy around here. Whatever was making the locals loco, to be on the safe side, he was going to order a gas mask for the rest of his stay.

"Boss you got a Smoothie Maker handy?" Squawky laughed fiendishly, hollering yeehaa a few times. "Yes sirree, we're gonna liquidate us a Penguin Flipper." He twisted Dorky's flipper even harder, "Gonna make us a Wise Guy Semantic Smoothie," and looked cold and sure, deep into Dorky's, tear filled eyes, "You know what I mean, huh?"

The squad of samurai penguins from Tokyo zoo, busy guarding Frosty, could smell blood, and started to go a bit crazy, squealing and cheering. Even Hotstuff got in on the action, like a voracious dragon, stepping up a gear.

"Enough," shouted William, "just get the Ice Rat out of here."

"What about the other's, sir," said Squawky, releasing Dorky. "What you want we should do with them?"

"Liquidate them all!" he commanded, waving them away.

"Come on," said Squawky to the Inspection Committee, "you heard the boss."

"Where are ye taking us?" asked Malachy.

"To swim with the fishes," barked Squawky, using Mafioso *lingua franca* for you are about to be killed.

"I can't swim," said Malachy, demonstrating that he was as semantically challenged as Dorky.

"Hold it there said Ryan!"

Outlining a special grievance against Séamus, he requested permission from William to kill the Ice Rat right here, right now.

Now this was a surprise. William couldn't believe Ryan had a stomach for violence. Séamus must have hurt him real bad. William had never killed a man before, never even seen one killed. He always kept a safe distance and never got his hands dirty. There was no need back in New York, when you had waste to disposal at your services. But out here, things were different.

William granted him permission, and Dorky gave Ryan a pistol, to carry out his foul deed.

"On your knees, you dirty, double crossin' Ice Rat," Ryan hissed, walking towards Séamus.

"Jaysis, Mary and Joseph," screamed Séamus, blessing himself a few times, before Dorky dragged him to his knees.

Ryan held the pistol to Séamus' sweating temple. "Now start prayin'."

"Jesus," screamed Séamus, "are yis blind, sure I'm already prayin'. But is there any chance I could use the oul' toilet, wha'?"

"Silence!" Ryan shouted, and he cocked the trigger, and pushed the pistol harder into Séamus O'Malley's temple.

"Don't worry about the toilet, so," said Séamus.

"Have you changed your mind?"

"No," said Séamus, squirming, and looking down at the small puddle surrounding his steel toe capped, boots, "it's just that, I t'ink it's too late."

A fan of Quentin Tarantino films, Ryan thought he would add a few appropriate words to mark the occasion. Poking the gun back into Séamus' temple, he said, "Ok then, Séamus O'Malley, close your eyes, you dirty Ice Rat, and prepare to meet thy maker, the Penguin God."

Chapter 52

Love Blew My Circuits

No rocking could be felt over in Murphy's On The Rocks, not yet anyway. The bog-boys were still whooping it up to some Irish céilidh on the duke box, while Mai-Ly whispered sweet something's into PaddySan's ear, explaining some of her erratic behaviour these last few days or so.

"So I broke your sword in two to save your life," she said, innocently. She'd already told him that she'd been sent by William The Third to assassinate him. He gathered as much, and this is why he was going to attack her first, back there in Technological Shenanigans.

"But," she continued, "when I heard about your heroic deeds, and how you helped save the people of Eirestown, I fell in love with you."

You'll not see two iShillelaghs blushing very often, but had you been in Murphy's at that moment, you'd have seen it alrigth. Mai-Ly gave a girlie giggle and carried on. She'd only seen pictures of PaddySan in DumbHK's iShillelagh catalogue, and he wasn't bad looking at all, although, she admitted, she felt the pony tail was very dated indeed, and might have to go. In real life, pony tail or not, PaddySan was even more handsome. However, more than anything else, "It was your spirit I fell in love with," she went on. "That compassionate, cavaliering, care free, courageous spirit."

"Love literally blew my circuits," she admitted, in buttery Kilkenny tones, blushing slightly again. Fortunately for PaddySan, didn't the blown circuits allow her to bypass the assassination programme William McCoy had put into her AI processor.

"Love conquers all," said PaddySan, dragging her down to the dance floor, where they both ducked as a pair of bog-boy's legs swung by.

"But," asked PaddySan, squeezing her a little tighter, his own circuits sizzling with passion, and about to blow at any moment, "why did you threaten the lads on the POP, and jump out with the parachute?"

"Oh you fool," she giggled. There were two reasons, she went on. The first was to somehow infiltrate William McCoy's organisation, and hopefully carry out the sabotage herself, without risking any other lives. She knew all about William's plans to melt the Ross Ice Shelf, but wasn't sure how he was going to do it. Sadly, having parachuted out of The Eirestown POP, it soon became clear that she needed some assistance. She'd searched the Antarctica for hours, and was almost giving up, having come to the conclusion that it was empty.

But then, out of the blue, a memory from her student days in Shanghai, where she'd trained before being shipped over to DumbHK, Silicon Valley, California, gave her a glimmer of hope. She knew that Irish pubs were to be found everywhere in the world. And, following a few sessions in Paddy

McGinty's Dragon over there on Nanjing Road, Shanghai, she also knew that the Irish were drawn to such establishments, much like iron filings to a magnet.

"Sure you couldn't write it," she said.

"What?" said PaddySan.

"Having made the decision to find an Irish pub in the most unlikeliest of places," she said, "didn't I bump into a rowdy, staggering group of penguins, flippers wrapped around each others' shoulders, and them all blowing green hiccups."

"Get away will yeh!"

"I'm not codding you, PaddySan," smiled Mai-Ly. "Following their directions, I entered Murphy's an hour later, and there they were, all the assistance I needed, drinking pints of White Stuff and eating Irish White Rabbit Stew, at the bar."

Luckily, it transpired, the the iShillelagh Irish Wolf Hounds had been reprogrammed by QuickMIC with limited success, and sent with Malachy Malarkey on The Eirestown Flash.

"I see," said PaddySan, giving the Irish Wolf hounds a thumb up. They were still at the bar, tucking into fresh bowls of Irish White Rabbit Stew.

"And as a bonus," she concluded, in the sweetest Kilkenny accent PaddySan had ever heard, "I found you again."

"What was that?" PaddySan released Mai-Ly, and looked anxiously at his feet, which were still wobbling slightly from the first seismic impulse wave. Before anyone had a chance to answer him, the lights flickered, the duke box went off and the whole pub started to shake violently.

In any other pub in the world, panic would have set in at the first tremor, never mind after a complete shake down, and people would have be running for the nearest exit, screaming and crying for their very lives, scared half to death. But, for the most part, the patrons in Murphy's remained relatively calm, many didn't even notice the fact that half the roof had just collapsed.

The bog-boys were oblivious of any shaking in any event, and the Wolf Hounds were only slightly annoyed because their bowls of stew started sliding down the bar which was starting to sink at one end, becoming lopsided. And when the lights and duke box came back on, the duke box blaring the House Of Pain's classic Jump Around, with steam seeping up through the floors, from newly formed chasms as wide as snooker tables, the whole place went mad altogether, some nearly hopping as high as the ceiling which was rapidly falling down around their ears. Murphy's could have shaken to the ground for all most of them cared.

"Come on quick," said PaddySan, grabbing Mai-Ly by the hand and pulling her out of harm's way as an ice rafter fell from the roof, "we've got to get back to The Erebus Hilton."

"But the Wolf Hounds?" said Mai-Ly.

"Leave them to me," PaddySan said, running over to where six fresh bowls of Irish White Rabbit Stew were about to slide off the rapidly sinking bar. Withdrawing his katana, he let the six bowls slide onto its blade, and ran out the door with them balanced perfectly, not even spilling a drop, shouting for Mai-Ly to follow him, the salivating Wolf Hounds hot in pursuit.

"Stew ... stew!" An hour later the Irish Wolf Hounds were tucking into their hard earned Irish White Rabbit Stew, while PaddySan and Mai-Ly continued to look for the entrance to The Erebus Hilton, underneath a basalt overhang, halfway up Mount Erebus.

PaddySan and Mail-Ly had made their way up the Hut Peninsula on a sledge, pulled by the Irish Wolf Hounds.

Just after they ran outside Murphy's, they found a pile of snowboards. Some of the Californian Geeks over at Mac Town liked to get around on them out here. They also found a disused penguin sledge, probably abandoned by some drunken penguin sledge-gang, who woke up with no memory whatsoever of the night before.

So PaddySan promised the Wolf Hounds that they could have the Irish White Rabbit Stew, which he balanced precariously before them on his katana, if they put on the harnesses and pulled the sledge up the Hut Peninsula, turned left at Sultans Head Rock, passed The Erebus Glacier Tongue and carried on towards The Erebus Hilton entrance, not far from the Three Sisters Cones. He'd made a note of the directions earlier, peeking out of a fold in Donn-Dubh's hat.

Moments later, the Wolf Hounds were a sleek rowing team, effortlessly bobbing up and down, in a wave like motion, accelerating across the snow. Well oiled Pistons on the end of a crankshaft, they were generating more horse power than a Formula 1 racing car. At the bottom of the downward stroke, they dug their open boxing gloves deep into the snow, using them as snow oars, and leverage, to hop forward, dragging the sledge along.

UP-DOWN-UP-DOWN-UP-DOWN-UP-DOWN, stroke after stroke UP-DOWN-UP-DOWN-UP-DOWN-UP-DOWN. They were shovelling so much snow that a huge Antarctica Category 1 Herbie, a White Out hurricane blizzard, was forming behind the sledge.

Coxswain PaddySan was at the helm, his new found love, Mai-Ly, beside him, encouraging the dynamic pistons with shouts of 'Stew, stew,' instead of 'mush, mush'. The Wolf Hounds were salivating so much at the thought of the stew that icicles were forming down the sides of their mouths.

"Stew... stew!" shouted PaddySan cracking a whip over their heads for effect. The Wolf Hounds kept pumping ferociously up-and-down letting out grunts and snarls and the odd howl, until they arrived at their destination where they lapped up their reward heartily.

"The entrance must be around here somewhere," said PaddySan. Sure a disused sledge, with remnants of chewed octopus lying all around it, and the sleek looking Icicle, hanging out of a pile of snowdrift, were signs enough.

In the distance Mai-Ly could see numerous helicopters flying along the Ross Ice Shelf, which was disintegrating along its edge in huge chunks, icebergs the size of Manhattan crumbling away like snowflakes, dropping 50 meters into the Ross Sea and creating min-tsunamis. Further in land, if you could call the lake filled, slushy regions of the ice shelf land, the shelf was collapsing in on itself, over-and-over again, releasing wafts of steam in the form of cumulonimbus clouds. These vertically rising behemoths, stretching as far as the eye could see, filled the sky.

"What was that?" Mai-Ly asked, wiping a drop off her cheek, and she looked into the sky.

"Warm rain," PaddySan said, holding his palm out. "Air temperature is rising rapidly, we might be too late."

"Stew ... stew" growled the Irish Wolf Hounds.

"Not now," said PaddySan.

"No look," said Mai-Ly. "They've found something, over there. Come on."

A second later PaddySan, Mai-Ly and the six iShillelagh Irish Wolf Hounds were looking into a deep ice tunnel.

"What do you think?" said Mai-Ly.

"Well," said PaddySan, "there's a smell of Irish stew coming out of it, alright."

Mai-Ly sniffed the air, "Not sure."

"If it's what I think it is," said PaddySan, jumping into it, "we're in."

The others didn't hesitate, Mai-Li jumped in after her new found love, and the Irish Wolf Hounds flew in to follow the Irish stew trail.

Chapter 53

Wawking The Plank

"Please!" Screamed Séamus, Ryan's gun digging into his temple, "hol' on a minute, will yeh."

"What?" said Ryan.

"Are yeh having a laff," said Séamus, "me about to cross over to the other side and all?"

"I don't understand," said Ryan.

"Jaysis," said Séamus in disgust, "a freckin penguin God? Sure St Patrick himself, may the Lord have mercy on his poor oul' soul, chased them oul' pagans out of Ireland along wit' the snakes hundreds of years ago. I don't know about your good self, but meself, I'm a Christian."

"Oh," said Ryan, "well close your eyes and prepare to meet thy Christian maker then. Is that ok?"

"Grand," said Séamus, "t'anks a million Ryan, sure that's much better." He closed his eyes, and joined his flippers before him in prayer. "I'm sorry about all tha' messin' wha', but I'd hate to end up in the oul' fiery pit, or penguin heaven even, if there is one."

"So am I," said Ryan.

"What?" said Séamus.

"Sorry."

"Ryan," said William nervously, becoming very concerned for his own safety, "why are you pointing that gun at me?"

"I can't let you do it sir," Ryan asserted calmly, "I can't let you kill my friends, and I definitely can't let you flood the world. Switch Hotstuff off, now."

"Ryan?"

"I mean it," he said waving the gun at William, "and tell everyone else to stand down."

"Ryan," pleaded William, "why?"

"Sorry, sir," said Ryan.

"You should be," said Captain James, holding a gun to the back of Ryan's head. James was just back from a brief surveillance round, to make sure no one was else was about to surprise them. "What did I tell you about this hippy sir?"

Captain James Bush took the gun off Ryan, and ordered one of the coal stokers to tie his hands.

"What do you want me to do with them, sir?" said Squawky. "Are we still going to liquidate them?"

"Yes," hissed William, "but I've a better idea, now."

"Better than liquidation?" asked Squawky.

"Much better," said William ominously.

Thirty minutes later with Hotstuff still hissing, and pumping away, Captain James had strapped a plank to the steel runway which extended across the chasm, joining the control platform to the tunnel platform.

"A diving board?" asked Squawky. "I don't get it."

"You never heard what they did to pirates on ships in the good old days," said William, "when it came to treason?"

Squawky shrugged his shoulders.

"They made them walk the plank into shark infested waters."

"Ingenious," said Squawky, "wawking the plank. But we've got no sharks."

"Therefore," said William, "we'll just have to settle for a river of lava. Get them ready, the Ice Rat can go first."

"You hear that, Dorky?" said Squawky. "We're gonna make them wawk the plank. That's real gangsta, that is, even Scorsese would be proud."

"Ahh come on now lads," said Séamus O'Malley, as Dorky and Captain James poked and prodded him over to the plank, hovering over lava flows hundreds of metres below. "Sure I've only just survived one death sentence, is that not enough?"

"Quiet," said Dorky, lifting Séamus onto the plank.

"Yis are wrong .. lads ... please." Séamus looked over the edge and screamed, "Jaysis lads, but I've an awful head for heights, come on now ... stop messin' will yis!"

"Move," shouted Captain James.

"Yeah," said Dorky, "get waddling."

Séamus stepped shakily along the reverberating plank, and Ye Olde Ross Ice Shelf Committee covered their eyes.

Following a brief workout, Shin was sweating slightly, but the muscles were now as supple as they were all those years ago. And now Shin O'Beef crept like the ninja Shin was along the Erebus Hilton corridors, heading towards the Industrial Boiler Room.

Shin had a rake of weapons hidden all over the body, including darts, knives and shuriken stars. A quiver full of tricolored arrows, with green fletchings, white shaft, and orange head, was tied next to an orange bow - a bow designed for sharp shooters, and therefore much shorter than the traditional yumi, longbow - down the centre of the back. Two three, pronged sais were tied either side of the quiver. Shin also had several smoke bombs to create diversions, having mastered the art of *Hitsuke* long ago, as part of the Minus 1 training.

It was going well. Shin moved along the corridors as if invisible, unseen, unheard, a tricoloured Antarctica ghost. The large riveted steel door was in sight now. The sign on it read "Industrial Boiler Hall", with a huge red warning: DANGER: RISK OF DEATH. This was the place alright. The ethereal tricoloured ghost floated along, almost there now.

What was that? A cracking sound broke the silence. How clumsy! But it was to be expected after all this time. Shin smiled and bent down to examine the source of the noise, a noise barely discernible to most, but to ears like Shin's, it was if a tree had fallen in a forest, crashing down, and taking another ten trees with it. Shin examined the detritus just trodden in, a bone dry, crunchy, brittle, fried ring of Calamari, courtesy of Séamus O'Malley, no doubt.

Shin O'Beef placed the calamari gently down and looked around one last time, before attempting to open the steel riveted door. The coast was clear, thank God no one had heard the calamari crackle and snap under Shin's foot. Shin stepped ever so quietly towards the riveted steel door and was about to turn the handle when something, which can only be described as a noise similar to a drum kit being rolled down a hill, exploded in the background. Shin spun around to be greeted by eight rapidly accelerating rolling pin balls, fresh out of an ice chute at the other end of the corridor.

As fast as Shin was, the collision couldn't be avoided; years ago, perhaps, but a nanosecond too slow today. Shin, carried by the eight pin balls, slammed into the steel door, and collapsed into a mangled heap on the ground.

"What was that?" William asked Captain James, when he heard a thunderous clap coming from the corridor which led back to the main entrance to the Industrial Boiler Unit.

"Hotstuff sir," said James, nonchalantly, "just some echo or something."

"Are you sure, I don't want anyone getting in here."

"I've got security placed everywhere, only a ghost could get in here," claimed James.

Séamus was slowly edging towards the end of the five metre plank. "Come on lads," he begged, trying to keep his balance, and not look down. "Sure I've a fantastic work record. I've never been late, not a day, and not one day off sick either, not .... whoooaaa."

Séamus lost his webbed footing, and fell off the plank into the lava stream below, falling to sure and certain death. Ye Olde Ross Ice Shelf Committee gasped, and then cheered. Séamus had managed to cling onto the side of the plank with one flipper, and was trying to climb back onto the plank, which was gently bobbing up and down.

"DROP, DROP, DROP," the samurai penguins started shouting repeatedly, and they were soon joined by the coal-stokers.

Outside the main door, Shin O'Beef didn't move a muscle as the rolling pins, rolled off one-by-one. PaddySan jumped up first, then Mai-Ly and finally the six Irish Wolf Hounds.

"A ninja," said Mai-Ly.

"A dead one by the looks of it," said PaddySan.

"Not at all," said Shin O'Beef, rolling backwards slightly, before kipping into an upright position, drawing both sais out in a flash and placing them across PaddySan and Mai-Ly's necks. "Just a little ninja, trick. You slow the metabolism down to feign death. They usually back off then. Then BOO, surprise, surprise. Now who are ye, and where are ye headed?"

It didn't take long for Shin and the rolling pins to realise that they were on the same side, both here to rescue Ye Olde Ross Ice Shelf Committee and stop Hotstuff flooding the world. So rather than Shin O'Beef running in there single-handedly and possibly committing suicide, they formulated a more promising, and elaborate plan.

Chapter 54

Sure Who Was You Expecting, Jackie Chan?

"DROP ... DROP ... DROP." The cheers grew louder as poor oul' Séamus only just managed to scramble back onto the plank, much to the chagrin of all those willing him to fall.

"Jesus, Mary and Padre Pio himself," implored, Séamus, "now that's the third escape." He clung onto the plank for dear life. "It has to be the third time lucky lads, sure I don't think I'm meant to die, wha'."

But Dorky had other ideas, and put one large, webbed foot on the other end of the plank, pumping it furiously, bouncing the plank up and down, and bucking poor Séamus high into the air.

And then the jeering resumed, "DROP ... DROP ... DROP."

"Stop," screamed Malachy, "Stop. He's no Ice Rat, he wasn't helping us." Fired up by Malachy the committee started screaming, shouting and pleading for Séamus' life.

But Séamus was losing his grip, Dorky jerking him more and more violently, "DROP ... DROP ... DROP." Then he was gone from the plank, leaving a cloud of steam and smoke behind him. A sure sign that it wasn't fourth time lucky for poor oul' Séamus and that he'd perished in the incandescent lava stream below.

Dorky, Captain James, the samurai squad, and the coal-stokers cheered with delight. Even William let go of the rail for a moment to applaud and cheer Séamus' demise.

Ye Old Ross Ice Shelf Committee and Frosty, still strapped into his chair, had tears in their eyes. "Bastards," screamed Malachy Malarkey, "Séamus wasn't an Ice Rat, he was a sound fella."

"If you think so highly of him," said William, "you can let him know how you feel personally."

Shouting over to James, William gestured back at Malachy and said, "Him next." QuickMIC screamed no, while Donn-Dubh and Ryan tried to beat off the coal-stokers, but the bog-boys had muscles of steel, and didn't feel a thing.

Malachy Malarkey edged along the plank, soon to join Séamus in the fiery pit below.

"DROP ... DROP ... DROP," went up the shout, and Dorky duly obliged, pumping on the plank again.

Malachy was wobbling, losing his footing. He slipped, then regained his composure, then slipped again ...

"Stop!" The control room door flew open, and PaddySan, Mai-Ly and the Wolf Hounds charged in, PaddySan screaming to halt proceedings.

"No ... Malachy ... NO!" PaddySan blared as Malachy was bounced off the plank by Dorky, and over the side, down to the fiery pit below. "Malachy!"

There was no time for cheering or grieving, the samurai penguin squad, twenty in all, surrounded the ill fated rescuers with swords drawn, followed by ten coal-stokers wielding base ball bats. Even the Irish Wolf Hounds knew the game was up, and gulped, holding their gloved hands up in surrender.

"Ahh," said William, "so glad you could join us. Just what we needed, a few more iShillelaghs to walk the plank. Bind them."

Squawky and Captain James tied their wrists, and shoved them all next to Frosty.

"Who's walking the plank next, boss?" said Squawky.

"Let me see," said William, "Ahh, yes, Ryan my boy, the other rat."

"Such a pretty one as well," said Squawky ordering the coal-stokers to drag him over to the plank.

"And him next," said William pointing to Frosty.

The coal-stokers hoisted Frosty and the chair up, and were about to carry him over to the plank when an unexpected tricoloured ninja fell out of the sky.

As part of their elaborate plan, while the rolling pins stormed through the steel door, Shin had gained access to the control room through a disused door, higher up the rock face, which had previously been used as entry point to access Hotstuff's upper piping. Shin O'Beef had been dangling from a wire above the proceedings, for some time now, slowly rappelling down, hoping to take them all by surprise. Unfortunately, it was Shin who was taken by an even bigger surprise. The tricoloured ninja costume may have survived decades in pristine condition, but the wire had been slowly corroding all these years, and half way down, didn't it snap. Fortunately, Shin O'Beef's fall was broken by William McCoy The Third, and William was now unconscious, slumped on the floor, James and everyone else in panic mode.

"Is that who I think it is?" said Malachy.

"Shin O'Beef," said QuickMIC, "Sure I don't believe it, the rumours are true!"

First the samurai penguins attacked, but Shin threw several smoke bombs to blind them, flipped into a summersault, and came down on a samurai penguin's head, hopping over another ten of them, knocking them all unconscious, with deft ankle flicks.

"Wow," said Ryan, as the diversionary smoke cleared, "Shin O'Beef's like that one from Crouching Tiger, Hidden Dragon."

Shin was running and hopping all over the place, off the walls, the doors, and even Hotstuff's control panel, where Shin performed a lightning speed set of elaborate moves, that looked like someone doing a hop jig, the fastest Irish jig known.

That was fascinating enough to watch, but Frosty's eyes nearly popped out his head when he suddenly realised that Shin was actually running over Hotstuff's dials, wheels and levers in an ordered way, which was actually Hotstuff's shutdown sequence.

Hotstuff groaned, clanked and hissed, shuddering for a few moments, before the lava sluices started closing, reducing the input power dramatically, and finally bringing Hotstuff back to stand-by mode.

Shin O'Beef was back on the ground, surrounded by the other ten samurai penguins. The penguins circled slowly, swords drawn. Shin drew up onto one leg, and started twirling like a ballerina performing a can-can dance, kicking the one leg in and out, and knocking all the penguins unconscious, in one circular sweep, which was executed faster than a blinking eye.

Seeing the penguins' plight, the ten coal-stokers rushed Shin from all sides, but Shin O'Beef performed a Matrix move, and, in slow motion, hopped high into the air, one knee bent, with arms raised, like some kind of predatory tricolored ninja bird.

It is not clear what noise the coal-stokers made as they crunched together like players in a rugby scrum, suffice to say that they didn't walk away unscathed. Several collapsed on the spot. The others staggered around groaning for a few moments, clasping their heads, before collapsing onto the same pile.

Shin O'Beef wasn't finished yet, and took out a few knives and spikes, dispatching them in several directions. Squawky was pinned to one wall, Dorky was pinned to a pipe, and Captain James where was Captain James? And William? Where was William? Gone?

Finally, Shin O'Beef ran at Frosty with a razor sharp knife. Frosty Oighear pressed himself back into the chair as far as possible, leaving a memory foam impression of himself in the upholstery. With Shin approaching faster than a bullet, Frosty screamed for his life, but rather than killing him, Shin O'Beef cut Frosty's gag away, and sliced through the strapping around his hands.

Frosty thought this was the end, and screamed out for his grandmother, "Máthair chríonna! ... Máthair chríonna help me!"

Shin O'Beef ripped the white ninja balaclava off, revealing their identity for the first time ever, to someone outside Minus 1, that is.

Frosty was dumbfounded, "Mother of God!"

"Mother of God?" Shin O'Beef, laughed. "Sure I've worked a few miracles in my time, but I wouldn't go that far."

"I mean," said Frosty, stammering in disbelief, at the newly revealed face, smiling down on him, "is that really you, grandmother?"

"Sure who was you expecting," said Frosty's grandmother, "Jackie Chan?"

Taking out a hipflask, Shin took another gulp of Jamaican over-proof white rum. "I'm telling you a stór, this stuff has taken the years off a-me. Here, sure you look like you could do with an oul' sup yourself."

Frosty burst into tears of joy, then succumbed to sheer hilarity at the thought of what his máthair chríonna, dressed as a tricoloured ninja, had just done. Not only had she saved them all, but hopefully Ireland and the world itself.

Ye Olde Ross Ice Shelf were elated but at the same time in fits of tears for Malachy and Séamus.

"They're dead," cried QuickMIC, "dead!"

"Sorry, about your friends, lads," said Shin O'Beef, "sometimes, I really wish I could work miracles."

Chapter 55

The New World

It was over, and they were safe, for now at least. Frosty was tapping away at the control panel, taking Hotstuff out of stand-by mode, and making sure she was completely switched off, never to be switched on again.

Samurai penguins and coal-stokers lay unconscious all over the floor, but some were starting to come round, so Shin O'Beef, the balaclava back in place, got busy tying them up with a series of complex, un-pickable, Ninjitsu knots. Squawky was pinned by a spike next to the door he'd been trying to sneak out of, but hadn't Shin O'Beef managed to stop him in his tracks, with throwing precision only a trained Ninjitsu warrior could aspire to.

Unfortunately there was still no sign of Captain James and William McCoy The Third. Ironically, Shin said, that they must have escaped when the diversionary, smoke bombs created dense layers of smoke.

After a few more taps, and switch throws, Hotstuff shuddered to a complete stop, and the control room became absolutely silent. Deep inside T1 and T2, distant rumbles could be heard, along with gushing waterfalls and creaks and groans, as the Ross Ice Shelf continued to melt and fragment.

QuickMIC and Donn-Dubh, with tears streaming down their faces, walked over to the plank where Séamus and Malachy had just perished, crying their hearts out. QuickMIC looked over the edge of the platform and shuddered at the depth of the fall down to the cooling lava rivulet below, which had now stopped flowing, the sluice gate closing it off. The lava was solidifying he assumed, entombing the remains of Malachy and Séamus.

"They'll be like yer ones from Pompeii," said QuickMIC.

"What," said Donn-Dubh, "Portsmouth football fans?"

"No you feckin eejit," said QuickMIC, "I'm talking about the residents of Pompeii, Italy, who were buried alive by Mount Vesuvius when it erupted two thousand years ago. Ironically, many of those residents were instantly frozen in time, caught doing whatever they were doing, by fast moving pyroclastic lava flow."

"Poor Malachy and Séamus," Donn-Dubh, sniffled.

"Séamus was rare oul' craic, altogether," said QuickMIC, "wasn't he?"

"'Deed he was," said Donn-Dubh, smiling as he remembered the talkative, little green penguin from Dublin.

"Yis're roight, o' course," said a voice from under the plank, "now are yis going to stan' there all day, or give us a hand, wha'?"

QuickMIC bent down to look under the plank, zoomed his brilliant white elated eyes, and shrieked with delight and joy. Underneath, half way along the plank, Séamus was dangling from his red bandana, which had caught on a large splinter, on the side of the plank, as he was bounced off it by Dorky. Fortunately cloud and steam from the lava flow below, had camouflaged the fact that he never actually fell to his fiery death. And hadn't Séamus managed to catch Malachy, who was clinging on for dear oul' life, from one of his green flippers.

"Howya," said Malachy,

"Howya Malachy," QuickMIC cried.

"I must admit," said Malachy looking down, "I'm enjoying the view, but I've a few reservations about the company."

"Wha'?" said Séamus.

"Sure I've never been fond of Ice Rats," winked Malachy.

"Go away will, ya," said Séamus, threatening to drop him, "we'll have less of that malarkey out of you, Malachy Malarkey."

Shin O'Beef was right. Captain James had used his military training to escape, carrying William, unconscious, over his shoulder. The smoke bombs had formed perfect cover, and within minutes of Shin deploying them, Captain James was in the main foyer of the Erebus Hilton, waiting for the lift.

Several thousand penguins were still in the foyer cheering, hollering and applauding, watching the Antarctica melting on the plasmas. News feeds from all over the world were reporting the unfolding devastating consequences, which had been triggered by Hotstuff. And they were ecstatic that all their hard work was starting to pay off.

One plasma showed a few hundred penguins outside sunbathing. You wouldn't believe it the reporter said, but the increase in air temperature had gone to their heads, and they were outside, slapping sun cream all over each other, before settling into deck chairs, eating ice cream, some drinking piña coladas. The reporter went on to say that there was also a strange rumour circulating. As well as shipping rubber dinghies, wellingtons and water pumps to places sinking deeper by the minute, Amazon had started the expedited shipping of vast quantities of penguin sun cream to the Antarctica. However, an Amazon spokesman was unavailable for comment. Unbeknownst to the reporter, virtually every Amazon employee was busy helping load the colossal sun cream order onto oil tankers.

Every ten minutes, all the plasma screens in the huge foyer switched station to GRABiT's own satellite channel, where two perky American reporters gave an overview of GRABiT's response to this global deluge, and their latest catalogue range, The New World. GRABiT were transmitting commercials all over the globe, reassuring the planet that even if the Antarctica and everywhere else melted completely, climate refugees of the world could take up affordable new housing from a worldwide selection in GRABiT's New World range of catalogues. And if they couldn't afford it, government subsidies were already in place to help them. Promises had been made by GRABiT's partners including the Federal Reserve, the IMF, the ECB, The People's Bank of China, the central Bank of The Russian Federation, the UN and numerous other global financial institutions and central banks, keen to re-house people as fast as possible, and avert the possibility of the complete anarchic breakdown of society.

GRABiT's reporters, promoting special offers from the New World catalogues, highly recommended places like New Venice, a stone's throw away from New Rome, New Pisa and New Florence. Cultural cities built conveniently together high up in New Italy's New Appennino Mountain Range. These New World Cultural Heritage cities had stunning new sea views either side, the New Adriatic on one, and the New Mediterranean on the other. And you could even walk along newly manufactured beaches, crafted from the finest sands, dredged from the bottom of the Old Persian Gulf.

All the Renaissance art and architecture, from the original submerged cities, had also been loving recreated in minute detail. However, due to GRABiT's conservative censorship policies, its alignment with The Tea Party, and following strict instructions from the Pope himself, over there in the New Vatican, pieces such as Michelangelo's Renaissance masterpiece David, had acquired extra blobs of marble, a fig leaf in this instance, to cover carnal flesh which had no business seeing the light of day in God's New World.

On a happier note, the reporter noted, the Leaning Tower Of Pisa no longer leaned, such was GRABiT's desire to recreate the deluged, old world perfectly.

Actually, you wouldn't even know you'd moved home at all, chirped one of the reporters. Previous Google Maps and 3D Technology had been used to recreate every detail of every house, street, building, cafe and every nook and cranny. No stone, announced one reporter gleefully, had been left unturned. Smirking, the other reporter stated that even turned over stones had been left lying around the new streets.

And over in New Rome, the reporters proudly announced, the Sistine Chapel's ceiling had been given a new theme. The iconic image of the hand of God giving life to Adam had now been replaced by the hand of William McCoy The Third giving a Fortune magazine, with GRABiT listed as number one in the Fortune 500, to his son, William McCoy The Fourth. The baton successfully handed over, the penguin audience went hysterical, as the camera gave a close up of the Fortune 500 list, emblazoned on the ceiling.

The GRABiT reporters went on to recommend many other areas around the world and focused on a special section dedicated to New Dublin, New Galway, New Claremorris, New Tipperary Town, New Templemore, New Limerick and New Cork. All of Ireland, including every Irish town and city, now that Ireland would soon be completely submerged, had been loving recreated in the New Appellation Mountains, once part the former USA, now known as the New USA, or NUSA.

But you'd better get your skates on, the Irish sales team advised. Two prominent Irishmen, the American president and the Taoiseach along with their families, had already taken up residence in the New Appellations, creating levels of hysteria and demand not seen since the Taoiseach promised every man and woman in Ireland free drinks.

You may rest assured, said another member of the sales team, that New Ireland, over there in the New Appellations, had also been lovingly recreated in the greatest of detail, and will provide all the craic of Old Ireland. Sure after a few pints of New Black Stuff, a New aul' sing song, a New fist fight, and a New black eye, you wouldn't even notice the difference, and would wonder why you hadn't emigrated here before the floods.

On and on the GRABiT commercials went: covering New New York, New Paris, New Milan, New London, New San Francisco, New Sydney, New Tokyo, New New Orleans, New Mumbai, New Beijing, New Hong Kong, New Moscow ... every country, city and town had been lovingly recreated. And, finally, if anyone wished to stay locally, of course they were always welcome to take up residency in Frosty's Town, New Antarctic. It certainly was a new dawn on a new day ... And on the seventh day, GRABiT rested.

GRABiT's commercials complete, the screens showed that most major cities were now knee deep in water, and many coastal areas were gone completely. Bangladesh had been the first heavily populated area to be submerged, and millions were on their way to a range of affordable accommodation in the Chittagong Hills in the South East, in the minutely replicated cities of New Dhaka and New Chittagong.

However, Old London was not falling as quickly as GRABiT had hoped, and New London, in the Grampian Mountains, Scotland, was almost completely empty, waiting patiently for new arrivals from Old Submerged England. Only a handful of GRABiT sales people were running around the New West End, on top of Ben Nevis, making last minute preparations.

According to a Times reporter, who'd been in London with Her Majesty, interviewing Her following Scotland's recent NO vote in the Independence referendum, the Thames Barrier was still holding up but not for long, and Her Majesty, having received advice from both Met Offices - the Meteorological Weather and the Metropolitan Police - was positively livid at the audacity of GRABiT's expansion plans.

The Times reporter realised this might be their last edition, so he was determined to squeeze every last drop out of the interview with Her Majesty. "Oh the indignity!" The Times reporter scribbled in a note pad, writing down Her Majesty's words verbatim. It was bad enough having to be manhandled into a yellow rubber dinghy, parked just outside Buckingham Palace, wearing Union Jack wellingtons, Her Majesty complained. All because Her Majesty's Ministers had allocated the army, navy and other auxiliary personnel to tackle flooding problems elsewhere in the country. But to lose Buckingham Palace and be left homeless: what an outrage! If Interpol could get their hands on William McCoy The Third, The Times reporter scribbled, Her Majesty promised them a swift resolution to the now half sunken Gibraltar. And, please note he hastily added, She had already ordered the Yeoman Warders to pack up The Crown Jewels, and prepare a room at the top of Tower Of London for its first prisoner since The Kray Twins. William The Third would spend his last days there, whether it was submerged or not.

Prince Philip's career in The Royal Navy may not have prepared him for such an unlikely scenario, The Times reporter wrote, turning over a page, but like the water around him, he was quickly rising to the challenge. While zealous crowds waved from office windows, safe above the water, Prince Phillip, not long off The Mall, stuck his paddle into knee deep water at Piccadilly Circus, turned the dinghy with a jolly heave-ho, and paddled ferociously towards Bond Street. Where, The Times reporter penned, he was going to drink a final farewell pint of the velvety stuff, and the Missus a half, in the only pub left open in London, an Irish pub by the name of Paddy McGinty's Corgi. A pub which, five minutes earlier, had been granted a Duke Of Edinburgh Royal Warrant, over a hastily convened telephone call.

Meanwhile, Her Majesty, clinging to both sides of Her yellow dinghy, Her Union Jack wellingtons ankle deep in water, made it perfectly clear to Her Prime Minister, who was in another dinghy beside Her, sitting next to The Times reporter, that GRABiT's licenses for luxury condos, roads, towns, buildings and any other kind of planning permission whatsoever in Her Majesty's Highlands, were to be revoked forthwith, and with the full refund of any bribes his officials may have taken. She made it perfectly clear that William McCoy The Third's money was no good around here, even if he had promised to mint New England banknotes with her face on it.

Further, Her Majesty informed the Prime Minister, She had taken the Royal liberty of phoning the First Minister of Scotland, to announce that She was on Her way, to take up residency in Her newly adopted home. And if Prince Philip kept paddling at this speed, they hoped to be there before dinner. Her Majesty's low lands would soon be lost forever, and She needed all the Highlands She could get her hands and dry feet on. Of course, as Queen of Scotland, or New England as She preferred to call it, She would be more than happy to make the Scottish First Minister, Her King in waiting, sixtieth in line to the throne. Her Majesty's Prime Minister almost crashed his dinghy upon hearing this, giving The Times reporter a mighty shock altogether.

Meanwhile, back in The Erebus Hilton, outside the see through elevator, Captain James waited patiently, with William hanging over his shoulder, praying that the elevator was still working.

He hadn't noticed it, but the volume on all the plasmas had been turned down, and a murmur was rippling through the thousands of penguins, who were ecstatic now that they were all wealthy share holders in GRABiT, and would soon be relocated to luxury condos of their choice.

At first, the chant started as a faint whisper, but because it was started by a few lads from Tipperary, it didn't quite go to plan, and what should have been a heartfelt send-off, once again became a cause of embarrassment and comedy:

"William The Turd ... William The Turd ..."

And when James turned around to see what all the fuss was about, the chant became a tumultuous blast altogether. Sure the penguin's nearly triggered another Mount Erebus eruption:

"William The Turd ... William The Turd ..."

Conscious now, but hanging over Captain James' shoulder, William still had that mantra going around in his head, when they left The Erebus Hilton by the rock basalt entrance. Fortunately the Icicle was still there, and more importantly, still intact. They dragged it out of the snow pile, turned it around to face the right way, jumped back in, fired up the solid fuel jet boosters and flew back down the Hut Peninsula to Mac Town and freedom, for now anyway.

An hour later, Captain James received clearance from Mac Town and pulled the Bombardier BD-700 into the takeoff profile. William McCoy The Third was in the passenger seat, evaluating what he still hoped could be the dawn of a new Genesis, as the Bombardier BD-700 slowly climbed.

Captain James gently turned the Bombardier BD-700 one more time, to give William an overview of the apocalypse he'd created. Across the Ross Ice Shelf, melt lakes the size of small seas had formed on the surface, and some of the waterfalls gushing over the edge were ten times bigger than Niagara if not bigger.

It was clear that Hotstuff had done a lot of damage in her short life, even Mount Erebus was erupting intermittently, but it remained to be seen if the planetary weather system had been destabilised enough to ensure Genesis' success. With the Ross Ice Shelf imploding and bellowing out steam clouds and ice bergs, William and James headed for one of GRABiT's office blocks, over there in Wellington New Zealand.

William closed his eyes, hoping to take a little nap. But the demons which haunted Frosty were now haunting him, and voices circled inside his head. Sean Water was right, what a turd William was ... a self-deprecating turd at that! Captain James had told him everything when he came round. He'd been outwitted by what? Something, or someone, falling out of the sky onto his head? A crazy old bat ... who also happened to be an Irish Ninja granny?

He truly was a turd ...

Chapter 56

A Continental Refrigerator

'Murphy's On The Rocks,' was in full session. In one booth Ye Olde Ross Ice Shelf Committee was sat with Séamus, Frosty and his grandmother. PaddySan and Mai-Ly were holding hands, whispering sweet nothings to each other.

When the group first arrived, Séamus O'Malley downed three Green Avalanches faster that the bar tender could make them up. "Sure the oul' green colour needs topping up lads," he claimed, adding that walking the plank had scared the colour out of him.

The Cracker Craics were on stage, and yer one wearing the Galway shawl was in fine form, singing Ruby Murray's version of 'If You're Irish (Come Into The Parlour)'. The Uilleann pipes were on top of the world, now that the world itself had been saved, and was back in dry dock, unlike most of the patrons of Murphy's, who were submerged in a flood of drinks.

"So tell us Frosty, wha'," said Séamus O'Malley, sipping his fourth Green Avalanche, himself greener than a savoy cabbage, "how did you do it?"

"Sure that was easy enough," said Frosty modestly, proving once again that the Irish have more geniuses per square metre than Mensa. "With Hotstuff switched off, the ice sheets stopped melting and entered into a state of stasis."

"Stasis?" inquired Séamus.

"A state of inactivity," said Frosty, "basically it means that she'd stopped melting."

"Be Jaysis," said Séamus, holding up another Green Avalanche, "if I drink any more of these yokes, I t'ink I'll be entering a state of stasis meself, wha'."

"She was in state of equilibrium, so," said Frosty, "and assuming she stayed there long enough, sure the rest was easy.

"It was?" said QuickMIC, taken aback.

"Well there were a few problems, and it was touch and go for a few days there lads," admitted Frosty. "But Hotstuff was still fully functional, and, thanks to the SAM dynamic matrix architecture, even with large areas of the ice shelf gone, there was plenty of intact piping running up and down T1 and T2. Therefore it became a simple thermodynamic problem."

"Ter'mo'dy-na-Mick, wha'," said Séamus O'Malley, blowing a green bubble and emphasising the word Mick louder each time he used it. "Ter'mo'dy-na-Mick." He giggled to the others, "Do yis here tha', wha'?" He gulped another mouthful of Green Avalanche, looked at the glass and said, "Is it me or is it the freckin' drink?" Shaking his head he continued, " Ter'-mo'-freckin'-dy-na-Mick. I mean to say, I've met a few Micks in me time, including a QuickMIC," he nudged Malachy, "who isn't that quick," and went on, "but I don't t'ink I ever met a Ter'Mo'Dy-na-Mick. Would he be one of the new Polish lads Frosty, over there in Dublin, by any chance?"

They all laughed, and when they settled down, Frosty explained that a heating system is pretty much like a refrigerating system. "However for refrigeration, you need a suitable coolant gas to fill the pipes, instead of hot water."

"A gas like sulphur dioxide, for instance?" surmised QuickMIC.

"Good man yerself, QuickMIC," said Frosty. "And wasn't there plenty of it to be had from Mount Erebus," he carried on. "Sure Erebus produces it in vast quantities, and that's why The Hilton Erebus always had that eggy smell lingering in the air. As soon as the gas supply was rigged up," Frosty went on, "sure it was only a matter of implementing a few more bits of technical magic." He paused to think of an example, "Like converting the condenser into a compressor, stuff like that."

"So basically, you reversed the thermodynamic equilibrium," said QuickMIC smugly, only to be met with black stares.

"He means," explained Frosty, "the heat exchange went into reverse, and Hotstuff became a continental refrigerator instead of a continental heater."

"Are you sure it will work Frosty?" asked QuickMIC.

"I don't see why not," said Frosty confidently. "The Ross Ice Shelf was the weak link in the chain, as soon as she started refreezing, the rest of Antarctica, including the other ice shelves, began to fall into line. Then the global domino effect started to reverse."

"Amazing!"

"'Deed it is, QuickMIC," agreed Frosty. "Just as soon as the planetary weather systems return to their previous stable conditions, and they're on the way now by the looks of things, we can switch Hotstuff off altogether and destroy her."

"Jesus," said Malachy, "Donn-Dubh was right about that continental refrigerator after all."

"He was?" asked Frosty, and Malachy told him about Donn-Dubh's madcap idea back in Eirestown, to get the Chinese to create a continental size refrigerator to refreeze the Ross Ice Shelf.

"I was right," said Donn-Dubh sipping on a Green Short Back and Sides, "but it wasn't the Chinese who made a fridge the size of a planet, it was the Irish."

"Jaysis," said Séamus, "don't mention those frisky freckers to me."

"Who?" said Ryan, "the Irish or the Chinese?"

"You're a freckin' genius, Frosty," said Séamus, ignoring Ryan. "I haven't got a freckin' clue wha' you just said, but all I know is tha' whatever yeh did worked, cos' it's snowin' outside."

"And ye don't even have to be outside to know that," smirked Malachy, holding out his hand to catch a snowflake.

They all looked up at the holes in the roof, through which snowflakes were gently tumbling into Murphy's, to be swept around the bar every now and then by gusts coming through the revolving doors. Although repairs to Murphy's were ongoing, they had been prioritised. The cellar, where the drinks were held, had been repaired first, then the bar was propped back up, then the dance floor. There were still ongoing discussions about the roof, and so many people loved the nostalgic feel of the snowflakes coming in, that it might never get repaired at all.

And even though it wasn't Christmas, what with everyone looking up at the incoming snowflakes, the Cracker Craics starting singing the Fairytale of New York.

"Bagún.... Bagún!" The Irish Wolf Hounds were sat at the bar, tucking into their third plate of Cabáiste agus Bagún. They were sick to death of Irish White Rabbit Stew, having found thousands of white rabbits these last few hours, and were taking a break from that Antarctic delicacy.

Back in the booth, Ryan was explaining how he'd been blackmailed into going to Eirestown by William McCoy The Third, and then to the Antarctica.

"You guys saw what he was like," said Ryan, defensively, "he was ruthless. I had no other choice. But I just couldn't go ahead with it when I met you guys, and cut off all contact with him,"

"Ohhh myyy days," said Squawky, returning from the bar with a tray full of drinks, "am I glad to see the back of that ruthless, double crossing, back stabbing gangstaaaaa, William McCoy The Third." He placed the tray on the table. "You know what guys, ruthless is an understatement, you just couldn't trust him." He closed his eyes, furrowed his brow in anguish, placed a flipper over it and added in a mournful Brooklyn accent, "I think I'll be in therapy for the rest of my life."

Squawky had dressed especially for the goodbye party, and was sporting a pink Armani Sabre Tooth Parka, off-pink thermal bottoms, a daring colour he'd once seen on the end of particularly cold penguin's flipper. A luxurious DKNY pick cashmere sweater, and brand new Christian Louboutin, multi-coloured spikes. On top of this fashion extravaganza, he wore a pink Ralph Loren baseball hat, with the beak turned up and slightly tilted to one side.

"I'm telling you," said Squawky, raising a flipper to his anguished temple again, "no one was safe. The things that monster made me do." He looked at Ryan as a mother might look at a five year old who'd just fallen over and scraped a knee, "I feel it for you hun, I really do."

"Don't get too carried away, you" said Frosty's grandmother. "You just fulfil your end of the bargain, and we'll never have to meet again – Kapish?" Then she came over all Shin O'Beef, pulled a knife out from God knows where, and threw it at Squawky, slicing the beak off his pink Ralph Loren baseball hat.

Squawky nearly shed a tear when he bent down to pick the beak up, "Kapish, Shin ... I mean Sean ... I mean ..."

Squawky and Dorky had been given two options after Shin O'Beef had demolished the samurai penguins and coal-stokers. Either walk the plank, or hang around until the Hotstuff had completely repaired the Ross Ice Shelf, after which they were to destroy Hotstuff and The Erebus Hilton.

Squawky complained that walking the plank in brand new pink UGG boots was not a very practical proposition, so they chose the latter option, and Dorky was back in the control room, waiting for Hotstuff to complete the freezing process.

"By the way, Frosty," said QuickMIC, "there's still one thing I don't understand."

"Go on."

"Why were you so surprised to see your grandmother when she took off her ninja mask?"

"To tell ye the truth lads," began Frosty, "I had no idea that it was máthair chríonna wearing the ninja suit."

"You didn't?" said QuickMIC.

"Not at all," said Frosty's grandmother, "sure I'm Ireland's best kept secret."

"Are you not worried that you've now revealed you true identity as Shin O'Beef?" Donn-Dubh asked her.

"Let me get this right," she answered, patting her grey bun with one hand and taking a sip of Jamaican over-proof, white rum with the other. "Am I worried that a group of people from Eirestown, a place no one has ever heard of," she took another sip, "who have just saved the world from flooding, with the help of a few iShillelaghs, I might add," she nodded over to Malachy and QuickMIC, "and some double crossing talking penguins," she raised her fist at Squawky, "know my real identity, and the fact that I work for Minus 1. An Irish secret service, which is so secret that no one knows it exists. Is that what you're asking me?"

"Yes," said Donn-Dubh, "I think so."

"No," she smiled, "I think my secret is safe, don't you?"

Donn-Dubh and the others thought for a minute, then the penny dropped, just after a few more snowflakes, and they all started laughing.

"Jaysis," said Séamus O'Malley, the green talking penguin from Dublin. "Yeh roight, o' course, Shin, sure who in their right mind would believe that load of oul' cod-ology?"

The time had come. The whole of Murphy's On The Rocks were outside, waiting to wave off the Eirestown heroes. Hundreds of geeks from Mac Town had also come along to say their goodbyes, or so they claimed. But they'd use any excuse to get out of that hell hole and have a drink in a warm, homely place they officially denied existed.

Sledges were going to carry the Ross Ice Shelf Committee, Frosty and his grandmother to The Eirestown Flash, because Malachy now thought he remembered where he parked it.

Donn-Dubh's hat had proved invaluable. The sledges were going to be pulled by robotic iShill-huskies, which QuickMIC had invented and packed into Donn-Dubh's hat as part of the supplies.

"Mush, mush," Donn-Dubh shouted, cracking a whip above the little, grey and white iShill-huskie heads. And the sledges took off, slicing through snow and ice.

Séamus shouted after them, "Stop! Hol' on a minute, wha'," and Donn-Dubh pulled on the reins to stop the sledges. Séamus ran after them and gave each of them a hug, "Yis are great ... the best friends a penguin could ever have, wha'! T'anks a million for everyt'ing, and have a safe journey home." Wiping a tear from his eye, or perhaps it was a wayward snowflake, he added, "Yis saved me life and I'll never be able to pay yis back, but ... always remember ... I'll be eternally grateful."

With that Séamus started waving them off, and the farewell party outside Murphy's On The Rocks started singing a specially composed song for them, to the tune of The Leaving Of Liverpool:

'Farewell to Murphy's on the Rocks,
Fare well to you Mac Town,
We are bound for beloved Ireland,
a place where we belong ...
'So I'll see you soon, my own true love,
When I return, united we will be.
It's not the leaving of Antarctica that pleases me,
But my darling when I think of thee.'

Soon the sledges were out of sight, and the farewell party went back into Murphy's, where The Cracker Craics were waiting on stage.

"Welcome back lads," said Paddynini into the microphone, the oul' Paddyvarius up on his shoulder, "are they gone?"

"They're gone alright," shouted Séamus O'Malley. "Good riddance and all."

"Grand," exclaimed Paddynini. "I bet ye're glad to see the back of those trouble causing Irish feckers from Eirestown, eh? Sure they were an unholy shower altogether."

"We are of course," screamed Séamus, raising his glass in the air, and asking for three cheers and hip-hip-hoorays. When the hip-hip-hoorays subsided, he added, "Would you be havin' the belivin' of that shower. Sure they nearly got me kil't stone dead, wha'!"

"The rotten, good for nothing interfering do-gooders," roared Paddynini, nearly swallowing the microphone whole. "They should have stayed at home, altogether. Never mind yourself, sure they nearly got us all kilt stone dead, or drown-ded. And I don't know which would have been worse."

"They should have stayed at home, alright," agreed Séamus. "It's not the freckin' immigration into Ireland that the Irish should be worried about, wha'. It's the freckin' emigration ou' of the mad place that the rest of the world should be worried about."

The Irish were all the same agreed the Cracker Craic, also in a Dublin accent. If they weren't drinking, swearing, singing or fighting in their own pubs back home, they were off causing trouble somewhere else around the world.

Séamus concurred that the Irish were mad and that they should knock down Hadrian's Wall and relocate it elsewhere, a bit closer to home.

"It was the wrong Celts Hadrian was trying to keep out," announced Séamus, now on the microphone beside the fiddle player, knocking back his eighth Green Avalanche, the crowd cheering him on. "Hadrian should have built a freckin' wall around the whole of Ireland instead, and done us all a favour."

As the cheers and whoops grew louder, didn't Séamus turn bright red, an anatomical wonder for an oul' green penguin, keel over, fall off the stage, and roll across the floor, where another penguin bent down to check his pulse, giving the anxious fiddle player the thumbs up.

Paddynini breathed a deep sigh of relief, the last thing they needed now was an Irish wake. A leaving party was bad enough, but a wake, sure there'd be murders. He spat into his hands, rubbed them together, threw Paddyvarius back up onto his left shoulder, and struck up almighty, fierce jig altogether. Didn't the fiddle strings themselves smoke, as he started bowing the bejaysus out of them.

With Séamus O'Malley rolled under a table to sleep it off, the whole pub went crazy altogether, the bog-boys flinging each other all over the place like acrobats from *Cirque Du Soleil.*

Chapter 57

Eirestown Was Éire

"Mush ...mush!"

"Stew ... stew!"

Ye Old Ross Ice Shelf Committee were lost, and not for the first time.

Worse, the Irish Wolf Hounds hadn't spotted a real white rabbit for hours. Sadly, the last one turned out to be a snow mirage, a pile of snow blown into the shape of a rabbit, which they only found out when they pounced on it, coming up with mouthfuls of snowflakes, instead of white fur. Then they were gone. Just before they left, one of them said, "T'anks a million lads, it's been great craic and all. But we're away to find White Rabbit paradise."

"White rabbit paradise?" called QuickMIC after them.

"Yes," said one of the iShillelagh Irish Wolf Hounds, "White Rabbit Paradise. Frank the oul' penguin from Kerry told us that it was out here somewhere. A place where there are more white rabbits than there are Irish."

"What?"

"Sure it sounds a bit farfetched we know," said the Wolf Hound. "A location on earth where Irish migrants are outnumbered by another life form but," he seemed a little hesitant, uncomfortable even, "me and the boys, without wishing to offend ye ..."

"Go on, so," said QuickMIC.

"Well," the Wolf Hound continued, "rather than go round in circles and starve to death with ye eejits, looking for an invisible vehicle, we're going to pin our hopes on White Rabbit Paradise." And off they went, pulling their sledge, pistons pumping away as they left a blizzard behind them.

It was true, Malachy didn't have a clue where The Eirestown Flash was, and had spent the last hour or so walking though imaginary doors, in the hope that he was walking into the invisible vehicle. It was funny at first, because whenever he walked through a door that wasn't there he'd asked the lads, "Can you still see me?"

Once or twice they said no, even though they could, and Malachy started fumbling around, believing he was back inside The Eirestown Flash, trying to grab a switch, to take her out of stealth mode.

Like the Irish Wolf Hounds, the others were convinced that the sledges were going round in circles. Exhausted, Ryan suddenly recalled the tablet in Donn-Dubh's hat, and asked Donn-Dubh to check his Sat-Nav device. Donn-Dubh whipped it out of his hat and they all cheered when he fired it up.

"One moment, lads," said Donn-Dubh, "before I check our location. Let's take a selfie, but we'll call it a shelfie. Get it?"

"A shelfie?" said Malachy. "Sure that's a good one alrigh. We're on the Ross Ice Shelf and ..."

"Ok", snarled QuickMIC, "we get it."

So they all huddled around Donn-Dubh, smiling, and he held up the device, pressed a button, and the camera gave an almighty flash.

"Grand," said Donn-Dubh, "I'll check our co-ordinates now," and they all cheered again, hoping that they were about to find out where they were.

But the cheers quickly turned to groans when the power-on LED flickered briefly, before the Sat-Nav switched itself off.

"You've run out of power?" said Ryan.

"Yes," confirmed Donn-Dubh, shaking the Sat-Nav manically. "That shelfie must have drained the last of it."

"And you have no more batteries?"

"I don't think so."

"Are you sure, now?"

An hour later, having emptied his hat, Ye Olde Ross Ice Shelf Committee found almost everything you could name, including a few kitchen sinks; everything that is, except batteries.

"I'm sure now," confirmed Donn-Dubh, shoving the contents back into the folds of his hat, complaining that he couldn't be expected to think of everything.

So back to circles it was. Then QuickMIC came up with a fantastic idea to discover if this was actually the case, were they really going around in circles, and they all agreed on his plans. Twenty minutes later, Ye Olde Ross Ice Shelf Committee, PaddySan, Mai-Ly, Frosty and his grandmother were all inside an ice cavern, trying to get some protection from bitter winds, on the very edge of the Ross Ice Shelf, implementing the first stage of QuickMIC's plan.

"It's great idea, QuickMIC," said Malachy. "Just like yer one, Ariadne and that thread of hers. We'll leave markers, and if we are going around in circles, we'll soon know."

"Ariadne, who?" said Ryan.

QuickMIC had been telling them all about Ariadne who was from Greek, not Irish mythology, which was probably why very few people in Ireland had ever heard tell of her. "Anyhow, she gave her boyfriend a ball of thread," continued QuickMIC, "and he went into a labyrinth."

"Ah," said Ryan, "I remember it now. And if he got lost, he could follow the trail of string to find his way back out."

"That's it," said QuickMIC relating more of the story to them.

The others were all so enthralled by QuickMIC's story of Ariandne, Theseus and the Minotaur, that it was not until they smelled burning, that they all turned around to find Malachy with a blowtorch in his hand, carving huge initials into the ice.

"What the hell are you doing?" screamed QuickMIC. "And where in the hell did you get a blowtorch?"

"Creating a marker like we agreed," said Malachy. "I got the blowtorch out of Donn-Dubh's hat. Sure you should see some of the stuff he's got tucked away in there."

Malachy carried on his handy work, melting a dot at the bottom of an exclamation mark. The dot complete, he stood back to admire his marker, which had been written in three foot high letters, burned deeply into the ice:

EIRESTOWN WAS ÉIRE!

"Eirestown was *Éire*, get it?" said Malachy, the blowtorch swinging by his side, still cutting away at the ice. "What do ye all think, sure it's a nice play on words, eh?"

"Are you mad?" asked QuickMIC, "we're on the Ross Ice Shelf ... for God's sake will you turn off that blowtorch!"

"Sssshhh," said Frosty, "what was that noise?"

"Sssshhh," repeated Malachy, mimicking him.

"Not that noise you eejit," said Frosty, "listen."

They all became silent, and only the soothing hiss of the high octane blowtorch, which was still swinging from Malachy's side, could be heard.

"Will you turn that thing off!" screamed QuickMIC again.

It is hard to describe the cataclysmic noise they heard next. You could say that it sounded like an ice berg being ripped from the side of the newly repaired Ross Ice Shelf, because that is exactly what it was.

With an almighty thunderous, reverberating, screeching, cracking, rumble of a noise altogether, loud enough to wake every penguin for miles around, their very own iceberg split from a newly formed section of the Ross Ice Shelf, along the very line Malachy had been swinging the blowtorch over. The Iceberg stowaways clung on to each other, and any bit of ice they could get their hands on as they crashed into the Ross Sea, with a tsunami generating splash. Speechless, they all watched in dismay as the Ross Ice Shelf receded into the distance.

"That's torn it," mumbled Malachy.

"Will you put that thing out before you sink us," screamed QuickMIC, grabbing the blow torch from Malachy, and quickly extinguishing the flame.

"What are we going to do now?" asked Frosty.

"Will the ice melt?" said Malachy nervously. "Sure I can't swim."

"No," said Ryan, "judging by this ice bergs size, we're in for a long ride."

Malachy couldn't understand why the ice wouldn't melt, and Ryan told them about the good oul' days, the days before refrigerators had been invented, when they had ice farmers in Wisconsin and other places in the late 1800s.

"Ice farms?" said Malachy.

"Yes," explained Ryan. "The Wisconsin lakes froze every winter and ice harvesters would cut out 700lb blocks of ice, and store them in an ice house, between layers of sawdust. The ice would last the whole year, stored like that. The ice trade was huge, and ice could be shipped anywhere in the world."

"So how long do you reckon we have?" said Frosty.

"Oh," said Ryan, gauging the iceberg once more, "I'd say at least three months, ninety days, thereabouts."

"Three months," gasped Malachy, "school starts in one."

They all started panicking. Ryan had to get back to America to find a new job. Frosty and his grandmother had to get back to Templetuohy to make some taayyyy and ham sandwiches. QuickMIC had to get back to make sure Eógan hadn't wrecked Technological Shenanigans. And Donn-Dubh had a new Jiggy-Reggy CD to record for Louise Walsh, sure he'd been signed and everything a month before he left Eirestown. Only PaddySan and Mai-Ly couldn't care less about how long the iceberg was going to be around. They were too busy smooching and cuddling in an Irish, country style, cottage igloo PaddySan had just built, by cutting ice blocks out with his katana. Weren't they nice and cosy in there altogether, with Templetuohy turf infused smoke, wafting out of the chimney.

As the iceberg bobbed up and down, pandemonium was setting in as its passengers suddenly realised their fate. And what if, God forbid, Ryan's calculations were wrong?

"Come on now lads, calm yerselves down," said a familiar, soothing voice. "Sure there's only one thing ye can do at a time like this."

"What's that?" they all asked in unison.

A familiar dishevelled figure stepped out of an ice nook, and starting playing his Paddyvarius. He was quickly joined by a few more musicians, and a lady with a Galway shawl, wrapped extra tight since it was so cold.

"Sing a song," declared Paddynini.

The uilleann pipes took up the tune and the lady began to sing a gentle lullaby:

"It's a long way to Tipperary,
It's a long way to go ..."

Within a few beats, didn't they all calm down, and join in. Soon, five thousand penguins swam up behind the iceberg humming the song with them, and started pushing with all their might, pointing the ice berg in the direction of Ireland, heaving away and giving it an almighty burst of momentum.

The Eirestown Berg, as it quickly became known around the world, would soon pick up currents in the Amudsen Sea. Then winds would carry it round the bottom of South America, around Cape Horn, and into the Scotia Sea, where it would join old clipper routes, and follow in the wake of Ferdinand Magellan and Sir Francis Drake. From here, the Atlantic Ocean would beckon and guide them home along the South America coast line, over the equator, passed West Africa, and further north, to where familiar European waters waited for them.

Well that's what the five thousand penguins hoped for. And Good riddance to the trouble causers. They may have saved the world, but the oul' bankrupt penguins would be glad to see the back of these interfering do-gooders, now that their GRABiT shares were worthless. They were also pushing the Eirestown Berg so hard because any day now the penguins were expecting a few container ships full of penguin sun cream from Amazon.

Unfortunately, what with Antarctica freezing cold again, the sun cream lotion would have to be relabelled for human use. Sure the last thing the oul' penguins needed was this interfering lot sniffing around, asking questions and disrupting sales channels. To make sure the Eirestown Berg got as far as the

Atlantic, as fast as possible, the penguins had enlisted the help of four blue whales, who were to pull the berg like tug boats, until they were well clear of the Antarctica.

"Ahh look-it lads," said Malachy, when the blue whales took up the strain, "sure the penguins are waving us off."

"An' don't come back ye interfering Irish freckers," one irate penguin shouted.

"What did yer one over there just say?" said QuickMIC. "Him there on that block of ice."

"Him with the green swimsuit and green hardhat on?" asked Malachy.

"Himself," said QuickMIC.

"Sure I can't hear him," said Malachy, "there's too much noise coming from the waves hitting the iceberg."

No one else could hear the penguin either, but they all started waving back at him anyway.

"Yis're roight, o' course," said the penguin, "start waving like the freckin' eejits ye are, wha'!"

"He's a mighty wave on him for his size," said Ryan.

"Yis have been worse than a freckin' curse," the penguin shouted, waving a vigorous penguin fist at them.

"Ahh, now, look at that wave," said QuickMIC, "he's giving it everything he's got. Sure he must be awfully sad to see us go altogether."

"And if yis ever come back," said the unidentified bitter, green penguin, "I'll kick yis all up and down the Ross Ice Shelf, and beat the living daylights out of yis meself! Do yis hear me, wha'?"

Chapter 58

The 28th County Of Ireland

Once again, the world's media had descended on Washington, D.C. In the Oval Office, fresh from his Appellation Mountain retreat, the America President was sitting in front of a camera, about to address the world, with Ireland's Taoiseach standing behind him, along with one or two other officials, including oul' Nibbler.

A makeup artist was carrying out a few last minute checks, busy fixing the President's hair, sweeping down his lapels, brushing some foundation onto his face, and ... the director shouted: Action.

The cameraman zoomed into the President's composed, and freshly made up visage:

"People of the world, this is your President speaking," began the President, in a presidential manner. A concerned looking official minion, tapped him on the shoulder to stop him, bent over, and whispered into his ear. The President sighed under his breath, and corrected himself:

"People of the world, this is the President of the original United States of America speaking."

After a few rounds of loud applause, he continued to thank everyone for their patience throughout the recent global ordeal. "Rest assured," he continued, "the Ross Ice Shelf is frozen solid again."

Then the other half of the double act, the oul' Taoiseach, decided to get in on the action, "About as solid as your fiscal policies," he joked, giving the President a pat on the back.

"Thank you," said the American President, scowling at him off camera, before he added that nearly all flood waters had receded to pre-deluge levels.

"I'm also delighted to inform you," the President carried on, shifting through a few sheets of paper before him, "that 99% of all climate refugees have returned to their homes, however," and he gave the Taoiseach a here's some payback for you me oul' boyo look, "it seems that the Irish never know when to go home."

The poor oul' Taoiseach didn't know where to put his face, until he had an oul' brainwave, "Sure don't worry yourself, Mr President," he said, smiling and giving the American President a look which said, we'll see who's the wittiest one here me boyo, "my tickets are booked. And I've booked one for your good self, just in case you've forgotten where you came from."

Ahem. The American President, of Irish ancestry himself, and in America all his life, cleared his throat and got away from the subject as fast as possible. "And you'll be glad to hear that planetary weather systems are almost completely readjusted, and back to their pre-flood conditions." The Polar Jet stream was up and running, he went on, keeping equatorial weather systems at bay, and thermohaline circulation was stable again, with El Niño back in its original, oceanic groove.

All was well with the planet.

"However not since the Enron scandal," the President reluctantly admitted, "had an American Corporate acted so negligently, and so greedily, bringing untold shame on this great nation of ours." He shuffled a few more notes and announced, "You may rest assured that the perpetrators, one William McCoy The Third, ex-CEO of GRABiT, along with ex-USAF Captain James Bush have been arrested, and placed in a floating maximum security prison. Where they'll stay," he promised, "until the waters in Lower Manhattan's East Lake fully recede to become the East River again." After which time, they would be hauled before a judge and jury.

Finally, he stated, GRABiT's assets had been frozen, "A bit like the Ross Ice Shelf," he nodded, "not my fiscal policies," he added, smiling and winking back at the Taoiseach. "Further," he announced, "GRABiT's assets would be used to pay the hefty compensation claims, which were currently pouring in, if you'll forgive the pun, from all over the world."

The President smiled into the camera again, and winked reassuringly, before concluding: "So thank you all for your patience, all your support, and all your courage, strength, determination, faith and compassion during the apocalyptic circumstances we have just passed through. Not only does it make me feel proud to be human, but it reaffirms my faith in the dignity of man." He finished by raising a salute and said, "The people of America say thank you, people of earth!"

The President shuffled a few more papers on his desk, then, turning to Ireland's Taoiseach, he stretched out a hand, and in a sincere gesture of praise said, "But if there are one people we need to extend a special thank you to, not only for their sacrifice, their courage and their ingenuity in resolving this global crisis, it is the people of the 51st State of America ... IRELAND!"

Everyone in the room started clapping, and cheering, and the millions gathered outside in the National Mall, garbed in green, orange and white went mad altogether. Over in New York and Boston, the out of season painting of the green halted, and several million stopped to share app screens, or watch giant advertising screens. And they, too, went mad altogether, as the Tricolour was slowly raised over the Whitehouse, to join The Star Spangled banner.

But despite all the celebrations, the American President couldn't understand why the Taoiseach was still frowning at him. The 51st State of America? Surely there was some mistake, thought the Taoiseach, and he bent down to whisper to his distant Irish cousin, the American President. A sudden recognition of horror came over the President's face. His Irish ancestors were not happy, insisted the Taoiseach, not happy at all.

The President flew back to the camera lens, immediately, where, he cleared his throat again, and corrected himself once more: "But if there are one people we need to thank more than any others, for their sacrifice, their courage and their ingenuity in resolving this global crisis, it's the people of Ireland." He nodded back at the Taoiseach, and added, "And we the people of America, are proud to be their 27th County!"

Forty million Irish Americans gasped, and then the second biggest party the world has ever known started. However, unlike the Taoiseach, despite his liquid fiscal policies, the President was not about to promise free drinks, and bankrupt his country.

A few moments later, the President stood up and offered his chair to the Taoiseach, the duly elected President of the Irish American Union.

With great reverence the Taoiseach looked directly into the camera and began, "Well lads, we thought the Antarctica was banjaxed, and it almost was." He looked over his shoulder at the Vice President of the newly founded Irish American Union, the President of America, and said, "America might be Ireland's 27th County, but if there is anyone to thank, we must all raise our glasses to the people of Ireland's 28th County, Eirestown!"

Nibbler wasted no time bending down to nibble the Taoiseach's ear. "And not forgetting the oul' Technological Shenanigans and iShillelaghs over there in Eirestown," the Taoiseach added with a nod. "Please don't forget to send me one of those yokes QuickMIC. Oh and send one to the Whitehouse, I'm sure that our American cousin, the President, would love an oul' Cantankerous Cabbage."

"I think I'd prefer a Crafty Oul' Sod, QuickMIC, if you watching," said the President, bending down to whisper the rest of the sentence directly into the Taoiseach's, "a bit like yerself."

Nibble ... nibble ..."Oh, and more one t'ing, lads," the Taoiseach concluded, "this time the drinks are not on Leinster House."

Chapter 59

Fibrillatory Neuro-Amnesia

"Did you hear that trollix," said TongueSlinger, putting down his glass, "I'll not be raising my empty glass to that eejit."

"Neither will I," said Paht, ignoring TongueSlinger's attempt to get another free drink. "The 28th County of Ireland is it. Sure he's a fine memory on him now alright."

"You know," said TongueSlinger, "I wish I was out there in Antarctica with our very own Eirestown heroes."

"Our heroes, now is it?" said Paht. "I thought they couldn't stop a fridge defrosting?"

"Ahh, now," said TongueSlinger, "that must have been the drink talking."

"That explains it then," said Paht, giving him the nod.

"It's only a pity the drink's not talking at the moment," said TongueSlinger, looking dejectedly into his empty glass.

"Anyway," said Paht, continuing to ignore TongueSlinger's efforts to get a free refill, "why do you wish you were out in the Antarctica with the lads?"

"Sure I had a rare oul' session last night," said TongueSlinger, caressing the empty glass before rubbing both temples, "and I've the head of a polar bear on me this morning."

"You have?"

"'Deed I have, never mind the hair of the dog," he said, picking up the empty glass again and shaking it in Paht's direction with a smile, "sure I could do with the oul' hair of a polar bear."

"You'll be waiting a long time for a polar bear round here, you trollix," said Paht, himself with the head of an oul' grizzly bear, adamant that TongueSlinger was getting no more freebies.

"Ahh, now, come on Paht," pleaded TongueSlinger, "don't be an oul' trollix, yerself. Sure it's not my fault the Taoiseach won't pay up."

TongueSlinger was watching proceedings on the television in Paddy McGinty's, where he'd been hoping to help Paht drown his sorrows. However, whether you needed the hair of the dog, or had a polar bear's head on your shoulders, even if Christ himself came into the bar after forty days and nights in the desert for an oul' sup of water, Paht was reluctant to give anything away for free at the moment, especially drinks. Sure hadn't the Taoiseach gone and reneged on his free drink offer.

"But can you believe the excuse the Taoiseach came up with not to pay the nation's tab," groaned Paht. "Fibrillatory Neuro-Amnesia? I've never heard the like of it."

"Sure you have to hand it to him," said TongueSlinger, "he's like a compass."

"What do you mean?"

"He's himself covered from all angles."

"So what if the world has been saved from flooding?" grieved Paht, ignoring TongueSlinger's attempt to humour him. "What about us? Sure every pub in the land is drowning in debt now. And that's more of a disaster than the fehking Ross Ice Shelf melting, I can tell you."

"It is," agreed TongueSlinger, lifting up an empty glass, which was an even bigger disaster in his eyes. "Sure the whole country's on its knees, and they're not paying for the drinks they promised us desperate, honest, law abiding citizens."

"You're desperate alright," said Paht.

"And awful thirsty," smiled TongueSlinger, lapping at the rim of the glass until it was dry.

"And it's all t'anks to that fehkin' Taoiseach's 'Drinks Are on the House speech'," moaned Paht. "He should have kept his fehkin' mouth shut."

Ireland's pubs were on the verge of bankruptcy, all of them. Paht was right, what an excuse the Taoiseach had used not make good on his promise to pay for the nations free drinks. Leaving them with the biggest hangover Ireland had even known.

It had taken Paht a while to get the Taoiseach's excuse out of yesterday's copy of The Eirestown Press. Even after he dangled it over the open range, the paper played it real cool, and showed no sign of giving him the headlines.

"They've me printed on fireproof paper now, you oul' baldy, trollix!" said the paper, sneering up at Paht, the flames lashing away at the edge of his pages. "I can't feel a thing, sure you may lower me down all you want, but you'll not be getting any news out of me today."

"Won't I now?"

"'Deed you won't," said the paper, basking away in the flames, with an awful brazen attitude, altogether. "Sure I wouldn't waste my ink on a baldy, ignoramus like yourself."

"We'll see about that, now," said Paht menacingly, putting the fear of God into the little oul' paper. Didn't he take up the defiant Eirestown Press, and throw it into the back of the freezer for a few hours, slamming the door behind it. And the next time he looked in, sure wasn't the poor oul' paper shivering and ruffling its pages, trying to keep itself warm, "Jaysis, but you're a desperate scoundrel altogether, Paht," said the paper when the freezer light came on, himself chattering away with the cold. "The lads told me to expect the worse, but this is worse than worse. Sure your nothing but an oul' newspaper sadist, you trollix!" Paht was about to close the freezer door again, but the paper begged him to leave it open saying, "Ok, I'll tell you everything, just let me out of here quick, before I catch my death."

A few minutes later, having held the paper over the range to warm it up, Paht had it open on the kitchen table, where it became complicit in an intricate weave of blarney, fresh from the Taoiseach's very own neurological spinning wheel.

Suggesting that the Taoiseach had refused to pay the nations bar tab was not quite correct, the paper revealed. What the Taoiseach had actually claimed, following advice from The Minister for Health, was that the almighty shock of knowing that Ireland was about to sink had caused a rash of fibrillatory neurological, fibrillations somewhere between his ears. Sure, as you can imagine, the paper revealed, that was bad enough, but didn't the oul' fibrillations upset the neuro-chemical balance of his neurotransmitters, causing his brain to go haywire altogether.

"Not only had the fibrillations interfered with my memory lads," the Taoiseach explained in an interview with The Eirestown Press reporter, "but they also created a momentary lapse in common sense."

"And sound financial prudence," interrupted Nibbler, "make sure you print that, in bold if possible."

"'Deed we will," said the reporter.

"But be sure to tell your readers that he's over the worst of it now," said Nibbler, "and they needn't worry for him."

"Over the worse of it, the dirty lying, good for nothing trollix," said Paht, grabbing hold of The Eirestown Press, and threatening to cut it into shreds with a chain saw.

"Come on now, you can't blame me," pleaded the paper, when Paht fired up the chainsaw. "Sure you said it yourself, I'm only the messenger."

Paht powered off the oul' chainsaw, composed himself, apologised to the paper, and placed it gently back on the table, where it ruffled its pages again, grateful to be in one piece and more than happy to reveal the next section of the Taoiseach's interview.

"Further," the Taoiseach added, the reporter transferring his weave, thread by thread, onto a new loom in his laptop, "this extremely rare condition, known as Fibrillatory Neuro-Amnesia, or FNA to the lads over there in the health service, was also worsened by altitude sickness, out there in the Appellation Mountains. Where you can rest assured, I was overseeing oul' Ireland's very survival."

"Aren't we lucky," Nibbler interrupted again, placing a caring hand on the Taoiseach's shoulder, "that the Taoiseach's FNA, although a very rare and lethal condition, has now been completely cured. Sure we should all be thankful that the Taoiseach came through it in one piece."

"However," typed the Eiretown reporter, one of the Taoiseach's legal team having joined the interview, placing a caring hand on the Taoiseach's other shoulder, "it means that any promises the Taoiseach made during the time when FNA had him in its grips, like a banshee determined to suck the very life out of him, were made *non compos mentis*."

The fact that yer one from the legal team spoke Latin, had not gone unnoticed.

"*Non compos mentis* me hole," Paht said, grabbing hold of the paper again, intent on doing it some serious damage.

"Latin? That's exactly the kind of blarney they spin when there trying to swindle ye," said the paper, agreeing with Paht. "Fibrillations?" the paper shrieked. "Sure he's a tricky oul' scoundrel, that one."

"I'll give him a good fehkin fibrillating if I ever get my hands on him," said Paht, placing the paper back down, "and that little mousey fehker beside him."

"I'd beat the living daylights out of that mousey fehker meself," said the newspaper. "Sure I'd give him a merciless beating altogether."

The Taoiseach was over it alrigth, a picture of health up there on the screen in Paddy McGinty's. Fully *compos mentis* and larger than life itself, now that he'd manage to squirm his way out of paying the nation's bill.

But poor oul' TongueSlinger was far from such a healthy picture, what with his dry tongue flapping around his empty glass like a raspy piece of sandpaper, and Paht still refusing to give him a free drink.

"Just look at them," said Paht, flicking a beer mat at the screen. They were at it again, the Taoiseach and the American President, congratulating each other, patting each other's shoulders, and welcoming in a new dawn on a new day. Perhaps the shock of a global catastrophe might wake the world up and make it a better place after all, said the American President, shaking the arm off-a his Irish American cousin.

"And won't the GRABiT compensation fund be a great platform from which to grow this new found brother and sisterhood," the Taoiseach added, thanking his cousin for such a magnanimous gesture.

Having made the comment about the compensation fund, the blood drained out of the Taoiseach's face and he staggered, struggling to maintain his balance. Millions all over the world gasped, as the Whitehouse camera zoomed in on his pasty looking face.

"Look-it, TongueSlinger," said Paht, flicking another bear mat at the television where the Taoiseach was on the verge of collapsing. "Sure his oul' neurotransmitters must be fibrillating again with that Fibrillatory Neuro ... now what's it called?"

"Amnesia," said TongueSlinger.

"Thanks for the reminder," said Paht, "I think I've a touch of it meself."

"Sure he must be going haywire again," said TongueSlinger. "You never know, perhaps he'll promise us the drinks again."

"You're right," said Paht, rubbing his hands together, excitely.

As if he'd fainted, the Taoiseach slumped back into the American President's executive chair and asked for a glass of water. The shock of the thought which had just entered his mind, a thought worthy of an Irish genius, had his neurotransmitters haywire alright, and himself fibrillating again, but for all the right reasons this time.

"Listen lads," the Taoiseach said, jolting up in the chair, and staring into the Whitehouse camera intently, "that's all my brothers and sisters over there in our fair oul' Emerald Isle. Pay close attention now ... especially ye who thirst for righteous and recompense from our Lord, over there in the highlands." He subtlety winked one of his angelic eyes, and every Irish man and woman in Ireland recognised the code words.

"Whist now," Paht said, "did you hear that?"

"Coded language," said TongueSlinger, repeating it back to him, "'Thirst', 'righteousness', 'recompense', 'highlands'."

Which every Irish person in the land knew translated as: "Sorry about the nation's bar bill lads, but I've reconsidered Leinster House's position. And I'm glad to inform ye that we would like to make ye all a new offer. Which I'm more than sure ye'll all be happy with, even the ones who contacted the Mapping Agency to report the dubious new co-ordinates of their fine establishments. So pay attention now lads, and let us show this shower the real power of GIDO, the Global Irish Distributed Office."

A silence descended over Ireland, and you couldn't even hear a glass clink, a cow moo, or a Cantankerous Cabbage tell a joke.

Out of code language now the Taoiseach continued: "The American President has been kind enough to inform us that the GRABiT compensation fund will be opened to Irish residents first. And anyone and I do mean anyone, who lost anything whatsoever, will be able to make a full claim against it, without the need to provide receipts."

No receipts? The American President gave him a questioning look.

"Because," the Taoiseach said, answering him directly, "the integrity of the Irish throughout the world is surpassed only by their generosity. And," he continued, speaking once more to his dearly beloved Irish brothers and sisters across the television airwaves, "talking of our generosity: I can imagine that many of ye spent what ye thought were your last hours in the pubs of our great land. Where our generous landlords no doubt provided all the drinks for free, rather than see it go down the drain. Therefore I'm ecstatic to announce that those generous landlords of our great land will also be able to claim all their drink bills as legitimate business expenses against the oul' GRABiT compassion fund."

Although it was over 3000 miles away, after that announcement, the screams of joy emanating from Ireland could actually be heard in the Whitehouse.

"Now I'm away lads," said the Taoiseach, "but I'll be staying in America to process the compensation claims meself, and sign them off personally. But don't forget me when I come back home in two weeks time, to campaign for the oul' elections."

"Did you hear that?" said TongueSlinger. "Sure he'll win the election by a landslide."

"Hear it," Paht said, jumping up out of his chair like a hurdler, "I'm away to the polling station to get my vote in early." He snatched TongueSlinger's empty glass out of his hand, "But here, let me fetch you a refill before I go!"

Chapter 60

When Irish Eyes Are Smiling

And lo it came to pass ...

The Eirestown berg, propelled from Antarctica by thousands of penguins humming an Irish lullaby, and later tugged through the Ross Sea to the Atlantic Ocean by blue whales, had survived, just as Ryan had calculated, for exactly 89 days and nights. Bobbing and weaving across calm and treacherous seas, the barren, icy-cold leviathan had fulfilled its promise, carrying its grateful passengers back to their home.

With the world in such turmoil, there had been no time, nor services, available to carry out a rescue mission for the Ye Olde Ross Ice Shelf heroes. However, residents in many countries, whenever possible, and when tide and weather permitted, sent out supplies of food and various essentials to keep them going, on their long journey home. And when food was running short, they threw out fishing lines. Fortunately, before they left The Erebus Hilton, Donn-Dubh managed to stack a rake of Templetuohy turf in his hat, and, for weeks on end, the taste of turf smoke infused fish became a welcome delicacy.

Flowing through Dublin, down the Liffey, had been great craic altogether. As they passed under O'Connell's bridge, people dropped flowers, shamrocks, black thorn shillelaghs, food, sweets, drinks, money, tricolours, anything and everything except kitchen sinks, which would have sunk them on the spot.

Frosty and his grandmother disembarked just after O'Connell's bridge. Didn't she have an appointment at G2's Intelligence Headquarters, where she was to be decommissioned yet again. Following that, Frosty and herself were off down the country, to their beloved home in the bogs of *Teampall Tuaithe*, where they would enjoy an oul' sup of taayyyy.

At last Eirestown was in sight, but time was running out. Ryan's calculation had been spot on. But with the heat steadily increasing, the Eirestown Berg was shrinking faster by the lengthening day. Sure it was almost a sliver of ice now, tossed up and down in the river Laffy.

Conditions were so bad that Malachy, Donn-Dubh, QuickMIC, Ryan and even Mai-Ly and PaddySan, now that their love nest, the igloo, had finally melted, were presently huddled together, clinging on for dear life on top of the last few square meters of ice, the tips of their noses almost touching.

"Whew," said Ryan to Donn-Dubh, "you really do need to brush those fish stained teeth"

"Carry on now," growled Donn-Dubh, nerves getting the better of him, "and you won't have any teeth left to brush!"

"Come on now lads," said QuickMIC, "keep still, sure you're rocking the berg."

"I'll rock the head off your shoulders, QuickMIC," said Donn-Dubh, "if you don't shut up and stand still."

He couldn't swim either, and the panic was setting in.

Not far now.

A platform came into view, and it looked like the whole of Eirestown, including King Cormac, were standing on it and waving at them.

"We'll not make it," screamed Malachy, closing his eyes, and clinging onto Donn-Dubh's legs, "we'll not make it."

But there was no need to worry. Sure everything had been taken care of.

"Look-it," said Ryan, "a jetty."

A jetty had been built which extended into the Laffy, allowing them to step off the Eirestown berg, just as it finally dissolved into the river.

"Whew," said Malachy, "that was close."

At the end of the jetty, hundreds had gathered, and the King waited to award them the highest honour in Eirestown, miniature gold shillelaghs on Connemara marble plinths.

"Fáilte ar ais," said the King hugging them one-by-one, and handing them their golden shillelaghs.

"Sorry your majesty," said Ryan, "but I don't speak Gaelic."

"Same here," said Donn-Dubh.

"Sure neither do I," said King Cormac, giggling, "but the oul' tourists love that one."

"Welcome back," said QuickMIC.

"Thanks," said Donn-Dubh, returning the compliment, "and welcome back yourself."

"No you eejit," said QuickMIC, his UTU functioning perfectly for once, *Fáilte ar ais*, it means welcome back."

"Now before we go any further," said King Cormac, "could I just have a moment with the real hero?"

QuickMIC proudly stepped forward, but the King waved him back and looked invitingly at Donn-Dubh. "Me your majesty?" Donn-Dubh stammered, stepping forward. "It's very kind of you to recognise me like this, and I'll welcome anything of value you wish to give me. But I couldn't have done it ..."

"Not you, you feckin' eejit," snapped the King. "Sure you were only carrying the luggage. I said the real hero." And he reached into the folds of Donn-Dubh's hat and pulled out an extremely humbled and bashful Snippy.

"People of Eirestown," the King declared, raising Snippy way up above his head on his open palm, "I give you our hero."

Snippy started bowing and snipping in time with the cheers and clapping of his adulators.

"Here now," said King Cormac, giving Snippy an oul' fishy treat which had been prepared by An Cabáiste agus Bagún Deli, "this is to thank you for all your service." Snippy was overwhelmed with the gift, and snuggled back into Donn-Dubh's hat where he wouldn't have to share a morsel.

"Hiyis," a familiar voice said. "Jaysis, but it's great to see yis all again lads."

They couldn't believe it, it was Séamus O'Malley himself, the holy, green, living show of a VIP penguin from Dublin.

"How?" stammered QuickMIC, taking a double look to make sure it really was Séamus, "How on earth did you get here before us?"

"And why are you dressed as a zoo attendant," asked Malachy, "and carrying that net?"

"Sure yis couldn't write it, wha'," said Séamus. But he tried. After they left Antarctica, his poor oul' heart was broken. The Eirestown lads were the best friends he'd ever had, not only that, but they had him homesick something rotten. And with no family, or job, what with the The Erebus Hilton destroyed and all, didn't he decide to take after them. So with his head in bits, he staggered out of Murphy's, hoping to follow their tracks.

"But yis wouldn't believe it, or perhaps yis would," he said. "Didn't I bump into the iShillelagh Irish Wolf Hounds. And yis wouldn't believe what they were doing, either."

"What?" asked QuickMIC.

"Weren't they were filling The Eirestown Flash with white rabbits," he continued. "I bumped into them returning from their thirtieth visit to White Rabbit Paradise, and they had the sledge stacked as high a house."

"They found it then?" said QuickMIC.

"'Deed they did," said Séamus, twitching and looking around nervously. "Sure I nearly broke me oul' neck trippin' over a few of the little, white freckers, wha'. It was freckin' unreal. I'm not coddin' yis, they were everywhere."

He looked around nervously again, and waved a net, as if expecting someone or something to hop into it.

"With The Eirestown Flash full to bursting," he went on, "meself and the Wolf Hounds got into her, pressed an oul' button that said HOME, and didn't we arrive back here in Eirestown, like her name suggests, in a flash, wha'."

"So why are you dressed like that," asked Malachy again, "and what's the net for?"

"Now that they're home," explained the King, "the Wolf Hounds are mad for the oul' grey rabbit stew. They've lost all interest in the white rabbits altogether, which has left us with a bit of a problem."

"A problem?" said QuickMIC.

"A problem," whispered Séamus, putting a finger on his beak and sneaking a glance over both shoulders. "I'm sorry to inform yis, but yis have a white rabbit infestation here in Eirestown. And I'm not coddin' yis, they're freckin' everywhere. And with them big oul' floppy ears sticking out of their heads, sure they can hear you comin' from a mile away. You have to be trained for this job, me boyo."

"And, thankfully," said the King, "using that training, Séamus has kindly offered to round up the little pests, and take them off to Dublin Zoo when he goes back."

"Sure only an expert like meself could sneak up on them, wha'." He waved the net through the air dramatically from side to side, and swatted the ground a few times, "I'll catch them alroight, roight!"

"And when you do, you're off back to the zoo, so?" said Malachy.

"'Deed I am," said Séamus. "The oul' compo from Trinity College came through in the end, and I'll be able to live like a king back in the penguin enclosure."

"So the Chinese pandas have left the penguin enclosure?" said QuickMIC.

"They had no choice," said Séamus. "Some fertility drive, wha'. Sure the oul' lad had no lead in his bamboo, and the missus got sick of waiting."

"Get away will yeh," said Malachy.

"I'm not coddin' yis," said Séamus, "she ran off with a grizzly bear in the end. Said she fancied a bit of rough. If only she'd have only waited until I got home. She'd have had septuplets in no time whatsoever."

"You'll be around for a while then?" said QuickMIC.

"I might," said Séamus, looking around anxiously, with a baby white rabbit peeking out from under one side of his zoo keeper's hat, "these white rabbits breed faster than the Irish me boyo. Yis've got to keep your wits about yis with these furry, white freckers alright." As his head twisted from left to right, another two baby white rabbits popped their heads out of each of his jacket pockets. "Sure there's no tellin where they'll hop out from next." And yet another one popped its head out from underneath the other side of his hat, and didn't two sets of white floppy ears start dangling from either trouser pocket. "But I'm ready me boyo! So remember," he looked around again, his net primed to pounce, "if yis find any of them little white rabbits wha', just give me an oul' shout, and I'll be back in a flash with this net for them."

QuickMIC was about to say something, but Séamus was off scouring Eirestown, waving his net, and leaving a trail of white rabbits behind him, what with rakes of them hopping out of his hat and pockets.

"Can I have your attention please," said a voice over a microphone that was suffering a little feedback. "Welcome back and all lads," said the Cracker Craic, "how's the craic?"

"She's mighty," shouted Malachy.

"Grand so," said Paddynini, standing on a huge stage. Throwing the oul' Paddyvarius up onto his shoulder, he started playing, and was joined by the other Cracker Craics. "Well we've a surprise guest for ye," he said, smiling from ear to ear, "join in if ye know the song."

"And its home boys home, home I'd like to be,
Home for a while in my own country."

"Look-it," screamed Malachy, "it's Eógan."

On stage, Eógan, dressed as a sailor in white middies, with a green collar and green trimming around the cuffs and waist line, started singing Home Boys Home, a hearty shanty of old.

"Ohhh myyy days," said QuickMIC, his UTU mimicking Squawky perfectly and his eyes turning bright red.

"Didn't you know he could sing?" said Malachy.

"I knew that alright," said QuickMIC. "But take a closer look at the dancers."

"Ohhh myyy Eógans," said Malachy, clapping in time to the song …

Dancing around Eógan, in marching formation, were rakes of 30cm high iShillelaghs, also dressed in middies. Every now and then they started doing star jumps, and stanky legs.

"Sure they're all the spitting image of Eógan," Malachy concluded. "It looks like the oul' lad's been busy back in the shop."

"Busy," cried QuickMIC, his eyes turning black. "Never mind the white rabbit infestation, it looks like I have an Eógan infestation over in Technological Shenanigans."

And just when QuickMIC thought it couldn't get any worse, several of the iShillelagh Eógan dancers, sprang out of a huddle to reveal …

"Sweet Jaysis," screamed QuickMIC, blessing himself a few times, "it's Jezebel. And will yeh look at the cut of her."

Jezabel was dressed as a female buccaneer. On her head she wore a green tricorn, with yellow and white feathers embellishing it, and she was strutting around provocatively in black, thigh-high pirate boots, beneath a swallow tail, cascading, green lace dress, on top of which she wore a leather basque, which was at least two sizes too small, by QuickMIC's reckoning.

"Are you sure she's not for sale?" asked Ryan, with the eyes popping out of his head.

Everyone was up dancing by now, clapping in syncopation. Even the King, as most of the heroes joined in, shimmying and marching up and down the jetty, giving and receiving high-fives.

However, PaddySan had other ideas. As Eógan was just starting his second verse, PaddySan had the music stopped. He apologized to the town and all those here present then whispered into Eógan's ear. Eógan smiled and passed him the microphone.

"Once again, 'deed I'm sorry for the interruption and all," said PaddySan, with some of the hushed crowd wondering whether the journey had sent him crazier or something.

"Good man yerself PaddySan," a few people shouted. "Ye've the key to the town now," another shouted, "you may do as you please, so."

"T'anks a million," said PaddySan modestly, in his velvety Tipperary accent, "but I promise not keep ye long, lads." Then he called for Mai-Ly to join him up on the stage. You couldn't hear a pin drop as he got down on one knee, and asked her to marry him, holding up a shiny piece of Templetuohy turf that he'd whittled and polished into a claddagh ring, during their journey home across the seas.

"Yes," she said, slipping the turf ring onto her finger. PaddySan handed the microphone back to Eógan, who started the song from the beginning again, and didn't the whole town go mad altogether.

"And its home boys home, home I'd like to be,
Home for a while in my own country."

Ten minutes later the party burst into Paddy McGinty's Goat, carrying Ye Olde Ross Ice Shelf heroes, and everyone was still in an awful happy mood altogether ....

"Well?" said Paht, interrupting the clapping, bringing the celebrations to a standstill.

"Well what?" said a few of Ye Olde Ross Ice Shelf Committee.

"Did ye bring us back an oul' bucket of ice?"

"'Deed we did," said Donn-Dubh, and he started pulling buckets out from the cool section of his hat, one after the other, passing them along a human chain. Even Snippy got in on the act, picking up any ice cubes that fell back into the hat. Soon the kitchen, landing and bar was full of buckets of green ice.

"Be the lovin' ..." said Paht, scratching his chin. "What happened, did ye bring the Ross Ice Shelf home?"

"It was a leaving present from Murphy's On The Rocks," said Donn-Dubh. "By the way, they couldn't believe there was an Irish pub in Eirestown called Paddy McGinty's Goat, so your Irish pub guide came in very handy."

"Sure what will I do with all this ice?" said Paht.

"Don't worry yourself about that, sure you'll be needing all the ice you can get," announced King Cormac, following in behind the crowds. "By Royal Decree I declare that the drinks are on Paddy McGinty's Goat!"

A few minutes later Paht came round, stretched out in the middle of Paddy McGinty's, where he'd been carried for a bit of fresh air after he collapsed. TongueSlinger was crouched over him, fanning him with a promotional flyer from You'd Be Mad To Go Anywhere Else, and QuickMIC was checking his pulse. Sadly, he'd feinted behind the bar after King Cormac's declaration. No one could refuse a Royal Decree, well you could, but it meant five to ten years inside King Cormac's dungeons. Sure this was going to cost poor oul' Paht a fortune, and himself only just promised a refund by the Taoiseach for the Leinster House fiasco.

"Pass me over a bit of that ice," said QuickMIC, and he proceeded to rub Paht's temples with a few green ice cubes, fresh from the Antarctic.

"Sorry," said King Cormac sincerely, holding one of Paht's hands, "that must have been a dreadful shock to your system."

"You could say that," said Paht, panting and heaving, his eyes barley open. "Sure I think I'm not long for this world, now. The forefathers are waiting for me, I can see them beckoning through the haze."

The crowd became very hushed altogether as the moaning and groaning coming out of Paht filled the bar.

"TongueSlinger," whispered Paht, "is that yourself?"

"'Tis meself, dear oul' friend," said TongueSlinger, just back from the bar, having taken the opportunity to sneak himself a free drink, "is there anything I can do for you?"

"I'd like to leave you a personal message before I go," said Paht, straining to get the words out. "Kneel down here so beside me, my dear oul' friend."

"Grand, so." said TongueSlinger, moving in close, hoping he was about to become one of Paht's heirs.

With TongueSlinger's mingy ear hovering over his mouth, Paht yelled, "Now get back up to that bar and pay for that drink, you dirty, robbin', thievin', good for nothin' little intransitive trollix."

Even TongueSlinger didn't have the heart to berate poor oul' Paht as he lay dying, and he ran over to the bar, making sure Paht, and everyone else, could hear the till opening, and his money dropping in.

"Good man yerself," said Paht, shaking with the fever, the melting ice cubes on his temple making it look like he was sweating profusely. "Now if ye don't mind," he went on, his breathing barely discernible, "I'd like to shut up the oul' pub and cross over to the other side peacefully." Raising his hand, didn't he turn his head, twist his face in an unholy grimace, and add in a woeful voice, "*Cóiste bodhar* is on its way, I can see it in the distance, and it's driven by an oul' *dullahan.*"

An eerie chill filled the bar as several women wailed, "The death coach," and scrambled over each other to get out, with half the bar running out behind them. Just in case the dullahan, the oul' headless coachman, made a mistake and took the wrong passenger.

"Paht," said King Cormac, clearing his throat and pulling out his mobile phone, "before you leave us, I've the Taoiseach himself on the line. He wants a word with you." He fidgeted with the phone, connecting it by the wonders of WiFi to the plasma television, so that everyone could see and hear the message, while Paht was carried to a prime viewing chair.

"People of Eirestown, Ireland's 28th County," began the Taoiseach, his smile filling the screen, "I'm calling to give ye a personal thank you. A million t'anks actually, on behalf of our great nation."

The bar erupted in cheers and applause, and settled down when the Taoiseach spoke again. "And I've a message for Paht, landlord of Paddy McGinty's Goat." They all started cheering again and Paht perked up a little. "Now Paht, I won't be keeping you long, I'm sure you all want to be celebrating the lads' homecoming. I just called to say that such is the nation's gratitude we'd like to reward you."

Paht shot up, the news of a reward fortifying him like a sniff of smelling salts.

"So," said the Taoiseach, "the drinks really are on Leinster House this time!"

The Taoiseach couldn't understand why his offer was met with absolute silence in the bar, so Nibbler bent down to his ear and whispered. "And," added the Taoiseach with a wink, "ye may rest assured that I've already wired over the necessary funds to Paddy McGinty's Goat."

Paht leapt of the chair, not even stopping to thank the Taoiseach.

"It's a fehkin miracle," said TongueSlinger, as Paht covered the barroom floor faster than Paul Hession, Ireland's sprinting champion.

Quick as a flash, Paht was back, having confirmed on the phone that the funds were in his account, "Drinks are on Leinster House for the rest of the week lads, at least," he shouted punching the air.

King Cormac had been teasing Paht all along, having already spoken to the Taoiseach before he came into Paddy McGinty's.

"That was an amazing recovery altogether Paht, I hope there'll be no relapse?" said King Cormac. "By the way, shall I cancel cóiste bodhar?"

"Not at all," said Paht, "let the oul' dullahan in for a drink. Won't he have a terrible thirst on him after that journey, and I'm sure he'll need to sit down. Especially when he finds out that he's come all this way for nothing. "He looked around the bar with a glint in his eye and added, "And who knows, he may decide to do us all a favour, and take a few of these miserable fehkers instead."

"Grand, so," said the King.

"We've only one problem now," said Paht, back behind the bar, scratching his chin.

"What?" replied everyone in the bar.

"What with all the free drink, we may not have enough ice, after all."

They all groaned.

"Here," sniggered Paht, "sure I've a great idea altogether. It's the perfect solution to our ice shortage."

"What is it?" they all asked.

"All we have to do is melt the Ross Ice Shelf, then we'll have as much ice as we need."

A moment later, didn't he find himself with more ice than he needed alright, cowering under bucket loads of green ice cubes, which had been deposited over him by everyone in the bar.

"Jaysis," shouted Paht, popping his head from out of the pile of ice, an ice cube flying out of his mouth, "but ye have me nearly frozen to death."

"Now you know how I felt," said the Eirestown Press, which was folded up on a shelf beneath the counter, where it was still defrosting.

"Ahh come on now lads," said Paddynini, gently bowing the oul' Paddyvarius at one end of the bar, with the rest of the Cracker Craics behind him, "sure we'll sing an oul' song to warm our hearts and souls ... and put a smile back on Paht's icy face," and he started singing.

By the time the Cracker Craics sang the first chorus, Paht had served everyone a drink, including the oul' dullahan who, despite Paht's best efforts to get him to take TongueSlinger away, would be leaving with an empty coach.

And as they reached the last chorus, the whole bar had joined in singing, waving drinks in the air, and grinning from ear to ear:

"When Irish Eyes Are Smiling, sure 'tis like a morn in spring.
In the lilt of Irish laughter, you can hear the angels sing.
When Irish hearts are happy, all the world seems bright and gay,
And When Irish Eyes Are Smiling, sure, they steal your heart away.

Author's Note

Did you enjoy the first Eirestown féile? Sure I hope you did. And I also hope that you've not become too friendly with any of the characters. Remember, Eirestown is a very hard place to find, but it can be an even harder place to leave.

But isn't it grand that we can all sleep at night, safe in the knowledge that the people of Eirestown care so much about protecting the world, and its residents. And themselves not yet even on the map.

So look out for the next féile, coming to a town near you soon. Sure you never know what the lads will get up to next.

In the meantime you might also like to read an up and coming series of books about Malachy and QuickMIC's escapades, aimed more at the younger audience, but aren't we all big kids at heart. So any age should enjoy them

The first in the series is called, The Eirestown Matinee, where every Sunday afternoon, all the children of Eirestown gather in Technological Shenanigans for the Sunday Matinee. Here Malachy Malarkey and QuickMIC perform for them, show them a movie, give them a story, or, if they are really lucky, actually take them all on an adventure!

Get updates on all oul' the up and coming new stuff over there at:

www.eirestown.com
www.eirestown.ie

'Till then .... *ádh mór ort!*

Michael Collins